Lynn

Merry Christmas

MW00744654

Gotcha!

(Smoke & Eagle)

2nd in the 'Smoke' Series
As told by
Master StoryTeller:

Robert Preston Walker

Robert Preston Walker

Dream Merchants International Inc.

Mr. Smoke Describes a Victim Turned Hero!

This Exciting and Original Novel by Robert Preston Walker weaves a Tale of How One Man Becomes a Terrorist Fighting Sensation!

After decades living in fear, a newscast brings Damon Gray out of his shell and turns him into an international sensation in the crime-fighting world. Years earlier, he and his parents were victims of a terrorist bombing. His mother and father died, but he was revived at the scene. Before the accident he was a talented concert pianist with extraordinary psychic abilities, but such a traumatic event masked his gifts. Years later, after his grandparents die in a plane crash, he hits a new rock bottom – until seeing a news report about a terrorist act jolts his abilities and gives him the power to avenge his family.

Damon quickly becomes a hero – a terrorist bomber assassin dubbed "Mr. Smoke" by one of his Irish terrorist bomber victims. As Mr. Smoke, Damon hunts down terrorists, but yet another group is hunting him. Damon is an Enhanced Human, and each of these gifted individuals has been hunted by the Enhanced Human Exterminators. One of Damon's would-be assassins offers a fun sub-plot, as she fails in her attempt to assassinate him and eventually joins the Smoke team as "Misty Smoke". In their adventures, the Smoke organization encounters beings from other dimensions that add an extra layer of intrigue to this compelling novel. Robert Walker's riveting plot line is also propelled by a cast of characters that help Damon fulfill his mission. Two of his closest friends are American Sylvia Brighton and her husband Michael, head of the British Anti-Terrorist Control Unit and a Lord of the Realm. His assistant, Garret Hastings, an ex-military man, would lay down his life for Damon in a heartbeat. A truly delightful and action-packed novel that pits good against evil, Mr. Smoke has accumulated rave reviews from readers. It's a hero's story that weaves international, and inter-dimensional, action with one man's pursuit of justice.

***

Gotcha!

ISBN 978-0-9835962-0-2

Gotcha!

is dedicated to my wife, Karen Lynn Walker.

Karen, thank you for your kindness and patience, and for listening to me read (and reread, and reread, and reread) you the story as I wrote, to make sure it flowed properly.

And thank you for laughing in all the right parts.

With Love,

Robert

Acknowledgments

Many thanks to my editors and test readers; Karen Walker, John Isherwood, George Etheridge, and Joe Peery.

I would also like to thank Dream Merchants International Inc, my publisher.

Thanks also goes out to Kimberly Martin, at km@self-pub.net, who

formatted Gotcha!. What a pleasure it continues to be to work with her.

I really don't know how to show my appreciation to each and every one of them, except by thanking them in print.

Special thanks, again to my beautiful wife, Karen, for her vital and impartial input. Well .... not *really* impartial. A bigger fan, I've never had. Can you believe she still wants an autographed copy of the first run? Now that's a fan!

All three sons, Damon, Brandon and Tanner are expecting one also.

The only one who hasn't asked for one, yet was beside me all the way, is Grace Catherine Walker, our cat.

Eyes closed in contemplation, Grace would patiently sit be me for hours as I worked on the story of Gotcha!, and never criticized. I wish each and every one of you out there could have the kind of support that I have had with my labor of love, called Gotcha!

Robert Preston Walker

Gotcha!

(Smoke & Eagle)

2nd in the 'Smoke' series

A new novel Novel by
Robert Preston Walker

Scene 1

"**D**ammit!"

"Daddy!" piped up his shocked seven year old daughter from the back seat of their Landrover. "You shouldn't say *that word*. Mommy gave me heck when I said it. Remember mommy?" Her mother smiled and nodded. Brandon grinned down at his daughter.

"Sorry Angel. We're running *late* and daddy *almost* forgot some important papers in my office that I *have* to take and drop off to Stefani at InterGlobal *today*." apologized Brandon Thomas, Angel's father. Turning to his wife, he added, "Char, why don't you back the car out of the garage while I run in and get the files that I need. We're late enough as it is. I'll lock up and meet you out in front, okay?"

"Sure thing, darling. Scurry away." Charlene smiled with love at her husband and waved her slender hand at him as if she was shooing him away. He smiled and threw her a kiss as he darted away. She knew how compulsive he was about being on time. And they were late for an important meeting. A meeting with Q, and *they* didn't tolerate or react well to tardiness either. She finished seat belting their daughter and then got in the driver's side and punched the remote to open the garage door. Once it was fully opened she turned the key to start the car.

***

Brandon was in his home office, located behind the laundry room which was directly behind the Garage. He was behind his steel desk, picking up his brief case with the papers that he needed so desperately. He needed to drop them off to Robyn, his secretary at InterGlobal Travel Agency, before he met with Q. She would know what to do with them. He was bent over and going through the open case to make sure that the file with all the documentation was in there. It was. He closed the case.

At that instant his wife turned the key in the ignition. The car bomb attached to the underside of the Landrover exploded. The garage, acting as a gun barrel, shot the twisted Landrover out to land in the middle of the street. The blast vaporized the walls connecting the laundry room and the office, driving the washer and dryer into the metal desk and into Brandon.

***

Brandon Thomas awoke to find himself coughing and choking, with white everywhere. It got into his eyes. He blinked. It was the debris vapor, smoke and drywall dust from the explosion from the blast. He must have been knocked senseless for a few moments. He staggered to his feet and stood stunned at the sight of the front of his house blown away. He saw his vehicle in the middle of the street. An agonized groan escaped from him as he staggered over the rubble and ran to the twisted wreckage.

No one had come out of their homes. They were either at work or terrified. He gripped the bottom of the glassless front drivers window. He looked into the front seat. Parts of his wife were splattered everywhere, but miraculously, her head and face were untouched. Her head and neck looked at him from the passenger seat with an innocent surprised look. She looked like she was going to speak to him. He waited. Then he shook his head and looked with dread in the back seat.

His daughter, Angelina Thomas, was limp in her car seat. She was covered in blood. Whether it was her mothers or hers, or both, Brandon could not tell. She did not look to be breathing.

Brandon heard a soft whistle in the background. He turned around. Four Police cars and two ambulances had arrived with lights flashing and sirens blaring. He felt a light tap on his shoulder. He turned to find a paramedic talking to him. He shook his head violently. His hearing returned. The noise was deafening. He covered his ears with both hands.

"Turn off those bloody sirens!" roared an authoritative voice. The noise stopped.

"My daughter." Brandon stated quietly to the paramedic.

"We are working on her now, sir."

Brandon looked, nodded, and allowed himself to be lead away by the paramedic to a waiting medical vehicle. The sirens were turned off. Silence reigned as the paramedics took down his information and checked him out.

"You may be in bad shape Mr. Thomas. I can't tell for sure." said the young man that had brought him to be checked. "We need to get you to a hospital immediately. Please get in the ambulance."

"What is your name, son?" Brandon asked.

"Al, sir." came the surprised respectful response.

"Well Al, *we* are not going anywhere until I find out about my daughter." Brandon stood up and walked over to the vehicle, just as the medical emergency unit personnel removed the tiny girl child from the back shattered window and placed her limp form on a stretcher. They gently strapped her down and proceeded to put her in the nearest ambulance.

Brandon touched his Angels arm. It was still warm. He could see her little chest rising and falling slowly, almost imperceptibly.

One of the rescuers smiled at him. A young woman. She touched his arm and spoke.

"She is *alive* sir, but only *just*. We have no time to spare. We need to get her to surgery *stat!*" Brandon nodded. Two paramedics lifted and rolled the stretcher into the ambulance.

A police officer stepped up to Brandon. "We need to get a statement from you sir."

Ignoring him, Brandon stepped forward and said to the paramedic. "I'm going with my daughter."

The police officer said politely yet firmly. "I'm sorry sir, but we need to get a statement from you *now*. You can follow in the other ambulance shortly. There is nothing you can do now anyway."

Continuing to ignore him, Brandon stepped toward the ambulance. The police officer grabbed his arm.

Brandon stopped. He looked down at the hand on his arm and then up at the young police officer. "Let go of my arm, youngster. I am going with my daughter. You can take my statement at the hospital."

"I don't think so, *Mister Thomas.*" said the *youngster* grimly. "I need help over here!" he called to his fellow officers. Three other officers, that were close by, came running over to lend a hand. The one holding Brandon produced a set of handcuffs. The four converged on Brandon. Within four seconds all four officers were unconscious on the ground. The one who had been holding him was handcuffed with his hands behind his back.

Brandon Thomas looked out at the remaining four police officers and said quietly, flatly, with no emotion. "I am going with my daughter. I will give you a statement at the hospital. Is that understood?"

"Yes sir!" said all four officers at the same time. None of them reached for their guns. They saw the look in Brandon's eyes. Something had changed in them. And in his face. Gone was the plain ordinary looking man, a man that would not stand out in a crowd. Something had dropped from him. It was if a curtain of gauze that had been surrounding Brandon Thomas, until this very moment, had vanished. In its place stood *something* or someone else. Someone or *something* very, very dangerous.

Contrary to popular law enforcement media propaganda, not all police officers are willing to nobly risk their lives in the line of duty, and these four were *not* foolish, witless *or* noble. Not one of them was going to mess with a deranged father who could render four veteran police officers unconscious in less than a few heartbeats.

Brandon stepped into the ambulance and closed the doors behind him. The ambulance raced off, sirens again blaring.

Brandon sat beside his terribly injured daughter, holding her hand. For a long time he just stared at her, then he squeezed her hand lightly and closed his eyes.

"Hang in there Angelina." he whispered to her, putting all his love in his plea. He opened his eyes and looked down at the peaceful face of his daughter. Suddenly his breath caught in his chest.

Angel opened her eyes and smiled up at her father through the clear plastic oxygen mask.

"Mommy says to tell you that she has always loved *only you* since she first met you daddy. She said she would be around as long as you needed her."

"I love you, Angel." Brandon leaned forward and whispered.

"I know, Dadd..." She closed her dark blue eyes. Brandon wiped her black curly hair off her pale alabaster child's face.

"Please don't leave me, my little Angel. I couldn't bear to lose both of you." Brandon whispered to his daughter. Unconscious tears rolled down from his eyes, creating flesh colored tracks through the chalk dust covering his face. "I really couldn't." Angel didn't respond.

Gotcha!

The two paramedics looked at each other. (That was the strangest conversation that they had ever witnessed. They talked about it later. The little girl shouldn't have been able to talk at all, as sedated as she was.)

Brandon sat holding his daughters hand while the ambulance raced through the streets and had flashback after flashback.

***

Scene 2

Brandon Thomas was a deep cover penetration and information retrieval agent for an ultra secret government organization named Q. He was their top information gathering field agent. Q operated globally. They did what the other agencies couldn't or wouldn't. No country was beyond their jurisdiction, not even the United States. The Head of Q reported directly and only to the President of the United States of America.

Brandon had been recruited right out of high school. He had been an honor student. He had achieved one hundred percent on every test since grade two. At Q, his skills were legend. If any information was needed that could absolutely not be gained, attained or found, they called in Brandon.

He considered himself an information gathering loner. He always worked alone. It was alone that he did his best work. When they first asked him to choose a code name he chose the name IGL (pronounced Iggle). It stood for Information Gathering Loner. The person asking misunderstood, thought that it was his accent, and his code name became Eagle.

Eagle was an orphan, of parents unknown, dropped off at the orphanage when he was only days old with a note stating that his name was Brandon Thomas, no middle name. Not that not having a middle name was a bad thing. He never missed it. He had never been adopted. Prospective parents always seemed to pass him by. He grew up in relative obscurity in the orphanage and the New York City school system. Even though he scored one hundred percent on his tests since grade two, when he turned seven, he always seemed to blend in. Everybody took him for granted. Upon high school graduation, Brandon had been awarded a small scholarship to a nameless Midwestern University.

Although he had perfect test scores, Brandon Thomas did not stand out in a crowd of people.

Computers, however, were another matter. He could not hide from them.

***

An Organization, named Q, found out about Brandon's test scores through their computer sorting system. Q was always on the lookout, or searching, for fresh and unique talented recruits that they could test, then train and then harvest the results. Most were culled through the various phases of the process. They brought in Brandon Thomas, no middle name, and tested him.

Brandon had no idea, at that time, who or what the company or organization was that had recruited him. Although small for his age, young Master Thomas turned out to be exactly the type of person that Q was looking for. They found, through the testing, that Brandon operated best alone. That was fine with Q. They needed agents who could operate alone. Most couldn't.

Only one, other than Brandon, worked alone. Her Code Name was Kameleon. Kameleon was the only one who matched the Eagle's success rate. But then again, she didn't do what Brandon did. She had been in a different Division. She had been in the KOLD (Killers On Leash Division). No longer was she with

Q. She had gone Independent. She was now Q's top Free Lance Assassin. Her code name was Kameleon. They had never met, though Brandon had heard rumors of her throughout the years. The rest were the ones who needed the moral support of a partner. Q spent over twelve million dollars in the next three years training the Eagle. They considered it a bargain.

***

Brandon Thomas flashed back to the present as the ambulance swerved recklessly around a corner. He automatically stabilized Angel's stretcher and smiled. The ambulance driver was doing his best to get them to the hospital in record time. In time to save a little girls life.

Angel's daddy had another flashback. A more recent one, this time.

***

Brandon Thomas had just recently returned from Red China from another FFM (Fact Finding Mission). An extremely sensitive one this time. Although almost all were extremely sensitive, this one, on a scale of one to ten, was a ten. Most were eights. He provided his information on his assignment to his Reporting Superior, who was also his Controller. His Superior looked like his code name. He was short and round of body and face. The top of his head was bald and he combed the sides of his head hair straight up. Those, combined with his oversized round glasses, made him look exactly like his code name. His code name was Owl.

When Brandon had supplied all the information he had on his target assignment, Owl asked if there was any other information that he would like to share. Brandon said no. He was dismissed and he went home.

The Eagle knew what Q wanted to know, what Owl was fishing for, although he didn't come right out and ask. He knew, before he went in to give his report, that Q had been told by more than one highly reliable source that Brandon had been privy to an ultra top secret security file. The COW file. A file that supposedly had information that could bring the United States Government to its knees! Right up to and including the President of the United States of America. A file so scandalous and dangerous, that its very existence was rumored to be a myth! Apparently not!

He also knew that Q had been told that Quan Chi Hanoi, Red China's purportedly Immortal Emperor, had put a *'Burn'* Contract on the successful identification and death of the agent that had somehow pierced China's ultra top security measures and gained the ultra secure information that Q wanted.

The very same information that the Eagle had just garnered and supplied to the Owl. That was the only name that Brandon was known as in the smoky murky world of international espionage; the *Eagle*.

China's contract on the Eagle was an open one. Anyone could collect the bounty if they could provide a body and proof of identity. Named after him, the Emperor Quan Chi Hanoi also had his own handpicked agents Secret Covert Organization Red China, Hanoi, known as SCORCH in the espionage world.

Scorch was also seeking the identity and destruction of the infamous Q agent, the Eagle. Because Owl didn't specifically ask, Brandon felt no need to broach the subject. It had nothing to do with his assignment. He never reported items that were not directly related to his assignments. He had been told, when first recruited, that adding superfluous information only muddied the waters.

"Just report the facts on the mission at hand, nothing else." he had been instructed. He had understood and complied. Brandon never revealed his sources. He was not expected to. It was too easy for a leak to destroy his information pipeline. Or that of any of the other field agents, for that matter. All Q cared about was results. They didn't want to know all the particulars. Plausible Deniability they called it.

Top Agents were almost impossible to find, so Q guarded them jealously. None of the field agents knew each other, only their Controller. Although Q or Owl never told him, Brandon knew that the Eagle was their top producing agent in the FFD. The Eagle was the only one in the FFD (Fact Finding Division) to achieve one hundred percent results. Nobody else even came close. Therefore, the Eagle was used only on the IFFM (Impossible Fact Finding Missions). Information Gathering Missions that other top Q IG agents had been unsuccessful at attaining or achieving.

Q did not want to waste Brandon's special *Talents* when others could do it. The Eagle was kept very busy.

Scene 3

As Brandon was sitting in the ambulance, with one of his hands absently covering one of his daughters *(his left hand, sporting a simple muted titanium wedding ring encasing a dark oval ruby on his wedding finger)*, Brandon reviewed the recent events ...

The Eagle knew without question or doubt that Q would declare that the Red Chinese had planted the bomb in his garage. All the evidence would point to it. Garage terrorist bombings were a favorite of SCORCH. It was one of their signatures. The bomb fragments would be of Red Chinese design, of that he had no doubt. And there supposedly *was* the SCORCH *Burn* Contract on his life to back it up.

Brandon, the Eagle, added these facts, along with many others he had checked into these last few days, and he came to the *only logical conclusion.*

Plausible Deniability. One of Q's favorite phrases.

Q had tried to kill Brandon and his family!

Brandon almost couldn't believe it. *Almost* being the key word. All the evidence that he had uncovered in the last few days led him to believe that it *could* happen, but he just couldn't bring himself to believe that it *would* happen. And though one of the Eagle's *instincts* felt it, but he just couldn't bring himself to believe in it enough to act on it.

Q normally protected *all* their agents and personnel to the *nth* degree. Logic and Q's past performance lead him to override his instincts. He had thought that he was too valuable to Q. He was their golden haired Boy Wonder. When he had been told by Owl to report in, he thought it was to confirm his knowledge of the mythical *COW file*. That had waylaid his suspicions and overrode his *instincts*. Brandon's head unconsciously dropped slightly, as though hung in shame and agony at that thought. His wife had been murdered and his daughter's life was hanging by a thread because he had *not* followed his instincts this *one* time. Even the best of the best weren't perfect.

Pale lines of skin showed through the chalk white, as unconscious tears coursed their way down his motionless face from unseeing eyes. One of the paramedics glanced over at him at that moment. He later told his partner that Brandon's face looked as if it was cracking apart.

At that exact moment in time, Brandon Thomas looked very much like he felt; a betrayed, broken hearted clown.

That moment did not last long. As the paramedic relayed that moment later to his partner, something subtle inside Angel's father *changed*. Slowly his head rose and *something else*, or *someone else*, looked out. Someone or something *not* quite sane.

That cold predatory *look* scared the paramedic in a way he could not describe. He quickly looked away.

The *Eagle* noticed the reaction of the paramedic as he looked back down at his daughter. That caused him note the change in himself.

***

When the ambulance arrived at the hospital, Angel was immediately rushed to surgery. Brandon Thomas gave his report to one of the police officers that had followed the ambulance in. The officers left immediately after the statement. They wisely forgot about the incident with the other four officers. All had recovered within minutes.

After signing the statement, Brandon immediately retired to the men's room to repair himself. He looked at his image in the mirror. The chalk covered figure that stared back at him, he did not recognize. What he saw was a dead man with dead eyes staring blindly back at him from a cracked face. A living dead man who should be with his dead wife!

"Oh, my god!" Brandon whispered hoarsely to the corpse in front of him. "Oh god, oh my god, Char is dead! My pure, loving, beautiful wife is dead! What are you going to do now?" he asked the dead man in the mirror.

The *Eagle* receded as delayed reaction set in. A shudder wracked his frame. Another followed. Then another. Each one stronger and more violent than the one before. Brandon grabbed blindly at the sink to stop from collapsing to the floor. The porcelain shattered to dust beneath such a grip. The white hunched figure in the mirror took on the shape of an eagle, the cracks in his face looked like feathers.

'Pull yourself together man!' the Eagle hissed savagely inside his head. *'So you screwed up! You lost your wife. It happens! You know that!'* The familiar inner voice continued and he listened like a drowning man clutching a life preserver, *'But your daughter still needs you! She still lives!'*

Brandon nodded imperceptibly. His face changed subtly as he relinquished command.

The *Eagle* was now back in control.

***

Scene 4

When Brandon Thomas returned to the waiting area minutes later, there was no evidence of the drywall dust on his clothing or his body. His thick chestnut colored hair was damp, but dried within minutes. Even an astute observer would have had a hard time finding any physical evidence that Brandon had just been a victim of an explosion or the meltdown that happened in the Men's Room.

He walked over to a chair that was backed against the wall with a full view of the room, sat down and waited. He picked up a magazine, opened and stared at it. Pages were turned but he was not reading. His mind was in overdrive turmoil, sorting memories. People passed him. No one spoke to him. It was like he was invisible.

Sometime later, possibly hours, Brandon didn't remember exactly, a woman in surgical scrubs walked into the waiting room and walked up to him and asked politely, "Mr. Thomas?" Brandon nodded and stood. "Please come with me sir."

With that, she turned and guided Brandon to a nurse's station. The nurse explained, as she escorted him, that that she was taking him to his daughters recovery room, which was located directly off and connected to, the emergency surgery room in IC that his Angelina had been operated in. When they arrived, Brandon took in the room at a glance. Numerous medical staff were scattered, seemingly randomly, around the room, most in surgical scrubs.

The glaring exceptions were the two large muscular men in conservative dark suits. One was in a dark blue suit, the other in a dark brown. One of the two men was conversing with a corpulent, balding man dressed in surgical scrubs.

Brandon recognized the two men in suits immediately. They had met at a briefing on one of his assignments, years ago, to give him needed information. They looked to be wearing the same suits that they had worn when they originally met him. The one in the brown suit had never spoken, only the one in the blue suit. No names had been used and the Eagle had not been told their status, but he knew them to be a top team of Q's hit squad, KOLD (Killers On Leash Division).

When Brandon first entered the room, one of the men - the one in the blue suit - looked up at Brandon, smiled and walked over to him. Brandon smiled back. They shook hands.

"Q sent us to protect you." *Blue Suit* stated in a quiet voice. Brandon nodded. "What the hell happened?" *Blue Suit* asked quietly, yet bluntly. His cold soulless eyes bored into Brandon's. Brandon's eyes did not waver as he answered, just as quietly.

"A *Red Chinese* SCORCH assassination attempt. Somehow they found out about me." The agent of KOLD nodded in understanding and something seemed to relax in him slightly, although it was nothing Brandon could see. He just *felt* it.

"Excuse me ... Mr. Thomas?" asked one of the men in scrubs as he approached him. It was one of the medical staff who had been talking to the other assassin, the Eagle noted. From the attitude, probably the surgeon. Brandon nodded.

"May we talk privately ... over here please?" The Doctor motioned and Brandon followed. He noticed *Blue Suit* walk over and say something to his partner, *Brown Suit*. Again he saw, or rather *felt*, something in the other man relax.

He turned a part of his attention back to the surgeon.

The doctor stopped a suitable distance away from prying ears. He turned to Brandon, started to speak and then stopped. He looked nervous. He didn't meet Brandon's eyes. He was sweating slightly. More of Brandon's attention focused on him.

"Yes?" Brandon asked quietly. Something in the way he said *'Yes?'* made the doctor jump slightly and meet his eyes. He started to sweat more. He took a breath, smiled and said to Brandon.

"Mr. Thomas, my name is Dr. Bogart. I have some good news and some bad news for you." He paused again to gather his thoughts.

"What is with this good news bad news *bullshit?* This is *not* a comedy sketch. What are you trying to tell me? Speak plain and fast, *doctor*. I have run out of patience." Brandon's attention was now almost exclusively focused on the sweating physician. The words were spoken very softly, but with great underlying force and passion. The *doctor* knew it.

"The good news is that we saved your daughter's life Mr. Thomas!" he said quickly.

"Then what is the bad news?" came the soft reply. Dr. Bogart trembled at the voice.

"Well, *(gulp)* you see, *(gulp)* it's like this Mr. Thomas, umm ... ahh ... the patient ... your daughter ... was in surprisingly good shape when she arrived. Oh, she had a lot of minor internal damage, but nothing that wouldn't heal on its own. With the exception of a ruptured artery, that is. She had lost a tremendous amount of blood. We needed to repair the artery immediately!" his voice gained in volume, as if trying to gain courage. "Your daughter was in critical need of a blood transfusion, Mr. Thomas. As you are aware, she has a very rare blood type. It is the same as yours. Because you were involved in the explosion, we could not use you as a donor in case something was wrong with you and you needed it. We happened to have her blood type on hand and we used it." He stopped speaking again. He was at a loss as to how to continue.

"And?" The word was spoken in such a way that the surgeon started to sweat more.

"Mr. Thomas, I don't know how to say this!" he said desperately. "I don't know how it happened. *It should have been impossible.*" He paused again, gulping like a guppy. He saw something change in Brandon's eyes. Something that scared him to death.

"One or more of the bags of blood was tainted." The doctor blurted quickly. "I'm sorry Mr. Thomas, but your daughter was given a bag of blood tainted with the SIM virus. I am *so* very, very sorry."

Brandon was quiet for a moment, absorbing this information. Q had trained him well. No expression showed on his face. His eyes took on a sleepy look. The Eagle was now in *full* control.

"You are telling me that you saved my daughter's life only to have infected her with the SIM virus, the deadliest known virus on the planet?" The Eagle spoke quietly, politely. He knew it was not the surgeons fault. His very actions proved that. The surgeon nodded numbly.

"I would like to see my daughter. Where is she?" Angel's father asked abruptly, yet quietly, in a strangely altered voice. The doctor jumped as if stung.

"In the room to your right." the surgeon answered automatically. "But you need to have a checkup, Mr. Thomas. Immediately. And your daughter won't wake up for awhile yet. She is still heavily sedated from the surgery. She won't even know you are there."

"I will go for a checkup *after* I see my daughter. Is that understood, *(there was a long pause)* Doctor Bogart?" the last said very softly, almost caressingly, in the same tone as before. "Yes, uh ... yes. I suppose that will be fine." came the faltering response. Suddenly angry at the situation, and his own reaction to it, Doctor Bogart turned and spoke abruptly to one of the nurses.

"Nurse, allow Mr. Thomas in to see his daughter for a few minutes and then see that he is taken and examined, *stat.*"

"Yes, Doctor Bogart." responded the stunned nurse as he stormed away.

Brandon turned and walked up to the two men in suits, *Mr. Brown and Mr. Blue.* As he approached them he *changed* slightly again, the Eagle still in full control of the situation. "I'm going to say goodbye to my daughter and then go for a checkup." His altered tone brooked no argument. As with the

Doctor, the two men nodded unconsciously at the subconscious authoritative implant. "After that, we'll go to Q and report in. Position yourselves outside the door to my daughter's room while I'm in there. The bomber, or bombers, may be in the hospital even as we speak. Call Q and have backup sent *immediately* to protect Angel."

Mr. Brown looked at Brandon questioningly. "Angel is my daughter." Brandon clarified.

In unison, both men nodded understanding. Mr. Blue walked across the room, took out his cell phone, and made the call.

As Brandon opened the door and walked into the recovery room to see his daughter, his eyes never lost sight of Mr. Brown until the door was completely closed. Unaware of this, Mr. Brown positioned himself outside the door.

A few moments after Brandon had gone in to see his daughter, Mr. Blue finished listening to whoever was speaking, said something in return, closed his cell phone and returned to his partner waiting outside the recovery room door.

"Our controller says to wait and take him out on the way to headquarters for the usual debriefing. That way, his guard will be down." Mr. Brown nodded.

They waited patiently for a few more minutes. Then Mr. Blue started to fidget. He felt it! Looking down at his watch he suddenly declared, "It's been *too long*. Something's wrong!" He looked at his partner. "Shall we take him out now and be done with it? I was told on the phone that he has had all the training *and more*. To wait could kill *us*. What do you think?"

His partner looked at him for a moment, and then reaching under his coat, Mr. Brown surreptitiously pulled out a silenced gun and said in a surprisingly high voice for one his size. "Let's do it." *(No wonder he didn't talk much!)*

Together they burst into the recovery room, guns at the ready, only to find Angel asleep on the hospital bed with a note pinned to the sheet on her chest and the window wide open. Brandon Thomas was nowhere to be seen. Mr. Brown dropped into a military crouch and scanned room and the ceiling. Mr. Blue ran to the window and looked cautiously out, retreated and turned to Mr. Brown. In turning he rattled a tray of glass tubes. He heard a small crunch. He looked down and lifted his foot. A small empty glass vial lay broken under his shoe. He looked back up at his partner.

"Lock that door." he growled.

Mr. Brown locked the door. Mr. Blue walked over, unpinned the note and read it, then took out his cell phone and hit redial.

"The Eagle has flown. He left a note. What are your instructions? *(long pause)* Yes sir." He read the note, then listened again, nodding slightly. "Yes sir, we are on our way in. Shall we liberate the *Celestial Spirit* before we return? *(longer pause)* Yes sir!"

Mr. Blue closed his phone. "Let's go."

Mr. Brown smiled a happy smile and leveled his silenced gun at Angel.

"No!" Mister Blue said sharply. Mr. Brown looked at him in surprise, but did not pull the trigger. "Not today," Mister Blue said, in a little softer tone, "maybe some *other* time, okay partner? We need her as *bait* for now. " He knew how his partner *hated* to be disappointed. And he knew how to control him.

Well ... sometimes.

Mr. Brown's dark eyes lost their glow. His smile faded. His hand dropped slowly as he put his gun away. He nodded acquiescence.

Mr. Blue put the note in his pocket, closed the window, picked up the broken pieces of glass, put them in a plastic baggie and put it in his pocket. He casually dropped it in one of the garbage cans on their way out. There could be no red flags. No hint that anything unusual had occurred in Angelina's hospital recovery room.

***

Scene 5

One week after he had exited through the hospital window, Brandon Thomas sat in a corner booth in a small café in Paris France. *Le' Café Cappuccino.* A corner booth at the *back* of the Café.

It was mid morning. Not many customers were in the cozy little café. Too late for breakfast, too early for lunch. Brandon was sipping on a cappuccino and working on a small hand held PDA cell phone when a stunningly beautiful woman walked through the door. With a walk that defied description, the flawlessly pale alabaster skinned woman approached his table. She was wearing an exquisite outfit. A knee length, softly shimmering, amethyst colored dress accented her glowing emerald green eyes and long, wavy, flaming red hair. The few patrons ignored her.

She stood at the table for a moment as Brandon continued with his work on the PDA, seemingly not noticing her.

"Aren't you going to invite me to sit down?" she asked softly.

Brandon looked up, as if surprised to see her. His hand reached up and touched his bluetooth earpiece.

"Hello! But of course! Please, be my guest! Nice of you to come calling after your vanishing act last night."

"You're not fooling me, Mr. Thomas." she said as she slid onto the seat across from him. "I know you saw me as soon as I walked through the door."

Brandon smiled. "Yes I did, didn't I? Shall we carry on from where we left off last night?"

"By all means, let's continue." She paused for a moment, waiting for him to continue. He paused for a moment, waiting for her to continue. Finally Brandon broke the silence.

"Well, what did you think of my POA? Do you have any thoughts on it?"

"I think it's a great POA, Mr. Thomas." she said seriously. "And though I can find no flaw with the *premise* of your *Plan of Action*, I can think of a thousand and one ways you could be joining me if even *one* thing goes wrong."

"Joining you?" he asked, puzzled. Then his face cleared. He smiled. "I do keep forgetting that you're a *spirit*, don't I Charlie? Well, you can't blame me. I can feel your feathery fingers when you touch me. I can touch you ... well, almost. I can hear you clearly. You can hear me clearly." He paused for a moment looking at her. "And I did notice, Char. You are wearing different clothes today. Every time I've seen you since you die... since the explosion, you've been wearing the outfit that you wore on that day. Nice outfit, by the way. *Stunning* would be a better word."

"Thank you, my dear loving husband. I thought you would like it. It's too bad that you are the only one here who can see it." She smiled her special *'I love you'* smile. The smile that she had only ever smiled just for him. Angel got a different *'I love you'* smile. A mother's smile.

Brandon touched his hand again to the bluetooth in his right ear. With the PDA cell phone on the table, to everyone in the Café, he seemed to be talking to someone on it.

"Getting back to the POA we were talking about last night. Have you thought about it? Do you have any ideas or suggestions as to who I could contact to purchase the equipment that I need?" he asked his spectral wife. She shook her head slightly, hair swishing to the movement. "And speaking of last night, why did you disappear so suddenly?"

"It's funny, I was *just now* wondering when you would get around to that, dear." She saw his look. "Not *funny haw haw*, but *funny* as in *strange*. Not that what you asked was *funny*, but what happened last night *was* and *is*, and I need to talk to you about it." She paused and looked at her husband intensely. "I was in the room of the terrorist bomber that was killed last night. One second I was talking to you about your Plan of Action and *poof*, *(she snapped her fingers)* the next instant I was standing in his room. He was the one, the bomber I mean, that was on TV around midnight."

"The Mr. Smoke *smoke*?" he asked incredulously. His voice rose slightly in pitch. "You witnessed a *terrorist bomber* get *smoked* by Mr. Smoke?"

"Oh, don't look so surprised. *And keep your voice down!* People are looking at you!" she said urgently. "And don't worry. They couldn't see me. Or should I say, the *bomber* couldn't see me. The *other three* did."

Brandon laughed as if someone had made a joke on the phone. "Oh, you mean you saw it *on* the News!" He surveyed the room without anyone noticing. The customers went back to their own world.

"I doubt if one of them, other than the waiter, speaks English. They just heard the name Mr. Smoke." he said softly.

His wife laughed delightedly. "You really *are* good! I'd almost forgotten. Gosh, let me think ... I haven't seen you in action for a long time, since .. um .. before Angel was born. I love it."

He grinned slightly, and ignored the compliment. "The *other three?* I thought that Mr. Smoke hunted alone. From all the information I was able to garner on him, he works alone." Brandon continued quietly.

"He does. He is three beings in one body."

"Whoa! Three beings in one body? Where, in the twilight zone of your mind, did that come from Charlie?"

Charlene tried to look indignant, but finally gave up and grinned when Brandon did not respond. "What I *meant* was, I think he may be a paranoid schizophrenic with multiple personalities! He had *three distinct auras,* Brandon. When I appeared, Mr. Smoke saw me immediately and two of them disappeared. Only one remained. I think I caught them off guard when I appeared on the scene. *In fact I know I did*. I think the other two just went invisible. I felt that they were still there watching me." She paused slightly, thinking. "But I may have been right when I unconsciously said that he is three beings in one body. I have never seen anything like it. They were all intertwined, totally blended yet distinctly different. I probably wouldn't have noticed if my aura sight hadn't become enhanced when I became a ghost."

Although Brandon was looking at her intently, he didn't see her. His mind was focused on what she had just shared with him.

Suddenly, Brandon frowned.

A man behind Charlene Thomas frowned back at him. Brandon smiled back at him and pointed to his phone and ear. The man understood the look was not at him and smiled back and turned away. He returned his focus to his wife.

"Wait a minute Charlie! Mr. Smoke saw you? How can that be? I thought that only *I* could see you. That *is* what you told me in the hospital, remember?"

"I'm a *ghost* ... not a ... a *goddess*, for crying out loud!" Charlene stated in exasperation. "I don't know *everything!* I am not *all-knowing!*" She used two fingers on each hand to make quotation marks before and after *all-knowing*. She then put her small fists on her hips. "In fact, I told you I don't know *why* I'm still around. *Remember?* I'm just your wife without a body."

"Just my wife without a body?" Brandon paraphrased. "What in the world brought that on? Why are you so upset Char?"

"Because Mr. Smoke asked me why I'm still around!" She stamped her small foot under the table. Brandon heard the sound. "And I didn't have an answer for him!" She looked ready to cry.

"I can answer that, if you want." Brandon said gently, and then smiled at his wife's surprised look.

Gone was her *ready to cry* look. "Can you really, sweetheart?" Her husband nodded. "Then, *yes please!*"

"You are here to help me as long as I need you." Brandon stated solemnly.

Charlene Thomas paused in thought for a moment, then said slowly, "You know, that feels right ... somehow. How did you know, Brandon?"

"Our daughter told me on the way to the hospital. She said that you told her to tell me. She also said that you told her to tell me that you have loved *only me* since we first met."

Charlene looked happy and sad at the same time. "She's right darling, but I don't remember saying it." she placed her fingers on her forehead in unconscious frustration. Her slender hands dropped in defeat as she looked at her husband imploringly.

"Brandon, why can't I remember saying it?"

"Because you'd just been killed?" Brandon suggested tentatively.

"Maybe," she said quietly, as if to herself, "but I have a feeling there is more to it than that." Suddenly she smiled at her husband. "Okay, I'll accept your premise for now. Let's hope you will always need me!"

"I will." he said quietly. His wife laughed. She knew him well. He didn't show it, but she knew that he was as frustrated as she was, with all the same unanswered questions.

"Alright ... back to our previous conversation," he said, "tell me what happened at the *Smoke* scene. From the beginning, this time."

Charlene arched her back and stretched, pulled back a stray lock of flaming hair and leaned back in the booth, settling herself in a more comfortable position. '*No wonder I think she's real and alive,*' Brandon thought to himself, '*she acts real and alive. I can even see her chest rise and fall slightly as she breathes. Not at all like one would expect a spirit to behave at all.*'

"I *am real*, darling. I'm a *real ghost*."

Brandon frowned slightly. "I take it you still have the same abilities, even as a spirit? The mind reading, and the seeing of aura's?"

"But of course. In fact, they seem to be a lot sharper and stronger in the spirit world. Oh, don't give me that *pretend* grimace. You *know* that my *abilities* have helped you in the past. And you *know* that I have never intentionally tried to read your thoughts. I know you so well I don't have to. You normally block your thoughts from me anyway." She paused in thought, and then continued. "I don't *think* I read your thoughts Brandon, but I just might have unconsciously slipped and done it without realizing I did it. If so, I'm sorry, darling. What can I say except that I'm just human ... well, almost!"

His grimace was replaced with a slight nod and a smile. She always knew how to make him smile. It was another of her *Gifts*. To Brandon, one of her greatest.

"The *Smoke*?" he reminded her gently.

She laughed her soft throaty laugh. "*Ahh yes*, the Mr. Smoke ... um, *Smoke!* Well, as I said, last night as we were talking ... pow!" She snapped her fingers again, "I was somehow instantly *transported* to the man who got *Smoked* by Mr. Smoke. The man who got '*Smoked*' was in his apartment, I assume watching television, when I appeared just as Mr. Smoke pulled the trigger. I stood frozen in horror at what I had witnessed. *'The man didn't stand a chance'*, I remember thinking in shock … not that he deserved it, the creep, after I found out what he had done!" the last was spoken with heat.

Her husband looked at her questioningly but didn't interrupt. He didn't want to break her chain of thought. She noticed the look.

"Sorry darling. Where was I? … Oh yes. Mr. Smoke just glanced up at me and then proceeded to arrange the body and take pictures with a small camera that magically appeared in his hand." She saw Brandon's skeptical look. "Okay, I *know* it wasn't magic, but it did seem to appear in his hand. When he had finished taking pictures, it …"

"More cappuccino, monsieur?" asked the waiter, who had suddenly appeared at the table, startling Charlene into silence.

"Yes please." responded Brandon in perfect French, covering his blue tooth as if still on the phone. *"And please bring me the lunch special."*

"Which one, monsieur?"

"You decide."

"Very well, monsieur." The waiter turned and left.

"How very rude! Did you see the way he cut me off? Why I've half a mind to …." She faded off as she saw her husband's smiling face. Then it hit her. She smiled in genuine good humor at the revelation. "Now *I forgot* that I am a ghost."

"I prefer the word *spirit* over *ghost*."

"I think there is a difference between them, Brandon. I think of a spirit as the *essence* of a person or ghost. To me, a *spirit* doesn't have form. A *ghost* does. That is why I consider myself as a *ghost*. I will call myself a *spirit* if you would prefer, though."

Brandon laughed. "Only you would think of that. Why don't we compromise and call you a *Tweener*?"

"A *Tweener?*"

"Yes, a *Tweener*. Right now you're *tween* heaven and earth."

Now it was Charlene's turn to laugh. "Only you would think of a word like that. What made you think of *Tweener?*"

"Well ... I have to confess Charlie that I used to think of you as *Tweener* when we were dating."

"You did?" she asked, surprised.

"Absolutely! When we were dating, I came over to your house one time and found you sleeping. You had no clothes on and only had a light filmy sheet covering you. After that, I often thought of you as naked '*tween* the sheets."

"Then *Tweener* I am!" she laughed. "Now let's get back to the Mister Smoke, *Smoke*. As I was saying *before* I was so *rudely* interrupted, I know that the appearance of the camera was not magical, but when Mister Smoke finished taking the pictures, the camera vanished! I was looking right at it when it happened. It was there one second and gone the next. After he was done, he slid his tinted eyeglasses up, on their swivel, to his forehead and his liquid golden cat eyes looked at me and he said, '*You can move on now, Charlene Thomas. I just Smoked the man who planted the bomb in your Landrover.*'" She saw Brandon nod slightly in understanding as to the passion and why she had called him a 'creep'.

"He was the … the *creep* who planted the bomb that killed me, Brandon! In that instant, my whole attitude changed toward the incident. That's why I said that he deserved to be *Smoked* unceremoniously! And the eyes that looked at me, Mr. Smokes eyes, weren't human, Brandon. He *must* have been wearing contacts, but I have to admit, they didn't look like it. They looked very, very, *very* real. What I saw of his face was black, but it was the matte black of makeup. His mask looked almost identical to that British television broadcast rendition of him. Then he lowered his glasses, turned away, and proceeded to search the corpse. I couldn't see clearly, but I saw him take a number of things off the dead man. Then he moved out of my range of vision, to search the rest of the house I guess. I just stood there still stunned at the revelation that the man he *Smoked* was the very man who tried to kill our entire family." She hugged herself and shivered at the memory.

At that moment she looked very fragile to her husband. And very much alive. His heart and soul ached to put his arms around her to hold and comfort her at that moment.

She pulled herself together and continued, "I looked down at him Brandon, and all I could see was a very *fit* Asian man in his late forties or early fifties. A very fit *dead man*. And I vividly remember *not* seeing his spirit leave his body. I somehow expected to, seeing as I was a spirit also and had aura vision.

That was when I started to figure out I was a ghost instead of a spirit. I walked around the room and saw pictures of him and of his wife, along with pictures of their grown children and young grandchildren. Turns out it was his ex-wife." She saw her husbands smile. "I checked around. No women's clothes in the house. No wonder. I imagine it must have made her sick inside to live with someone like that. I don't even classify the bomber as a him. He is a *THAT*. To me he is a someone like that!"

Brandon nodded in understanding. "You said he was of *Asian* descent? Please describe him to me. The television didn't show much, just an unrecognizable angle shot of his face. Usually a frozen, reaction formed dead face doesn't look, in death, as it does in life."

***

Charlene painted a verbal picture of the Asian in exquisite detail. Her verbal painting skills rivaled her phenomenal memory. Once finished, Brandon recognized him immediately. He had seen him at Q twice only. Both times, something about the man instantly repulsed Brandon. At first, he thought it may have been the inscrutable Asian face, but he *felt* that it was not. The second time, out of curiosity at the second feeling of repugnancy, and to test his skills, (part of which meant Q *not* finding out about it) the Eagle followed him and made it a test of his skills to find out all about him, without the slightest detection. He had succeeded.

The Asian was an Independent Contractor, an incredibly highly skilled *explosives expert* and assassin that could not be traced back to Q. And Q only hired the best of the best. He was not surprised that Q hadn't killed him after his botched attempt. They always forgave their best people the few times they failed. Brandon filed that thought away for later. '*Food for thought.*'

"Do you know what country you were in at the time?" he asked when she was done.

"The United States. New York City to be exact. 125 East River Drive." The surprised look in her husband's eyes made Charlene smile. "You're welcome. I thought you'd want to know."

Brandon returned the smile. "Please continue, Char."

"Well, after awhile, Mr. Smoke came back into the room, just to double check things on his way out, I think. Anyway, he stopped and looked at me again and asked, *'Why are you still here, Charlene Thomas?'* That is when I told him I didn't know."

Charlene smiled at the thought. "Somehow I knew he was surprised when I answered him. Oh, nothing changed about him, but somehow I *felt* it. He asked if there was anything he could do to help me. *'How very kind of him.'* I remember thinking at the time. You know darling, it came as a bit of a jolt to realize that Mr. Smoke wasn't a cold blooded killer. He came up to me, so close that I could *almost* smell his subtle, incredibly wonderfully sexy Cologne. He took off one of his gloves and put his hand on mine. His hand was large, well formed, and bronze in color. Well, large compared to mine."

She saw something in her husband's eyes. She grinned impishly. "Yes darling, I knew at *that* exact moment that he was either a white man with a great bottled or tanning bed tan, or of mixed heritage, or was an Asian. Narrows it down to about a hundred trillion people, doesn't it?"

"If ah done tole you once, ah done tole you a kazillion times, *quit zageratin' gurl!*" her husband said in a backwoods drawl.

Char nobly ignored her husband, closed her eyes for a moment in recall, then opened them and continued. "I remember that his hand had an incredibly beautiful tri-gold colored ring on the middle finger. It was somehow like his aura. There were different colored triangles embedded in it. They looked to be floating. It was an *impossible* ring. I have never seen anything like it. There can only be one of those rings in the world. If you find that ring, or who made it, you will find Mr. Smoke!" Charlene said it with a *'See how easy it is?"* tone and look.

Brandon smiled in amusement. "You could *almost* smell his *'subtle, incredibly wonderfully sexy Cologne'*? I didn't know you could *almost* smell *anything*. How can you, as a ghost, *almost smell* something, Char?' he asked kiddingly.

Charlene was not fooled. She answered seriously.

"I ... ah ... don't really know, Brandon." she saw an almost startled look cross his face. "What I am trying to say is that I don't know how to *explain* it. It wasn't *exactly* a smell, but it *almost* was? Oh forget it!" she finished in exasperation.

Brandon bit back another smile and said nothing. His wife composed herself and continued. "Back to his hand. It was a beautifully shaped hand, almost statue like. No calluses. Smooth skin but *not* soft. Very muscular hands with no superfluous flesh, does that make sense?"

Brandon nodded and lifted his right hand.

"How very silly of me! Of course it makes sense to you. Your hands are like that, maybe just slightly smaller." She paused as sudden realization struck, then exclaimed. "You and Mister Smoke are both about the same height, and your body type is similar. Your bone structure is slightly smaller, if your hand is any indication. And you both walk cat-like." Without changing gears she switched back to the memory. "And when he touched me, I could feel it Brandon! What a shock! His hand didn't pass through me like yours does. He gently squeezed my hand and said he wished me the best of luck. Then he replaced his glove, turned and walked towards the door. All of a sudden a cloud of smoke surrounded him and he vanished. I just *knew* it had to be a stage magician's trick, but it sure was impressive. Even his aura's disappeared. I couldn't see them anywhere. I've never seen anyone who could make their aura invisible. I'm sure he did it so that I wouldn't know where he went, so that I couldn't follow him. Or he teleported back to the *Starship Exercise*, which I highly doubt. I *didn't* hear him say *'Beam me up Banana Comb Eyes!'* And his hand was way too young to be *Captain Quirky*."

She shook her head slightly, in wonderment, at the memory, then continued. "After that, I checked out the house and the address. He didn't miss anything that I could see. Then I left and stood outside and watched as the police and news media arrived. And … that's my story of the Mr. Smoke … uh … *Smoke*."

"I'm not sure I understand Char. First you tell me you think that Mr. Smoke is a paranoid schizophrenic with multiple personalities and then you tell me you're shocked that he's not a cold blooded killer." Brandon quizzed.

She placed her hands on her hips and almost glared at him. "Just because he *may* be a paranoid schizophrenic with multiple personalities *doesn't* mean he's a *cold blooded killer*. To hear and see it on the News, you would think he was."

Her hands dropped as she paused again to gather her thoughts. "But *when* he touched me, Brandon, I *knew* he was *not* a cold blooded killer. I mean, *he may be one* when he's killing a terrorist bomber, but only then. Oh, never mind. Maybe he *is* a cold blooded killer to terrorist bombers, but he is *not* to anyone else. Does *that* make sense?" she almost sniffed at him.

Brandon couldn't stop himself. He laughed at her and at the situation. "Yes it does Char, but *only* because I know you."

Char started to say something, but whatever her retort was to be was cut off as the waiter abruptly appeared with the luncheon special and served it with a flourish. Brandon looked at the plate and laughed again, in spite of himself. The waiter looked confused.

"Is everything alright, monsieur?" he asked quickly.

"Yes, yes, everything is just fine. Thank you." Brandon said with a smile. He pointed to the blue tooth as if it was something someone had told him. The waiter nodded silently and left.

Brandon Thomas looked down again at the *luncheon special* that awaited him on the table. He couldn't help it, he laughed again. He had travelled from the United States to Paris France, asked a waiter in a small exclusive French café for the French luncheon special and staring up at him was a double cheeseburger and deep fried potato wedges.

Charlene caught the irony of it and laughed also.

"Where were we?" Brandon asked as he took a bite of the burger. Speaking around the food in his mouth, he continued, "Oh yes, I remember. Mr. Smoke is a pure upstanding sexy smelling citizen who kills terrorist bombers as a, what ... hobby? ... pastime? ... or..."

Seeing the look on his wife's face stopped him. He stopped talking and swallowed his food and smiled.

Her face cleared.

"Very good! You did that for *their* benefit!" Char said, motioning to the people in the restaurant. "An arrogant American businessman, with no table manners, talking on the phone with food in his mouth." Then her face clouded slightly and her voice dropped to match. "Very clever, husband. You know I don't like it when you talk with your mouth full of food and you found a way to get away with it. Not only did you *get away with it*, you even managed to get me to *compliment you* on it! OOOOOOOO" she fumed!

Brandon could not help himself, he started to laugh quietly.

"I couldn't help it dearheart. Your *Starship Banana Comb Fantasy* sparked it." This brought greater and darker storm clouds to his wife's face. Then, seeing the absurdity of the situation, as her husband did, her face instantly cleared as she joined him in the laughter.

***

On a more serious note he continued, *without food in his mouth,* "All jesting aside ... yes Char, I really *do* understand what you are trying to say. And I agree with you. I think it's obvious that Mr. Smoke is someone who has a consuming hatred for terrorist bombers. Someone close to him must have been killed by a terrorist bomb or he was a survivor of one. I'm glad I was never asked to find out who he was. I *like* what he does. Anyway, enough of my opinion of Mr. Smoke! Is that the end of your story?"

"Yes. Well ... almost. What I mean is that it was the end of the Mr. Smoke ... Smoke, but not the end of my story. As I was watching the News Media and Police at the scene, a large crowd gathered. I stood just inside the police barricade so I wouldn't have people walking through me. It weird's me out when that happens because I ... I feel *who* they are, and it isn't always nice." She smiled at her husband. He smiled back in empathy.

"Anyway," she continued, "as I was watching, I felt a hand touch my right arm. I looked to my right side and saw nothing. Then I felt a touch on my left arm and looked to the left. Again ... *nothing*. Although I'd just finished looking over the crowd, I turned and looked again. As before, they were all looking at what was going on, not at me. As I was looking, I noticed a good looking couple who had been standing directly behind me. I was surprised that I hadn't noticed them earlier. I should have. I felt I should know them, but I knew I didn't. They were *very* expensively dressed, the woman in particular. My god Brandon, she looked absolutely *spectacular*, but *nobody* seemed to notice. As I was trying to figure out *why* they looked so familiar, they *both* turned and looked directly at me. Not through me, Brandon, *at me*! That was when I recognized them. The shock must have showed on my face, because they smiled at me. 'Lord and Lady Brighton,' I blurted, 'what are you doing here? You're both dead! Aren't you?'

"'Call me Michael.' Lord Brighton said to me as he stretched out his hand. Instinctually I reached out and shook it. Brandon, I could touch him as I had with Mr. Smoke!

"Then Lady Brighton put forth her hand, which I also shook, and she said, 'And please call me Sylvia. Lady Brighton seems so formal, don't you think? And dead? What makes you think we're dead?'

"Brandon, right then I thought to myself, *'Oh my god, they think they're still alive!'* What I was thinking must have showed on my face because both of them started laughing."

"'Of course we know that we are Ghosts.' Sylvia said laughingly. Then she sobered and said, 'Do you know that you are one also?'

"'Of course I do.' I responded automatically, but I was dumfounded, Brandon. I remember thinking, *'What are they doing here?'* I must have spoken out loud, because Sylvia answered,

"'We are here to see you, Charlene. May I call you Charlene?' I nodded like an idiot. She smiled, patted my hand comfortingly and continued, 'I know dear, I know ... a million questions must be racing madly through your mind right now, so just take all the time you need to sort this out. When you are ready, ask whatever questions you have ... Alright?'

"Again I just nodded like an imbecile." Charlene mimicked the imbecilic nod. Brandon could not help smiling. Char responded with a smile, as she recognized what she had done, then continued.

"They just stood there patiently and waited for me to get my act together. I don't think it took too long, but I don't remember for sure." Charlene paused for a moment, putting events in order. She liked things in order. She knew that her husband could absorb it any way she told it, but he was always patient with her. That was one of the many things she loved about him.

"Finally I said to them, 'Why don't you just tell me what you are doing here and then I'll ask the questions. So *many* are running through my mind right now that don't seem important, but might be. Like, how were you able to see me when I couldn't see you? Or, why couldn't I see you until *after* you both touched me? I do know you both touched me. Or, why did you come here to see me? Or why am I still here? Or .....' Lord Brighton held up his hand and stopped me.

"'Good idea!' he said quickly, before I could start again, 'why don't we tell you the reasons we're here and you can ask questions later, say what?'

"'Yes.' I responded *unintelligently*. I didn't say another word Brandon, so that they could speak. That was when I suddenly realized that everybody was gone except Michael and Sylvia Brighton and, of course, myself! I don't remember any of them leaving. Strange."

Char frowned at the memory, then shook her head slightly. "Anyway, they proceeded to tell me that, in life, they were close friends with Mr. Smoke and still are. It turns out that Michael was the Head of A.T.C.U., which blew my mind. The A.T.C.U. is ...."

"I know what the A.T.C.U. is Char." Brandon said quietly. "I know that Sir Michael Brighton and his wife Lady Sylvia were brutally murdered, shot-gunned down by a man and a woman, in that media covered restaurant shooting. What a media circus that was!" he shook his head slightly at the memory. "No one, *or* organization, was ever identified, or even *implicated* for that matter. What I *didn't* know was that, previous to his marriage to Sylvia, International Playboy and Lord of the Realm, Michael Brighton was the Head of the ultra secret British Organization, the *Anti Terrorist Control Unit*. I was told the Head of the A.C.T.U. was a genius brilliant tactician before an accident killed him ... I would like to have known him." He added absently.

Charlene brought him back on track. "How silly of me! Of course you do, darling. That's right; you were the one who told me who they were, years ago. Anyway, it seems that Mr. Smoke asked them to check up on me and make sure I was alright."

"How in the world did they know where, or how, to find you, Charlie?"

Charlene nodded in excitement, "Why, that is *exactly* what *I* asked them! They told me that when Mr. Smoke touched me, he '*connected*' to me somehow, *whatever that meant*. He was able to pass that *connection* on to them. He also told them where he had last seen me. That's how they found me."

Charlie suddenly switched gears again. "They gave me this wrist watch to wear." She held up her left arm and showed Brandon a golden wrist watch that she was wearing. Brandon looked at it closely. The triangle dial was blank. Nothing showed on it.

"Char, the dial is blank."

"Of course it is, silly! ... Oh, I see what you're saying. Hmmm ...Well, it's not *really* a wrist watch. It's more like a ... um ... like a Dick Tracy watch, or" she repeated herself in her excitement, "or like the one that Lois Lane used to call Superman! It's really a sort of ghost telephone that I can use to contact

Michael and Sylvia. Well Michael really. It was Sylvia's. She's the one who took it off her wrist, gave it to me and showed me how to use it."

She saw Brandon smile at the use of the word *telephone*. "I know, I know, I *should* have said *cell phone* shouldn't I?" She ran her fingers artfully through her hair and shook her flaming locks lightly. "No matter how much I try to cover them, my Canadian heritage roots keeps showing."

Brandon smiled and nodded absently as his mind raced. He glanced casually around the room. It was filling with the lunch crowd. Suddenly his eyes focused on her and he said, "Let's continue this conversation back at the flat, shall we?"

Charlene nodded in understanding and rose immediately.

Brandon arose, paid the bill and left the Café.

***

Scene 6

It was evening.

Sipping on a coffee that he had just finished brewing, Brandon Thomas looked at his wife sitting across from him. What she had just finished telling him *staggered his mind*. If anyone else had told him what she had, he would not have believed *any* of it. It went light-years beyond incredible and into the unbelievable.

He recapped, in his mind, the silent walk back to his furnished flat and the story that unfolded after they had arrived. After many questions on his part, her chronicled puzzle pieces came together to form a complete picture.

He remembered the media coverage of the brutal killing of celebrities, *Knighted Lord of the Realm, Sir* Michael Brighton and his beautiful wife, *Lady* Sylvia Brighton. Who hadn't? It had been front page news around the world.

'Royal Ex-Playboy and Internet Porn Queen Star Wife massacred in exclusive French restaurant!' was one of the headlines that he had read.

He had no idea that the flamboyantly foppish Sir Michael Brighton had secretly been the Head of the A.T.C.U., which was the acronym in the IE *(International Espionage)* world for the *ultra secret* British *'Anti-Terrorist Control Unit'*. He knew, from personal experience, that it was one of, if not *the best* Anti-Terrorist Organization in the world. It was *the Organization* that all other countries around the world went to when they needed help with *their* fight against Terrorism. The A.T.C.U. was also rumored to have the most sophisticated computer system in the world. Hack proof as well.

He brought his mind back to what his wife had told him. "Let me encapsulate what you have told me Char, just to make sure that I have harvested and comprehended all the pertinent information, okay?"

Charlene Thomas nodded and smiled her special smile at him. She couldn't tell by looking at him, but she knew what her husband *must* be going through. Incredulity, wonder and a whole lot of other emotions! And rightfully so! She did, and she was the one who experienced it firsthand! She sat in silence as he spoke quietly, as if in contemplation and not to her.

"Michael and Sylvia came to check up on you and make sure that you were alright. And they did this at the request of their friend, Mr. Smoke, the international Terrorist Bomber Assassin. *The* Mr. Smoke who supposedly *only* Smokes Terrorist Bombers."

Although it was not a question, Char nodded. Her husband continued, "You trusted your instincts and had a long conversation with Michael and Sylvia. You told them of the circumstances of your death. Of Q and my position within it and why I feel Q tried to kill me. *(another nod from Char)* They know that I can see you, as can Mr. Smoke and both of them. *(another nod)*. They know of our daughter and her plight. You told them that I was working on a Plan of Action to try to remedy the situation, but gave them no particulars. They told you that most Ghosts, the ones that stay behind, can't see other Ghosts because they are so caught up in their own trauma. That is why they had to touch you to establish contact, the way that Mr. Smoke did with you. And finally, that Sylvia gave you her *triangle watch*, one of two or more watches that Mr. Smoke got from *another dimension* and gave to each of them to keep in contact with him and each other in case they got separated. Sylvia gave you hers so that you could contact Michael if you needed their help. Have I got all the highlights?"

Charlene nodded, and then shook her head. "Well, you didn't mention the parts about Sylvia teaching me to change outfits and Michael knowing of the Eagle and how impressed he was of your exploits. You are Legend in the International Spy Community, *IE Community* he called it. I'm very proud of you Brandon. I had no idea you were so famous."

"*Were?* I'm not dead yet!" he chided lovingly. Her face took on that startled look that she got when he teased her. She smiled her *almost* embarrassed smile.

"I meant *are*, darling. Sorry. I must have confused *you* with *me*."

He smiled back.

***

Scene 7

Click...Click...Click. Her cell phone took the pictures. She sent the three photos off and put the PDA cell phone away. She repositioned the body that she had just photographed from different angles. She straightened to her full five foot eight, one half inch height and backed up.

Kameleon's cell phone vibrated.

She slipped it back out of her vest pocket as she looked back down at the woman on the shower floor. Satisfied with what she saw, she looked at the incoming number on the cell phone screen and answered.

"Kamele speaking." Her voice was low and had an echoic tone. *This bathroom has* great *acoustics'* she thought absently as she awaited a response.

"True photographic masterpieces. The balance has been wired into the specified account, as per your instructions." the sexless mechanical voice intoned.

"Understood, and thank you for your prompt response."

"You're welc..." The voice was cut off as she disconnected the call.

Kameleon did one final sweep of the apartment, made a few minor adjustments to make sure everything was as she wanted, and then exited. She smiled as an errant thought flashed through her mind. Someone had once stated, a professor doing a lecture she had attended years earlier, that a *perfect crime* could not happen. When asked for class comments, she had responded that if a perfect crime *had* been committed, no one would know. The professor had not reacted well to that at all, which had prompted a delightful class debate!

Kameleon had committed a number of perfect crimes. This was but one of them.

The woman Kameleon had just killed was a Senators wife. Senator William Joseph Warden's wife, Rebecca Lynne Warden, to be exact. Rebecca, or Becki as she was known to her friends, had been unfaithful. Not that being *unfaithful* warranted being murdered. If that was the case, ninety eight point three percent of the top government officials would be dead. No, if opening her mouth to give blowjobs was Becki's *only* crime, she would still be alive. Opening her mouth to one of her lovers and passing on government secrets was the reason Rebecca was *not*.

Kameleon *liked* killing women. She enjoyed it even *more* than men. She thought that women, with the laws the way they were in this day and age, by right of their gender, were given unfair advantages over men. She considered herself an equal opportunity contract freelancer. She did not consider herself a killer or an assassin, which she was categorized as by the organizations that employed and utilized her skills. Or that of a terrorist, a predator, a patriot, a soldier, a soldier of fortune, or any number of other smoke screen names used by others to justify what they did.

Shela Pryce considered herself a *Valkyr*. No, not *considered* herself to be, she *was* a *Valkyr*. And to the best of her knowledge, she was the *last* of the *Valkyr*. And she was considered, by the many who utilized her specialized and varied services, as one of the best, if not *the best*, trained *killer* in the world. If asked, she would answer honestly, and with no boasting, that she could *kill* any*body or* any*thing.*

No one who had *ever* hired or utilized Kameleon for that service would disagree.

***

Kameleon's phone vibrated later that night. She was in the middle of *Almost an Angel*, one of her favorite movies.

She glanced quickly at the time and then at the incoming number on the phone display.

It was Douglas Chandler's *private* number. '*Interesting.*'

Shela hit the *pause* button on her remote.

"Hello?"

"Good evening Shela. IceMan calling. Did I call at a good time?"

"I was watching a movie. Is it important?"

"Yes."

"Then it's a good time."

"Great! By any chance, is Kamele there?"

"No, not right now. May I take a message?"

"Yes please. When you see her, would you *kindly* ask her to stop by the *office* for a cup of coffee tomorrow morning around *ten.*"

"I would be delighted to, IceMan."

"Thank you Shela. Sorry to have bothered you. I hope you enjoy the rest of your movie."

"You are both welcome, and thank you, I will."

Shela Pryce *(aka Kameleon)* hung up the phone, sat in silence for a moment in thought, and then hit the *play* button.

***

Scene 8

Somewhere in a nameless building complex in the Blue Ridge Mountains, Douglas Chandler (*aka* the *IceMan*) hung up the speaker phone and turned his chair to look up at the monster of a man standing beside him.

The Commandant General of the combined United States Armed Forces was looking, distractedly it seemed, out the window at the moonlit and starlit mountains in the distance, chewing slowly on a cigar gone cold.

The *IceMan* was not fooled for an instant. He knew that the Commandant had heard and understood every word spoken.

A few moments went by while silence reigned supreme, then the huge black head turned in his direction, the neck muscles cording like steel cables with ropey veins feeding them. The moonlight and starlight from the window reflected off of his hairless head. Albeit the eyebrows, a head bald, as if hair had never known presence there. Emotionless slate grey eyes regarded the IceMan from under heavy black brows. They glittered like stones under water. To Douglas he looked like one of the mountains he had been staring at. Unchanging, unbending, unforgiving and forever formidable. Douglas had known him for a number of years, but could never estimate his age. The Commandant hadn't seemed to age a day since the day they were first introduced.

The IceMan also knew that there was little to no body fat underneath the uniform. Chandler knew that the Commandant

General, at six foot three inches tall, weighed in at three hundred and ten pounds dripping wet. They had worked out numerous times at the Gymnasium together. The IceMan always wondered how a man so big could move with the liquid grace of a Jungle Cat. Douglas himself was tall and fashionably slim. He usually detested muscle bound freaks, and Powder was certainly one of those, but JD's amazing intellect more than compensated for that in Chandlers eyes.

Commandant Powder walked to the front of the desk, took the chair situated there and spun the seat so that it rose in height to his satisfaction. It had been significantly lower than the *IceMan's*. A prop designed to intimidate the person sitting in it, forcing them to look upward. Now it was higher. He sat gingerly on it, as if testing the strength of it. To Douglas it looked as if he was crouching, tensed, ready to spring into action at any moment. He looked down at the *IceMan*.

"Do you think she will take the assignment?" the Commandant rumbled quietly around his cigar, as if he didn't want to scare or startle Douglas. He unclenched his large chicklet white teeth, removed the cigar from his mouth and tucked it into a cigar case that he produced from inside his uniform pocket. Other partially burned cigars of varying lengths were in there also.

"It depends on if we do our job right."

"Explain." was the deep commanding response.

The IceMan looked closely at Commandant Jakk Donn Powder. Known as JD to his few personal friends and colleagues, Douglas knew that very early in JD's life, no one had *ever* called him Jakk, Donn or Jakk Donn Powder to his face; the birth name his addict mother had bestowed on him.

Rumor had it that she had named him after the song, 'A Boy Named Sue'. She thought that, like the song, the names would make him strong, unlike her, and that he would not get hooked on substance abuse.

With JD's father unknown, or unacknowledged by her, JD's mother instinctively *knew* that she would not be there for her son, not with all of her mental and medical addiction conditions. She had overdosed soon after the birth. JD had been raised by relatives.

'She would have been proud of JD, had she lived. It had succeeded beyond her wildest dreams.' was the IceMan's errant thoughts.

"Well?" demanded the voice of JD Powder.

IceMan was brought back to the present in an instant. He realized that the Commandant *might* have no firsthand experience or knowledge of Kameleon.

Shela had left KOLD and gone Independent just prior to JD taking on his new position (created for Powder *specifically* by the newly elected President) as *Commandant General* of *all* of the United States Armed and Secret Services (Second to, and reporting only and directly to, the President of the United States of America).

KOLD encrypted personnel files, as were *all* of Q's files, were stored in secure standalone SC's *(super computer's)* that could not be accessed remotely. After Shela had retired from active duty seven years previously, KOLD had only used her on the most sensitive assignments, and only specific ones at that. Assignments that KOLD knew matched *Kameleon's* particular *eccentric* criteria.

The IceMan mentally shook his head. No, in all probability, JD knew nothing of importance about Kameleon other than myth and speculation. He treated JD's demand for explanation as such.

He nodded slightly to JD in recognition of the demand for clarification and information.

"That's right, you *may* not know her story, Commandant. Metaphorically speaking, please allow me to provide you with a few selectively *cropped* pictures of Shela Pryce, highlighting only the important and pertinent facts. If you wish, I will un-crop them and fill in the details later." IceMan awaited approval.

JD nodded approval. IceMan continued.

"Shela Pryce, or Kameleon as she is known in *our reality,* was our top agent in KOLD. We recruited her out of a psychiatric juvenile detention facility. She was about to be charged with murder. After blinding him, Shela had slowly and painstakingly beaten her stepfather to death, using her bare hands, feet and an empty wine bottle. This was done immediately *after* he had killed her mother for striving to prevent him from attempting to rape her. How she came to our attention is not important. Suffice to say she did, and with high approbation. KOLD erased all the charges against her, and killed any and all news stories about the incident. Odds are that she would not have been convicted anyway. Shela Pryce is *ice cold* under fire. The *only one* in KOLD that worked best alone. *Totally self sufficient.* Unbelievable! I wish we could find more like her." Douglas shook his head slightly in amazement.

"But, to KOLD, it also meant she was not totally controllable. Highly prized by me but marginally acceptable to KOLD *only* because she never failed. At twenty eight, five years ago, she retired and went freelance. KOLD, well ultimately it was *my choice,* allowed her to retire because of her, hmm ... how shall I put this ... uh ... let's say... because of her *eccentricities*."

"*Eccentricities?*" rumbled the man mountain. "That's an *amusing* word to apply to a cold blooded killer. Besides not being trustworthy, what *eccentricities* did she have, other than being totally self reliant?"

"I did not say she was *not trustworthy,* Commandant. I stated that Kameleon was not *totally controllable.* If Shela Pryce was not absolutely *trustworthy*, she would be dead. She has served us well in the eleven years she worked for Q in KOLD. And, might I humbly add, she has more than repaid my instincts about her retirement as well, *many* times in the last five years as a freelance *contract killer extraordinaire. Kameleon,* as she still prefers to be called while on assignment, has *never* failed to complete a mission successfully and also as important, to our *exact* contract specifications. Since her retirement, Shela has, from time to time, supplied KOLD with invaluable information as well. It is also an extremely cost effective arrangement, from a business point of view. Plus the added benefit it provides KOLD; *Plausible Deniability* should the situation arise."

The Commandant nodded slightly at the subtle clarification.

"Continue." he rumbled quietly, without either inflection or emotion.

"Kameleon's main eccentricity is that she won't kill an *innocent*. And by *innocent*, I mean someone who, in accordance to Kameleon's own special criteria or reasons, she feels does *not* deserve to die."

"I can see how that could create ... *difficulties*. Probably a side effect of the rape. Has she gone out of her way to protect any of the *innocents* of the jobs she refused?"

"To do so would be to *seal her fate*, I think is the saying. No, Kameleon has an insanely intense *self preservation instinct*. And please do not misunderstand me, Commandant General. I am speaking as correctly as I am able. I did *not* say that Shela Pryce was raped. I *said* that her mother died trying to prevent her stepfather from *attempting* to rape her. *Attempting* as in *trying*, and as in *failing*."

JD's face smiled slightly at the implied chide. It was most definitely *not* a nice smile.

Douglas continued as if he hadn't witnessed it. "Shela was a virgin when we recruited her and our latest *Intel* confirms that, though highly doubtful, she may *still* be a virgin. And all this *Intel* is based on the fact that she doesn't date men for long. She gets tired and bored with them easily. A few men have claimed to have had sex with her, but none claimed they made love to her. They inferred she was an animal. The fact that they inferred it made it suspect in my eyes."

IceMan shook his head in disgust. "I personally don't think Shela is a virgin. In my opinion, the *only* way Kameleon could have accomplished some of her assignments would have to have been by sleeping with the enemy. But enough of that! You can make that decision for yourself when you meet her tomorrow." Douglas nodded his head. The Commandant reciprocated.

IceMan continued, "Onward and upward. Shela Pryce has an overwhelming *need* to cleanse the world of evil, usually people. KOLS's initial testing's confirmed that. As you mentioned, she *is* totally self *reliant* but she is not totally self *sufficient*. Even though she now freelances, she feels that she still *needs* us. We feed her *intense need* to purge the world of evil. She has *never* talked out of school." Here he paused fr effect.

"It is against *one* of her Core Principles. And Shela has *never* violated her Core Principles. It is also one of Q's. That is one of the reasons why I let her retire. She poses no threat to KOLD. Plus we pay well and keep her busy cleansing *her* world. As I mentioned previously, when she came across information she thought KOLD could use, she passed it on ... and at no charge, by the way."

JD nodded slightly, yet his eyes seemed to darken. "I take it you have to convince Kameleon that Brandon Thomas is in need of killing?" The Ice Man nodded. "And how, might I be so bold as to ask, are you going to do that?"

"We are in the planning process. That is why you're presence was humbly requested Commandant. We need your help and advice and we need it quick. We were thinking to leak the knowledge to the Red Chinese, through our *IE World Community* connections, that Brandon Thomas is the infamous *Eagle*. We were thinking that we would leak that he was in love with another woman and his wife would not give him a divorce, so he killed her with a car bomb." Douglas saw the Commandant's eyes flicker and smiled internally.

His daughter being in the vehicle was an unfortunate accident. She was supposed to be having a sleepover with a girl friend, but her friend got sick at the last moment. He viewed the explosion from a distance, then dirtied himself, rushed forward to view the remains and file his report to the police at the hospital. And that he blamed it on the Red Chinese to throw off suspicion and then fled with his girlfriend to parts unknown."

The Commandant nodded, whether in understanding or approval, IceMan could not tell. He continued, "The Red Chinese, *reportedly,* have placed a *five million dollar reward* on his head, *for his head."* Here the *IceMan* paused as he smiled an ice cold smile. A smile that never seemed to quite reach his eyes.

Stone faced, JD also showed no sign of a reaction.

Douglas continued, "Of course, Q is really the organization responsible for the reward. KOLD will also put out, in the guise of the Red Chinese SCORCH, that the Eagle had been suspected, by Q, of selling sensitive US information to third world parties for awhile. All who know the Eagle will know that the last is not true, but to the rest of the IE world it will lend credence to the first rumor."

The Head of KOLD felt something change in JD. Nothing visibly changed, but he felt it. The Commandant's next words confirmed it.

"Do the first only. If you put out the last part about selling secrets, some may believe it. Then they would want him alive, and that won't do at all. The fact that *we* know the Eagle has had *total* access to the COW files mandates that he *die*, not be captured. And it has to be done quickly. Collateral Damage Control must be activated. Here is what I suggest we do......" he paused for a moment, thinking.

Douglas smiled internally. The first had already been done. The last, the part about the Eagle selling sensitive information, had not been done, nor would it be. He had used it to bait the Commandant into the game. It had succeeded.

The Commandant suddenly stood up. "I will arrive here ten minutes before ten am tomorrow morning. I want to meet this *Kameleon*." He turned toward the door. "I need to check on some things before then. Be here when I arrive."

The Ice Man corrected him, "Shela will be here at exactly nine fifteen. Ten in the morning *meant* nine fifteen. If I had said ten *am*, *Kameleon* would have come armed for combat."

JD's eyes went cold. "Q's little quirks bother me." The cold left his eyes and a small, soft, fugitive breath escaped him. "But I do know that Q does get things done that no one else can." The iron came back in his voice, "I will be here at *nine oh five*."

Chandler nodded and said nothing. He touched a fingerprint reader button on his desk to unlock the door.

The Commandant opened the door, paused, turned, looked at the IceMan and rumbled quietly. "I know that you've already done the first part. I also have eyes and ears out there. But I am a curious man by nature, so I will ask. Did you *really* think I would fall for the last part, that bullshit, cock n' bull story about the Eagle selling secrets?"

Douglas actually laughed out loud. "Not for a second my old friend," he said between chuckles, "but you had me thinking you did."

Without expression, the Commandant General turned back and walked out the door.

***

The chuckle vanished and the smile drooped off the IceMan's as if it had never existed. With eyes far, far colder than Ice, Douglas Chandler looked thoughtfully at the door as it closed. After it had completely closed, he punched a button on his desk.

A moment later a stunning, statuesque brunette walked through the door.

"You rang sir?" The voice was throaty, yet incredibly precise. There was no hint of any kind of an accent.

The perfect voice of a telephone operator, Douglas mused. His eyes returned to normal as he produced one of his rare *warm* smiles.

"Please get the President on the line, Pearle. The sooner the better."

"As you require, sir." With that said, Pearle Whirley turned and left the room.

***

Scene 9

Shela Pryce rose, walked over and turned off the television and DVD player. She could have used the remotes, but she preferred the exercise. She loved all the subtle nuances in the movie. She hoped one day she could meet and get Paul Hogan's autograph.

She went into the bathroom, disrobed and turned on the sauna. Returning to the living room, Shela walked out onto her balcony and looked out over New York City.

To her, it was the only place to live. It epitomized the world to her. A breeding ground for all things good, bad and evil. Love, hate, courage, fear and indifference ran rampant throughout the city. Even the very air and walls reeked of it. Shela could see, smell, sense and feel all of it through every fiber of her being. Only the exceptionally strong or lucky flourished in New York. And the lucky smart ones moved on before their luck ran out.

Most Gifted Sensitive's would have been overwhelmed by the sensations that Shela felt. That is why the majority of highly Gifted Psychic's steered clear of New York City. The ones that stayed were usually limited in their Gifts and Abilities or, like Shela, had been raised in it from birth.

In a world full of extremes, New York City stood alone as a city of monumental excesses, both human and other. And Shela Pryce gloried in it. What was sensory overload to most barely whet her appetite. Her senses weren't dampened by the massive overload, they were razor sharpened by it.

Feeling the cool night breeze on her bare skin, Kameleon stretched out her arms and embraced the living, breathing City of New York. Had anyone been watching her closely at that particular moment in time, they would have seen, just for a moment, something feral, an elemental energy force, flash deep from within her glowing crystalline amber eyes.

The moment passed, although her eyes still glowed. They always did. Starting with her stepfather and countless times by other men and women, Shela had been told that her glowing crystalline eyes were one of her greatest assets. Those and her long, thick, natural pale platinum blond hair.

Slowly lowering her arms, she turned, walked back in, entered the kitchen and concocted one of her special nutrient drinks. Deep in thought, Shela strolled back and into the nine hundred square foot bathroom. It was a marvel of beauty, simplicity and functionality. She crossed to the sealed sauna door, opened it and stepped into the dimly lit room, drink in hand. Pure white steam billowed out as she entered.

Once inside she stood for a few moments until the cool of the night had been warmed and washed away by the intensely thick steam. After a few moments of intense satisfaction she reached down and touched a hidden knothole under the bench and the steam was immediately sucked away. She used her hands to sluice and wick off the excess moisture and then punched a series of knotholes and the floor and roof descended to the floor below where her training area awaited her. When it stopped Shela could sense the steam jets resuming above her. If anyone was to open the door and look into the sauna above they would see an identical room to the one she entered. A room that they couldn't fathom, as it would be filled with the thick, dense, impenetrable steam.

Kameleon stepped out of a matching sauna on the floor below. Even to her expertly trained eye, she could not tell that it was actually an elevator as well. The floor plan was more Spartan on this floor. Shela lived on the top two floors of the Silverwood Bankview in the heart of downtown New York. The top floor was the living quarters.

The lower level, as she liked to think of it, was one of the finest fitness, acrobatic, gymnastic and martial arts training facilities in the world.

She paused for a few moments and put her hair into a ponytail as she looked out over the equipment and revisited the colorful history of the building she owned, as well as her part in it.

***

Shela Pryce had inherited all of Lester Dunne's Estate when he died. Rachel, Shela's mother, had signed a prenuptial agreement stating what she was entitled to if they divorced, which was but a pittance. At the time Rachel didn't care. She didn't marry Lester for money. But if Lester died while married to her, Rachel inherited all of the Dunne estate. Lester had no surviving relatives.

At the time of its construction, the Silverwood Bank, as it was called at the time of its erection, was one of the tallest business buildings in New York City, with breathtaking panoramic views in every direction. The lower level floors, which were more easily visible from the street, were unusually enhanced by highly sculptural ornamentation, including putty, urns and rusticated stone.

Each balcony of the towering building was marked by pilasters, pediments and balustrades and was highlighted by large stone fleches which carried the viewer's eye upward along the buildings height. The top of the building was crowned by a raised solid brass pyramidal roof with a towering obelisk, further increasing the sense of height which was an imposing and important factor at the time that the building was constructed.

Throughout its history, the Silverwood Bankview had been home to some of the brightest stars, the wealthiest magnates and the most illustrious of public figures. And still was.

It used to be a bank in the distant past, when it was first built. An architectural wonder at the time, although few knew it. Upon completion, Mark Silverwood, paranoid builder and owner, would allow no press agents beyond the ground floor to view, or photograph it. He felt that to do so would give bank robbers and thieves too much information. It was a turbulent time in American history. The fact that he was paranoid and lived on the top floors may have had something to do with it. All the floors were slightly different heights inside but they all looked the same from the street. It allowed him to add an extra floor, second to the top, that would go unnoticed. He destroyed all but one set of blue prints to the building. Those, he had kept safely hidden.

When the Great Depression hit, his bank went under with scarcely a whimper, as did Mark Silverwood. Dressed in a silk Lounging suit, he jumped off his balcony to his death and was found with a broken piece of a wine glass stem in one hand and an ivory cigarette holder in the other, cigarette still smoking. His lover was devastated, that is, until he found another Sugar Daddy.

Needless to say, Mark left no offspring. The Silverwood Bank was purchased by one of the Robber Bank Barons of the time, for pennies on the dollar, and converted into condo apartments for the insanely rich. He added the word 'view' and it became the Silverwood Bankview apartment building. He also lived in the top two floors, as had Silverwood.

The apartment condo conversion was a big mistake at the time. The Robber Bank Baron (not his real name) didn't care. He loved the Silverwood Bankview building and lived in it until his death.

It sat vacant for many years after the Baron died, as his estate was contested by all of his surviving relatives.

***

When the smoke cleared, the Silverwood Bankview Apartment Building title was transferred to one of the offspring who promptly sold it to a backwoods oil tycoon by the name of Augusta Dunne.

A backward young hillbilly, Augusta had just struck it rich in oil and gas and wanted to impress New York's Elite. He never did. Augusta was too rough around the edges. He never did fit in. It puzzled and rankled him greatly, because he just couldn't figure it out. All his drinking buddies told him that he was a fine figure of a man!

Augusta's son, Lester Dunne inherited the Silverwood Bankview apartment building from his father in the early nineteen nineties, along with the rest of the Dunne Estate, when Augusta died hele-skiing in the Canadian Rockies. Few (if any) attended his funeral.

Of good looking parents, Lester Dunne was a good looking child who grew into a handsome man. Daddy and daddy's money had twisted him though. He was an only child and his mother had died giving him birth. The uneducated and rough cut Augusta never forgave his son for killing his wife and Lester's mother, Margaret.

Margaret was the only child of one of New York's Elite who had fallen upon hard times. Young and beautiful, Margaret was courted and wooed by many up and coming young men. Alas, all were poor. The rich ones did not want to, nor would, take on her families debts.

A dutiful child unburdened with undo intelligence, but with a sweet disposition, Margaret was married to Augusta when she was scarcely eighteen years old. Initially it was a marriage arranged by her destitute parents for promised monetary favors from Augusta.

A god fearing girl, Margaret was a firm believer in the commitment and sanctity of the marriage vows and did her best to please and understand her new unknown husband.   As understanding came, so did acceptance. Margaret came to accept Augusta Dunne as he was, and it was through that acceptance that she came to love him. Augusta came to love her in a way that approached worship.

Margaret's parents died of a flu epidemic shortly after the marriage. Their debts died with them.

Augusta was ecstatic at news that she was pregnant. He was devastated when his son lived and she died. Oh how he missed her. Would that it had been Lester who died instead! One time, as a young impressionable child, Lester was told, by his drunken father, that very thing. His father never remembered saying it and Lester never forgot it. In shame, he never mentioned it to anyone. Had he been able to, he might have avoided becoming the twisted excuse of a man that he grew to be.

Although never given much money, Lester was never denied anything in his life. 'Except the love of a father,' he raged silently, time and again. Lester felt the animosity, hate and blame the times father and son were together. In later years, it was usually when Lester came, hat in hand, to beg for money. From birth on, Lester was left to be raised by tutors and nannies. It perverted him horribly inside.

Twisted though he was, Lester was the only one who had cried upon the news of Augusta's death.

Deprived of the love of a mother and now eternally cursed by the hate of a father whose love he could now never earn, Lester took his rage out on the ones that he felt were the causes of all his pain. Women! Oh, how he loved and hated them. They were the reason his father had hated him!

With the death of his father came the wealth. No longer was it Daddy's money! No longer did he have to come begging to a man who hated him.

At first his newfound wealth, combined with his good looks, well educated and charming patter, sparkling blue eyes, dark curly hair and fit body, had the women flocking to him. But they never stayed.

Many were the times he had run-ins with the law concerning his treatment of women, but his lawyers were too slick for the prosecutors to make anything stick. He was known within the legal community as Lester, the Teflon Molester. Nothing ever stuck to him.

Lester had met Rachel, Shela's mother, when Shela was thirteen years old. He was immediately drawn to Rachel by her beauty and wit. He had to have her! Rachel was an Tax Analyst at one of the tax accounting firms he used. He wooed her relentlessly, but she would not make love with him. She had been burned and emotionally scarred years earlier by the father of Shela, a tall handsome blond haired soldier boy who had promised to come back from a mission and marry her. He never kept his promise. Soldier Boy never survived the mission, but twenty one year old Rachel was never told that.

Shela only found that out when she joined KOLD. Rachel had devoted her life to raising her daughter. When Lester came into the picture she tried not to be, but was almost swept off her feet. By then, Lester had learned to hide his true nature until, what he considered to be, the appropriate time. When she first introduced him to Shela, Lester was smitten.

Although her mother was a beauty, to Lester, Shela was the PRIZE. The one he must own! Shela was small for her age, but was astoundingly beautiful. Lester could see the promise of unearthly beauty upon maturity. Shela Pryce must be his!

Although she was initially treated as royalty, Shela was repulsed by Lester for reasons unknown. Because she could not understand or pinpoint any firm reason why she should dislike her new stepfather so intensely and her mother's obvious love for him, Shela kept her own counsel and remained silent.

Lester knew of these feelings by all the little betraying signs that a young girl would unconsciously afford. Lestor took it as subtle rebellion and rejoiced. He would painstakingly beat that high pure spirit out of her and groom her to be his totally subservient trophy bride.

He would, of course, have to kill or divorce Rachel in order to marry his stepdaughter.

He shook his head. 'No, not divorce.' he thought, 'I will not pay her a dime of my money, the bitch! I will have no choice but to kill Rachel when the time is right, and then marry my stepdaughter.' Lester positively glowed at the prospect. He promptly proposed to Rachel. She felt the fervor inside him and assumed that it was for her.

That broke her last barrier. She happily accepted. It was then that Lester had Rachel sign the prenuptial contract. He told her it was part of his inheritance stipulations. He even had fake documents created to prove it. Rachel never asked to see them.

After the small wedding, Lester personally destroyed the documents and the man who made them. He would give no one power over him again!

That was the beginning of the end for Rachel, Lester and Shela.

A sharp, whispered, small little voice, told Kameleon to stop the memories there! She did as the familiar little voice scolded.

***

Scene 10

Placing the nutrient drink on a small table, Shela went to a shelving unit and removed one of her training outfits and put it on; then walked over to the dais that was situated before the Gymnasium.

On the dais was a large ancient hard cover Tome with strange letters on it. She opened the Tome at random and read the page. Shela didn't have to. She knew the entire Tome by heart, word for word. The name on it translated to 'The Way of the Valkyr' or 'Way of the Valkyr', the 'The' being redundant, as in "Bring me the "The Way of the Valkyr."

When she had finished reading the page and finding no new meaning in it, Shela touched a button on the side of the dais and music subtly permeated the room. She walked to the middle of an open area. Slowly at first, Kameleon went through her stretching routine. Then, as the music picked up in tempo, she started going through a series of incredibly erotic movements, slowly twisting, kicking, turning, spinning and writhing. All the fluid movements were in tempo with the beat of the music. It was the Dance of the Valkyr.

She felt the world slip away as she entered the Valkyr Altered State (or VAS as she thought of it.). Gone were the lower level, complicated thought processes. In their place were the higher and heightened, psyche, awareness and stimulation states. In essence, within Kameleon, the three were one and the same.

Complete Harmonic Awareness blended with extreme yet constant Corporeal Psychological and Physical Stimulation. When in this state she could slow down time tremendously, thus increasing her reflex time. She could also use up to and including one hundred percent of her muscle power for short periods of time. Writings from the page she had been reading from the Way of the Valkyr crossed her mind, confirming what she already knew.

Most people only realize a very small percentage of their muscle power. Shela considered one hundred percent use to be just that, the ultimate or maximum effort of use. Effort, to Kameleon, was as much a mental state as it was as a physical force. When it came to effort, one hundred and ten percent didn't exist to her. If a person could give one hundred and ten percent effort, then they were, in her opinion, giving one hundred percent. She knew that the results would vary with effort. A one hundred percent effort of a tired muscle would not produce the same results as a one hundred percent effort of a fresh muscle. It was the effort measured that mattered to her as much as the use and results. With leverage, a weak muscle could achieve greater results than a strong muscle without leverage.

Whenever Shela came out of her VAS training routine, she normally felt drained but rested. If she was on a mission and stayed in VAS for an extended period, the wear and tear on her joints, tendons and muscles could be enormous. If she had an injury while in VAS and came out too soon, it could be devastating.

When in VAS, if she was injured or cut, her arousal state would instantly kick into overdrive and she was able to mend most superficial wounds in a short time, normally within minutes. Some of the more serious ones took longer. Then she would need to get to a haven to come out of it, as she would be totally debilitated.

It had only happened twice and then it was early in her career. The first time had almost killed her because she came out of VAS too soon after the healing, leaving her helplessly weak. Because of that, Kameleon was unable to re-enter VAS but was able to crawl, like a fish out of water, into a trash container and elude discovery until her incredible recuperative powers brought her back to mobility. Once she had recovered enough, she entered VAS and escaped easily.

Shela likened entering VAS to starting a car engine, the car and engine being VAS and her body being the battery. The battery needed a certain minimum amount of charge to turn the pistons and provide the spark to start the engine. Once started the engine provided all the power needed through the fuel line from the fuel tank. The VAS battery and fuel being Shela's body. Unlike a car, VAS could not recharge her body as a car did the battery. The second time, she made it to a sanctuary before she left VAS. Once in VAS, she could maintain it for a long time, but, like her car battery analogy, she had to be initially strong enough to get there.

Although she liked to work up to the Valkyr Altered State slowly, as in her exquisitely sensual training routines, if needed she could instantly mentally activate, or trigger, her preprogrammed mental switch and enter her VAS instantaneously. She likened her sensual training routines to a light dimmer switch, working up to full brilliance slowly, whereas flipping the other switch put her at full brilliancy immediately. It took much more energy to do the full burst to reach VAS instantaneously.

Shela utilized her gymnasium for well over an hour. Once done she checked her joints and tendons for damage. One tendon on her left elbow was slightly inflamed. She sat and directed healing energy into it until it was healed.

Once healed Shela then left VAS, showered and went to bed where she dreamed of a dreamless dream. When she awoke in the morning, she remembered the dream.

She dreamed that she looked down at her sleeping body that dreamed of standing on an open grassy plain. In her dreams dream, Shela looked up at the cloudless sky and saw a wonderful warm golden sun shining down on her. Suddenly she realized that it was not a sun, but a great glowing golden Cat's Eye, and it kept getting bigger. It seemed to be getting closer. Suddenly it changed, even as she watched, into a glowing swirling red sun. As in the dreams before, Shela Pryce grabbed her sleeping dream body and shook it awake. She then forced her own body awake.

She had only had a few of these dreams in her life and she knew what they portended. One had happened the night before she had killed her stepfather.

The glowing suns didn't scare her. She knew that the eyes meant her no harm. That is how she always thought of the glowing orbs. Shela somehow knew, deep within herself, that the glowing growing eyes always came just to warn her. Warn her that something Big was coming, or about to happen.

This time she felt it was different.

Before, it had always been just about her.

This time it was different. It included her, but encompassed far more than her mind could grasp. Whatever it was, there was no one or no thing in this world that could stop it.

Shela Pryce shrugged, dressed and repaired herself, and then left to catch a waiting plane to take her to the mountain Powder meeting.

***

Scene 11

Whilst in Denmark, finishing off her training with KOLD, twenty one year old Shela Pryce came across an ancient Tome called *'The Way of the Valkyr'* in a high end Antique Book Shop in Copenhagen. It was written in ancient Celtic. It was ridiculously expensive, but she negotiated the price down a bit (twenty percent) and purchased it.

It intrigued her because, from her mother's side of the family, Shela was the end product of a long line of pure Celtic descent. Much later, when she researched her biological father, it turned out that he was of pure Celtic descent also.

Popular belief theorized that Celtic was an ancient religious cult. This belief had been propagated by many self-proclaimed experts in modern times and was generally agreed upon as fact. In truth, at its prehistoric beginning, it was a distinct race of people, platinum haired, fair skinned, extremely *spiritual* and highly *gifted*. And for reasons unknown to Shela, a race whose purity, as far as she had been able to ascertain, ended with her.

The owner, Jorgen Reinholt only agreed to the twenty percent because he didn't think Shela, who looked sixteen, could afford it. Being a man of his word, he sold it to her for the agreed price. He was slightly mollified when she paid cash and asked for no receipt.

Three weeks later a man came in asking about the Tome. Jorgen told him that it had been sold. The man, thinking Jorgen was just trying to raise the price, didn't believe him and, posing as a buyer, offered ten times what Shela had paid. When Reinholt had convinced the buyer that it had indeed been purchased, the man presented himself as Jens Schulman, Licensed Crime and Fraud *Investigator*, working on behalf of the National Museum of Denmark in Copenhagen.

Upon request, he supplied Jorgen supporting documentation and offered him a substantial bonus if Mr. Reinholt would divulge to him the name and contact information of the purchaser. Jorgen was mortified to tell the *Investigator* that he had no idea who the young lady was, that it had been a cash transaction.

It turned out that the Tome had been in the *Stored Archives* of the National Museum of Denmark and a *cleaner* had absconded with a number of extremely rare and valuable miscellaneous volumes, substituting *size* imitations in their place. It had taken awhile to catch him and it took a longer while to figure out what was missing.

The *cleaner* always brought a book to work to read. Always a hard cover book with a jacket cover. The *cleaner* put *his* book in the place of the stolen one, put the cover jacket over the stolen one and then took it home at the end of his shift. The books he left had to be a close imitation of the ones he stole, so he could not afford be too choosey, therefore they were random thefts. It turned out that he had purchased the imitation replacement books at the very stores he was selling to. The *cleaner* sold the purloined volumes to various booksellers to avoid suspicion.

The *cleaner* was caught when a book that was to be put on display was one of the books switched. Once caught, the *cleaner* readily admitted to the thefts and told the police where he had sold the books. Almost all were recovered.

Jorgen's establishment had been the last because the Museum did not consider it a priority.
Only its rarity lent any real value to it.

It was a *one of a kind.* To the Museum's knowledge, no other *'Way of the Valkyr'* existed. There was not much documentation on it when it arrived, just the name, a few words, a category and a few initials.

The few words were, *Women Warriors,* and categorized as: *Celtic Fiction, Fantasy, Fables, Arcane Practices, Pictographic Exotic Fighting Styles,* and the initials that meant *Worth Keeping as a Novelty Item but Not Valuable.* It had been part of a fabulously wealthy Lady's death bequeathment to the Museum, countless years earlier.

At that time the museum curators knew little of, much less understood, Celtic Lore. In the misty distant past, pagan Celtic Spirituality understood that all of existence has a cyclical nature and that there was, and is, a direct continuity between the *material world* and the *other world.*

Druidic teachings, that had been passed down through the ages, recognized that there is an unseen world that interpenetrates and affects the visible world. Things are just not always what they seem. Everything exists on multiple simultaneous *levels.* It was taught that human beings can *understand* things as having *three* levels: the Physical, the Spiritual, and the Symbolic.

As thus, Celtic culture was integrated with nature, and expressed itself through the manifold possibilities of life itself. Ancient Celtic religion taught the reincarnation of all individual souls, and the appearance of *divine* beings on Earth. The *'Way of the Valkyr'* went way beyond that.

Because of the male dominated society at the time it arrived and that it was of Celtic origin, it was of no great wonder that it held no credence. Danish men did not wish to think of their women or the Celtic Spirituality concept that way. Women were supposed to be strong willed and free, but the *men* were the *warriors*.

The *cleaner* had only used Reinholt once and Jorgen happily provided the *Investigator* with a copy of the purchase receipt, along with a police report that it had not been reported as stolen, as well as a copy of a receipt of a book that the *cleaner* had purchased before he left.

Jorgen was a man who covered his *assets*. Reinholt assured the *Investigator* that he had every intention of reporting the sale. And he did. For fifty five Krone (ten dollars) more than he paid for it! He had wisely *not* told the inspector what he had sold it for.

The Museum never advertised the loss of the few books that went unrecovered.

The Museum did not want or need, at that time, the bad publicity it would generate. They could live with the loss. To them it was just an oddity that was worthless except for its rarity.

The Tome, *'Way of the Valkyr'*, was forgotten.

Shela never found out that the Tome, 'Way of the Valkyr,' that she had purchased from Jorgen was stolen.

If she had, conscience would have ruled and she would have returned it.

And the Kameleon, Last of the Valkyr, would never have come into being.

***

Scene 12

"**W**hat in *heaven's name* do you mean, '*We* can't seem to locate him'? Who the *hell and damnation* are '*We*' and *why* in the *flaming pits of purgatory* haven't the *god damned* '*We*' found him?" the white haired man raged at Commandant JD Powder. "He is only *one man, for god's sake*. Do you have any idea what the ramifications would be if the contents of the *COW* file became public?"

"The '*We*' is '*I*' and *I* believe I do, Mr. President." rumbled the standing Commandant quietly, with respect.

"Bullshit and Poppycock!" The trim, red faced man roared. "Nobody does! The United States of America could be destroyed, JD. Destroyed, do you hear? I'm talking total anarchy, not only within our beloved country's borders, but on a global scale as well. The very foundations of our country would be destroyed. The cornerstone of the entire world! Absolutely destro...." The last words faded off as William Lantern, President of the United States, struggled to gain control of himself.

Shakily, he walked over and sat down on the chair behind the desk that he had just recently flown out of in his rage. With the back of his hand, then the front, he wiped the spittle off his beard from the '*flaming pits of purgatory*' part of his tirade. He placed his elbows on the desk and put his head in his shaking hands. A few of his snowy white locks fell over his hands. Slowly the shaking stopped.

Suddenly he sat up, took a couple of deep breaths, ran his fingers through his hair and smiled boyishly at his friend. His friend smiled back. JD was one of the few, less than a handful of, people that William could absolutely trust in the world. They had known each other since their early days in the Armed forces. William Lantern was a General at the time and JD was the gigantic young man assigned to protect him.

Early in his armed forces career, William, or Bill as he was known back then, had orchestrated a highly successful undercover assignment for Special Ops, which had necessitated him growing his hair long and sporting a mustache and goatee.

Upon returning to camp Bill had gone to the company barber and had his locks, mustache and goatee trimmed. He was seen by many on his way in. Upon returning to duty William was nicknamed *Wild Bill* by the men under him. It was a fun twist that accentuated Bill's mixed Native American and English heritage.

Because of it, he went on to garner many military medals and commendations, one of them being the Purple Heart, the most coveted of trophies. It was the politically correct thing to do *at that time*. Wild Bill understood immediately what was happening and rode the wave with an inspirational ability born of genius.

He instantly went from hiding his mixed heritage to glorying in it. Many of the medals and commendations were bought, most at the price of him keeping his mouth shut on certain
activities that the medal *awarders* were involved in. He arranged it so that both parties benefited, him being viewed as the lesser

one at the time. *'After all'*, as many of the awarders thought, *'it was just a silly medal, wasn't it?'*

Fanatically motivated to surpass all rivals without causing himself any political or physical harm, he became wildly popular within the ranks and brass. Bill's star rose. When William retired to go into Politics, JD followed. On his meteoric rise from Senator to Governor, from Governor to the Presidency, William Lantern took JD Powder with him. The golden haired *boy wonder* was now the white haired President of the United States, the first Métis President in US history. And the single most powerful man in the world. He still wore his thick white hair Maverick long and sported a well manicured mustache and goatee. The press still referred to him as Wild Bill, the *Light of the Future* (a play on his last name). The public loved it. And he knew how to get things done. They loved that even more. *Wild Bill Lantern* was a shoe in for his second term.

"No JD, if the *'We'* had been you, that sonofabitch would be dead. You and I both know who the *'We'* are." He chuckled as he wiped off his hands with a handy wipe. "They are everyone *but us*, you and I. Where do we go from here, old friend?"

"Right now we go to lunch with the Prime Minister of Britain, Mister President. Then ... *WE* make a *plan of action*. We, meaning *Our* Plan of Action, Mr. President, not *the other 'We'* POA."

***

Scene 13

"We have got to get our daughter out of their clutches, Brandon!" Charlene declared to her husband, in a desperate voice.

"That's not going to happen right now, Charlie." Brandon responded gently. "They have her on the move all the time and by the time we found out where she was she'd be gone."

"But she's in danger! They are going to kill her Brandon. They are going to kill our daughter, my little Angel." Mirroring her husband's tone, Charlene responded just as quietly, but with a great deal more intensity. Her face unconsciously twisted slightly in anguish, giving it a dangerous feral look.

Sensing his wife's distress, Brandon impulsively reached out with his hands to unclench hers. His hands passed through, although as always, he felt the slight tingle and the subtle implied resistance of *almost contact*.

He knew what his wife was going through. He was handling it better because *this* was *his* world. This was the IE (International Espionage) world that he had chosen to enter to help his country. His country had more than equipped and trained him to handle almost all situations. He would need every single one of those skills and training that he had, to navigate through the treacherous waters ahead to a safe harbor. Plus *much more*. And *much more* Brandon had. He also had *other training* (paid for at his own expense and taken secretly) that Q wasn't aware of.

Training and studying that he had taken, and was still taking on an ongoing basis, ever since he had joined Q. Training that Q would not have approved of, because they refused to accept or believe in them.

Although, it was that very training that had saved him from total collapse, in the men's restroom, at the hospital, after the bombing. On top of that, Brandon had all of the hard earned invaluable experience that fourteen years in the field had given him. His fourteen years in the field equated to twenty six years of a normal Q agent. When you are the best, they keep you busy.

"Not while I am alive and free of them, Char. They will use her as bait to lure me to her. As long as I stay alive and out of their clutches, as you so poignantly put it, Angel will be the safest, most protected person in this world. " Brandon said kindly.

Suddenly Charlene's face brightened and her posture softened. "I think you are overlooking something dear."

"And what, pray tell, my dear, would that be? Are you inferring that I, the world's greatest *defective*, have missed something?" Brandon looked aghast, then smiled at his wife. Many times in the past she had provided invaluable *insights* on some of his *cases*, as he considered them. Q called them *Assignments*. He liked to consider them as *cases*. He referred to them later as *Case Files*. Calling them *cases,* in his mind, made it seem like it was his decision to take them. He liked to believe he had freedom of choice.

In theory it *was* his choice whether he took an Assignment or not. In reality, that is why they were called *Assignments*. They were *assigned* to him.

Charlene smiled back. "I wouldn't *dream* of it. It may be that my beauty has blinded you to the oblivious." She flipped her hair back and struck a provocative pose. She saw from his smile that he caught her *'oblivious'* instead of *'obvious'* intentional *slip of the tongue.* "And speaking of dreams, by the way, do ghosts dream? That's a rhetorical question, in case you were wondering. How could you know that? You are not a ghost. OOOOOOO." She waved her arms and tried to look spooky.

Brandon couldn't help it, he laughed in spite of himself. His wife was back to normal. Well, almost. The smile dropped off his face. His wife noticed. She smiled at him lovingly and in understanding.

"It's alright dear. I sometimes forget that I'm a *ghost* also. The *reality* of it hits hard, doesn't it?" He nodded.

"Well," she continued brightly "let's get to what you overlooked, *Master Defective.* I'd ask you to guess, but that wouldn't be any fun for you, would it? The obvious fact is that *I'm a ghost.* I can *blip* to my daughter in an instant, whenever I want!"

"You can? Why didn't you tell me?" Brandon asked amazed.

"Well ..... because I haven't *actually* tried it." Charlene said hesitantly. Then she said more forcefully, "But I *feel* that I can!" "Do you feel up to trying it now?" Brandon had seldom demanded anything of his wife. He tried to phrase it as a request. That was one of the reasons that they had a wonderful and fulfilling marriage.

Scratch the *marriage* word and put in *life* or *relationship.* In Brandon's mind *marriage* was just a piece of paper confirming to the legal profession that two people wanted to live together until such time as one of the parties wanted a divorce. Charlene agreed with his view. In the marriage vows they had said, "until death do us part", but had written in the document, 'until *divorce* do us part.' Both thought it was hysterical. The legal and religious communities were not so inclined. The couple actually drew up a Prenuptial Agreement that stated that, in the event of a divorce all assets would be divided equally, including any and all children. They both laughed hysterically when it was accepted by the courts. In a document accepted and approved by the court, in the distribution of all assets, they could legally cut their child or children in half.

"And what does *Blip* mean?" Brandon finished.

"To answer your questions in reverse order, *Blip* is an official *ghost word*, OOOOOO," again she waved her hands and tried to make a spooky face, "that I *just* made up to mean Ghost Teleportation, like when I was drawn to the *Smoke* scene. To answer your first question, I'll try."

With that said she closed her eyes and concentrated. Nothing happened. She opened her eyes and looked at her husband in consternation and frustration.

"What is going on Brandon? She is my daughter for crying out loud. I truly believe that I should be able to *will* myself to *blip* to her whenever I choose."

There was silence for a few moments while both pondered the situation. Brandon spoke first, as if speaking to himself, feeling his way along. Char understood this and let him speak without interrupting.

"Maybe *will* and *belief* are not the answer, darling. You don't need *will* and *belief* to drive a car, do you? You need to know *how* to drive a car. To accomplish that, in my opinion and experience, you have to have three vital things. Why three? Because it is *easy* to remember *three* things. In the Mystic Realm, *three* is the most powerful of the small, or lowest, *prime* numbers. And triangles have great numinous significance. You need Ability, Determination and Understanding. ADU, as I like to call it." He paused a moment in thought ... then continued.

"You can substitute *Desire* for *Determination*, because *to me* they both mean *wanting the same thing*. I just think *determination* sounds more forceful. The last, though, is the most important. Most would argue that *knowledge* is the key. Some would say *wisdom*. Without *understanding*, *knowledge* is useless, as is *wisdom*. That is why repeating, screaming or hollering at someone who does *not* understand what you are saying does not make them any wiser. If you don't have the key, the car is not going to start is it? If you tell someone to turn the key and they don't, it's because they don't know what a key *is*." Char looked a little confused.

Brandon picked up on it. "Now don't misunderstand me. You don't need to know how a car is made to drive it. You don't need to know how to fix a car to drive it. All you need to know is how to put gas and oil in it, how to put the key in and turn on the ignition, put it into gear and how to step on the gas, brake and steer. Only a few can make cars. All, with a little knowledge and ability, can drive them. You can get all that other information from a manual or someone who has driven a car."

Here he paused for dramatic effect, then said. "Maybe you should call on Michael and Sylvia?" It worked.

Charlene Thomas tried to hug her husband and ended up trying to kiss his cheek in excitement.

"That is why I married you," she exclaimed enthusiastically, "because *you* can put into words *all* my feelings and thoughts. I's purdy smart, *ain't I?*" The last she added with an innocent smile, hands behind her back, kicking at the ground.

Brandon did not take her last comment lightly, as it had been intended. He knew she was joking, and understood that it was a backhanded compliment to him. But he took exception this time and did not answer in a joking, but in a deadly serious tone.

"Yes you are Charlene, and not just smart, but unusually brilliant." Only then did his tone lighten. "And thank you for reminding me."

Charlene laughed and stuck out her tongue at him. Brandon's left hand flashed out and almost grabbed her protrusion, almost touching it before she whipped it back in her mouth. Startled, she giggled infectiously.

"My god but you're quick!" she blurted.

Her husband just nodded gravely. "Just remember that when you think of trying it again." He warned solemnly.

She started to do it again, but then hesitated at the smile lurking in his eyes. Although she knew that he couldn't really physically do it, she had a vision of Brandon leading her around the room by her tongue.

Grimacing at the thought she activated her triangle watch.

***

Scene 14

"**N**ow that I have the headlines, please provide me with the details." Mr. Smoke asked of the ghost and Lord of the Realm, Michael Brighton. Michael responded, looking at his friends mask, "On which parts shall I fill in the details, my friend?"

"All," stated the smoke colored hooded figure, "starting with when she called you. We can talk as I change." He was proceeding to do so even as he spoke. Michael talked as he disrobed, transforming from Mr. Smoke, skilled Assassin of Terrorist Bombers, into Damon Gray, internationally renowned Symphony Composer and Concert Pianist.

"Well, let's see. We, or should I say *I*, got the call on the triangle watch about three earth hours ago. As you know, time moves differently in the spirit realm. It ebbs and flows. Anyway, Sylvia was, and still is, off checking out the latest fashion shows in Paris. Both men's and women's. She likes to keep me in the latest fashions also." Seeing the look in his friend's eyes, Michael grinned.

"Ahhh, I see. You don't want the Directors Cut, or even the Theatrical Release version." He put his right hand to his forehead and his left arm stretched straight ahead, fingers open and reaching, as if searching blindly. His eyes were squinting, as if striving to pierce the mist his hand could not. Slowly his eyes widened, as if seeing some*thing* for the first time. "Yes (pause) yes, it's coming to me. What's this, only the pertinent facts? But of course! I can see it all so clearly now."

Suddenly he clenched his left hand as if holding onto something important and then paused dramatically. Lowering it to mid chest level and holding it tightly in his left hand, as if it held *the prize*, he reached forward with his right hand and held it also. In mime he examined and then opened what appeared to be an invisible book.

Michael looked down at what he held in his hands. He read it for a moment as if to make sure that he understood it. He then carefully closed the invisible book, although he held the cover open slightly with his index finger separating the cover from the first page.

As if in awe at the message that he had read, Michael Brighton lifted his black maned head, looked directly into Damon's eyes and announced with an announcer's voice, "You, Doctor Damon Gray, want the Readers Digest condensed version!"

At that, Damon smiled one of his rare *true* smiles. It transformed his face. He looked ten years younger.

Graced with a gymnast's or dancers seemingly slender body, with little or no body fat, Damon's lean, chiseled face would have looked almost skeletal except for his high cheekbones and full lips. Most women who had met him found him breathtakingly handsome with his strong boned even features, square heavy jaw, show business white teeth, and large liquid silver eyes, mixed with his artistically long silver blond hair. The EH Females who thought he looked slightly weird or spooky were drawn to him by his *imagined* smell.

In fact, *all EH* women were drawn to his subtle *Psychic Musk*.

Sometimes Enhanced Human Males also smelled it. To them it just smelled like pleasant cologne. It was a recent TAG that he had acquired. Damon could turn the *Psychic Musk* on and off

at will and with perfect control.

By slightly altering it Damon found that he could use the *Psychic Musk* on Female *Normals* as well. He soon found that Female Normals held little fascination for him, no matter how beautiful or brilliant they were. Because Female Normals held no interest or fascination for him, he did not continue to use *Normals Psychic Musk* on them.

Damon found that he was *only* drawn or attracted to Female EH's. To each EH Female, Damon's *Psychic Musk* smelled different, from subtle sexual stimulation to intensely demanding. He could increase it from zero to the point of intense sexual intoxication, but he needed to be close, usually within twenty feet of the person, for it to work.

The fact that he was fabulously and insanely wealthy had little or nothing to do with it. Because of his almost insanely intense need for privacy, no one, except for a select few, knew of the true extent of his entire global wealth. Damon Gray's net worth was more than that of some large countries. Those select few were his friends and Damon Gray had very few *living* friends.

He hadn't smiled for many years after his parents and then grandparents were killed by the EHE Society. The *EHE* initials stood for Enhanced Human Exterminators. With Catherine's help, Damon, as the Ghost Assassin, had dismantled that EHE Organization personally, and he hoped, permanently.

Concert Pianist Doctor Gray had started smiling again when he had met Michael and Sylvia. He had stopped smiling again when they were brutally slain after having dinner with him and Catherine in a restaurant in France. He had not been in the room when it happened and arrived back just in time to see the culprits flee. With all his precautions to protect his friends, with all his EH TAG's Damon Gray, aka Mr. Smoke, had been unable to save them. He had been devastated.

His smile had returned after Michael and Sylvia, for reasons unknown, had not moved on, but stayed, as ghosts, to help him recover and to help him on his *Smoke Missions*. But his smile did not come quite as often as it had before they were murdered.

These thoughts flashed through a part of his mind as he concentrated on what his friend was saying.

"Well, let me put the events in order." Michael continued as he touched his *triangle watch* in a special way. "As I said earlier, Charlene Thomas contacted me approximately a few hours ago and I met with her. She wanted to know how to *flash*, as we refer to it, or *blip* as she refers to it, to where her daughter is. It didn't take long to teach her."

Brandon paused and looked at his friend closely before continuing,

"Damon, Charlene Thomas has an incredibly brilliant and insightful mind. She is also tremendously Talented, with Abilities *and* Gifts." He saw Damon's eyes flicker in recognition of that revelation. "I started her off by using the TW you gave us," he indicated the faceless *triangle watch* on his left wrist, "and she quickly grasped the mechanics of it, taking to it like a duck to water, as you Americans say. She was finally able to utilize it to home in on her daughter and *blip* to her. She returned shortly, as Angelina was sleeping when she appeared at her bunk-side, and gave me a big hug and a kiss on the cheek. She thanked me and blipped off, I assume, back to her husband."

Michael paused for a moment to resort his thoughts; then looked at Damon and continued, "Damon, while I was teaching her to blip, she told me of the circumstances of her death and her daughters *near* death experience."

He then provided Damon with the Readers Digest Condensed version. He finished by saying, "Damon, I think we should help them." He looked at Damon expectantly.

"Michael, when you say *we*, do you mean *we* as in you and Sylvia, or *we* as in the Smoke organization as well?" seeing the small smile on Michael's face he continued, "Ahhh, I take it by your smile that you mean the Smoke Organization as well. As you know, Michael, I only *Smoke* terrorist bombers. Utilizing one of my TAG's, I *know* that they are guilty. This IE, or International Espionage world you talk of is far too murky for me. Sometimes the *good guys* are the *bad guys* and sometimes the *bad guys* are the *good guys*. I need time to think on it. How much time do we have, or do you know"

Michael shrugged his shoulders. "I'm not sure, but I think it is not much."

Without turning, Damon suddenly smiled and said, "Hello Sylvia how was the shopping?"

"How do you *do* that?" exclaimed a voice behind Damon. "Oh never mind, you'll probably just say, '*Magik!*' But Michael *is* right in this case Damon, we *have* to help her!" said a soft, breathy, melodious woman's voice behind Damon.

Sylvia walked around Damon and gave him a passing kiss on the cheek as she walked over to her husband. Michael she kissed on the lips. She then turned and smiled at Damon. In life, Sylvia Brighton had been a world renowned beauty, credited by many as one of the most beautiful women in the world. As a ghost, she had shed her earthly cocoon and metamorphosed into an unearthly creature of exquisite ethereal, physical and sexual beauty. Thick, long flowing honey golden blond hair draped luxuriously down over her shoulders and helped to frame and accent her elfin face with full pouty turned up lips that always seemed ready to burst into a smile and large luminous turquoise eyes that now had an internal glow radiating from deep within, and a fabulously fit and lush body that defied gravity. When she walked, Sylvia moved with a natural sensual movement reminiscent of Mary Lynne Munroe.

She flashed her pearly whites at him again.

This time Damon smiled back.

"And not just her, either!" she continued as if she had never left off. "We need to help Brandon save Angelina as well. That's their daughter." She saw her husband's look and laughed infectiously. "I know that Angelina is not a *'that'*, she's a *'she'*, but I couldn't resist doing my Indiana *thang,* sweetheart."

"I didn't say a word!" Michael responded indignantly in an upper crust British accent. "I'm mortally wounded that you would infer that it would bother me."

"How does a ghost get mortally wounded?" Sylvia responded intrigued.

Michael looked at a loss for words momentarily, then responded, "It's a very technical and complicated answer. I'm afraid I couldn't explain it to you in a way that you would understand."

"And why is that?" she asked, humoring him.

"Because *I* don't understand it!" All three laughed.

Damon went serious. "Alright, I will listen. I respect both of you too much to not give my full attention when both of you say the same thing. Explain the entire situation as you see it," here he sighed dramatically and looked at them, "and you had better give me the Directors Cut, Outtakes *and* Deleted Scenes."

***

Scene 15

Kai Akyi, pronounced *Ki* (the '*i*' pronounced as '*eye*') and Akee (as in '*ack key*') sat opposite and below the Emperor's raised dais, in lotus position. The Emperor looked down at Kai keenly. The lad had been with him a long time. Emperor Quan Chi Hanoi smiled inwardly at the use of the English word *lad*. Kai must be what, thirty nine or forty years old by now, with two grown sons?

'*No,*' he mentally amended, '*definitely* not *a lad anymore.*'

Kai Akyi was no longer the student of his father. His *deceased* father, Zuki Akyi, China's Dragon Lord, who had served his Sovereign faultlessly and flawlessly for many years, until his untimely death protecting his liege.

As the Eldest Son of Zuki Akyi, Kai had instantly assumed the mantle of the *Dragon Lord*, China's Protector, Defender of the Realm, and Emperor's Personal Champion upon his father's demise (as would the Eldest of *his* sons, upon his death). Kai had just turned twenty eight at the time.

Trained from birth, as all his brothers were, and as his sons would be, Kai's transition to Dragon Lord was seamless and flawless.

'*That was many years ago. Where does the time go?*' was the Emperor's errant thought as he looked down at his Champion.

"*Do you know what must be done, Defender, what we ask of you?*" his Emperor asked quietly.

Kai bent his head, and bowed slightly in silent affirmation.

"We cannot entrust this task to anyone else except you, Dragon Lord. Every single one of our Elite Serpent Corps that have been sent forth, up to now, have failed to kill, capture or even find the Eagle. He is, or was, Q's top information gatherer. Through poorly disguised means and for reasons unknown to us at this time, Q has informed us of the Eagle's hypothetical real name, no doubt an attempt to taunt and humiliate us into action. Supposedly it is a Brandon Thomas, although we are highly skeptical. Why would they give up their top IG agent?"

The Emperor sat in silence for a few moments in contemplation.

Maintaining silence, Kai sat immobile. He knew the question was rhetorical. Stepping outside of his body, he surveyed the room and then quickly passed through the walls and also investigated the immediate corridors leading to this Sanctum. Secure. He glanced at the two people, the Emperor and himself, seated opposite each other, before entering and rejoining his flesh.

Returning to his body was always slightly repugnant to him. His human body was so slow, so sluggish and confining compared to his astral form. He loved the feel of freedom when outside of his earthly shell. Although he was out of his body for less than a few seconds, he was refreshed. Though statue still, an errant thought caused an inward smile to lighten his mood momentarily.

To an onlooker, this scene would very much look like a centuries old painting of feudal China, instead of today's modern society. Both were dressed in the ceremonial garb of the distant past. An affectation of the Emperors. Quan Chi claimed to live in the past and present simultaneously, a living *Reincarnate*. His age was impossible to guess. In all the time Kai had known him, which was from birth on, the Emperor had not seemed to age at all, and Kai was a trained observer. Quan Chi liked to say *we* instead of *I*, because in his mind and being, he *was* China.

Kai understood and agreed. He who had been trained from birth to serve the Emperor of China, who *was* China. In serving and protecting the Emperor, Kai was serving and protecting China. To die protecting China was his greatest ambition. Then he would be free of his earthly form to ....

He was interrupted from his reverie by the Emperor's softly vibrant voice. The voice of one used to controlling billions of people's lives.

"It has been rumored in the IE world that it was we who tried to kill Brandon Thomas and his family. A rumor no doubt started by Q. We know that we did not. It is obvious to us what is being attempted by Q. They are attempting to thwart our revenge on the Eagle. We are being misdirected, maligned, manipulated and quite probably made a target of retribution. We are highly offended." Although his voice sounded offended, his face remained immobile. It was the face of one who controlled his actions totally while in the presence of others, even those close to him.

"Honor now dictates that we sent forth our Champion to show the worlds leaders that we will not *be mocked, or thwarted of our vengeance. All of the traitors in the information leak that the Eagle took back to America, both knowing and unknowing,*

have been questioned and ... ah ... appropriately dealt with. It is exceedingly strange and frustrating that they were unable to provide us an accurate physical description of the Eagle. All gave conflicting descriptions of him. All were truthful. We suspect that Q is sending us on a wild goose chase, *as the Americans say, to muddy the waters. Why would they want us to know the Eagles identity?"* He paused again in reflection, then continued, *"Tell us what we know of him, Dragon."*

Kai was silent for a moment in recollection, then responded.

"Brandon Thomas, thirty five, resides and owns a moderately successful travel Agency in New York City. He was married to woman, Charlene, now deceased, and had a seven year old girlchild in the hospital recovering from the blast of a terrorist bomb. Our Intelligence Operatives have uncovered nothing about him that is out of the ordinary. He was abandoned at birth and raised in an orphanage in New York City, never adopted. Average grades in primary school. Height; six feet, one half inch. Weight: one hundred and ninety five pounds. Eye color; Hazel. Hair color; Medium brown. Education; University Graduate with multiple Degrees. The travel agency that he owns, he started just out of high school. It did well enough to pay his way through college to earn degrees in business as well as degrees in several languages, again passing with average grades. The language degrees would seem to be a logical step in complimenting his travel business."

There was a slight pause as if considering whether or not the next piece of information was pertinent. He decided it was.

"There was a rumor that, at the blast site that killed his wife and injured his daughter, he rendered four veteran police officers unconscious when they tried to detain him for questioning. It turned out that rumor was all it was. No police report on any incident was reported. It has been verified that he accompanied his daughter in the ambulance to the hospital. It seems highly unlikely that he would be allowed to do that after incapacitating four seasoned New York law enforcement officials. His whereabouts are ... at present ... unknown."

"Had a seven year old daughter in the hospital?" the Emperor asked.

"Yes, Master. It appears that she ... ah yes, I remember ... her name is Angelina Thomas, has been removed from the hospital and into protective custody. She is small for her age as was her father. A late bloomer, his first New York Drivers License at age sixteen, stated that Brandon Thomas was five feet four, one half inch in height. Angelina's present whereabouts are currently unknown at present."

"So much is still unknown to us! How very frustrating! Find the girlchild, this Angelina, and use her as the Americans are, to force Brandon Thomas to come for her. Ascertain first if Brandon Thomas truly is the Eagle. We will not be a pawn for Q to eliminate him as a threat to them. If he is that, then it is in our best interest to assist him," the Emperor paused a moment in thought, then continued in a softer, deadlier voice, "but if he is indeed the legendary Eagle, the Information Gatherer for Q, dispose of what is left of his remains only after you have harvested all of his knowledge for us. Only after you have *accomplished* that *are you to send his daughter to him in the void. You know when to contact us. Inform us once it is completed. Have we been clearly understood, Dragon Lord?"*

"Completely, *Master. Would you like me to give my understanding of your orders?"*

"Did we ask you to bore us with them?" the Emperor snapped in an irritated voice.

"No, Master." came the quiet, respectful response.

There was a moment of silence, then Quan Chi continued in a softer tone.

"We trust in your judgment, Defender. You have always succeeded, even where others have failed. Arise, go forth, and do as you have always done for us."*

Kia Akyi arose, bowed formally, and left the room.

Quan Chi sat in silence for a few moments after the Dragon had left. He was very angry; angry and upset with himself at his abrupt rudeness to Kai. It was undeserving and unwarranted. The Dragon Lord had done nothing deserving of it. The question that he had asked, he had asked countless times before. And rightfully so! The Dragon Lord of the Realm was not one to make mistakes.

The Emperor wasn't normally rude, unless it was a calculated action to cause a response or reaction in others, but this situation was getting out of control. The Eagle had obtained extremely secret information on China's Attack and Defense System (CADS). Information that could make China vulnerable. How the *Eagle* had done it still wasn't quite clear.

That was why the Emperor's Dragon Lord was called in.

Quan Chi flowed to his feet and shed his ceremonial robe. Bare-chested, wearing only his silk pant and shoes, the Emperor of China went through a series of intricate exercises. Twisting, turning, writhing, jumping, kicking, spinning and punching, his golden slender body was that of a muscular young man. Bathed in a light film of perspiration (Emperors don't sweat), by the end of his routine all his visible muscles stood out in high relief.

Toweling himself dry, Quan Chi replaced his regal attire and sat back down on his dais, lotus position, and pondered the situation with a mind clear of bodily distractions.

'Six feet, one half inch tall Brandon Thomas was five feet four, one half inches tall at age sixteen? Interesting.'

***

Scene 16

The Eagle was agitated. Why, he didn't know. It was unlike him. Brandon had been pacing the room. He felt uneasy, as if unseen eyes were watching him. He *knew* that it *was* ridiculous, his location was secure and had not been breached, but it didn't *feel* ridiculous.

Now, standing off to the side of the living room window of his apartment, invisible to anyone outside, he gazed out into the night. The splendor of the moon and stars were somehow diminished by the glaring lights of the famous French city. He was waiting. He had been waiting thusly for three days. But that was not what was bothering him. He was pondering the situation, when, suddenly, *something* changed!

He *felt* her *coming* just a millisecond before it happened. It was enough to prepare him.

Blip.

Charlene appeared off and to his left. She smiled at him and without a greeting, started to speak excitedly.

"I want you to meet someone for me, Brandon. Someone *very* special, I think. Someone who *may* be able to help us. Someone Michael and Sylvia suggested."

"And who would that be, Charlene Thomas?" queried Brandon Thomas of his wife. "No ... no, let me guess." He theatrically held up his hands to block her reply, "You just now blipped in from *who knows where* to tell me you want me to meet with someone very special. No, no, don't tell me! It's ...it's ... it's ?" He looked at Char expectantly, hands turning the other way.

"Mr. Smoke!" she burst out enthusiastically.

"Aw .... Char, I was just about to say that ..." Brandon paused in mid sentence. "Whoa! Wait a minute! Did I just hear you say that I should meet with *Mr. Smoke?*" Char nodded happily. "*The* Mr. Smoke that is the Angel of Death to Terrorist Bombers?" Again the smiling nod. "*The* Mr. Smoke that the greatest minds in the world cannot seem to find?"

"Yes, darling, all of the above, and more." Char agreed gaily.

Brandon stared at his wife in wonderment.

"Where have you been, Blipper? You have been gone for three days. I was beginning to worry." he asked his wife seriously.

"Blipper? Don't call me that. It makes me sound like ...a ... a ... I don't know... like a porpoise!" she responded indignantly, unconsciously straightening slightly, in provocation.

"Sorry sweetheart. Bad joke." Brandon replied contritely, but Char saw the twinkle in his eye, betraying the lie. She graciously ignored it.

"Were you serious about my meeting with Mr. Smoke?" he prompted.

Charlene nodded imperceptibly, not quite sure that she had completely forgiven him. What Brandon said next washed away any doubts.

"Char, you are right, this could be great! Mr. Smoke may be just the man to help us acquire the equipment that we need, or at the very least, can direct me to someone who can. When can we meet him?"

"There is no time like the present." A deep, ghostly voice said from behind him.

Brandon checked his impulse to spin around. He turned slowly, smoothly, his mind and body in perfect balanced harmony, ready to react to danger, taking in every aspect of the room as he did so, mind working furiously. No wonder he had been agitated! He was agitated no longer.

Standing in a corner of the room, where he could not possibly have gotten to undetected, stood none other than the seemingly slender figure of Mr. Smoke.

Shock set in. Brandon took a moment to gather himself. Never, in his adult life, had *anyone* been able to sneak up on him without his knowledge or his instinct kicking in and warning him! That someone *could* do so was unsettling to say the least. Then he remembered his earlier uneasiness and relaxed. He had put it down to concern for his wife. Next time, if there *was* a next time, he would trust *his feelings more*. Brandon was not used to questioning his own instincts. It was unsettling. He felt lessened. He did not like the feeling. It would not happen again!

While he was gathering himself, he took stock of Mr. Smoke. He was standing just far enough away that any movement or attempt to attack could be thwarted easily.

Almost totally encased in a charcoal grey combat outfit, the seemingly slender body of Mr. Smoke stood with his arms hanging at his side, slightly bent. His whole posture was one of perfect, deadly balance. The only parts of his body showing were his gloved hands, booted feet and goggled facemask beneath the cowl.

The Eagle estimated Mr. Smoke's height to be close to his, maybe slightly taller. With the hood and mask it was hard to tell, possibly just over six feet. So still did he stand, that for an instant Brandon thought he might be a decoy, a mannequin. A small movement dispelled the illusion. What the movement was, Brandon was unsure of.

"You are in no danger, Mister Thomas." the soft deep mechanically altered voice continued. "I have been asked by .... mutual *friends* of ours, to meet and talk with you, and possibly render you a service. Shall we talk?"

"I would like that, yes." So saying, Brandon walked slowly away from the window to the center of the room to meet the approaching figure of Mr. Smoke. The floor of the ancient building creaked ever so slightly under his feet. Not so with Mr. Smoke. It was as if he was weightless, so silently did he glide across the room. A small ghostly shiver tingled down Brandon's spine. More like a mental shiver. An errant thought, no ... more a question, entered and flashed across the Eagles mind. Was this Mr. Smoke even human? Never had he met anyone or any*thing* like this.

"Very astute, Brandon. May we call you Brandon, or would you prefer Eagle?"

"Brandon is fine." he responded automatically. He was stunned! How in the world did Mr. Smoke know that he was the Eagle? And '*we*'? Who, in deepest darkest pits of hell, were '*we*'? And what did he mean by '*Very astute*'? His mind in turmoil, he almost missed the next sentence. It stunned him even more.

"Let us just say that we are *mostly,* or, more aptly, *partly* human, Brandon."

Mr. Smoke removed his right glove and with his ringed hand shook Brandon's.

And thus began the conversation.

*****

Scene 17

"What will you be wearing tonight?" Charlene asked her husband as he exited the shower in the Hotel Excalibur in London, England, his muscles still pumped from the workout.

"Does anyone wear tuxedos anymore?" Brandon responded, wrapping the luxurious white bath towel around his waist, after using it to towel himself dry.

"The tickets say Semi-Formal attire."

"Then I'll wear my dark pewter Armani suit and go monochromatic with the accessories."

"Great choice, darling. I am surprised that you received *two* front row seat tickets at the exclusive, Invitation Only, 'sold out' concert. Who do they expect you to bring with you?"

"You."

Charlene laughed. "There is no way that a 'sold out' concert of thousands and thousands of people would allow a front row seat to be vacant. The promoters would go crazy. It is just not done. It has to do with publicity photos, I think."

"Normally, you would be right, but in this case, not so. If you remember, Damon Gray allows no photo's to be taken at the concert. One empty seat won't be noticed. And the room seats one thousand, one hundred and twenty people, not '*thousands and thousands*'" He looked at her face in the mirror as he shaved. "How is it that I can see your reflection in the mirror, Charlie?"

She hesitated for a just a moment, in thought, then suddenly announced with great conviction. "Because I'm *not a vampire!*"

Both broke into laughter at the same moment. When it died down, she continued, "I'm flattered that you think my being a ghost makes me so much smarter, and I hate to burst your bubble, husband, but..." she raised her arms in surrender as if to say *'What you see is what you get. This is it.'*

"Can *you* see *your* reflection?"

"What do *you* think, Mr. Eagle eyes? You *do* see the makeup and lipstick I'm wearing, don't you? Of course I can .... Wait a minute ... Wow! You are right on the mark, dear one. How *can* I see my reflection? Hmmm." she pondered, as if to herself.

"Are you asking me, is it a rhetorical question, or are you just talking to yourself? If you *are* talking to me, I ... don't ... know ... either!"

Both laughed again.

Suddenly Charlene stopped and exclaimed, "I know, I'll ask Michael and Sylvia! See you at the concert." She blew him a kiss and vanished.

"I hate it when she does that." he mumbled to himself in a joking manner, as he affixed a mustache, goatee and matching sideburns to his clean-shaven face. He then attached the receding hairline thinning haired wig. He added a few wrinkles around the eyes. One of the last things that he put on his face was a small mole on the end and to the side of his nose. The mole had a few short hairs imbedded as if they had cut and had grown out slightly. Then he applied makeup to all the visible hair areas until the blend was unnoticeable. With a special pen he added a number of fine varicose veins to his nose and subtly applied and blended rouge over top. He finished his face by doing a poor job of applying cover-up makeup on the hair covered mole and veins. He then produced two pink gelatinous pads and tucked them in his mouth, one in each side, between the teeth and outside wall. He smiled a wide smile. They blended perfectly.

Brandon then strapped on a gelatinous belly that added a good ten inches to his waist. Two large caliber non-metallic handguns were taped into matching indentations in the false belly. The shirt was designed to fit loosely and normally while large enough to just cover the false belly.

The large chest pockets on the shirt camouflaged the openings that allowed him instant access to the guns. The custom made Armani suit pants were a low-rise non-pleated style, with a stretchable and elasticized waistband, designed to be worn under the potbelly or without. The matching suit jacket could not be closed with the *belly*, but looked almost unnoticeable and acceptable open. Again, designed to be worn both ways.

Lastly he added colored contact lenses that turned his piercing hazel eyes into a dull, mossy, forgettable nondescript brownish color. He stood back and took stock. He added an ornate walking sword cane, altered his stance and attitude to that of a strutting peacock. He looked like a vulture trying to impersonate a peacock.

He was satisfied.

The person looking back at him was that of a paunchy, puffy faced, middle aged, jaded, alcoholic, slightly balding, bleary-eyed English Professor, striving to look dapper and on the prowl for a gay partner.

***

Charlene Thomas stood off to the side of the large crowd in the waiting area of the Oliver Theatre inside the National Theatre in the heart of London. The room was packed. She was amazed. It *was* a '*sold out*' show. Brandon had told her that their seats were A22 and A23, dead center in the first row.

She searched the crowd for signs of her husband without success. A number of people drifted into the corner she was standing in. She shrunk back to avoid contact. A few were starting to crowd her.

"Oh my lord, would you look at the buns on him!" a slightly slurred educated voice exclaimed in admiration. "Buns of steel, you could crack an egg on either one of them!"

The voice came from one of two men almost touching her. Char looked to see a paunchy, slightly inebriated man talking to a man who was obviously shocked and embarrassed by him.

"Do you know him?" the voice continued. It was the voice of one striving to talk soberly, that is to say, slightly slower and clearer, so that the words wouldn't slur. Char revised her opinion. He was drunker than she had originally thought.

The drunk put his hand on the man's shoulder and leaned in slightly.

"Could you introduce me to him? I'll make it worth your while, old chap. What do you say?"

The man shrugged the hand away with horror and distain and hurried away into the crowd. The drunk stood for a moment, baffled. Then he turned his bleary eyes to Char and winked.

"You've got way better buns anyway." He said to her and smiled lecherously. It was the smile that gave it away.

"That was very funny, darling, but then I knew it was you from the start!" Charlene stated indignantly.

"No you didn't." Brandon said without a hint of inebriation showing in his voice. He unobtrusively blocked the area she was standing in.

Charlene bit back another comeback, paused for a second, then admitted, "You're right, I didn't." She smiled. "Wow! Brandon, that is the best disguise that I have *ever* seen! It blew me away when you turned and winked at me. I was tricked right up to your smile. Your smile gave you away."

"Really?" he said quietly.

"You *don't* mean to tell me that you can change your smile also?"

He gave her another lecherous smile, one that she *didn't* recognize.

***

Scene 18

Two Back Stage Passes were issued to Brandon Thomas when he had presented his *one* ticket to the usher.

He noticed that others, seemingly randomly selected, received only one Back Stage Pass *per ticket*.

At first it looked like he had been handed one, but when he took a closer look later, the one Back Stage Pass was really two. The two had been moisture stuck together. With English humidity the way it was, it didn't surprise him. He pocketed both and made no comment. Brandon did not wish to attract *any* undue notice.

He made his way to his two paid seats, running interference for his wife. The extra seat beside him, Charlene sat in. It remained vacant for the entire performance. As Brandon had surmised, no one seemed to notice.

Brandon looked up at the bare stage. The stage floor glistened beautifully with the light of the overhead bulbs sinking in and rebounding off them.

After most of the audience had almost been seated, and before the lights went out before the performance, he heard a clear voice pierce the hubbub noise of the crowd arranging themselves in their seats. The sweet voice of a child. Brandon and Charlene were some of the ones still standing until the last minute.

"I sure hope I get to meet Doctor Gray. I just love his music. Doctor Gray's music is *Magic* Music! Were you able to get

Passes to see him? You promised me you would try your *very* best, and I saw you talking to someone and I saw them give you something after you gave him some money. Well, *did* you get them?" Almost directly behind him, he heard the sweet clear sound of a child's animated voice. The accent and gender he could not define. (*'A small child, judging by the piping voice, striving to be heard'*).

Brandon heard a man's deep gravelly voice (*'an educated American by his accent'* Brandon surmised) respond, "I am *so* sorry Tasha, (*'Ahh, it was a* girls *voice',* Brandon amended) but I was only able to purchase *one* Back Stage Pass from someone who had to leave early. Maybe we can meet Doctor Gray next time, okay?"

"Ohhhh." the little voice moaned. Then abruptly she stopped and piped out, "Oh, I'm sorry! Don't look so sad Mr. Hastings. I know you did your *very, very best*. I am sure you will get *two* Back Stage Passes next time. I - I just know it!" the last was said with a forced bravado that Brandon knew she did not feel.

'Cool kid!' Brandon thought to himself.
Charlene turned her head and looked back. "Oh Brandon, she is absolutely adorably divine!" enthused his phantom wife. "Give her *my* ticket! The extra one that was stuck together."

"No Char. I don't want to be conspicuous!" His lips did not move and his soft voice was just under the crowd noise, yet forceful. No one, except Charlene, heard him.

"Just turn around and look at her ... for me ... please, *darling?"* She smiled her *I Love You Smile* and his shoulders seem to sag slightly. He turned and looked.

It came as a shock!

Wearing a lavender trimmed snow white dress with matching leggings and shoes, the petite girl's eyes came up to meet his as he finished turning. Pure lavender eyes captured and held his. Never had he seen eyes that color. The rest of her face and body slowly came into focus. It was the face and body of a four to five year old girl. The porcelain smooth face, framed by the thick lustrous curls, could have graced the cover of any parenting magazine. (*'The hand tied lavender bows in her hair were a nice finishing touch'*, the errant thought flashed across his attentive mind.)

She was beautiful. As beautiful as his own daughter, but in a completely different way. Brandon noticed a doll, wearing a dress matching hers, sitting very properly on the chair behind her, as he tore his gaze away from her and looked back up at her Guardian.

And he *did* look like a Guardian. Brandon surmised *that* from Tasha's use of his name. *'Mr. Hastings'* she had called him. Brandon's quick, seemingly casual glance was deceiving. His glance told him everything he wanted or needed to know. Hastings looked, and was, every inch the bodyguard type.

"Is your name by any chance, Mr. Hastings?" he *almost* gushed, in his *slightly inebriated trying to act sober* Upper Crust English accent. The bodyguard's head nodded slightly, but the eyes remained cold.

"Someone was telling me that a Mr. Hastings was looking to purchase two Backstage Passes. Did I just hear a snippet about *'Maybe we can meet Doctor Gray next time'*, or some such words?" Again the nod and no smile. "Well, I don't know how much use *I* can be, but I *can* offer you *one* Pass, my ... um ... er ... ah ... *friend's* Back Stage Pass. As this empty seat testifies, the little slut said that *he* couldn't make it. And at the last minute! I know who he's with, the tart! He's with ... Well, never mind that. Sorry about the bad word, dearie." he said to the *girlchild* condescendingly. The *girlchild* whose eyes had not left him.

"It's *not* polite to stare, young lady." he enunciated each word slowly, sternly. Turning back to Mr. Hastings he tried to smile a boyish smile. "Oh never mind that, I never was much good with .... *children*. Never could stand the little *monsters*." He shivered slightly. The word *'children'* sounded like a curse word. He fumbled inside his jacket pocket. "Anyway, onward and upward! What say, maybe you can purchase another one during intermission." With that said he produced his second Backstage Pass with a clumsy flourish and offered it to the bodyguard.

Mr. Hastings did not respond, "How much do you want for it, sir?" he asked politely.

"Are you single?" Brandon leered. Hastings did not respond in any discernible way.

"Well, I'm *willing* to take that chance!" he announced as if reaching his own decision.

"It is *free of charge*! My gift to you ... you, big, beautiful, strong, hulking, handsome man, you." He proffered the Pass again. Again the man did not respond.

Brandon felt a mysterious sensation pass through his body as a small hand pulled his ticketed hand down, while the other relieved him of the Pass.

"Oh, thank you, thank you." piped up the girl child gushingly. "I just *felt* when I first saw you, that you were a good man. *Now I know it.*" The feeling vanished, as if it never happened, the instant her hands lost touch with his.

"It's not for you, miss grabby girlie girl." he almost growled at her. "It's for him!" he almost purred at Hastings, striving in vain to suck his stomach paunch in. "Anyway, I do hope you get a second one for the brat! I mean the ... *little darling.*"

As he started to turn away, he witnessed an amazing transformation in the bodyguard. Mr. Hastings suddenly smiled, reached forward and gripped his hand in a friendly grip. The smile transformed his face. He went from *enemy face* to *friend face* in the blink of an instant.

"Thank you, sir. You don't know how happy you have just made this little girl! And myself as well."

"Maybe lunch sometime ...?" he ventured leeringly again.

Hastings just smiled.

At that exact moment, the theater went black!

It was dark! Black dark! Cave dark!

The audience sat.

Silence reigned supreme. You could hear a pin drop.

Damon Gray's concert was about to begin.

Eleven hundred and nineteen people waited in excited expectation.

The timing was flawless.

Suddenly *one* spotlight flared on.

Where seconds before there had been a bare empty stage, there now reposed, Cocoa brown and glistening in the limelight, a magnificent magnum opus, *custom made for Damon Gray to his specifications; a Bosendorfer 290 Imperial Concert Grand Piano* sat off center and to the right of the stage, with the performers stool before it and to the front. To many piano experts, it was living proof of pure artistic genius, and a true masterpiece of workmanship, that dominated the stage.

A second spotlight blazed down highlighting a second breathtaking masterpiece of sculpture and workmanship. Not to be outdone by the Bosendorfer, off center and to the left rested an Italian *Fazioli Concert Grand Piano* in a dazzling black diamond finish (*again, custom made for Damon Gray to his specifications*).

It was, in every way, the equal of the other.

The empty Master Pianist's Bench was situated directly between the two pianos. The pianos were angled in a wide V configuration, making the empty stool the focal point.

Thirty *long* seconds passed before the rest of the lights brightened slowly to reveal a stage empty of all save the two Grand Piano's and Damon Gray's empty Master Pianists Bench.

The moment the lights reached full power, everything went black!

It only lasted a few seconds before they flashed back to full brilliance. The audience gasped. The entire back of the stage was filled with musicians complete *with* all their instruments! Before the audience could gather their wits, the lights flashed off and on again in a heartbeat.

The primed, anticipatory audience *erupted*. They roared, clapped and cheered with a mixture of high enthusiasm and disbelief!

It was unbelievable! It was impossible! It ... was ... magic! Seated on the Pianist's stool, between the two pianos, holding a custom made *Damon Gray Violin and Bow,* was none other than the Master Composer and Pianist. That the Master Pianist held a *violin* told the audience that tonight's performance would be special.

Tucking the namesake USA custom made *Damon Gray Violin* into place, Damon Gray arose in one *impossibly* fluid motion to greet his audience.

***

Scene 19

"**Y**ou might as well be the one to start, Gunner. Please begin with your intercourse with the Eagle and finish with your evaluation of him." Damon Gray took a sip of his energy drink as he awaited a reply.

Hastings looked at his boss, then at Catherine on his left and finally down at the small form of Natasha on his right. She was still holding on to her doll. She smiled up at him. He smiled back.

They were seated in the library at *BlackStone*, Damon's residence in England. Natasha sometimes called it *Castle* BlackStone, and to her eight year old mind, it was.

Damon had just returned from a meeting with Brandon Thomas. Damon had sent for Hastings and Catherine to attend a Council of War to see what, *or if any*, action should be taken.

He was going to send someone to get Natasha when they had arrived. She had been put down to nap as soon as she arrived home. Damon wanted her to get extra rest. He needn't have bothered.

Natasha was already seated in the library when they entered. Natasha was highly *'Gifted'*. She *'knew'* of the meeting and *when* to attend. She knew she was needed and it excited her. Deep inside, she glowed. *This was the first time that she had participated on a Smoke Mission!* (Even though Damon told her it was definitely *not* a *'Smoke Mission'*, to Natasha, it was.) Small for her age, she seemed dwarfed by the leather chair she was sitting so properly in.

Hastings shrugged his muscular shoulders and shook his head slightly, chuckling.

"Very apt phrasing, Commander. At first contact I thought the Eagle had switched tickets with someone, to protect himself. Commander, his disguise skills rival yours." Damon nodded in agreement, not taking offense where none was intended.

Hastings continued, "I knew that you purposely gave him two tickets and two Backstage Passes so that I could ask to buy one from him. I knew I had spoken loudly enough for him to hear that I had purchased one earlier and was unable to secure a second one. He threw me off a little when he turned around and offered one."

With the occasional clarifying question from Damon, he went on to replay the entire sequence of events from his perspective.

He finished with the Backstage Pass transfer, then added, "Only when Natasha touched his hand and said he was wonderful, did I let my guard down and accept who he was and that he was no threat to you, Commander. You asked that Natasha and I *not* compare notes until after we had talked with you. So, if it meets with your approval, Commander, I'll reserve my answer to your question until after Natasha has had her say. I need to hear what her observations were and add them to my own. Then I can finish my evaluation."

"As you wish." Damon nodded to Natasha.

Her concert meeting story matched Hastings but continued on. "The Commander didn't give the Eagle two sets of tickets just so that we could offer to buy a Backstage pass from him so I could touch his hand for you." she explained turning to Hastings. "The empty second seat beside him on the front row was for his wife. She sat in it. She sure is beautiful."

Hastings mouth almost dropped open. He turned and looked at his Boss.

Damon nodded. "Yes she is." agreed Damon. "Continue Natasha Gray."

Natasha giggled infectiously, turning her attention back to him. "Natasha Gray! I love it when you say that, Commander." She then put her little forefinger to her chin and frowned. "Now, where was I. Oh yes, the reception! I was turning to answer a question that someone asked me when I noticed *Mrs.* Thomas, Mr. Thomas's Ghost wife, dancing *just for him.* No one else in the room was dancing, only her. I couldn't help but look! Gosh, Commander, she danced wonderfully, just like an Angel."

Her lavender eyes blurred momentarily in remembrance then focused again. "Suddenly I saw Brandon's wife's clothes disappear right off her body! It shocked me into looking right at her, I mean right into her eyes. The moment our eyes touched, her clothes reappeared. I'm sorry Commander. I knew I wasn't supposed to let her know I knew of her. I didn't look at her for the *almost all* of the rest of the evening, even though she *was trying* to ... *read? touch*? No, not read or touch ... *probe* my mind? Yes, that's maybe a closer word! *Probe!* Well ... maybe all three."

"*Almost?*" Damon prodded gently.

Natasha giggled. "I just knew I wouldn't get *that one* by you, Commander Gray." Her face sobered and she continued in a very serious tone, "Well, I just *knew* she must be lonely as a ghost, so on my way out, I asked my dolly if she thought it would be alright with you, Commander, if I could be her friend. Dolly said it would be alright with you, so I turned and looked right at Charlene Thomas and *after* I looked at her *right in the eyes* to let her know I saw her, *then* I gave her two thumbs up for how beautiful she looked."

Natasha stood, bent forward and turned slightly to add emphasis and repeated the pose. Damon could not help it, he smiled. Natasha straightened as if finished, then suddenly looked at Damon, as if she had just remembered something important, and blurted, "Oh, and then I waved goodbye to her as we left. Did I do *good*, Commander?" she asked excitedly.

"Yes you did, Natasha. You did *do good*." Damon said absently.

***

"I see major issues with it, Commander. If what Brandon Thomas said is true, it does seem that he and his daughter are in desperate circumstances. If indeed he truly *is* the *'Eagle'*, and I do believe that he is sir, that alone could cause us *major* problems. From all my sources, the Eagle is, or should I say *'was'*, Q's top *information retrieval penetration expert*. He is Legend. He has always been absolutely loyal to his country and his organization. In my opinion, he still is. If his situation gets resolved with our help and he goes back to work for Q, we could be *compromised*, Commander." He rubbed his dark, stubble shadowed face absently. "Not to mention that of the Smoke Organization, if he ever finds out that you *are Mr. Smoke*. I don't know that we can trust him that way, but I also don't know whether that should be an issue. I agree with what you said earlier, Commander. In the world of International Espionage, nothing is as it seems. It is as twisted as a nine headed hydra."

Damon finished his energy drink in silence and then stood. The audience energy from the concert still vibrated off him three hours later. He almost glowed.

He had told them of his Mr. Smoke visit with Brandon. "Thank you Hastings. I have a lot to think about. I will let you know what we will do tomorrow. Come, Princess. Bedtime." Natasha laughed with delight as he scooped her up and headed for the door.

"The Commander *is* going to help them. Goodnight..." she called back, over Damon's massive shoulder, as they headed for the doorway. She managed a wave and a kiss to Catherine and Hastings before fading into the dark.

"How does she *know* those things?" Hastings muttered to himself as he waved goodnight.

"How should I know?" responded Cat, thinking the question was for her.

"Pardon? Oh ... well, she *is* your daughter."

"Not anymore." Ms Nipp responded quietly and with great satisfaction.

She arose and smiled at him. Hastings was always amazed at how Cat Nipp could make the act of standing up so incredibly sensual that it bordered on the extreme exotic erotic. She turned slowly and stretched, her signature white cutout micro-mini dress rising to within an inch of Hastings rising temperature. Without a backward glance, one of the most beautiful and the absolute sexiest women Hastings had ever known or seen glided out of the room.

Hastings was sweating. "Dammit," he growled softly, "I hate it when she does that!"

He heard her throaty laugh in the distance. He had forgotten about her incredibly keen hearing.

"Shit!" he muttered, even softer, his color darkening slightly.

Again, from farther away, the laughter.

***

Scene 20

"Tasha can see ghosts." Charlene announced matter of factly, as Brandon was eating his breakfast with a relish he hadn't felt for a long time. "And hear them too, I think."

Brandon looked up at her in surprise; fork paused halfway to his mouth. Slowly the fork went down, forgotten, along with his appetite.

"Explain please."

"Remember at the Backstage Reception when I told you how proud I was of you for giving them the Pass?"

Brandon grinned at the memory. "I sure do. Distinctly! You said you wished that you could kiss me, and I replied that in place of that, you could do a striptease for me." He smiled again at the memory. Then his smile disappeared.

"Do you mean to tell me that you think Tasha *saw* your clothes vanish for those few seconds before they flashed back on again?"

"I don't *think* she did darling, I *know* she did. It happened after I impulsively flashed off my clothes and was doing my exotic dance for you." She also smiled at the memory. "I guess I was glorying in the fact that you were the only one who could see me. "Out of the corner of my eye I noticed that Tasha had stopped talking to someone and was turning to talk to someone else just as I was doing the *imaginary pole dance routine*. Her eyes widened for a fraction of a second as her eyes met mine. And when our eyes met, I felt a ... a *something* go through me, probably the same feeling you described when your hands first met. It felt like I was ... oh, I don't know" she paused again, struggling to put into *speech* what she had *felt*, shrugged helplessly, and then continued, "like I was somehow *touched inside* ... or something."

Brandon nodded in understanding agreement but didn't interrupt. "I flashed my clothes back on immediately. She did not seem to see me for the rest of the night, but as she and her bodyguard were leaving, she turned at the door, looked right into my eyes to make sure I knew she was looking right at me, smiled the most beautiful smile, gave two thumbs up and then *waved at me* as she left! I quickly looked behind me to make absolutely sure and no one was looking at her. She had looked directly at me!" the last was said with an *ah ha! that proves it!* tone. Concrete evidence.

Brandon smiled, but did not doubt her. He knew better. "Is there *anything else* that you haven't told me?" her husband asked gently.

"I think she controls her aura." She saw Brandon's look.

"How can someone control their aura, Char?" he asked seriously.

She shrugged her shoulders helplessly. "I don't know. I didn't notice at first, but as I was *sensing* her and watching to see if she would look at me again, I noticed that her aura was extremely stable, even when she talked excitedly with someone. That is definitely *not* natural. Definitely *not*! Everyone's aura automatically reacts to their emotions to some extent." She paused for a moment, then added, "I also think she's older than she looks!"

That was just too much for Brandon. He burst into laughter. His wife looked at him with a confused look on her face. When she realized how it had sounded, she broke into laughter too.

Finally Brandon managed to say, "She's a Midget?" then broke into laughter again. Charlene only smiled condescendingly at that comment.

"You know what I meant! What I meant was, I just think Tasha is small for her age. I watched as she mingled with people at the reception. She looks four or five, but she acts much, much older."

"Like six or seven?" Brandon said with a straight face. She saw the twinkle behind it and laughed softly.

"I know it sounds silly, darling, but there is something about her and the way she acts that makes me believe that she has had too much life experience for a four or five year old. She reminds me of Angle. Angel is small for her age too, but Angel has led a sheltered life. I *definitely* don't *feel* that Natasha has led a sheltered life. Not that it makes one bit of difference. I still think Natasha is a beautiful child, both inside and out. It was just an observation. And you *did* ask if there was anything else, remember?"

"I did, and do, and thank you. I will file that away for future reference." There was no hint of humor when he said that.

Char knew that he meant it. She knew who he was and what he did. He was the Eagle. She knew that his cognitive, deductive, recollective and intuitive powers were second to none, and in point of fact, surpassed all the known boundaries that Q had tested him on, *before* and *after* they had hired him. No one in his *IG* Division had ever matched his test results or, for that matter, even came close. When Brandon had mentioned it, Charlene had teased him that the Eagle was the best there ever was and that Q was lucky to get him. She loved to tease him in a positive way. It was another of her traits that he loved about her.

Charlene Thomas remembered that Brandon had corrected her on that and told his wife of a woman in Q who had matched his test results, though it was in a different Department, KOLD. Char knew what KOLD stood for. The Agent's code name was Kameleon. He hadn't told Charlene her real name. She had never asked. It was just part of a conversation, or briefing, that Brandon had with the Owl many years ago. It had been in context to one of his assignments that the Owl had mentioned Kameleon's name and her test scores.

There were three reasons that Charlene remembered it so vividly. The first was the fact that Kameleon worked alone, like her husband. The second was that she matched Brandon's test results in her area of expertise. But it was the third that had made the impact on her. Brandon had told her that he had breached all of Q's security systems and had found out everything he could on Kameleon. Something about the way that the Owl had talked about Kameleon aroused the Eagle's suspicion and curiosity. The consequences of that act, if discovered by Q, would be the immediate *Extermination* of Brandon and his entire family.

That was so like, yet so unlike Brandon, that it had left a deep-rooted impression on her. He had never explained why he had engaged in such a dangerous act. Again, Char didn't ask, but she knew that it would have to have been for something extremely important to Brandon, for him to risk imperiling the lives of his family.

The Eagle's breaching of Q's security didn't alarm his wife. She knew that Brandon would never have attempted it if he thought that there was even the slightest risk of being discovered.

Why he had done it *scared her to death*, and she did *not* scare easily.

Charlene remembered that it was one of the *few* times that she had been sorely tempted to read his thoughts. It was the *results* of *what she might find* that stopped her. That thought instantly brought her back to the present.

"There is one more thing, Brandon."

"Another? Well I'll be darned! And what would that *thing* be, Inspector *Columbus*?" was the innocent, quiet response. She bit back a retort, smiled sheepishly and continued.

"Well, when I was watching to see if Tasha would look at me again, I took a calculated risk and tried to read her mind. "Children's minds are so simple, yet so powerful, because they are so uncluttered. They are fairly easy to read because of that. The walls or barriers erected by life's experiences, has not closed them off. Another one of the reasons that I think she is older, is that I *can't read her mind.*"

Brandon absorbed the implications of what she had told him. "Why didn't you tell me last night, Char? This is important information."

"Yes it is darling, but with all that was going on last night, I felt you were too tired to absorb it fully. You had enough on your mind. Besides, you needed a good restful night's sleep. I didn't want it to disturb your sleep, plus I knew I would be here this morning. It also gave me time to sort things out in my mind."

Knife and fork still in hand he returned his attention to finishing his meal. Brandon looked down to an empty plate! He had absently finished his breakfast of bacon, eggs, toast and jam. He placed the useless utensils on the empty dish.

"It started out tasting good, so it must have finished being good, because I would have known if it sucked. Oh, well." He poured and mixed another cup of coffee and retired from the kitchen to the living room.

"What were your impressions of last night? I want and need all of them to finalize my POA." He sat down on an overstuffed leather chair and took a sip of coffee. The "ahhh..." meant that it was good coffee. Charlene sat in the matching chair, opposite him.

***

Scene 21

"**I** know that I painted the canvas in broad strokes, Hastings. Are you now ready for the detail strokes, or do you harbor any questions or suggestions before we start?" Damon asked quietly, the next morning in the library.

"Yes I do Commander. First let me see if I understand the bottom line of this picture correctly. You have decided that you are going to provide *all* the equipment that he needs, at no charge, and then you are going to help Brandon Thomas in the rescue his daughter from the clutches of one of the most dangerous organizations in the world. Correct?"

Damon nodded but said nothing. He knew from the slight shaking of the head and his tone, that Hastings wasn't finished speaking. He was right.

"Ain't gonna happen, Commander. Nope, it ain't gonna happen!" The last said forcefully yet with respect.

"And why not, Gunner?"

"You know very well *why not*, sir. You know how I feel. You are not going into this on your own ... and that's final! Sir."

"What in the world makes you think that I am doing this independently?" asked Damon, genuinely surprised.

Now it was Hastings turn to be surprised! "Well ... you said, and I quote, *'I have decided to supply Brandon Thomas with all the necessary equipment, without charge or fee, and though not asked, will also be willing to provide aid in the rescue of his daughter, Angelina.'*"

Hastings paused for a moment as if that statement answered everything. When Damon didn't respond, he elaborated.

"You didn't say *'WE'*, sir."

Damon smiled an apologetic smile. "Yes I did, didn't I? My mistake, Hastings. I have been consciously trying *not* to say *'we'*. You had mentioned that I had unconsciously done it a few times. I suppose I overcompensated. Let me rephrase it. *'We'* will lend assistance, and the 'we' includes you, Catherine and, if need be, Natasha." He saw Hastings look and headed it off. "She wants to, my friend. She says her *Dolly* feels that Angelina is a lot like her and that Natasha can help her."

Hastings gave him a knowing look.

"I know, I know. I will check into it someday, just not now. That aside, she loved helping us at the concert, Hastings. She said she now felt like she was finally a *true* part of the family. That sealed it for me. Believe me when I say that *'we'* will let nothing happen to her. And you know who that *'we'* is."

Hastings relaxed and nodded. That *'we'* included two, *foreign yet not, sentient energy beings, self named as Golden and Garnet, (added parts,* Damon called them) that comprised but a small component of the total makeup of Damon Gray, Concert Pianist. *aka Gray Ghost* to the news media because he would allow no photo's to be taken of him. *aka Mr. Smoke,* Killer of Terrorist Bombers. *aka EH (Enhanced Human). aka 'Ghost Assassin',* Killer of EHE *(Enhanced Human Exterminators).*

"Are you alright with it now, Gunner?"

"As long as I'm involved in it with and for you, Commander, any and everything is alright with me. Think of me as a canvas and start applying the fine brush details."

"Let's finish the conversation in the gym?" replied Damon seriously, ignoring the tease about painting in broad strokes.

Hastings repressed a grin and nodded. He looked at Damon as they headed down to one of the subterranean caves that housed the Gymnasium. His boss tended to be a serious person. He was an artist, albeit a musical one, and his tendency was to think in terms of pictures. He knew that Damon had a love for puzzles. Hastings felt that he was born with that love.

An itinerant memory wafted across his mind's eye, a memory of a time when Damon was a young boy. He had told Hastings that the very *fabric of life itself* was a puzzle and that once completed, you went on to the next one, a bigger more complex one. Hastings had *almost* understood him on that one. Most he didn't, but that didn't bother him. He knew he was highly intelligent. He also knew that Damon's IQ was off the charts. He loved being challenged by his employers thought processes.

Damon knew he was being scrutinized by Hastings. He had come to know him like a book over the course of their relationship. Hastings looked like a bodyguard but he was anything but. He astounded Damon countless times with his insights and his
intelligence. Although he scored highly in both the physical and mental abilities in Damon's mind, it was the flux in Hastings intellect that intrigued him. Sometimes Hastings intuitively grasped things far beyond his mental abilities and capabilities.

They entered the cave that housed the gymnasium. Every type of exercise equipment imaginable was present.

Damon and Hastings changed into their workout outfits and began their routine.

Throughout their workout they discussed the plans to help Brandon. Hastings asked at one point, "Are you going to inform him of the Smoke Organization?"

"I am not sure at this time, Hastings. At some point it may be necessary, but until then, it will remain untold. One thing does concern me. Charlene has seen Mr. Smoke. She may have seen the body movements, and by that I mean the little movements that cannot be disguised because they are that person. They are as good as fingerprints. If she recognizes me, that may force the issue. I took that into account when I designed the Smoke outfit. It was designed to camouflage a lot of the small movements that a body makes. Initially its design purpose was to mask body attack signals to an opponent. Hopefully the outfit accomplished its disguise purpose with Charlene Thomas."

"I doubt that she would Commander. You move differently as Mr. Smoke than you do as Damon Gray. I have seen it myself. Once you put the outfit on, something happens to you. You *become* Mr. Smoke. You *walk* differently, you move differently, you act differently ... you *are* different. Even without the electronic voice scrambler, your voice changes. It is colder somehow. Even I do not recognize it."

Damon smiled in understanding. "Yes, you are probably right. The fact that I die *with* each of the Terrorist Bombers that I *Smoke* might have something to do with that."

Hastings eyes widened as the import of what his employer had told him sunk in. "You DIE when they do?"

He saw Hastings alarmed expression. "I should clarify that statement. As you know, when I see a newscast or story about a Terrorist Bombing, I somehow connect with that Terrorist Bomber. Because I am connected to them, I know where they are *every second of every minute of the day*. What I have never shared with you, Hastings, is that *when* I kill them, I *experience* their death *with* them. I pay a very large price for *murdering* them. I die with them as they do. Although I don't actually die in body, I do in my mind."

"You don't *murder* them Commander, you *cleanse* the world of the vermin." Hastings stated emphatically.

Damon shook his head slightly, "No my friend, I do not cleanse the world of *vermin*. I *murder* Terrorist Bombers. They are human, I have found out. I consider it *murder* because I give them no chance to fight back. To do otherwise would be beyond foolish. To accomplish my goal of ridding the world of Terrorist Bombers, I *cannot* afford the *noble concept* of giving them any chance to harm me. To harm me would do the same to my quest. When they die, I do not experience their *life,* Hastings. I experience their *death*. I *murder* Terrorist Bombers and I pay an unspeakable price for it."

A thought popped into Hastings mind, and he asked without thinking. "Do you also die with them when Misty Smoke kills them instead of you?"

Damon's head dropped slightly in affirmation. "I am connected with them Hastings. I know Death intimately. On more than one occasion I have experienced the death of a Terrorist Bomber that committed suicide because he knew I was coming. Or Shot themselves.

Hastings controlled a shudder. He had no idea that Damon experienced his victim's death. He could scarcely envision it. He felt a hand on his shoulder. He looked up in surprise. Damon had materialized beside him.

"Do not pity me, my friend." he spoke softly, gently putting his hand on Hastings shoulder. "It is a cross I *gladly* bear. Let us not talk of it again. Instead let us speak of the Eagle and his hurdles, agreed?"

Hastings nodded mutely. His employer, and friend, never ceased to amaze him.

"Hurdles? You call his mountains *hurdles*, Commander?" Hastings demanded.

Damon smiled. His ploy had worked.

***

Scene 22

Somewhere, in a huge nameless building complex in the Blue Ridge Mountains, Commandant JD Powder looked at the Kameleon. He just couldn't make himself believe it! *'Bullshit,'* he thought to himself, *'there is no way that Shela Pryce is a virgin.'* Suddenly another thought flashed across his mind, *'Unless she is a dyke!'*

At that *exact* moment Shela turned her head and looked straight into his eyes with her dull ones of a nondescript cow brown color.

"Not a nice word." she stated quietly.

Powder felt a slight rise in his body temperature. Nothing showed on his face. It was as motionless and emotionless as a cloudless winter sky, but something deep within him was shocked!

"What *word* would that be Kameleon?"

"*Gay* is the word they use now. And for your information, no, I am not. I prefer the company of men. Most women disgust me." she answered softly.

"I'm not sure what you mean." JD responded in the same tone. His calm exterior remained, but inside he was taken aback again. *'Is she a mind reader?'* he mused uneasily. *'And if so, did she just admit to* not *being a virgin?'*

Kameleon smiled a closed lipped smile. "No … no, of course you don't, Commandant. My mistake."

JD did not respond. But he did try to shield his mind.

Although Douglas Chandler was seated behind his desk, the Commandant was standing when Shela had entered the room and had been introduced by Douglas. He always used every advantage in every situation. Her hip movements made her entrance walk memorable. No hand shaking or saluting had occurred. He had bowed his head slightly in acknowledgement.

Kameleon seemingly glanced casually around and by, not directly *at* him. Then, taking off her slightly tinted glasses, she looked around the room as if seeing it for the first time. Obviously, his Herculean size did not seem to impress her. She *couldn't* be as vacant as she first appeared to be. Shela looked slightly cross eyed.

Without appearing to, he looked her over closely. Initially, what he saw didn't impress him. He had requested her file when he had arrived at eight ten am. He had been denied, not that it bothered him. He had wanted it for later, to compare with his experience. He favored to not muddy his instincts and intellect with the information overload of someone else's opinions as to who or what Shela Pryce, aka Kameleon, was.

His first impression of Kameleon *altered*. Maybe *all* was *not* as it seemed. He took a long, quiet, unnoticeable breath. Gone was the momentary *uneasiness*, banished as if it never was. It was instantly replaced by his eternal and questing natural competitive nature, his genius intellect and instincts quivering with an intense eagerness.

'*Ah, good ... a challenge!*' He took stock of her a second time.

Shela Pryce was wearing a short black skirt that had a slit cut up on one side to an unseemly height. It was obvious that she was not wearing any kind of underwear under the black patterned pantyhose. *'Probably the crotch-less kind, judging from the look of the rest of her attire'* he surmised.

Tattoos adorned her legs and ankles. *'Born to be Ridden'* was on the motorcycle wings of one of them. The hose pattern distorted the shape of her overly muscular legs, making them look heavy and slightly bowed. JD couldn't tell for sure. Or maybe they were bowlegged and the patterned hose made them look straighter.

The pattern subtly highlighted instead of camouflaging the plethora of small spider and varicose veins, as Shela thought they did. Her feet were sheathed in expensive plain black, genuine alligator high heeled pumps. They matched her sling purse. They were both glaringly out of sync with the rest of her sartorial ensemble.

A white, high neck scarf top, hanging loose, covered her chest area down to the start of her hips, neatly camouflaging her thick waist. Although the material was thick, JD observed dark marks, probably bruises or more tattoos, beneath the fabric. The pushup bra did nothing to flatter her physique, instead it gave her the appearance of being soft, mushy and top heavy. The scarf top dropped over one shoulder and part of a bruise peeked out.

Shela's long auburn locks were artfully messy, flowing down and around her face in disarray. They also looked slightly greasy. Using her little finger, she brushed back one of the loose curls back that had dropped over one eye. Her teeth, he could not tell. When she spoke he saw the nicotine stained bottoms of them. Her closed lipped smile told him the rest of the story. Shela did not like to show her discolored teeth. Her face was a little plump. JD's stone colored eyes easily discerned old acne scars, barely noticeable underneath the heavy makeup.

A curvature of the neck spine made her seem shorter than she was, almost making her look predatory. That was probably why she didn't look directly at people. '*It must bother her neck*', he surmised.

One of her long calloused hands rested on the shoulder strap of the black alligator sling purse that was hanging from her shoulder. JD could tell from her hands that she practiced martial arts a lot to have calluses that thick. With one broken on her little finger, the '*French Tipped*' stick-on nails were accented by a plethora of oversized rings, whether precious metal or costume, Powder could not tell. He expected the latter, judging from the rest of her attire. The oversized rings made her hand size hard to figure out.

'*Clothing and makeup aside, Shela Pryce could be quite attractive if she lost a little weight and firmed up.*' was the Commandant's errant thought. As it was, in JD Powder's final assessment, Shela looked *exactly* like what she was. A little overweight, though still sexy in a hardened way, Kameleon was every inch a veteran killer of the first order. Someone to be taken very seriously.

One thing bothered him. He chewed it over in his mind. The IceMan had assured him that Shela was *Secure*, that she could be trusted not to talk out of school.

On both muscular arms were old needle scars, barely discernible beneath the cover-up makeup. Some were covered by tattoos. Those scars concerned Powder. *'Once an addict, always an addict'*, was JD's axiom. An old adage that had proven *accurate* too many times for him to doubt it. In JD's mind, Kameleon had a weakness that could be exploited. Shela Pryce was *not Secure.*

"How do you know who I am, Shela?" she was glancing around the room again. ".... or do you prefer Ms. Pryce ... or Kameleon?"

The slight cross-eyed glance came finally to rest on his face. She replaced her tinted glasses.

"My eyes are light sensitive." she explained matter of factly, as if she perceived disapproval in JD's placid face. She ignored Douglas. She *knew him.* JD Powder, she did *not.* "And Shela is just fine, Commandant General Jakk Donn Powder."

JD's face didn't change, but the room suddenly got colder.

"That was only one of the questions, Shela." JD grated in an arctic cold voice.

There was a slight pause.

"I know." Kameleon responded quietly, yet distinctly.

Another pregnant pause, longer this time.

"Well?" JD finally demanded bluntly, *command* in his voice.

"What are the United States International Defense Missile computer login passwords and launch codes." was her, *out of the blue,* calm response.

JD Powder was nonplussed. *'Where had that come from?'* Not to be deterred, his voice rumbled automatically and brutally: "That information, young *lady*, is *only* divulged to specific people and then on a strictly Need to Know Basis. And you sure as hell, DON'T NEED TO KNOW! It is none of your business."

"Exactly." She said succinctly.

JD Powder was staggered, speechless ...

Kameleon continued as if unaware of his stunned silence,

"*Asking* a question is a request. It does not mean that it will be answered ... and *demanding it* is like pissing into the wind, *embarrassing* when it blows back in your face...."

Suddenly, JD laughed. A short one to be sure, but it was a genuine laugh. And the Commandant was not one to laugh.

Shela's face remained calm as she finished, "I know that you are JD Powder, Commandant General of all of the United States Armed Services, Secret and otherwise. You need to understand that I am no longer in any of those Services. If you feel the need to categorize me, you can liken me to that wind I just talked about."

JD nodded in understanding. His assessment of her *altered* yet again. He noticed something else. "Is that gum that you are chewing?"

"Shall we move on to the prospective assignment?" Shela suggested softly.

This was definitely not going as Powder had envisioned. JD Powder pondered the situation. He was quiet for some time, watching her reaction to the power of silence. He noticed that Kameleon showed absolutely no reaction to that silence. It was unnatural. It turned his blood cold. Finally, the silence got to him. He made a decision. Getting into a pissing contest would accomplish nothing.

Rather than be the one to break the silence, JD turned to Douglas Chandler and nodded.

The IceMan took over.

***

Scene 23

It was lunch time. The briefing was over. Douglas handed Shela a small high GB memory card encapsulated in a clear plastic case no bigger than a quarter. It contained all the pertinent information and details of the *proposed* assignment.

Still holding the encoded and encrypted flash drive, she turned to leave. Suddenly she stopped. Facing away from the two men for a moment, JD observed that she seemed to run her left hand down her right arm. She then turned and approached JD. In her left hand she held, what appeared to be a *cigarette*. Of the memory card there was no sign. It had vanished.

She presented the *cigarette* to the Commandant. He accepted it without hesitation.

"Who was it that said, *'Don't judge a book by its cover?'*" Her voice had changed somehow. She did not wait for a response. None was given.

The IceMan punched the button and the door unlocked.

Kameleon turned and left the room. Her walk had also changed.

Douglas watched as his Superior brought the object closer and intently scrutinized it for a moment or two. His face cleared. He slowly unrolled the cigarette to reveal a thin piece of synthetic skin with faded needle tracks on it.

JD cursed, then laughed, then ran to the window and looked out. People on lunch, smoke or coffee break were out, milling about with their colleagues. He did not see Kameleon exit the building and he could not discern her among the crowd.

Something caught his eye in the parking lot. No, not some*thing*, some*one*. The distance blurred the fine features.

"Do you have any binoculars, IceMan?"

"Of course." responded Chandler. He reached into one of his drawers and produced a set. JD noticed that they were the best that US tax dollars could purchase. He adjusted the focus. The figure became crystal clear.

Bent over slightly was the back figure of a young girl. She was sporting a long, thick, lustrous, platinum blond colored ponytail that hung halfway down her back with part over her shoulder. She was wearing a long black dress with an off center slit up to just above the knee, showcasing one of her muscular bronzed legs.

She was in the process of opening the driver's door of a sleek black nondescript sports car.

She straightened and turned, again highlighting the spectacularly muscled leg. JD revised his opinion. It was not a dress. It was a two piece combination. The waist length, black blazer fit like a second skin, downplaying her broad shoulders, blending in seamlessly to the skirt, accenting her tiny waist and extremely full hips. She was wearing a white blouse tucked into her skirt. Her breasts were camouflaged beautifully. He could not tell their size. Large, dark tinted sunglasses covered a large portion of her upper face, but her lower face was trim, flawless and with full relaxed lips. The black alligator shoes and matching handbag was a perfect match to her outfit. JD recognized them instantly.

Kameleon looked right at JD, smiled a dazzling white smile and waved one of her slender *non-callused* hands at him. How she knew he was watching her, at that precise moment in time, he couldn't fathom. The outside of all the building's windows were a mirror finish.

Shela Price then entered the vehicle and sped away.

***

Scene 24

"**W**hy did you *not* give me any warning, IceMan?" demanded the Commandant General, eyes glittering dangerously.

Q *was* part the US Armed Services/Forces. KOLD *was* a Division of Q. Douglas Chandler *was* the Head of KOLD. Douglas *did* know his parameters.

Unlike Kameleon, the Iceman *did* answer the question.

"Because I felt that you needed to see her in action, Commandant. To do otherwise would be to tarnish the experience. If you had known beforehand, your *true* perspective would have been altered to a false one. You needed to see it as others would, therefore making you more aware of how *talented, gifted and dangerous* Kameleon is."

JD Powder absorbed the information in silence. He finally nodded in agreement. He saw a question lurking in the IceMan's eyes.

"You have something to ask, Douglas?"

"May I speak freely sir?"

"You may."

"Am I right in assuming that, at some point in today's meeting, you were deciding whether or not to dispose of Kameleon after this assignment, should she accept it?"

JD smiled. "You continue to astound me with your insights Douglas. Yes I was. The President asked me to evaluate and recommend. He thinks this is too important an assignment to *not* tie up any and all loose ends. I assume you have a reason for asking, so please continue."

"This time it is not as *great an insight* as you assume, JD." he said heavily. "I have had the same thought many times." *Did he see the flicker of an eyelid?* He proceeded as if he had. "I know that I told you Kameleon is *Secure*. I maintain that assurance. I maintain everything I told you about her. I also believe that Kameleon has secreted away files on *every* single assignment and contract that she has ever done. Files and documents with *all* the *particulars* in them."

"You have evidence of that? That *alone* is reason to *expunge* her after the mission." JD's voice dropped in timbre to a grating growl. It was proof to Douglas that the Commandant was *looking* for a reason, *any* reason to kill Kameleon after the mission. He didn't like the way she had treated him in the briefing *(or* not *treated him, more likely)*.

Douglas had to *assume it was so* and thusly, *treat it as so*. He followed his gut instinct.

"No, no evidence, sir. Nothing concrete … it's just a … feeling, an instinct, *and*" again he paused for emphasis then continued forcefully, "I *always* believe my instincts and feelings. They have *never* failed me." He softened his voice, "The fact, or *threat*, that she *may* have the files does *not* deter me from eliminating her. In fact, like you Commandant, it *rankles* me greatly."

JD couldn't help it, he smiled at the *'rankles me greatly'*.

"You *can* say it '*pisses you off*', Chandler. And you're right, it *does* piss me off!"

Douglas smiled with him and continued. His voice now unconsciously rose *ever so slightly* in real passion. "I feel that we *need* to protect *our own*, and we do. They *should* reciprocate, *dammit!*" He shook his head slightly, "The sad fact is sir ... they do not. They mouth the words, but there is no *soul* behind them, if any of them *even have a soul*. We accept it, even though we don't like it. *Killers On Leash Division* is aptly named. We do *not* have normal people working for us JD."

"I know *all* about KOLD, Douglas." JD said softly, dangerously.

"No ... you ... don't ... sir." Douglas replied just as softly, yet respectfully. "And you can thank whatever god you pray to that you never will. You are a soldier. You have no idea what KOLD does on a daily basis. And though you have seen much death, what you have seen is snow white compared to what we do. Most of our agents are beyond insane. What KOLD's teams love to do would make you sick Commandant General. When your President is long dead and gone, KOLD will still be here, replete with their *insane* teams."

JD Powder did not know how to respond to that, so he did not. He listened and learned.

Douglas continued in a normal voice, but Powder knew it was the IceMan talking.

"At *first, my feeling* that Shela *may* have secreted those files *sorely* tempted me to eradicate her. You know that *all* agents are supposed to destroy *all assignment* files and documents, as well as any pertaining to KOLD or Q. That also applies to Shela, even though she is freelance. And she knows it applies to *all Freelance Contract Killers* as well! Though it is highly doubtful, her files could *conceivably* compromise us." He shrugged depreciatingly. "To what extent, I don't know. Nothing *in* them implicates us directly." He paused in thought, then continued, "No, that is *not* what stays my hand Commandant."

"Continue." The Commandant was a *real good listener*.

"What *stays* my hand, Commandant, are the things I mentioned to you before, all her strengths ... plus the *deciding factors* that tip the scales in her favor." Douglas again paused to gather his thoughts. From here on in, he had to tread softly. His house of cards would crumble with one wrong word.

"Might I be so bold as to ask what the deciding factors are that tip the scale?" the Commandant asked curiously.

"As I told you, Shela has an *insanely strong* self preservation instinct. If she perceives a threat, she eliminates it. Remember the Houssay incident a few years ago?"

"I remember it well. It was a bloody media circus! If memory serves me, it was *one* of the underground terrorist, *Ailibaba* to be exact, strongholds in a small European mountain town called *Massenet*. The media claimed that sixty seven were executed, shot once in the center of the forehead and then mutilated. The actual body count number was seventy two. We later learned that the media were not informed of the identities of five of ... how shall I put this ... well let's just say, *certain individual's* deaths. The United States was, of course, blamed, but to my knowledge, we were not responsible. We never did find out the identities of people or organization responsible." JD paused as a thought came to him. He looked keenly at the Iceman.

"Are you inferring that KOLD *may* have had something to do with it?" he demanded, incredulously.

Douglas shook his head slightly, yet emphatically, "No, I am *not*. We had nothing to do with it." He looked at Powder. How far should he go? *'What the hell,'* he thought, *'in for a penny, in for a pound.'*

"Kameleon is the one who killed them all." He stated it flatly, with no inflection, as an irrefutable fact. He *felt* the Commandant's disbelief. He laughed a small understanding laugh and continued,

"I will just give you the pertinent facts, Commandant. That is all I am allowed to give. I am sure you understand?" JD nodded. Douglas continued, "Kameleon had killed one too many of the *Ailibaba* Leaders. As you know, we don't know all of them. The ones we that we *did* know with certainty, Kameleon killed for KOLD, on *contract assignment*. KOLD had her leave her calling card each time, for the obvious reasons."

"What was her calling card and how many times was that?" The Iceman ignored the questions, and continued as if he had never heard it. JD maintained his silence for awhile after that.

"Many, though *not all*, of the *Ailibaba* leaders attended the *top secret meeting* at *Massenet.* Along with their private bodyguards, they each brought their top killers and assassins along. The meeting was to have *all* present pledge a *Blood Oath* to identify, locate and kill the Kameleon. A *Blood Oath* to them meant they would hunt Kameleon until death, *theirs or hers.*

Somehow Kameleon got wind of it and attended. When all had pledged, *she killed them.* Every single one of them!"

He acknowledged the disbelief in his superiors mind. "I would not fault you for disbelieving, sir. I would have also, if Kameleon hadn't called immediately after the kill and informed me. She also informed me that she had left her calling card on each of them. Many of the media claimed that they were mutilated with an *X* crisscrossing the bullet hole in the middle of their foreheads. The balance of the Ailibaba leadership knew that it was a K, for Kameleon. They were quick to put out, via the IE *(International Espionage)* grapevine, that there would be *no more* Blood Oaths on her life."

Here, the Iceman paused for effect, then finished with, "And that is just *one* small example of what she is capable of doing if she feels threatened."

It worked.

"One *small* example?" JD exploded, "Are you telling me that … that instance is just one small example? You actually expect me to believe that?"

"Do you know what this pad is, embedded on my desktop?" countered Douglas, pointing to a glass-like screen on his desk. JD nodded, puzzled at the counter. "It's a AZ11X Lie Detector. According to experts, one hundred percent accurate."

Douglas placed his hand over the pad, about an inch above it. "Am I telling you that the *Massenet Massacre* is just one small example of what Kameleon is capable of, if she feels threatened? My answer is a resounding …" Douglas Chandler lowered his hand squarely on the glass. It glowed to a *white* life.

"Yes." he finished quietly, his voice almost a whisper. The screen *now* radiated a bright green, signifying *truth*.

It wasn't the green glow that convinced JD as much as the whispered voice. The degree of volume and tone of voice validated that this was a *truth* that did not need to be shouted to the heavens to instill belief.

JD believed. And, in belief, asked the next logical question on his mind.

"What exactly are you implying, IceMan? As you know from experience, I don't like guessing games. Speak bluntly, or as plainly as you are *allowed* to, without all the innuendos, subterfuge and *bullshit*!"

Douglas *pretended* to stop a rebuttal to the *'allowed'* word, then moved on.

"Bluntly put Commandant, Kameleon *has* to have *Asylum* from us. By *us*, I mean all of the *United States Armed Forces*, both *Public* and *Secret*, and all affiliated *Agencies* and *Offices*, up to and including the President of the United States."

"Are you insinuating that *one girl* has the power to demand *Asylum* from the most powerful Nation in the World?"

Douglas touched a place on his desk. A small hum permeated the room. Powder knew a *silencer* when he heard one. No listening devices could penetrate it.

Douglas leaned forward, placed both hands on the table, one resting on the *Lie Detector,* and spoke quietly.

"I am not *insinuating* anything, sir. I am stating a fact as I see it. If threatened, one such as she could and would dismantle the United States Government, one piece at a time. And you know what I mean by *dismantle*. By the way, as far as I know, there is only *'one such as she'*, and that *'she'* is *Shela Pryce*, aka the *Kameleon*. You asked for blunt and you will get blunt." Again, the little pause for effect, just short enough to allow *no* interruption.

His hand remained on the desk, surrounded by an steady, glowing, brilliant emerald green light. "If you *should* decide to put a Contract on Kameleon and fail in the first attempt; if there even is the *planning* of a first attempt; you will be unwittingly signing a plethora of needless death warrants, *yours* and your Boss's being the first. Kameleon believes in taking the prime instigators out first."

"You think she could take *me* down, my friend?" JD smiled a deadly smile, ignoring the green light. An ice cold smile that had intimidated *all* who saw it. Until now.

Without batting an eyelash, the IceMan calmly looked JD Powder in the eye. Then, as if he had made a sudden decision, replied with a similar smile and in the same tone.

"I have something that you need to witness in order to understand my position and statements."

He moved his hand from the lie detector and punched another series of buttons on his desk. A screen came to life behind him and another appeared on his desktop. Douglas liked to view the reactions of the viewers as well as see what they were seeing.

His forefinger hovered just over the *'Play'* button.

"Commandant, allow me to preface this video by saying that this incident happened approximately nine months ago, in the *Epilogue Room,* with a group of six of our prospective *Elite*.

Q's current *top* Agent Graduates. They were there at the behest of their Close Mortal Combat Instructor, Eli Walton."

He witnessed, with an intense inward satisfaction, Powder's eyes unconsciously narrow in concentration. He continued with no noticeable change in his voice. Chandler knew that JD knew Eli Walton well. According to the IceMan's latest intelligence reports, Walton was, reportedly, the only human being on the planet that JD respected as a fighting machine equal to him. His reaction, small though it was, suggested to the IceMan that Powder feared Eli might have a slight edge on him. Both were of the same age, height and size. Both bald, they could have passed as identical twins except for their skin color.

Douglas marveled at the *possible* fact that JD could fear *anyone.* He filed the thought away for future consideration and continued.

"The *Epilogue Room* houses the Final Phase of the prospective *Elite 'Close Mortal Combat Training'* Course. We refer to it as CMCT. Only the top Graduate Agents from *all* Divisions of Q are invited to attend the *Elite* training course. It takes them another full year to complete, but *Elite* status has its rewards. Although we have had many fail to achieve *Elite* status, we have had no one refuse the invitation. Their very *attitude* assures it. All *Elite* share this particular attitude.

"After graduating their academic courses, which takes place in the *Final Chapter Room,* the prospective *Elite* gather in the *Epilogue Room* for the CMCT *Final Test.* They have passed all *Elite* tests but this. They are told it is Q's final *Elite* test. What they are not told, but *know,* is that it is *also* the *final test* for their

Elite status. If successful, they pass from being an Agent to being one of the *Elite*. This Final Phase is a *Full Contact, Close Combat Battle to defeat or victory*. It has rounds and scores. All things being equal, every combatant has a good chance of passing."

The IceMan went on to explain that, during a Q Agent's training and testing, *full contact* combat training was *not* allowed or tolerated. *All* participants wore protective gear for combat training. If any prospective Agent or Agents were caught engaged in *full contact* combat training, they were dismissed immediately. No exceptions. Few ever did. Q would *not* risk damaging a fully equipped, functioning, trained, field Agent. It allowed the prospective Agent to realize and achieve their full combat *potential,* without fear of crippling damage, as well as a slew of other documented reasons that he didn't go into, but inferred.

The *prospective* Elite were excluded from this *full contact* restriction. Though they still wore protective gear, it was much thinner and much less protective than the Agent armor. Q felt that the *Elite needed* to know and experience *full contact, up-close, deadly mortal combat*. And Q *needed* to find out if there were any *hidden* weaknesses that had been missed. Once in awhile it happened, but not often. The few who did not gain *Elite* status stayed at *Agent* status. They lost nothing and received invaluable training.

"You call this '*blunt*'?" JD interrupted.

"I'm sorry Commandant General, were you aware of our complete training program?"

JD did not respond.

"That is why I explained it. You will see why in a moment. As well as being the top of their class in their fields of expertise, the six prospective *Elite* that you are about to see, are the *best* trained killers *slash* assassins *slash* self defense experts... in ... the ... world," He paused in thought, then corrected himself, "with the possible exception of their trainer, Eli Walton."

Again, no response. Douglas *knew* his time was short. The *interest leash* was a different length for every individual. Douglas was sure that JD's *interest leash* was a short one. Chandler recognized it, but he did not hurry. He knew that *silence* was, and is, the *greatest* mental pressure that can be exerted on a person. He had only this *one* opportunity to hold sway. To *rush* was to *lose*. He knew that JD knew of the power of silence and used it to his advantage, but IceMan saw with Kameleon, that JD didn't like it used on himself. Even though he was a man of intellect, JD was first and foremost a soldier, a man of action. IceMan bore the silent pressure with the calm control of one who has many years of experience, thus expertise. Although he estimated his opponent to be of a superior intellect, the IceMan knew he did not have his IE training.

"Continue." JD finally muttered.

Douglas Chandler was a graduate *Elite*. He inwardly smiled at his small victory, but took nothing for granted.

The IceMan proceeded carefully.

"I attended Kameleon's Elite confirmation many years ago. I was invited by her instructor, who shall remain nameless. He was *ecstatic* about her. His exact words were, *'Shela Pryce is what I have dubbed a PPP, or triple P. Agent Pryce is a phenomenal phenomenon* among *phenomenon.*'" A soft smile in his voice accompanied the memory. "I remember laughing at this Veteran Instructors enthusiasm. As you may well be aware of sir, there are many Final Phase *Instructors*. As you will soon see, Eli was *not* the *Instructor* for her group. Miss Pryce was but one of seven. Only three became Elite. It was Kameleon who damaged the four beyond the ability to continue." Douglas indulged himself a small satisfied grin at the memory.

"I had a suspicion that Kameleon had *continued* her training after attaining Elite status. Disappointingly, only a very few do. The ones that *don't,* think they know *everything*. They assume that they had been taught *everything here.* They are *Elite*! *Elite* status *alone* is *validation enough* in their minds. Needless to say, I was curious as to Shela Pryce's skill level after so many years in the field. It was during an *Assignment Briefing* with Kameleon that I arranged what you are about to view.

"Kameleon and I were about to take a lunch break when I received an *orchestrated* phone call to attend and view the Final Phase CMCT competition and graduation. Because I had attended hers, it was camouflaged as a *'Ritual Attendance'.* Therefore Shela would have no reason to question it. She didn't. I invited her to join me. She accepted. I knew she would. I had accessed and reviewed her trainer's observations during her training." He paused in thought and then continued.

"In the transcripts on her progress, I noted that every time Shela had a chance to view and analyze *any* and *all* potential *Assignment* threats or competitors, she did. Unbeknownst to all parties involved in this Final Phase Testing, including Eli Walton,

I recorded the Test. This was the first, and quite possibly the last, time of any Final Elite combat test being recorded. Q *Mandates* that Elite *identities* and *skills* are not to be compromised in any way. I know it well. I was the one who instigated and implemented it." he nodded at JD's look at IceMan's damaging admission.

"Yet, in clear violation of my own Mandate, I secretly recorded this session on my own. I had witnessed her mind staggering performance at *her* Elite confirmation, heard too many rumors by *reliable* sources about a Miss Shela Pryce, during her training with KOLD and then later in the field. Although I could have destroyed if after viewing, I kept it. I have watched it on occasion." Here he paused again and looked meaningfully at JD Powder before continuing.

"Commandant General, you are the only living being, other than myself, to view what I am about to share with you. I am now entrusting you with this knowledge. After you view it, as with your meeting Kameleon for the first time, your perspective on this situation *will* change. And that comes with a one hundred percent money back Guarantee. Have a seat, sir."

JD sat.

With the stage now set, the IceMan hit the play button.

The room darkened.

***

Scene 25

"**I** have seen enough!" declared the bull voice of Commandant Jakk Donn Powder.

The IceMan hit a couple of desk buttons. The room lights returned to normal.

Commandant Powder sat for many moments in silence. Suddenly he arose from his seat and paced the room, hands clenching and unclenching, head bowed in thought, struggling to come to grips with what he had seen. He was not bothering to hide his feelings. He knew that the IceMan had experienced them, probably *every time* he'd watched the video.

Douglas watched the pacing. Now it was *he* who was again applying the dreaded power of *silence*.

Finally the Commandant turned and approached the desk.

"Make me a copy of that video. I will need it to review again before I can make an informed decision."

"I'm terribly sorry Commandant, but I'm afraid that's impossible." was the surprised response.

"I just gave you a direct order, Chandler. You *really* don't want to refuse a direct order from *me*, now *do you*?"

"I am not refusing a direct order from you, Commandant. I would never do that." ejaculated the IceMan fervently. He pointed, over his shoulder, to the fading screen behind him.

JD stood thunderstruck as he read the *still* highly discernible words *'File Deleted and Virus Destroyed'*. The IceMan's voice filled the void.

"I have viewed the video file many times Commandant, so when you said you had seen enough, I deleted and destroyed it. It had served its purpose. Destroying the video file was for *my* safety. No copy now exists. None ever did as far as I know." He smiled a genuine smile at JD; then finished earnestly with, "Now, if you had asked me to copy it *before* I had hit the *'Delete and Destroy'* button, I would have had no choice but to obey you. And I would have sir."

Powder was not deceived. In retrospect, he would have done the same. In point of fact, he reminded himself, he had many times.

Now it was the IceMan's turn to be staggered.

JD Powder laughed.

"Well done, IceMan, well done." he said after he caught his breath. "I do believe you when you say that now no copy exists, but I think you forgot to add *'in Q's system'*." He noted the hurt, innocent, surprised look in Chandler's face. JD waited for a response, but Chandler did not speak. JD turned suddenly serious.

"I will take what you have shown me to the President. He will have to take my opinion on what I have just viewed. Are there any words that you would like me to convey to him?" The last was asked as a courtesy, more rhetorical than literal.

To his surprise, Douglas responded.

"Tell Bill that his decision *will be known* by Kameleon. Believe me when I say that she has friends in *every* department of the government. Friends who value her friendship and goodwill more; much, *much more,* than that of any *temporary* President of the United States of America. Tell him that as long as Kameleon has Asylum from the United States, in my opinion, she poses absolutely no threat to us." He paused in thought.

JD remained silent. He knew there was more to come. He was right.

"In fact," Iceman continued in a deadly serious voice, "Q, through KOLD, will continue to utilize her services on a contract basis. Tell the President that he would not be in office now if it were not for her. He will remember. Tell him that his *savior* on that *December* day two years ago was none other than Kameleon. And finally, JD, just a reminder that you were sworn to secrecy when Kameleon's real name was revealed to you. Kameleon's identity stays with *you only*."

JD witnessed IceMan eyes turn as cold as his name, as he continued, "Understand and remember two important facts Commandant. Kameleon *knows* that you know her identities. The reason that she didn't act surprised when you called her by her name is that I had already told her that you knew. The second is that Kameleon *also knows who you are*. In all probability, she has more information on you than we do on her."

Something in JD changed, ever so slightly. IceMan recognized the look. He had been waiting for it.

In a soul chilling *soft* voice, KOLD's IceMan responded first.

"Words spoken in haste or anger cannot be taken back, sir. Please do *not* say *anything* that *could* cause *any* lament, my friend. It may help you to *value* what I am saying if you *understand* that *my* first allegiance is to the United States, then to Q, then to KOLD. In that order and only in that order. I also remind you that we try to protect our own to the *best* of our considerable abilities and resources. All in Q believe that. Even the Eagle does. Barring extreme exceptions, it is true. That is why, upon *your* direct order, Commandant, KOLD contracted out the Eagle and family's *'fubar'* death attempt for that very reason. Even now, the Eagle must still think that Red China is responsible. News reports of the Mr. Smoke assassination of the Contractor validated him as an *'Asian terrorist bomber'*. I agree that we have a major *'situation'* on our hands. I *also know* that in this ever changing world of ours, there is a certainty that you should *also know* as well, JD. As I mentioned before, Presidents come and go. Remember that. And make *goddamn* sure that Bill *also knows*."

Those quiet, deadly, softly spoken words stopped *any* attempt to *posture* from JD. He stood undecided. Finally he shook his head slightly, relaxed and responded.

"You are aptly named IceMan. Personally speaking, Q's policy to protect its own warms this old soldiers heart. And you were correct in your assumption that Kameleon pissed me off."

Although the IceMan showed no reaction, JD smiled ruefully, as if it was he, JD Powder, who had been *mind read*.

"My lofty *new* position does seem to have gone to my head, doesn't it? Hell man, I never ranked more than a sergeant in the army. Now I'm the Commandant General of all the US Forces, armed and otherwise. That rank grants me the power to get the President's wishes done. Things that he can't legally, morally or ethically do, I can. *And do.* I am, and always will be, Wild Bill Lantern's Aide. I do what he tells me to do. Don't *you* forget *that* IceMan. I also need to clarify a few points. Number one, I am *quite* aware of the boundaries that my oath of silence necessitates, concerning Kameleon's identity. Secondly, I appreciate the reminder of my oath. Thirdly, I understand it for what it was, a reminder only and not a threat."

JD smiled. This smile made the IceMan's blood run a little colder.

Suddenly JD leaned forward and placed a huge hand on the gleaming white Lie-Detector. "Fourthly, I take all my oaths to heart. I have never broken an oath." The light radiated a bright green. Keeping his hand on the desk he continued, "I will advise the President of your wishes *and because* I respect your judgment in this matter, Douglas, I will support them." He lifted his hand from the green plate and continued.

"I have decided *not* to inform the President about the video. I have no wish to appear a fool. Without proof he would not believe me. Hell, even with proof, if I was him, I wouldn't believe me. I'd think it was a doctored special effects movie. It shall remain our secret Douglas." Abruptly he turned and headed for the door.

"Now turn off that irritating *silencer* and open the door. You may not believe this, but some people think I'm an important person. I have places to go, people to see and things to do."

At the door JD turned.

"I will let you know the Executive Decision as soon as I receive it." JD laughed a small depreciatory laugh and parted with, "I must be getting as paranoid as Q, because I noticed that your hand wasn't on the Lie Detector when you said there were no more copies of the video out there." He pointed out the window vaguely and shook his head.

"How silly of me."

***

Scene 26

Douglas Chandler sat for a moment after JD left. If JD Powder could have seen him now, he would not have believed that this was the same soulless, ice cold, calculating, past and present *master* of international espionage and intrigue. What JD would have seen was, what looked to be, a perfect picture of a slumped and beaten man, a man old beyond his years.

Such was not the case. Douglas Chandler was a rarity, the *Exception* to the *Rule*. When in battle, he could maintain his composure *almost indefinitely*. He had never been taxed *beyond* his limit, although many times he felt he had been pushed *to* it.

This was one of those times. He was *not* beaten, he was recouping after a battle. He knew when to rest and did so on those occasions.

He pushed a button on his desk that transmitted a *'No Calls or Interruptions'* to *his* Aide outside his door.

He then punched a series of buttons, rose and entered the open doorway that had magically appeared in the supposedly seamless wall. He entered a large bathroom and took off his jacket, then his shirt, then his bullet proof vest. He was now down to his t-shirt. He removed the sodden article, then folded and wrung it out over the shower by hand. He put it in a clothes hamper.

After disrobing down to his shorts, he put on a powder blue work-out outfit and entered an adjoining room, his private gym.

He completed an intense forty five minute workout. His hand wrung sopping shorts and gym clothes followed his t-shirt into the hamper. After showering he retrieved a fresh t-shirt and shorts from one of the cupboards, changed back into business attire and re-entered his office.

He pressed a button that removed the *'Do Not Disturb'* earlier message. Immediately the phone rang. *'You may not believe this, but some people think I'm an important person. I have places to go, people to see and things to do.'* ran through Chandler's mind. The IceMan smiled as he reached to answer it. He also had things to do, places to go and people to see.

A small voice whispered across his mind like soft warm summer breeze, halting his hand for a split second. *'The real reason you saved Kameleon's life is that you are in love with her ... isn't it?'*

"Rubbish!" he announced coldly, ruthlessly, out loud. His hand continued forward, "Absolute bullshit and garbage. Why, I'm old enough to be her.... Hello? ... No ... please excuse me sir, I wasn't talking to you. I was talking to someone else...

Still, a ghost of the question lingered.

"Pardon? ... No, now is *not* a good time to talk. You'll have to excuse me sir, but I'll have to call you back.... Yes, yes, thank you, that would be fine. Till then."

Scene 27

Damon Gray sat alone in contemplation.

He was seated lotus position in the exact center of a gigantic triangle. He had been so seated for some time. Surrounded by the intense solitude of the Triangle Cave, was where Damon Gray loved to meditate. It was, to him, the ideal location. The impossible Triangle Cave, Gateway to Other Places, *somehow* helped him to focus his minds and abilities.

To some, meditation was a clearing of one's mind. To him, an open and actively questing mind was the fastest way to enlightenment. Years of intense study led him to this belief. His hungering questing *need* had set in motion things that he was *still* striving to *understand*. He had found out that he was unique in a lot of ways. To say Damon Gray was extremely highly *gifted* and with many *Talents*, *Abilities* and *Gifts* would be like comparing the sun to a candle.

Damon was not satisfied to just drive a car. He had an unquenchable *need to understand* everything possible *about* the car. Damon Gray also had this same insane *need*, this ravenous *need to understand* all his *Talents Abilities* and *Gifts*. For many years he had been denied them.

Although some religions, cults and spiritualists practiced the art, the thought of shutting one's mind down to receive enlightenment was an indescribably revolting concept to Damon Gray. He had died and been brought back to life, a life bereft of all of his *Talents, Abilities* and *Gifts.* He had survived and been fortunate enough to recover all of his *Talents, Abilities and Gift's ... and much, much more.* He likened the experience to that of a man suddenly cast into a dungeon deprived of all light, when he had known sunshine all his life. It was crippling in a way that no one could understand.

Then, just as suddenly, the walls were sundered, allowing him to step forth to feel and see the earth beneath his feet, the sunlight bathing him, the stars in the heavens, the universe and lo, *even the multiverse,* in ways that he never had before. In a way that no one *on earth* ever had before. Because Damon was different, he *chose* to keep his mind open and questing, instead of shutting it down.

But these were *not* the thoughts that were running through his mind at present. Those thoughts were in the past, embedded in his photoneumonic memory, ready for *instant total recall* should the need or occasion arise.

No, he was contemplating his next *course of action*, should the need arise, on the issue of assisting Brandon Thomas. His next *course of action* would be followed by a *plan of action.* Then, the *action* would happen. Damon Gray did not plan reactions. He planned *actions* to *actions.* In his opinion, to *react* to an *action* or circumstance was to invite defeat. That meant that you were under *someone else's* control, even if that *someone else* was *Coincidence* or *Chance.*

The Triangle Cave operated *outside* of earth time. Damon had learned its perimeters and how to manipulate them. Although many hours passed in the TC, as he called it, only minutes had passed on earth. It gave him a tremendous advantage in times of stress.

And now was a time of stress.

Above all, Damon tried to protect his friends to the best of his considerable TAG's. To help Brandon Thomas meant the possible compromising of his and his friend's safety and well being. No, he corrected; not *possible*; *inevitable* was a word closer to the truth.

Each member of the *Smoke Organization* had full disclosure of the situation and all were in agreement to lend assistance with their leader, Mr. Smoke, (Commander they all called him by mutual consent, so as not to compromise his identity) Once sure that they all understood the risks and agreed, Damon retired to the TC to weigh the options.

He reviewed his meeting with Brandon and Charlene Thomas as Mr. Smoke.

***

As he walked across the room to meet the Eagle, he removed his right hand glove. He extended his camouflaged hand at the appropriate distance. His timing was faultless. As he had expected, Brandon responded instinctively.

Brandon shook his hand. At the end of the shake he had turned Damon's hand slightly before letting go. Damon knew it was done to look at the tri-colored triangle ring.

"Charlene said you were wearing an incredible ring. It is light years beyond *incredible*. It defies description. Those floating embedded triangles appear to be three dimensional. Although it looks like tricolored gold, it must not be. It looks new, yet I can tell that you've worn it for many years."

"What makes you assume that?" was the mechanical sexless reply.

"It is almost embedded in your finger, it sits so flush."

Mr. Smoke nodded noncommittally but did not respond verbally.

When he did speak it was to the point.

"In order for us to make an informed decision, please tell us all the information, pertinent and otherwise, that you know of this situation. We will determine *what* is pertinent to us, *if* we decide to help you, Brandon Thomas."

"If? ... *IF? Why in the world* would I reveal Classified US Government Ultra Top Secret Information on an '*IF*' promise?" Though the Eagle spoke softly, quietly, Mr. Smoke heard and felt the Saracen Steel beneath the velvet glove of his voice. "In fact, other than the basics, the *need to know* information that *you* need to know to make a decision, why would I reveal *any* Classified Government information regarding any of my Assignments?"

The mechanical voice disappeared and a human one replaced. A deep melodious one with a slight Irish accent. "You misunderstand us. That is unacceptable. There must be understanding by both parties. You are correct when you *imply* that your Assignments do not concern us. The Assignment particulars that put you in your present predicament *do*, as they could cause concern to us also. And that concern needs to be minimized to the utmost. Wouldn't you agree?"

There was a long pause, while Brandon struggled with the situation.

"Darling, might I suggest something?" his Ghost wife asked softly.

"Of course you can, Char. You know that." was the response. Damon, through the eyes of his entwined twin *entities*, could actually see the psychic love waves passing between them. It amazed him. This was a first for him.

He was brought back when Charlene Thomas turned to him and asked politely, "Mr. Smoke, do you *three* promise to *not* reveal to anyone what you are told here today, without Brandon's or my approval?"

Now it was Damon's turn to pause in thought. He was not shocked at the use of the word, *'three'*. When Charlene Thomas had first appeared at the *Smoke* scene of her Terrorist Bomber, he had a feeling that she had seen his two bonded intertwined inner beings. The two inextricably blended entities, self named *Golden* and *Garnet* that were now an integral part of the fabric of Damon's very being.

"I will agree to the following understanding. Of what you share with me today, I will need to share some of that information with the Smoke organization. I will only share what I feel is *absolutely* necessary. That *has* to be left to my discretion. I will not call you every time a situation comes up. One thing I can promise and I will never break this promise or allow it to be broken, to the best of my abilities. I can promise that what I share with select members of the Smoke Organization will be treated as a *sacred trust* and stay *only* with those individuals in the Smoke

Organization, that which is shared here today." He paused in thought for a couple of seconds and amended,

"I also promise that we intend you no harm, as long as there is honesty and trust between us. We need and want you to know that we understand that your concerns are as real and valid to *us* as they are to you. You *both* must now understand and validate *ours*. The Smoke Organization is being hunted by every Government Anti-Terrorist Organization and every Terrorist Group … in the world. We *must* protect ourselves. It is the best that we can offer. The decision is now yours."

"Why do you need the particulars when all I am asking for is equipment that I am willing to pay top dollar for?" Brandon countered.

"The information received, shared to us by your wife and *other sources*, leads us to believe that you may require *much more* than equipment. Brandon Thomas, you have no reason to trust us. You do not yet know us well enough to, but I *feel* that you need to make some hard decisions fast. I do not envy you. Your wife had great abilities in life that have become even greater in death. *She* trusts *us*."

Brandon looked keenly at Mr. Smoke.

"What am I missing here? Why would you and your Smoke Organization be willing to offer more? I have not requested it." Brandon demanded in that soft deadly voice.

"Because *I* requested it, darling." was his wife's quiet response.

Damon remained silent as Brandon turned to his wife in disbelief.

"*You* did? You can't ask someone *you don't know* to put themselves in mortal danger for someone *they don't know*. It's not right Char. I have *no* right to ask that."

"You didn't," Charlene replied pertly, "I did. And, to put your mind at ease, they haven't said NO yet, have they?"

"What in the world does that mean?" Brandon responded, confused.

"I think it means that you *might* need the Smoke Organization's help to survive this Mission of yours." replied Damon, for Charlene.

"See. *They* understood!" Charlene stated with an '*ah-ha!*' tone, as if it had made perfect sense. Brandon smiled in spite of himself.

She had succeeded, Damon noted, the tension had eased. His already high estimation of her rose again.

"He said, '*I think*', darling." her husband responded chidingly to her. Turning back to Damon, Brandon sighed and continued,

"You are both right. I have operated *alone* so long that I tend to think in those terms." Damon remembered that the Eagle's eyes seemed to pierce right through his eye coverings as if they didn't exist. It created an unsettling, exposed feeling for Damon.

"Mr. Smoke, I felt something when we shook hands. My wife trusts you. I trust in her and her abilities. I will put my trust in you to keep your word. I will share all I know regarding this matter."

Damon remembered Brandon's head dropping slightly for a moment, as if in defeat, then rising in battle scarred conquest, although still slightly bent from the almost crippling, mental wounds of betrayal.

"I never would have believed that I would break my *Sacred Oath of Allegiance* to Q and the United States of America, and yet I do so now without any guilt or regret. I feel guilty about that lack of guilt. Why is that, do you suppose?" he muttered to himself, shaking his head slightly in wonder.

Damon knew it was a rhetorical question, but felt the need to answer it. He instinctively *knew* that Brandon *needed* closure in that area.

"I believe that it is because your *Sacred Oath of Allegiance* was based on a *Lie,* Brandon. *That Lie* being their *Oath of Allegiance* to you. Our many informed sources confirmed what your wife told us. Charlene told us that they, *they* meaning the US Government, through the Organization you pledged Allegiance to, called Q, tried to have you and all your family *murdered* on the basis of an unsubstantiated rumor." He shook his head slightly, whether in disgust or amazement, Brandon could not tell, then Mister Smoke continued.

" Brandon, they have since put, in the guise of Red China, a five million dollar reward on your head, for your *head only.* They not only failed to protect you, as promised, they are even now actively hunting you. They are also holding your daughter *ransom* to draw you out to kill you *both,* again in the guise of protecting her from Chinese agents. What you owe on your *Oath of Allegiance* to them, is now for *you* to decide, not them. They no longer hold sway over you."

"You are right!" the Eagle stated softly, suddenly calmed. His posture straightened to that of full height, the inner turmoil now totally defeated, battle scarred but still whole. "Thank you for that, sir."

"Call us Smoke, for now." Damon responded in a Scottish accent. He knew that Brandon heard the smile in his voice and responded.

"Who is the 'we' and 'us' you both keep referring to?"

The Terrorist bomber Assassin paused for a moment as if in contemplation, then spoke.

"You do not need to know at this time. Let us continue, shall we?" Mr. Smoke answered in yet a different voice.

Or was it voices? Damon thought back again. Yes, it was definitely three voices in one.

The Eagle had not responded to it. He may have thought it was the voice scrambler. Hopefully that was the case.

Hastings had also mentioned that Damon used the 'we' word a lot instead of the 'I'.

'We will have to be more careful', Mr. Smoke reminded himself. He suddenly grinned in chagrin behind the mask.

'I mean that 'I' will have to be more careful!' he amended.

***

Scene 28

"**C**ould I have your attention, *pul-ease*."

"I repeat ... could I have your attention, *pul-ease!* Would a Mr. Samuel Singh *pul*-ease return to the last booth *you-all* were at and purchased something. *You-all* left something very important behind ... I repeat ... Mr. Samuel Singh, *pul*-ease report to the last booth you were at. *You-all* left something *very important there!* And just to remind *you-all* ... the Louisville Street Rod Nationals Show will be closing in fifteen minutes. *Pul*-ease finalize all purchases and exit the building. Thank *you-all* for coming. We will reopen tomorrow morning at ....."

Kai Akyi paused slightly as the announcement carried on. He smiled inwardly at the hometown *southern* accent, especially the '*pul*-ease' and '*you-all*'. It seemed to make everyone feel cozy and welcome.

Kai was *aware.* He looked around casually. He felt like a sardine in a sardine can. The Louisville Kentucky Fairground's annual Street Rod Nationals Show was jam packed with people from around the world. Customized cars from eighteen ninety one to nineteen eighty were on display. From the extremely beautiful to the extremely bizarre, and everywhere in between, there were customized Street Rods of every design and description imaginable. Enough to suit any car addicts tastes.

It was quantum light-years beyond zoo-like. The NSRA had recently elevated the *entry year* to nineteen eighty from nineteen forty eight. There were tens of thousands *more* cars present than any previous year. Cars and Street Rods arrived from all over the world, French, German, Swiss, Chinese, Japanese, and Italian to name but a few. Louisville, Kentucky hosted the largest Street Rod Nationals convention in the world, for many years. This year went far beyond their wildest dreams. There were an estimated *thirty five thousand* Hot Rods being exhibited, for sale and everything in between. It was wall to wall people. Everything and everybody seemed to move at the slowest persons pace.

Except for the *Dragon Lord*, China's *Defender*. Dressed unremarkably, a nondescript Kai resumed movement, weaving his way quickly and seamlessly through the crowd, without causing the slightest ripple, arriving moments later at a hot dog stand at the edge of the parking lot area where many of the Hot Rod owners paid to park their MotorCoaches for the duration of the Hot Rod Show.

Kai again looked around, seemingly casually, like an overwhelmed tourist. No one noticed him. They were not supposed to. If anyone of importance had noticed, they would no longer *be* anyone of importance. And Kai did not want that. He did not want bloodshed. That was not his goal. This time.

For three days, he had paid several of the transient workers, ones who would do almost anything asked of them for a reasonable price, to wear miniature remote cameras and monitor the comings and goings of the residents of seven characterless oversized Coaches, having them pay particular attention to one in particular. The one in particular was a nondescript oversized MotorHome positioned between six matching oversized nondescript MotorHomes, all of which were situated inconspicuously among the countless other MotorHomes and Trailers.

They were KOLD's *Monolithic Seven.* Designed, manufactured and constructed specifically for KOLD. It was but one set of their Mobile headquarters.

The three matching MotorCoaches on either side were decoys, although they were not to be discounted. Kai had executed his usual legendary *due diligence.* From the information garnered from the cameras of *his* decoys *(the transient workers),* the *Dragon Lord* intimately knew every occupant in the Seven Monoliths. Q's Comp Tech's didn't concern him, those he could handle easily. It was the balance of them that commanded his utmost attention, the balance being the *Killers Off Leash.*

The Seven Coaches housed a number of KOLD's Elite. Four of the Motor Coaches housed eight of the deadliest killers of KOLD, four of them had Elite status. Kai rated these eight, four two men teams, among the finest and best Killing Machines in the world, with three of the four teams better than China's best.

Kai excluded himself from that equation. He *knew* himself to be in a league of his own. The other two LandYacht's housed two Contract Killer teams. They were *at least* as deadly as KOLD's Elite, though the KOLD hierarchy would not admit to it.

Kai knew not *how,* but more importantly *in his mind,* knew *why* they were deadlier. They were *loose cannons.* Unlike KOLD's killers, they had no loyalty except to their partner, and sometimes, not even then. Much as Kai despised them, he whole-heartedly respected the damage that they were capable of. He turned his attention back to the Coaches.

The Coaches were positioned in such a way so as to draw the eye away from their monolithic size of just one of them. Everything was done to downplay their size.

To a casual observer, they looked like the rest of the Coaches, Toys for Big Boys, which is to say that they were *the LandYacht's* of the owners showing off their Hot Rod Masterpieces.

To that same casual observer, the Monolithic Seven, as he had named them, looked to be landlocked.

Kai knew better. The middle one was situated in such a way that it could exit easily. Once the middle one was through, the other six could easily follow in a staggered formation.
KOLD was harboring their little *detainee* in plain sight

Kai was there to *alter* that circumstance.

Kai was there to *appropriate* their little *detainee*, unharmed, without getting caught.

Angelina Thomas, seven year old daughter of the world's most wanted man, was the little *detainee* in the center Coach.

Kai Akyi, *dreaded* Dragon Lord and Champion of the Immortal Emperor of China, ambled inconspicuously towards the Monoliths.

***

Scene 29

"The call you were expecting is on *line one*, sir."

"Thank you Pearly Anne." Douglas replied.

"You are welcome, sir." responded Pearle Anne Whirley. The IceMan punched the top level hack proof security line, line one.

"Report please."

Those abrupt two words were actually code words to signify that the IceMan was alone, that all was secure and that it was safe to speak freely. What they didn't know is that Douglas secretly recorded all incoming and outgoing calls.

The IceMan listened without interruption. When the voice finished, the IceMan spoke coldly yet clearly.

"What are you doing and what are your plans to reverse the current condition?"

The voice continued. Douglas could see the voice *stress level* rise on one of his flush mount desk screens. That was recorded also. When the voice ended, IceMan responded.

"No, no orders at this time. Continue to do what you deem best, Elite. That is what we are paying you for. Until later."

The IceMan hung up the phone.

He punched another button.

"Yes, sir?" responded Pearle's crisp voice.

"Please get the President and Commandant General *both* on a secure conference line for me, Pearle."

Bill paused for a fraction of a second then continued.

"Make it security conference line *one*."

"Yes sir." The line went dead.

Although his voice remained the same, always polite, Pearle Whirley knew that when Douglas called her Pearle instead of Pearly or Pearly Anne, it was important! She punched the secure conference line one and dialed.

Moments later, "Both parties on secure conference line one, sir."

"Thank you Pearle." The IceMan punched the speakerphone on his desk and automatically punched the record button at the same time.

"Mr. President ... Commandant General ... we have us a situation. We need to talk immediately ... *privately,* just the three of us, *no one else.*" Immediately the two voices started to argue, stating their hectic schedules.

"Gentlemen!" he interrupted sharply, "I have just received word that the *Hatchling* has *just now* been *appropriated* by person or persons unknown."

Silence reigned supreme at the import of that statement. Wild Bill Lantern, Elected President of the United States, was the first to break the silence.

It was a controlled, soft, smoothly *deadly* voice that spoke.

"We are at your disposal, Iceman."

"Three hours, SCC One." The IceMan stated.

"Done." replied the President.

All three lines went dead at the same time.

***

Three hours later, in a *supposedly nonexistent* Secret Control Center, named SCC One, the three men convened in a secret room, deep beneath the earth's surface. An ultra secret complex that only a select few knew about. The SCC One personnel had just been vacated for this visit.

JD looked around. This was not his first visit to SCC One, but he was still impressed, as he had been each time previously. He understood *little* of the purpose or function of the superfluity of equipment that filled the scope of his vision. The titanic high domed circular room looked like something out of a Star Wars Battle Star. Positioned in the exact center of the room was a raised seven step circular Dominion Dais, topped with a large swivel/rotating Command Chair decorated with an overabundance of buttons knobs and equipment.

JD always wondered when and how SCC One could have been built *secretly* when it was located *directly beneath the Oval Office of the Presidential White House.*

It was one of seven identical secret *Command Centers,* all situated strategically around the country, and built expressly to house the President of the United States in *Conditions of Extreme or Dire Circumstance.*

This was one of those *Conditions.*

Instead of taking to his Command Chair, President Lantern led Powder and Chandler to a private circular conference room situated *(for lack of a better description of a circular room within a circular room)* off to one side. Inside the room was a large round oak table surrounded by comfortable oak chairs. Attached to each chair were wonderfully padded seat and arm cushions, studded and encased within buttery soft, burgundy colored leather. Directly facing the door, one chair was larger, bulkier; *almost* throne-like.

JD and Douglas chose a chair on each side, *after* Bill took possession of the Command Chair. Bill touched a button in front of him and a soft, almost silent, non-distracting buzz permeated the room. All within knew the *Silencer* had been activated. No electronic listening device could penetrate the room while it was on.

Yet even with it on, the silence was deafening. The tension in the air could be cut with a butter knife and was felt by all.

"What the hell is going on, dammit?" demanded the President, finally. Nobody answered.

"Well, Douglas?"

"I'm sorry sir, I misunderstood. I didn't think the question was directed at me." the IceMan responded quietly, respectfully.

"You are the one who demanded this meeting, Douglas. Who the hell did you think I was directing it to, if not you?"

"If I'm not mistaken, it was to someone called '*Dammit*', sir." Douglas responded quietly.

William Lantern's face went dark with blood. Then he saw the small, almost imperceptible, *grin* on the IceMan's face. Instead of erupting in anger, Bill erupted in laughter. The situation changed in the flicker of an instant. The tension was gone, the explosive situation defused by the expertise of the IceMan.

Douglas continued. "Well, Mister President, I gave you the highlights when I spoke to both of you earlier. As '*Dammit*' is unavailable at present, allow me now to fill in the details." Again the small grin caused the other two to smile. Unchallenged, he continued. "As you are both aware, Angelina Thomas, the Eagle's daughter, code name Hatchling, was abducted out of the hospital and kept under sedation." Douglas paused slightly as he noticed the Presidents almost invisible reaction to the word *'abducted'*.

The President held his tongue.

Douglas knew Politician's hated *compromising* words. He knew Wild Bill didn't mind that Angelina had been *abducted*, when in fact he had personally ordered it.

The President had just couched it in different terms, using *no* politically *compromising* words. Douglas smiled inwardly at all the smoke and mirrors that went on in the political arena. And he did know that it *truly was* a political *arena,* and that one misstep or mistake could spell physical, political, financial ruin or suicide, or all of the afore mentioned. Chandler mentally shrugged. He didn't have time to choose his words. He continued.

"The Hatchling, as I shall refer to her from now on so that we don't lose focus on whose daughter she is, was placed comatose, by strictly measured and medically monitored chemical sedation, in one of a group of seven identical MotorCoaches that we own. Q likes to refer to these particular vehicles as *Mobile Units One* through *Seven*. Field Agents like to refer to them as M Units or *Munits*. Since Hatchling's removal from the medical facility to one of them, the M Units have been constantly on the move around the country, with short layovers for maintenance. The Louisville Hot Rod Show was one of those maintenance layovers." He saw the question in both of their eyes.

"*These* seven Mobile Units, externally identical in appearance, are many years old and have been refitted many times. It would be prohibitively expensive to replace them every few years. Most, if not all, have well over a million miles on them. It was found to be more cost effective to refit than to replace." That answered their look.

"It was *never* an issue before this. There were three of the seven M Units that were in line to be refitted at the beginning of this FUBAR situation. Four had been finished."

Douglas noticed both Lantern's and JD's quizzical looks. He enlightened.

"Because the Munits are so monstrous, we like to send out at least five to help camouflage their size. Due to the importance of the situation, the three that had not yet been refitted were conscripted, for added security. Smoke and mirrors gentlemen, or more aptly put, a version of the old shell game. Under which shell is the pea?" He smiled at their understanding. "No one would know for sure in which one of the Munits the sleeping Hatchling was residing ..."

"Why is she being constantly sedated?" interrupted JD. "Surely not to lower the chance of her trying to escape. She is seven years old and in a debilitating recovery state from the explosion and the surgery."

The IceMan did not respond. He sat in silence for a moment and then turned his head and looked directly at the President.

The President paled slightly.

"I do apologize, JD." responded the President immediately, to cover the gap. "I thought I had briefed you on everything pertaining to this case. Apparently not so! I can't for the life of me understand how I could have forgotten to mention it. Let me rectify this IceMan." He looked at Douglas as if asking permission. All present knew and were aware of the subterfuge.

IceMan nodded. Bill continued.

"JD, the Hatchling was infected with a bag of tainted blood during the operation, when it was initially confirmed that her injuries would *not* prove fatal. That bag of blood contained the SIM virus. Sedation minimizes the chance that the Hatchling would awaken and bite one of *ours* in an effort to escape." and then added as an afterthought, "In essence, it was also done for *Damage Control,* to prevent the Hatchling from disclosing any part of the COW file to any *listener,* and in so doing, cause the end of *that listener's* existence."

JD knew that William Lantern only used the name *'Hatchling'* to minimize the despicable act that was done to an innocent seven year old girl and to help reinforce the importance of the *situation*, which was to use her as bait to lure her father to *their* destruction.

The *'their'* meaning *Brandon*, code name *Eagle* and his daughter *Angelina*, code name *Hatchling*. Both had to die, and die soon, *before* Brandon became aware of who was *truly* responsible for the bombing that killed his wife and injured his daughter.

'But the SIM virus? Why the SIM virus?' JD pondered silently. The IceMan spoke next, again raising the question in JD's mind whether or not the IceMan was truly a mind-reader or was it

that he had caught the flicker of the undisguised revulsion, disgust and distaste on JD's normally immobile features.

"The reason for the infection of the SIM virus was in case something; no not *something* – *'exactly'* is the correct word; *'exactly'* like this happened. No matter what, the Hatchling must die. A healthy SIM infected adult would succumb and die within three to six months. Because of her young age, thus her small weight and weakened state, once the Hatchling awakens and reaches full consciousness, the SIM virus, until now held at bay by her almost deathlike comatose state, will kill her within the next sixty days or less. The SIM virus, short for SIMIAN Virus, is the deadliest virus known to man. Whether or not the virus was originated by man, no one seems to know for sure. As you are no doubt aware, there is no known cure for the SIM virus. It was a shame it was discovered so soon and that the Eagle was informed."

"Why would you say that?" JD queried, seeking confirmation of an idea.

"As with any operation, Q does not like to show *any* of their cards. Although highly unlikely, at the hospital we might have been able to lull the Eagle into going with the Contractors we sent to take care of him ... but we trained him *well* gentlemen." he added with quiet pride. "Instead he bolted, knowing we would have no choice but to protect the Hatchling for him. One thing *is* in our favor, though. The Eagle now knows how little time his Hatchling has left, and will be desperate to recover and save her, if he can." the IceMan concluded.

"How is that in our favor?" JD prompted.

"The Eagle is famous for being a loner, although that is a bit of a falsehood. He always had Q behind him to call on for whatever he needed materially or financially. His vanishing act from the hospital proves to me that he no longer completely trusts Q with his well being. The Eagle *must assume* that there *must* be a mole in Q's midst. How else would the Red Chinese have discovered his name and address to plant the garage bomb? He is alone and desperate. Circumstance has forced the Eagle into that scenario. Desperate people take desperate measures." IceMan smiled. It was not a nice smile. It was a cold smile. "That, gentlemen, is when mistakes happen."

"As did *we,* when we foolishly rushed into that FUBAR garage car bomb attempt and the botched attempt again, at the hospital." reminded Wild Bill wryly. Suddenly his voice went sub zero to match the IceMan's smile. "Not to mention the recent loss, or theft or whatever the hell *other fancy words* you want to call it, of the '*Hatchling*'. This whole god damned situation is becoming intolerable! We were desperate to plug a leak and mistakes were made. Mistakes that could cause *catastrophic* damage to the USA. Explain NOW, Douglas, exactly how the '*Hatchling*' was stolen out from under our very noses and why you called this emergency meeting."

IceMan Douglas Chandler knew he was skating on extremely thin ice at the moment.

"Initially it is unclear as to *how* and by *whom* it was done, but we've since ascertained that it was China's *Dragon Lord* that boarded the 'Hatchlings' *Munit* and drove it away unnoticed. The Munit and crew have not yet been located." the IceMan stated.

Stunned silence reigned as the President and his Commandant absorbed this tidbit of information. JD was the first to react.

"*The* Dragon Lord, as in *Kai Akyi, the* Dragon Lord, Champion of the supposedly *Immortal Emperor of China?* That Dragon Lord?" he exploded incredulously.
The IceMan nodded.

"*Swell* ... that's just ... *swell*." The look on his face and the way that JD Powder said *'swell'* made it seem like the foulest swear word imaginable.

Unable to hold the frustration in any longer, the President stepped in to the fray. The stress in his voice, barely controlled, was evident to the other two.

"Douglas?" the hoarsely growled words reverberated like they were coming from *another entity* existing *inside* the Presidents body. "I will only say this once. First, you *need* to explain the *'At first it was unclear'* statement and *then* you *need* to continue and *then* you *need* to *not stop* until you have spoken *everything* you brought us here to say." Here he paused significantly. "Speak." he commanded as if to a dog.

Douglas knew when to be a *wolf* and when to play a *dog*. The stage was set to his liking. Now was the time to play the *dog*.

A flash drive magically appeared in the IceMan's hand and he started speaking as he inserted it into a convenient computer port. And though the IceMan obediently *acted* the part of the *dog,* all present knew *without any doubt* that it was a *wolf* who spoke, and the IceMan did not stop speaking until he had spoken *all* that *he* felt *needed* to be understood, *all* that *he* felt *needed* to be seen and *all* that *he* felt *needed* to be said.

And though all present knew the IceMan's words and actions were precisely scripted, they were listened to, watched, understood and heeded.

***

Scene 30

Shela Pryce put the PDA down and picked up a cell phone. It was a *very special* cell phone. She flipped it open and hit the send button.

"Hello Kamele. Have you come to a decision?" asked the *altered* voice.

"Please turn off the voice scrambler, IceMan." Shela ignored *his* question. "Does the PDA, that I received from you personally, contain *everything* that you have on the *situation*?"

"Unfortunately, yes." responded Douglas Chandler's natural voice.

"Are you sure the information you supplied is accurate?"

"Why do you ask?" the IceMan answered, now countering *her* question.

"The Eagle is ... correction ... *was* the cream of Q's FFD. *Elite* status, if memory serves. I find it hard to believe that what I viewed *actually* happened."

"I was assured that it happened. It is the reason that we need to *seal* the breach." He paused for emphasis. "Circumstance dictates the necessity of *permanently* sealing it ... immediately."

"After what I viewed and heard, I understand completely." Kameleon agreed.

"There will be a double *fee* bonus for a quick *resolution* to Q's problem."

Kameleon's tone changed subtly.

"You don't need to sell me, *sir*. I had already decided to take the Assignment. In spite of that, I will *accept* the bonus. Just to clarify, when you stated that there would be a *double fee bonus* for a quick resolution, I expect a double fee *as the bonus*, in addition to the usual fee." Here she paused for a response. None was forthcoming.

She continued. "Though I understand the need to execute a quick and final termination, I will not be rushed. To do so could prove disastrous to all concerned. Granting priority status, I will fulfill the assignment in an expedient fashion, subject to my standard clauses."

Douglas heard the *sir* used respectfully yet coldly. Red flags flew across his mind.

"Ahh, you misinterpret Kamele. I understand your need to prepare. I would expect no less. I assumed you understood that. My apologies Kamele."

"Accepted. Send all subject and pertinent information immediately."

"It is in your PDA mailbox, even as we speak." Although nothing showed in his voice, Douglas mentally exulted. *'She took the Assignment!'*

"Damn, am I that predictable?" Kamele's voice was troubled.

"Only when it comes to a *Triple 'A' Mission*, which you already know translates to a Kameleon *worthy:* Assignment, Adventure and Adversary." Douglas acknowledged assuredly.

"Well ... I guess I can live with that." but the voice did not have the sound of surety.

**

Douglas Chandler hung up the phone. One less obstacle to overcome.

With the *doctored* and *fabricated* evidence she had been presented with, Shela had been convinced that Brandon needed, and deserved, to die. He knew that if she *ever* found out of the deception, he could plead ignorance.

Knowing her the way he did, he knew that she would not believe him and that in all likelihood, he would die a horrible death. The IceMan did not fear Death. He was in the Death Dealing business. What he did fear was *how* he died. There were a few people in the world that he feared in this way. Shela had not been one of them, until now!

Intimate knowledge of what the Kameleon was capable of conjured vivid images in Douglas's mind. He understood, all too well, the dangers of panic and how it debilitates.

He took immediate steps to correct the condition.

In the Ice Chambers of his mind, the IceMan girded himself, snuffed out the tiny candle flame of panic, and rose to the circumstance. He mentally shook his head, then physically stretched, settled himself and smiled. It was time to move on.

He depressed a button on his desk and *again* watched a video of a group of Tour and Transit Busses exiting the Kentucky Fair Grounds.

He remembered well the mystified looks on the President and JD's face when he had first showed them the video. They hadn't noticed anything out of the ordinary. They did not notice a blandly colorful, nondescript, two storied Tour Bus amidst the other exiting Transit and Tour Busses.

How their faces changed when he enlightened them. He enjoyed the mixture of emotions that crossed their faces as understanding unfolded. The two of them reacted in different ways, as had he when he had first figured it out.

That ordinary Double Decker Bus was none other than the perfectly camouflaged missing *Monolith* that housed the sleeping 'Hatchling'.

He smiled at the memory. Then the smile faded. He portrayed the video as a victory to the President and JD. And a victory it was, but a hollow one. Knowing how it was done did not alter the fact that one of the deadliest men in the world, China's *Dragon Lord*, now had the sleeping 'Hatchling' in his possession and no one seemed to know where in the world they were.

All the Monolith's tracking devices had been debilitated, and the cloaking devices had been activated. Kai Akyi, China's Dragon Lord, one of the deadliest humans alive, with full United States Diplomatic Immunity and Privileges, had accomplished what was thought to be impossible. He had disarmed and disappeared with one of the Munits containing the *'Hatchling'*!

Douglas knew that the Kameleon would take care of the Eagle in a timely manner. Of that he had no doubt. It was the risk, slight though it was, of her discovering the deception that concerned him.

The IceMan *never* bought lottery tickets or ever *wished* to win a lottery. He had absolutely no interest in them.

But right then, at that *precise* moment, the IceMan felt like the most *addicted* lottery player.

Lord how he *wished* that he had someone *other* than the Kameleon, someone who possessed her unique abilities and achieved her results.

Someone *without* her goddamned Warriors Code, to *hunt* down and kill the Eagle!

***

Scene 31

T he Eagle sat in contemplation. He was using but one of his many *TAG's* that he had first started acquiring at age seven. As with his other *Talents, Abilities* and *Gifts*, it had matured in seven year stages and reached, what he felt was full cumulative maturity, on or about age twenty eight, almost seven years previously. His thirty fifth *official* birthday was in a few weeks.

His *actual* Birth Date was not known, only the date he was dropped off at the orphanage, which was logged as his *Official* Birth Date. He compared this *Talent* of his, recalling a memory or memories, to that of standing in the middle of a High Definition Three Dimensional movie set, surrounded by all the actors, complete with theater Surround Sound. Charlene had told him she thought of his Memory Talent as *Mind Viewing* and Reviewing.

He was Mind Viewing and Reviewing the meeting with Damon Gray at the reception, after the Concert:

***

Wearing a charcoal grey monochromatic outfit and his signature tinted eyeglasses that disguised his eye color, Doctor Damon Gray had approached the Eagle without seeming to do so intentionally. When close enough he turned, as if seeing the Eagle for the first time, and bowed his head slightly, arms hanging loosely at his sides, negating the rise of Brandon's hand to shake.

'*In all probability to avoid people crushing his pianist's hands*' was his first notion. Brandon understood how shaking a lot of people's hands could cause problems for someone who performed with them.

'*Like a surgeon*', was his errant thought.

Brandon Thomas likened this *Talent* of his to: living and reliving, experiencing and re-experiencing, viewing and reviewing a real life experience or memory; as participating in a *finished* three D movie. He would occasionally rewind and review certain scenes from different angles, striving to achieve a new perspective.

The Eagle turned his focus to Damon's hands. Hands devoid of ornamentation. Well formed muscular pianist's hands, he noted, larger and longer than they had appeared onstage. But then, Damon looked much larger in person than he had appeared to be earlier, onstage. Like an epiphany, *understanding* suddenly dawned in Brandon's mind. Damon must have had the pianos and violin *custom made to his own specifications*, slightly oversized, thereby downplaying his own size and dimensions to the audience.

'*Very clever*', he thought. '*No, not clever. Brilliant!*'

Brandon had originally estimated the height of Damon Gray to be about five foot eight inches to five foot ten inches tall, when he had first viewed him onstage. He now *correctly* estimated Damon's height at just over six feet. Dr Gray was large boned in a way that made him look and *seem* almost slender. That was why Damon's hands looked slender. Unless someone shook his hand they wouldn't notice their size. Another paradigm shift!

'*Damon didn't shake hands, because to do so would draw attention to them. It had little or nothing to do with damage to his hands*'.

To reinforce his new opinion, Brandon noticed that Damon's French cuffed shirt had larger cuffs that dropped down slightly over his wrists helping to camouflage them.

Brandon knew that Damon was someone who intensely valued his privacy, hence the media moniker '*Gray Ghost*', because *none* had been successful in obtaining a clear photograph of him.

"Ah, Mr. Sparrow, it is a true pleasure to meet you!" Mr. Sparrow was the name on the tickets and backstage passes. Brandon inwardly mused at the apt name analogy, and wondered, '*Did Damon Gray know that he was the infamous Eagle, or was it a coincidence?*' Brandon Thomas was *not* a strong believer in coincidence.

"I agreed to meet with you because a mutual acquaintance of ours, someone I trust, suggested we meet. How can I be of service to you?" Doctor Gray continued.

Brandon performed an elaborate bow, almost a curtsy. "Wonderful performance, Doctor Gray. Truly splendid, say what! Intoxicating!" The drunken English Professor spoke slowly, loudly, enunciating each word carefully. Striving to suck his stomach in and failing miserably, he leered at Damon. "How can you be of *service* to *me?* ... well, good looking *(again the leer)* ... like the insatiable thespian that I am, let me masticate on that morsel for a moment." People standing close by suddenly turned and moved away in embarrassment. The Eagle noticed. He also noticed that Damon reacted *not at all!*

Brandon's voice suddenly dropped to just below the crowd noise and he continued on in a coldly sober voice. "I am in need of some very specialized micro miniaturized equipment, Doctor Gray. Some will need to be computer created and computer controlled and assembled. Some will need highly sophisticated micro-*miniaturized* computers. One hundred thousand angels on the *point* of a needle micro-*miniaturized*."

"I am going to need specifics, of course."

"But of course, Dr Gray. I have in mind what I need, but I don't know if they exist. I was informed, *by our mutual acquaintance*, that you were the only one to go to. I was told that if it didn't exist, you could, in all probability, *make* it exist ... or at least *have* its existence created by someone else."

Damon Gray smiled at that last remark. Really smiled. Brandon was amazed at the transformation. Damon Gray became *alive*. Until that moment, Damon had seemed to be *elsewhere*. With a *nip and tuck* show business handsome *face and body,* he seemed nothing more than a shallow minded pseudo *intellectual*, albeit gifted with a *phenomenal* musical talent.

Brandon had not really noticed, until that smile, just how devastatingly good looking the pianist was. It somehow reminded him of Charlene. Although he knew she was physically appealing in a pinup poster way, it was *who* she was *inside*, her *vital essence* that took her to the realm of true heart stopping, breathtaking beauty.

There was much more to this composer/pianist/showman than his highly erroneous first opinion.

Brandon's first opinion of Damon, as he watched him mingle with the small crowd at the reception after the concert was that; albeit a breathtakingly brilliant and gifted consummate concert pianist and entertainer *onstage*, Doctor Gray was nothing more than an attractive empty vessel *offstage*.

Damon continued in a slightly friendlier voice.

"Let us agree that our acquaintance was being very ... *sanguine*. I was informed, correct me if I'm wrong, that *time*, or lack thereof, is a vital component?"

"Your information is correct."

"Is money an issue?" Damon's voice went back into the business mode.

"It shouldn't be." Brandon responded in the same vein.

"What is your budget cap? Please be forthright."

Brandon smiled outright. He liked the *no* gobbledygook, mumbo jumbo attitude. It would make things much easier if there was honesty between all parties in these business negotiations. Most businesses did not understand that *alien* concept. The successful ones did. It usually evolved into a win-win relationship for all involved. He knew that *his smile* told Damon that he welcomed it, just as he knew that Damon must know that *he, Brandon Thomas, felt* that there were really no *other* viable choices in this situation.

"I have immediate access to a little over five hundred thousand US dollars."

Damon Gray paused for just a moment. Whether in contemplation or in shock, the Eagle could not tell.

"This must be exceptionally important to you." Damon's voice was now warm. "Let us retire to more suitable surroundings, shall we, Mister SparrowHawk?"

'SparrowHawk?' Brandon pondered incredulously in retrospect. *'Damon went from Mister Sparrow to Mister SparrowHawk! What in blazes does that man know? Does he know that I am the highly sought after 'Eagle'? And, if so,* how *does he know, or more correctly, how did he find out?'*

He filed these thoughts away for future consideration and continued the memory. What else might he find that he missed the first time?

As they proceeded to an obscured egress, Damon commented, "I liked the part about the *'hungry actor chewing on the morsel'.*"

Brandon laughed, "I always wanted to use that one but could never find a way to insert it into a conversation." He paused in thought. "Speaking of which, I'm hungry, are you?"

Nodding in agreement Damon answered, "As a matter of fact, I am. Come to think of it, I *do* know of a private place where reticent thespians congregate to masticate."

Both laughed as they exited the room.

***

Scene 32

BlackStone: after the concert.

In the library.

Brandon Thomas was impressed, and he did not impress easily. The ride from the concert to BlackStone was remarkable. The vehicle they traveled in was slightly oversized, although not enough to draw attention. Viewed at a distance, it was of a nondescript charcoal grey color and style. Only upon closer inspection did the paint job show the depth and brilliance of a decadently expensive paint job.

In retrospect, Brandon marveled that he had not noticed more about it. There were no hood ornaments or identification marks of any kind on the vehicle. At first glance, it looked like a version of *every* nondescript aerodynamic bubble car on the market. Ten car experts would give ten different answers as to the type of car and manufacturer that it was, and they would all be wrong.

It was only *after* Brandon Thomas entered the back suicide door of the car for the first time that he became aware that he was sitting in no ordinary car. The driver and his front seat passenger were introduced to him, by Damon, as Hastings and Natasha. No last names. They were the two that were directly behind him in the theater that he had given his Back Stage Pass to.

"Where to Commander?" Hastings asked respectfully to Damon.

"BlackStone, Hastings." was the reply from the Commander.

"As you wish, Commander."

'Commander?' The Eagle silently pondered at the usage and inflection of the name, or title, *'Commander'.*

Being the best of the best, and thus true to form, the Eagle had done his preparatory homework and research on the young looking Master Pianist, prior to their first encounter. Brandon was unaware of Damon ever having held any kind of military rank or designation, other than Doctor, of which he held a multitude.

'Maybe it is a musical title, like Maestro.' he thought and then mentally shook his head. *'No, more likely a title bestowed on him by Damon's Personal Assistant and ex-military weapons specialist and combat expert, Garrett Hastings.'*

Brandon had viewed Hastings file and knew all about him before he had joined the Gray Family, wheelchair bound and sexually impotent, twenty plus years earlier. There was no information on him after that. Zero!

The Eagle was a *Prime Observer,* which was one of his *TAG's.* To him, Hastings did not move or react like a person who had been medically diagnosed and classified as a paraplegic over two decades ago. The Hastings that Brandon had observed the movements of that evening was that of pure liquid grace on two feet. Poetry in motion, Hastings had moved with the seamless blend of dancer and warrior movements. Seemingly ever vigilant, Garrett Hastings smoothly muscular body, to Brandon's practiced eyes, seemed always in balance, with body and mind never out of symmetry. The way he had interacted with the women at the reception denied the sexual impotence noted in Hastings file.

'*Was he even the same man or someone who had assumed his name, or even a different man altogether?*' the Eagle wandered.

And to add to his dilemma, Brandon had absolutely no idea as to who the little lavender eyed girl, Natasha, was. Nowhere, in his prelim, had there been any mention of her. It had surprised the Eagle that, with all of his contacts, connections and today's internet information plethora, there was so little *solid* information to be garnered on Doctor Damon Gray or, for that matter, *any* of his entourage.

'*Extremely frustrating.*' he thought in quiet frustration.

After the seat belts were fastened, Hastings hands quickly flew over a series of buttons and switches on the seemingly ordinary consul. From the back seat where he was positioned, Brandon saw the consul fold in on itself and transform into what appeared to be, before the privacy window separating the front from back seat shut off the view of Hastings flying fingers (with Natasha seated beside him, twisted around in her seat, waving and smiling back and up at him with her large, glowing, luminous lavender eyes), a dashboard command consul that would rival and in his opinion, put even the most sophisticated airplane consuls to shame. And being an avid aviator, Brandon intimately knew of some incredibly sophisticated and convoluted airplane consuls.

He returned Natasha's smile.

The ride itself was both pleasurable and unusual. The car seemed not to be moving at all, so smooth was the vehicles suspension system combined with the commanding driving skills of Hastings. There seemed to be no stopping or starting, so smoothly did Hastings weave through the traffic. Impenetrable, the tinted windows made their nighttime journey untraceable to the *Eagle*.

He had no idea where they were they were going. Not that it mattered. He had heard of 'BlackStone'.

And when Brandon arrived, BlackStone came as a bit of a shock!

It used to belong to a globetrotting ex-playboy, a Lord of the Realm and his wife. They had both been brutally murdered by unknown assassins. It made headlines around the world.

Their names were Michael and Sylvia Brighton, to be exact. The Ghost friends of his Ghost wife.

'Things are getting weirder and weirder.' Brandon thought to himself.

Damon did not speak throughout the entire journey. Brandon watched him keenly. Brandon felt that Damon seemed totally *aware* of him, but felt no need for any unnecessary conversation. Brandon was a little uncomfortable with that, and that kind of *uncomfortable* was a new feeling for him. He came to the conclusion that the Master Pianist was far deeper and more complex than even he originally suspected.

When they arrived at BlackStone, Hastings parked in the garage. A white haired butler had been awaiting them and opened the doors for them. They all exited at the same time, yet Hastings somehow magically appeared *between* the Eagle and his 'Commander'.

That, along the quiet comfort between them, told the Eagle that the bond between Hastings and Damon was far deeper than that of an employer/employee relationship.

Upon entering BlackStone proper, Damon excused himself, including Hastings and Natasha, explaining courteously, yet with quiet authority, that they would meet Brandon in the library in sixteen minutes. Who the 'they' were, the Eagle was unsure of. Initially, Brandon had been thankful for the reprieve. He had wanted time to gather himself and review the evening.

All of those noble intentions went out the window, along with the trash, upon entering BlackStone.

Brandon was instantly enchanted by it. He hadn't seen much of it from the outside upon their arrival because of the tinted windshields and BlackStone's exterior lights being out, but upon entering the building itself, the Eagle experienced the enchantment of BlackStone and was almost overwhelmed by the occurrence.

"Oh ... you can feel BlackStone's beauty and magic also, can't you?" a piping childish voice enthused. He looked down in startled surprise to see Natasha beaming up at him, her incredible lavender eyes aglow with excitement.

Stunned by her insightful observation, the usually unshakeable Eagle hesitated slightly to gather himself. As he started to respond, Brandon was politely interrupted and escorted immediately to the library by the butler introduced to him by Damon Gray, as *Whitner*. Brandon wasn't sure if it was an intentional interruption or an unaware one, by Whitner. ("Just *Whitner*, sir." Whitner had informed him when he responded with a *Mister* in front of Whitners name at the initial introduction by Damon).

His last view of Natasha was of her head tilted, looking up at and talking excitedly, hand in hand with Damon Gray heading the opposite way down a corridor. Just the instant before they passed from sight, Natasha turned her head and waved her free hand at him.

He didn't have a chance to wave back before she vanished from sight.

***

Scene 33

"**I** take it from what Natasha said, that you like BlackStone?" Damon spoke the statement/question as he walked through the library door exactly sixteen minutes later. Brandon automatically started to rise to greet when his host motioned Brandon to continue to sit. Damon chose a chair and settled lightly on the cushion facing Brandon.

Brandon returned Damon's smile. "She certainly is highly … *insightful* … or should I say *gifted*?" he responded carefully and then paused, looking away and into himself, delaying the answer, giving himself time to think.

Damon seemed to be in no hurry for an answer. Patiently, motionlessly, he sat across from the Eagle, awaiting a response.

Finally the Eagle reached a decision and spoke. "It's the *damndest* thing, Damon. There *is* something terribly weird and wonderful about BlackStone. Without knowing why, I was absolutely *enchanted* by BlackStone upon entering." He smiled wryly, "If, in fact, a Heaven exists - and to a lot of people, I am sure it does - to me it would look exactly like your library." He paused again in thought, then added, "Well, not '*exactly*' like your library … you *are* missing a *few* volumes."

Damon laughed in genuine good humor. "I know the feeling Brandon. It happened to me also. And I agree with you … and the missing volumes, whatever, whenever and wherever they may be, will be added … eventually."

Now Brandon chuckled and added, "It had been rumored that BlackStone was purchased off the Brighton's by an international corporation that uses it to entertain certain celebrity and influential clientele." He paused for a few seconds, as if remembering. "When not in use, rumor has it that the corporation rents BlackStone out for a ludicrously high fee." Brandon added, *almost* as an afterthought.

"Ahh ... yes ... the Rumor Mill is a busy company, isn't it? The President, Mr. Rumor has never been successfully sued, has he?" Both smiled at this. "Did the rumor say how long the waiting list was, to rent?" Damon queried curiously.

"Supposedly years! At first I didn't believe it, but after seeing but a small part of it, I wouldn't doubt it now. How did you manage it."

Damon flipped his long hair back and shrugged his shoulders elegantly. "What can I say? If I *had* to hazard a presumption, I would, in all likelihood, presume that the principals are music lovers."

"Ouch! I guess I asked for that one." Both smiled.

Without seeming to, the Eagle viewed the muscle play under the jacket when Damon had shrugged slightly. What he had assumed as shoulder padding was none other than pure rock hard muscle! When Damon flicked his hair back, his neck revealed thick corded muscles.

'Not a normal man, from the little that I've seen.' Brandon filed the thought away for future *3D mind viewing*.

"Now back to business. Please tell me all the facts, theories and suppositions that come to mind as well as your planned course of action, or more aptly described as, Battle Plan."

Brandon knew he had little or no choice in the matter. Damon was his only source at present. *'Be honest with yourself!'* he told himself sternly, *'he is the only source of help, PERIOD, for what I need.'* He finished with, *'and if I was in his shoes I would insist on full disclosure also.'*

He also admitted to himself that he respected Damon for insisting on full disclosure to protect his friends and loved ones. Brandon felt … no, more like *understood* … on a deep instinctual level, that Damon's concern was more for his friends than for himself. That alone convinced the Eagle.

The Eagle spoke. Damon did not interrupt.

When the Eagle was finished he sat in silence, body slumped, showing the unconscious tell tale signs of high stress and fatigue, head slightly bent, yet he still watched Damon with an *almost* veiled fierce and focused concentration.

Some moments passed as Damon also sat in silence and absorbed what he had been told.

Suddenly Damon Gray stood, in that impossibly fluid motion that Brandon had seen on stage earlier, and stated gently, "Thank you."

Damon put forth his hand to shake and Brandon instinctively reached forward to accept it.

"Are you truly the *infamous* Eagle?" Damon asked as his hand started to enclose his. Brandon's hand paused for a fraction of a heartbeat and then continued forward to be engulfed by the pianists' hand. It felt like he was gripping a hand made of spring steel. There was absolutely no give in the hand at all, yet it was warm and the pressure was light as a feather.

'As if to avoid crushing my bones to dust' was the errant thought. That thought was in his mind when he unconsciously answered the question.

"Yes." He paused, then spoke again. "You are very good, Doctor Gray. I now remember that you have many Degrees and Doctorates in human Psychology. It seems they are more than paper degrees." Damon smiled, still holding his hand. "Now do you believe me?" the Eagle finished softly.

Damon carefully released the hand still placed unmoving in his. That Damon heard the last question, Brandon was sure of, although Damon's next words belied it. They were spoken as softly.

"You must be exhausted Brandon and exhausted people don't think clearly. I suggest you spend the night at BlackStone and we will meet you for breakfast at seven fourteen, then?"

"Yes, you are correct in what you say. Seven fourteen would be fine, Doctor Gray. Do you mind if I use BlackStone's gymnasium for a quick workout before I retire? It helps me unwind."

***

Scene 34

"**H**ow would Brandon know that we have a Gym?" Hastings asked of Damon Gray.

"He noted our physiques and came to the obvious conclusion. I also believe that Brandon Thomas *is* the Legendary *Eagle*." Damon replied.

Hastings raised an eyebrow. "Commander, over the years I have kept in contact with my old army buddies. Some of them have risen to the top of their fields. Through them I have heard of this Legendary *Eagle* that you say Brandon Thomas claims to be, and from what I've heard, why ... he'd have to be in his late sixties to have done all that has been credited to him!"

He saw the look in the Commanders eyes and responded. "No, I am not disputing what you say Commander, just a little incredulous that someone so young could have done so much. I saw him out of his disguise when he was on the way back from his workout. He looks to be in his early twenties."

"I understand your skepticism, my friend, but the math does work out. He is old enough to have done all that has been accredited to him. And I think you will find that he is much older than he looks. When I went to shake his hand earlier, I asked him if he was the legendary *'Eagle'*. He paused for an instant, before placing his hand in mine, then continued the motion, somehow knowing or intuitively guessing what would happen; that while I was in physical contact with him, I could tell if he was lying or not.

He acknowledged that he was. I should have said *'I knew'* he was the *'Eagle'* instead of *'I believe'* he was the *'Eagle'*. I'll try to be more precise ... *although* with words, it is not so much *what* is said as the *way* it is said or a combination of the two. " Here Damon paused for a moment, then added, "He is an *EH*, but I'm not sure he knows it."

"How can you tell that, Commander? Are you now able to spot an *EH*? Do you now have *EH* sight *also*?" piped up a small melodic child's voice.

Damon slowly turned his head and glared down at the dark massively curled head of Natasha peeking out around the corner.

"How long have you been listening young lady?" he growled very, very dangerously.

"You know *perfectly well* that I have been here the *whole time!*" Natasha giggled at his *pretend,* over the top, theatrical growl and stood up from her pretend crouch and entered the room at a run holding her dolly in her right hand. About three feet from Damon she left the ground in a flying leap and he caught her and lowered her to his lap.

She straightened her Lavender and white nightgown and then checked the coordinating lavender ribbons in her hair. Then she took a quick glance to make sure her dolly hadn't lost *her* ribbons and then turned her face up to look at Damon. She could feel Damon's chest falter slightly in breathing when their eyes touched. She didn't need to touch him to know that he loved her. She smiled up at him and his pretend frown disappeared and a breathtaking smile took its place. It was his *Natasha love smile* and it was unconsciously reserved for her only. *Why* her Guardian loved her (Damon Gray was *not* her biological father) she didn't know or care. To know that he *did* was enough for her.

"No, I can't always tell at a distance if someone is EH, Natasha. I sometimes can with a *highly gifted one* if I touch them. With Brandon I knew before I touched him."

"Wow!" she spoke in a hushed voice. "How did you know Brandon was an ... *Extra Human* ... is that the right word for EH?"

"No, but you're close. It's *Enhanced Human* ... and who has been telling you about EH"s?" he asked softly.

"Oh ... you know." She stated softly. Without moving his head in the slightest, Damon's eyes looked down at her *'Dolly'* and then back up at her. She nodded almost imperceptibly. He understood.

"Am I missing something here?" Hastings demanded. "Did you two just go off somewhere just now and leave me behind? Did I miss the answer?"

Damon looked up and smiled. "Brandon said he liked my Cologne." he stated simply.

Hastings looked confused for a moment, then a burst of comprehension crossed his face and he exclaimed, "I understand completely. Ahhh yes ... he liked the smell of your cologne!" he smacked his head theatrically with his left palm as his right arm raised up as if to grab something out of thin air. His voice raised in pitch with the rising of his arm. "Why didn't I think of that? It makes perfect sense! He *has* to be an EH if he likes the smell of your Cologne ... of course ... of course ..." His voice faded in relation to his right hand dropping.

Looking Damon in the eye, he announced quietly, "This may come as a shock to you Commander, but ... you ... don't ... wear ... cologne! You say it exposes you."

Damon smiled with almost boyish delight. "Exactly, Hastings! You've got it!"

Hastings and Natasha both looked at Damon in confusion, then at each other, then back at Damon again.

Damon caught the looks. His smile disappeared. "I apologize, really I do Hastings. I thought you understood. I wasn't trying to confuse you; I just forgot that I hadn't mentioned it to you yet." He saw the waiting looks on their faces. He sighed.

"I do use a *special* cologne on occasion. It's ... a ..." He looked down at Natasha. He bent down and gave her a kiss on the cheek, placed her on the floor and said firmly "Bed time young lady."

"Ohhhh ..." Natasha said in exasperation, stamping her small foot in frustration. "Adult talk, I just knew it!"

"I'll tell you someday, when you're older." Damon said kindly, still bent so that he was on eye level with her.

"Really?"

"Really."

"Well, I *guess* I can live with that." she stated in her tiny *grown up voice*. She then leaned forward and kissed Damon on the cheek and gave him a big hug. She received one from him in return. Then Tasha jumped off of Damon's lap and repeated the same process with Hastings. He also responded in kind. Then she jumped to the ground and straightened her clothes and her hair.

"That's all I came down for anyway!" Natasha stated loftily, "My goodnight kiss and hug from both of you ... What's that ..?" she stopped, bent towards her stuffed friend and listened to her Dolly for a moment. Then she continued to the door.

At the door, she turned, smiled at Damon and announced, "Dolly said that if you didn't tell me when it was time, she would. Goodnight!" With that she turned and skipped off down the hall.

Damon's head dropped slightly at the last remark, as if in shock or thought. Then it raised and Damon looked at Hastings in a distracted way, his silver eyes not focused *at* Hastings, but at some distant point behind him.

Hastings knew that look. He likened it to the inward, distracted look that one acquires when one has received shocking information and is in deep thought about it.

"Alright Commander, out with it." Hastings prodded gently.

Damon smiled as his eyes refocused to Hastings. "Delayed reaction, my friend. I was just wondering what Natasha meant when she said *'also'*. Did she mean had we acquired a *new Gift,* the *Ability* to tell an *EH* from a *Normal* or did she mean a gift like *hers* or something altogether different? I'll ask her later on that, as well as what her 'Dolly' has been telling her. We will need all the help we can get." Damon was silent for a moment, thinking about it.

"Well ... thanks for that confusing tidbit, Commander, but I was *talking* about your new ... fragrance?" his eyebrow raised in question.

"Ahh yes, my friend ... sorry. Let us continue. Where was I? Oh, yes ..." Hastings knew it was an act, Damon's way of trying to seem more human. He released the frivolous thought and focused as Damon continued.

"I am not sure how to explain it, my friend. I found out recently that we can send off a subtle psychic scent that EH's are drawn to. They think it is a smell that all can smell. I did some initial testing and though it was only females that were drawn to it, I felt that male EH's could smell it also. I now have conclusive evidence that they do, since Brandon recently noticed and commented on it."

"A psychic scent ... as in cologne?" Hastings was struggling to understand.

"Well, no, not exactly." Damon responded. He paused in thought.

"Well, *what* exactly?" Hastings queried bluntly.
"More exactly, a *Psychic Musk*. Much like Cat has for *Normals*." Damon smiled at Hastings surprised look. He knew Hastings had experienced Cat's many sexual *Talents* on more than one occasion.

He raised a hand and continued before Hastings could respond.

"Initially when I experimented with it, I found that *EH* females were unconsciously drawn to me sexually. As you are aware, Cat's sexual *Talents* work on all males, *EH* and Normals."

He saw the acknowledgement and question appear in Hastings eyes.

"No Hastings, we have not *physically* changed in that way. We still cannot experience an orgasm of our own. It is still physically impossible. We can still *only* experience the female EH's orgasm, as long as we are in physical contact with them. I think because they *are EH's,* they are much more sensitive than *Normals.* What I found is that when having sex with the EH females, the Family Jewels somehow excited the EH's to an ultimate and *total* orgasm. When this happened, *for just a flicker of an instant* all their defenses were totally down. When this happened, we instantly Copy Slash Pasted their Talents, Abilities and Gifts and into us, along with the full knowledge on how to use them. I think that I have no desire to copulate with *Normals,* as they provide nothing of interest or value to me. At the beginning I tried a couple *Normals* and the experience seemed somehow ... shallow and disappointing ... not for them, but for me. EH's, on the other hand, have their TAG's. Interesting. I will need to experiment more and re-evaluate."

"Are you saying that you are some kind of *psychic Talent, Ability and Gift thief*?" Hastings asked incredulously.

"If you are asking: *Do I absorb or take away their Talents, Abilities and Gifts?* The answer to that question is a definite NO."

He paused for effect. "The EH Females lose absolutely *nothing* in *that* way. All that happens is that, at that moment of *complete and total orgasm*, for that *infinitesimal* instant that all their defenses are down, the Jewels Copy and Paste their *TAG's* into me. Much like a computer copy and pasting."

"Kind of like a Psychic *TAG* Vampire..?" Hastings stated, almost a question, in partial understanding.

"I guess you could say that I am a Psychic *TAG* Vampire, only I don't hurt or in any way, injure the EH victim. As a matter of fact, I give ultimate satisfaction as payment. And unlike Vampires, we retain all their *TAG's*. Their *TAG's* become a permanent part of our makeup." Damon paused as another realization struck him.

"So in a sense, we both benefit, albeit I found that theirs is a memory that fades quickly. Most notice nothing, but some of them looked like they felt something *was* taken. They soon dismiss the notion when their *Talents Abilities* and *Gifts* function as normal. But they are *not* wrong, Hastings. They *have* lost something. It seems that, because of the Jewels, when they reach the *ultimate orgasm,* they *lose* that *flicker of an instant* that their *Talents, Abilities* and *Gifts* are *transferred,* or should I more correctly say *copied and pasted* into and become a part of us. That is all they lost. That flicker of an instant. And that is a good thing."

"What do you mean by that?" Hastings asked, suddenly concerned. "Why is that a *'Good Thing'*? Are you in any danger when that happens?"

Damon realized that he had to tread softly here. Hastings would lay down his life in a heartbeat for his employer. He was much more than an employee to Damon, much more than his *'Personal Assistant'*. They were bonded in *Friendship*. Hastings would never knowingly allow anything harmful to happen to Damon if he could help it. Damon respected that, but still had to go his own way. Hastings also knew that, much to his fear, anger and frustration in those instances. He did know that Damon usually shared everything he felt was important with him and did take every precaution he could think of to protect himself and his loved ones.

"What aren't you telling me Commander?" Hastings insisted when he received no prompt response.

"I am not trying to evade any of your questions Hastings." Damon said this with a soft voice, with no reprimand in it. "I am just trying to understand it also, as I go along. Talking with you helps a lot. Just be patient my friend."

Hastings nodded and remained in silence.

Damon continued, "I say *'that is a good thing'* because I feel that I almost *die* and am *reborn* in that *flicker of an instant*." He saw Hastings grow suddenly pale."Wait Hastings, let me continue." he said with raised placating palm. "The pain of their Talents, Abilities and Gifts being integrated into my body in that *Flicker of an Instant* in time is incommunicable. My whole being is ripped asunder and then reintegrated or reassembled with all the added pieces or parts, or as I like to describe them, *Talents, Abilities* and *Gifts* along with all the EH's knowledge of how to use and control them. Most times I have more control. Who I am ... my whole being is completely restructured in that instant. I think the *only* reason I survive is because Golden and Garnet hold us together at that moment."

At that instant Damon's eyes changed. One eye became a brilliant, swirling, miniature blood red sun, with no pupil or white showing. The other eye transformed into a large glowing golden cat's eye completely filling the eye socket cavity, again with no whites showing.

"It's about time we get a little credit where credit is due." two distinct yet similar voices rumbled out of Damon's throat at the same time.

Hastings smiled at Golden and Garnet. "Well hello Garnet, hello Golden. It has been awhile. Thanks for taking care of the Boss for me."

"*NO* PROBLEM Hastings," the voices rumbled in laughter, "or should we say *UH-HUH?* We used to think *You're Welcome* was the correct response, but we hear so few people say it anymore."

The red eye changed to match the golden cats eye as *Golden* took over and went on in a more serious tone, "Relax Hastings, we know how to take care of ourselves ... well ... at least in *this* instance. The first time *almost* killed all of us. When it happened the first time, it caught us by surprise and we had to scramble, but after that we were fine. She is one of, if not *the* most powerful EH's we have encountered to date. She had TAG's that she was unaware of. For some reason, we were, and are, aware of them and know how to perfectly control them. She now can also. During the Copy Paste process we automatically integrated and strengthened her natural Ability to control her buried TAG's. That hurts like hell too." Golden smiled at Hastings. Hastings smiled back.

"We assume that it was, and is, a small *gift* in exchange for Copy Pasting TAG's into us. She was happy with the trade. She now has new TAGs that she didn't know she had and the Ability to use them. That seems to be part of our TAG's or makeup, which is in Damon also. I've said enough. Take over Boss." The golden eyes turned back to liquid silver.

Damon took over."We have since found we can control whether we bring their buried EH TAG's to fruition, but to date we have not stopped it. We feel that it is fair compensation. Golden and Garnet let me take the majority of the pain, so that *they* can hold ourselves together and take care of the rest. And don't even bother to ask what that means. There are no earthly words to describe it."

Garnet's eyes and voice took over. "Oh yes there is, just not in the human tongue."

Hastings smiled and nodded. He pretended to have a clue. He never really understood most of what Golden and Garnet were ever talking about, because most of the time *the words* they spoke were permeated with many layered meanings. All he did was nod and smile, and ask Damon later to explain. After what he had just heard, he knew that he would be doing it again soon.

***

Scene 35

At one time, Damon had told Hastings that *Golden* was a *Prime Instinctual* and *Garnet* was a *Prime Emotional*. Damon had explained that they had told Damon that they were two *missing* parts of him, or rather, two *added* parts that completed him.

'*Whatever the hell that means!*' Hastings remembered thinking at the time. '*And I sure as hell don't know what a Prime Instinctual or a Prime Emotional IS!*' he thought as he looked at them now. Garnet's eyes blurred and vanished and returned to the Commanders liquid silver color.

"How many times have you *fed*, vampire?" he demanded in an iron tone. "How many victims have you *ravished* and left *depleted*?"

Damon could not control himself. He started laughing. Hastings couldn't hold a straight face for much longer either and he burst out laughing too.

When Damon got his breath back he responded, "Not many, my friend. There are not as many EH's as you would like to believe. Most were killed over the centuries by the EHE's *(Enhanced Human Exterminators),* but the bonus to that is ... only the Best of the Best survived. The ones that are left, at least as far as I have been able to ascertain, are tremendously strong in their *Talents, Abilities* and *Gifts.* My research dictates that most EH's rival other EH's in TAG strength. In a strange way, it is like

Mother Nature weaned out the weak and infirm Enhanced Humans, leaving only the Strong to grow and flourish."

Hastings smiled. He liked it that Damon challenged Hastings mind with new concepts.

"Are you implying that this world, this earth of ours *is*, *possesses* or *has* an independent intelligence? That ... that ... what, that a *Mother Nature* is an *actual* thinking, distinct and individual entity?" He stumble said it in a jovial manner, though not really meaning it as a joke. Damon understood.

"You mean like Golden and Garnet and I existing in one body? How absurd!" was the soft response.

Hastings was staggered by the concept. It had not even entered his head. He knew *what* and *who* Damon was inside *only* because he had personally experienced it *happening* to Damon and watched it happen as Damon changed and grew from the man he was to the multi-unit entity he was now. Damon broke his train of thought.

"Yes, Hastings, I do believe that there is a Mother Earth *Entity,* much like *Golden and Garnet*, although many times more complicated and complex. We have *felt* her recently when *we* had returned from Elsewhere. *We,* as in Golden, Garnet and I. It was like she missed us and was happy to have us home. A strange feeling. Somehow she knows that we feel her and that makes her happy. She even likes Golden and Garnet, even though I somehow *know* that she fears them because they are not a piece or part of, and are outside of ... this space and time. I like to think of Mother Nature or Mother Earth as a *SHE* or of the *female persuasion* because the *female* of the humankind species is the BirthGiver and usually the Primary CareGiver. Therefore, more loving."

Hastings responded in the same *almost joking* timbre, "You talk as if HumanKind is a separate species from you, now that ..." he paused when he saw a flickering look in the Commanders Eyes. Had he imagined it? He joking tone stopped.

"Okay Commander, I'll concede that you are a special case, but a *real* Mother Earth? Why doesn't *Mother Nature* squish us? She sees what we are doing to her. If I was her I would!"

"I understand your feelings Hastings. At one time I might have agreed with you, had I thought about it. If you understand that human kind is but a quick blink of one of her myriad of eyes, in the time of this world. As with the Dinosaur, Caveman and Atlantis, we too shall pass. That *She* will morn our passing, I am sure of."

"Wait a minute, Commander! Doesn't having a *Mother Earth* negate the God concept?"

Damon looked puzzled. "In what way, friend? If you were God would you leave the running of this world to ManKind?"

"Well ... no! I'd ... *really* Boss, I'd squish us like an ugly bug." Both laughed at that.

"Do they come back for more?" Hastings asked curiously, returning to the previous subject. "I mean the Eh females, they should be flocking to you if they experienced the ultimate orgasm with you."

"You would think so, but the answer is *no*. Something happens when they reach that point. I discovered that they can't seem to remember it exactly, maybe because it is so intense. They remember up to it and after it, but not the actual event. And it disturbs them. Something happens to them and they lose interest in me quickly."

"Why would that happen if you have the *psychic musk?*"

"That, Hastings, is exactly the answer." Damon said with excitement.

"I *don't* understand." Hastings muttered.

"Don't be hard on yourself. Neither did I, at first. Upon further experimentation, I discovered the answer." Damon smiled at the memory. "With the exception of one, the ultimate *Event,* as we call it, *(referring to Golden and Garnet)* made the *EH* women *immune* to our *psychic musk.* That is why they were attracted to us in the first place, and that is why they lost interest after the *Event.* They could still smell it, but it held no sway over them. In fact it seemed to do the opposite."

"Opposite? You mean they hate you? Commander, that could cause serious problems if that's the case." Hastings interjected in a worried tone.

Damon smiled at the concern. "I didn't say that, Hastings. Further investigation showed that, after the *Event*, their feelings for us changed to those of a *brother.* Although they couldn't *consciously* remember the *Event*, they somehow *knew, deep* within their inner being, their soul of souls, that I did not react or feel the same as they about the Event. They *felt* the difference. On a primeval level, most if not all women feel the act of sex is really the art of making a man love and want to be with them."

He saw Hastings quizzical look. "A mating or bonding instinct?" He clarified. He still saw the quizzical look on his friends face.

He illuminated further, "Instinctively the EH females *knew* that *we* were incapable of feeling the type of interest in them sexually or romantically that they needed. Thusly, they no longer had any sexual feelings for us. We were *eunuch* to them. Which was fine with us. After they almost killed us with the *Event*, we had and have absolutely *no* desire to have *sexual relations* with any of them again. They still *like* us; they just no longer *desire* us."

Hastings laughed with relief and in humor. "That's pretty funny, Commander, seeing as how you *never* feel the sexual urge at all."

That statement startled Damon. "Just because we never *feel* any sexual urges or needs doesn't mean we don't enjoy it when it happens. We do experience *their* physical feelings as they reach orgasm, but to a lesser extent because we are not connected to their Psyche, only to their physical and psychic entities. And only then because we are in personal and direct physical contact with them while it happens." Damon paused in thought, then added,

"And I know we don't feel the full sensation that they do, only about ninety one point six three percent of what they feel, which is still close enough for me to understand the balance ... why are you grinning, Hastings?"

"I just noticed you switched out of the 'we' and into the 'I' on a couple of occasions. Plus I love your statistics. Do you know that research shows that seventy six point ... uh ... three five eleven percent of all statistics are made up on the spot?"

"No I didn't. Who came up with that statisti .... oh I get it, you just made it up!" Damon laughed as he was saying the last part. "That is funny! I'll use that in my performances, if you don't mind." His stage voice came on, "I recently heard that research shows that seventy six point ... uh ... uh ... three five eleven percent of all statistics are made up on the spot. No, I stand corrected ... it's eighty four point two three five seven percent." Both laughed at that. Damon then continued in a more serious tone.

"The reason for the switching between the 'I' and 'we' or 'us' is that we three are one, yet separate. Sometimes 'I' speak separately from 'us', meaning myself, Golden and Garnet, just as they sometimes come forward and speak, either separately or in unison as they just did. Sometimes it just slips out, though not as often as it used to, thanks to you. Does that clear that up?"

"Clear as mud, Commander. By the way, you said 'with the exception of one, all EH females were immune to your scent afterwards'. Who was the one?"

"The one, as you so eloquently put it, is none other than the one I acquired that Gift from as well as the all the rest of her Talents, Abilities and Gifts." Here Damon paused dramatically. Hastings went for it like a fish to a fly.

"Well, who was it? Do I know her?" he asked impatiently.

Damon smiled knowingly.

"Unbeknownst to me at the time she was my first Psychic Vampire victim. The one that almost killed us with the copy slash paste of all of her Talents, Abilities and Gifts that were transferred into us."

"Unbeknownst? What in the world did you mean by that? Did she know what happened or was she like the rest?" Hastings asked, sidetracked.

"She was like the rest, in that she lost that moment of the Event, but she did know that something had happened to her, but for some reason, maybe because she *was* the first, it didn't affect her as it did the rest. She does not think of me as a brother. That part is missing. And she still wants sex with me ... as usual."

"As ... usual?" Hastings repeated slowly, as realization dawned on him. "Are you telling me that Catherine Nipp was your first Psychic Vampire Victim?"

Damon smiled at the look on Hastings face. "Yes I am. We can talk more about this later, Hastings. I will answer all your questions then. Right now we have other fish to fry."

Hastings nodded his head slowly. "I agree, Boss, it can wait till later. I'm starting to feel just a little out of my depth here and more than a little punch drunk. Let's move on to something that I *can* wrap my mind around and that is Brandon Thomas and his dilemma. Bring me up to date on the situation."

***

Scene 36

"**O**kay." Hasting stated. "Allow me play the Devil's advocate for a moment. *I* do *believe* that *you* *believe* that Brandon Thomas, the Eagle, told you everything. But why would he do that, Commander? It goes way, *way* against the grain of any Q Agent would do. Commander, with your TAG's, don't you *feel* that it is more than just a little strange that Q's top Information Gatherer would do that? My gut instinct tells me to beware, and I am just a *Normal*. Wouldn't he hold at least a little back, just to cover his options? I mean, he doesn't know us does he? Why should he trust us? He doesn ..."

"Whoa, Hastings! Slow down; one question at a time." Damon smiled and put up his hand to ward off any more words and to take away any sting to his words, as well as the interruption. He liked to let people finish their sentences.

"And you are *not* just a Normal any more than I am. You are more an EH now than you are to a Normal, because of the *enhancements* I made in you." He saw Hastings surprised look, and with it came a nod of agreement on that statement.

Damon continued. "I do understand what you are trying to say, my friend and you are correct to assume what you are assuming, *if* this Eagle was a normal Agent of Q. It is the '*IF*' you are missing. We need to think outside the box, as Brandon does, my friend. Brandon Thomas is *not* a normal or ordinary Agent of Q. That is why he *is* the *Eagle*. The best IG Agent that Q has ever had or probably ever will. He was not brainwashed with, or by, their propaganda when he joined them. To him it was the obvious choice of profession for someone with his particular *TAG's.*"

"Got it. It even makes a weird kind of simple sense when you tell it like that. Continue, sir." Hastings smiled, then nodded and added, "Think outside the box. Huh ... who'da thunk? I think I may try that sometime."

Straight faced, Damon pretended to pretend to graciously ignore this little jibe and continued. "The reason that the Eagle told us everything is that he has nothing to lose, absolutely nothing, and everything to gain by giving full disclosure of the situation."

Here Damon paused for a second, then continued in an introspective voice, as if talking to himself. This time Hastings remained silent. This was not the time for levity. He listened and learned.

"And the Eagle would not talk of any *other* assignments, only the last one because it was the only one relevant to this situation. Hastings, Brandon gave full disclosure because *he has nowhere else to go* and no one else to turn to who could help him in this situation and ... he wants to win this one . no ... he needs to."

Damon looked at Hastings keenly.

"What would you do if it was Natasha?" Damon asked softly.

Stunned, speechless, Hastings paled at the thought.

Damon nodded in agreement and at his friend's new perspective and continued, "Brandon loves his daughter as much as we love Natasha, Hastings. He doesn't want to lose his little Angel to the deadly SIM virus *or* to Q, and that includes anyone or any*thing else that could cause her harm. And* the Eagle *will* do *any and everything* to prevent it, as long as there is breath in his body. Brandon wants his daughter to live a long, full life. *And* he will do whatever is necessary to accomplish that goal. Do you now see why I believe he has told us everything?"

Hastings nodded as understanding suddenly dawned within. Damon had changed his perspective with just a few words. Hastings now looked at the situation in a vastly different way. What was, at first, an assignment to supply a paying client for help, to that of helping a drowning man caught in a tidal wave, save himself and his daughter from almost certain disaster. And a good man, on top of it all, by what Damon had told him of Brandon Thomas.

"Is there any way, with the help of your computer genius, to convince Q that the COW file does not exist, except as a myth? That may get them to call off the dogs on Brandon's case."

"Great idea if it would work. But it won't. Proving that something doesn't exist, that *does*, is far more difficult than proving that something does exist that doesn't."

This brought about a pregnant pause in Hastings. Finally he burst out,

"Now it's my turn to say whoa! Commander, could you rephrase that in language that I understand?"

"What part don't you understand?" Damon asked.

"I almost understood the part about proving something exists that doesn't ... in other words, Boss, almost none of it!"

Hastings stated in exasperation. Suddenly, partial understanding dawned.

"Hold it!" he exclaimed suddenly, "Wait a minute. Commander, are you actually saying that a COW file, *the* mythical COW file actually *does* exist?"

"Isn't that what I just said? ... And you said you didn't understand. What a kidder you are Hastings."

Hastings ignored the jibe. "What makes you sure the COW file exists, Commander? I have heard rumors of it for over twenty years and no one has yet to come forward with proof."

"That is because I have had no need to use or acknowledge it ... until now ... and that *'now'* is only a *maybe*." Damon stated quietly, all joking timbre gone from his voice.

"You have the COW file? I mean ...You created the Cow File? Why ... why didn't you ever tell me Commander? The very existence of that file puts your life in *terrible* danger." Hasting stated heatedly.

"Any more in danger now than thirteen seconds ago?"

Hastings was again, speechless.

"The reasons I didn't tell you are obvious, but I will state some of them for you now. There was no need for you to know of its existence. It would have put you in needless danger. It would have upset you to know that I had created and had access to the COW File because you would feel that it would put me in danger. And another ..."

"Okay! Okay! Okay! I get the message, Commander." Hastings stated hands raised in the air in surrender. Then he continued, "Actually, Commander, after I got over the initial shock, I realized that you did the right thing, all things considered." He paused a moment in thought, then continued, "Wow! So, the mythical COW file *does* exist! There are too many questions running through my mind right now. If it meets with your approval, sir, we will revisit this later?"

Damon smiled a small smile. "I expected no less from you, Hastings. Yes, of course we will talk later. Right now let us discuss our next course of action to help Brandon Thomas. First though, call in Catherine Nipp. We will need her input and suggestions and of course, to utilize her incredible skills."

"Speaking of Cat, Commander, have you figured out why she is not affected towards you as the others EH women have?"

"You mean, feeling toward me like a brother" Hastings nodded in confirmation. Damon continued, "I have, Hastings. Because the psychic scent was one of *her* TAG's, she was not affected as others. I tested the theory with other female EH's and found it to be true to form in them, as well. I won't go into it, suffice to say that it is the reason that she was unaffected as they were."

"Does you scent work on Normals? And can you turn it on and off like Cat?"

"Yes I can *alter* it slightly to use it on Normals if I choose to, but it has to be a conscious act. Probably because of my lack of sexual desire ... let's just say it gets complicated. And yes, I can turn it on and off at will."

"Enough said, sir." Hastings confirmed. "Oh, by the way, I assume by the way you said it, that you haven't told the EH women of the, uh ... *transference*. Did you tell Cat?"

"You are correct on your first assumption, and the answer to the second is: Yes I did Hastings. I told Cat because I didn't know what the hell had happened. I felt I had to. Remember, it was the first time for me. I felt I had no choice in the matter, if I wanted to protect her. And before you ask, she didn't care one whit, in fact she said it turned her on. And as a foot note, she hasn't reached *Ultimate Orgasm* again. I tried and can't seem to accomplish it. I assume it's a *onetime thing* that the *Symbiot* does to facilitate the transfer of the TAG's."

"Symbiot?"

"Family Jewels."

"Gotcha … 'nuff said Commander. I'll go get Cat."

***

Scene 37

A soft bell tone sounded in the room.

"Enter Whitner." Whitner entered soundlessly.

"Mr. Thomas, sir." he announced to Damon.

"Good morning, Brandon. I trust you slept well?" Damon asked, as a refreshed looking Brandon Thomas entered the dining room slightly behind Whitner.

Brandon was adorned in a tasteful monochromatic dark silver beige outfit, replete with coordinating shoes and belt that had been delivered to him upon waking that morning. All fit perfectly.

Brandon opened his mouth to reply, and to thank him for the change of clothes.

Brandon paused, and remained openmouthed in astonishment, as he absorbed the room for the first time. The high ceilinged room was spectacular. It looked to him like a room out of a Fairy Tale. It was a room of wind and fire *frozen in time and space*, spacious seeming, yet comfortingly cozy at the same time. The focal point of the room was the dining area. A large Crystal Flame Chandelier, seemingly magically suspended over the dining table, lighted the room with a soft, yet clear, full spectrum light. The room seemed alive and vibrant, waiting to entertain.

Damon was seated facing Brandon, beneath the chandelier, at an exquisitely crafted, round dining table made entirely of a non reflective glass or crystalline substance. Made of the same material, the arm chairs looked sturdy, yet with the same exquisite simplicity as the table.

The chairs seat and arm cushions appeared to be of a clear substance that were either of that substance, or had a clear covering with a core filled with a matching clear gel like substance. It looked to be the former, to Brandon. Each chair was distinctly different, imbued with their own individual personality, yet with every one of them unmistakably bearing the family resemblance.

Although the table and chairs reflected no noticeable light, all their intricate details stood out clearly. The table was set with four place settings and all of the settings and other items on the table were made of the same substance as the table and chairs.

"Amazing." Brandon breathed, almost to himself.

He closed his mouth and continued into the room after taking a quick three sixty look around.

"It took my breath away when I first saw it, also." Damon acknowledged, rising to meet him. They shook hands briefly as Whitner pulled a seat out for Brandon off to the side, almost facing Damon but still with full view of the doorway. At present he was the only other person at the table.

Whitner appeared and poured him a steaming cup of coffee from a clear coffee pot, mixed it to Brandon's taste, then turned and left the room.

Brandon brought the clear glass cup of coffee to his nose and sniffed it, then took a sip.

"Mmmmm Hmmmm!" came the satisfied sound. "Mind if I ask how Whitner knew of my preferences in coffee? This rare blend is my favorite." He took another sip, "And it is mixed exactly how I like it."

"Not at all." Damon responded quietly.

There was a brief silence as Brandon took another sip.

"Well?"

"Well what?"

Brandon suddenly smiled, *"You are a deep one, Doctor Gray."* He sang softly in the tune of the Grinch song. Then he continued in a serious voice, "And how did you know my sizes in clothes? Thank you, by the way. They feel incredible ... no, wrong word ... *wonderful* is a more appropriate description. I've never worn anything like them. The shoes feel like I've worn them forever. Oh, and how *did* Whitner know of my preferences in coffee, Damon?"

"You are welcome, Brandon. And just because I said I didn't mind you *asking*, didn't mean that I would *answer*."

Just then, as if on cue, the bell tolled again.

Whitner entered and announced, "Gentlemen, Ms Catherine Nipp." He turned and left. It was only after Whitner had *completely* exited that the person in question walked in.

Damon rose to greet her. Brandon sat spellbound in his chair, staring at Catherine Nipp as she glided across the room toward them. Never had he seen a walk like that, all her movements were in perfect balance.

"Brandon Thomas, Catherine Nipp. Cat ... Brandon."

Embarrassed, Brandon surged quickly to his feet, righting an almost spilled a glass of water with his left hand while putting forth his right hand to enclose the one Cat had raised to where his hand *would be* when he was standing. A brilliant smile travelled up to her incredible, slightly oversized, pure ice blue eyes. Brandon stood there mesmerized, tongue tied.

"Good morning, Brandon. A true pleasure to meet you. I have heard some wonderful things about you." came the soft, full, throaty voice out of the most sensually, sexy, and beautiful woman he had ever met.

"Uh … thank you …"

"Cat, turn it off! He's married." Damon stated softly, yet with authority.

Instantly something happened and the woman before him was transformed into just an incredibly beautiful woman. Gone was the incredible sex appeal. Brandon could think again.

'*She walks and acts like a top runway model*', Brandon thought errantly. '*No, definitely not a runway model with legs like that, more like a top rated body building, gymnastic or fitness celebrity!*' he amended as he took stock of her rock hard physique and incredible muscular development.

Catherine looked at Damon and smiled that breathtaking smile. "Aren't all the good ones, Commander? Besides, his wife is dead." she looked down toward Brandon's belt line, smiled, then back up at her boss. "He's not!"

Damon smiled back at her. "But her ghost is here."

"Right now?" Cat asked eagerly, glancing around, her long, silky, undetectable platinum blonde wig continually framing and reframing her face as it flowed with her head movement. Then she stopped and frowned prettily at Damon.

"What does she look like? Introduce me."

"No, she is not yet here, Cat; and yes, I will introduce you to her when she does make an appearance."

Brandon was glad of the banter going on between them, as it gave him time to collect himself. He had a feeling that this was not the first time that Damon had done this to allow people to recover themselves. It was a little unnerving to him that it had even happened. He filed the thought away for future study, composed himself and then restudied Catherine Nipp.

A wonderful mass of contradictions, Cat's muscular yet firmly rounded development was breathtakingly beautiful, almost slender yet full bodied at the same time. Never had he seen such exquisitely developed calf muscles. *'Sheer liquid, flowing, living perfection. A sculptures dream, a body to be captured in Marble and displayed in a museum.'* was the thought that entered his mind. *'No, not captured in marble,'* was the errant update as he noted her glowing golden skin tone, *'more like captured in gold or golden bronze.'*

Well formed feet were encased in top fashion designer footwear made of clear plastic. Brandon recognized the designer. The obscenely expensive spiked high heeled open toe sandals beautifully showcased her tasteful French Tipped toenails.

Catherine was wearing a fantastically scandalous, almost illegally short white dress with seemingly random patterns cut out of it. Brandon could tell at a glance, as could anyone with eyes in their head, that she was completely nude under it. Highlighting and showcasing every curve and muscle of her light golden body, it covered slightly more than a swimsuit bikini and then only *just,* barely covering her private parts.

He noticed that she had spread a cream containing golden sparkle dust on her skin to give it that glow. *'She doesn't miss a trick. Maybe there is more to her than meets the eye … and that's saying a lot!'* He smiled internally at the private jest and tucked the thought away for future consideration.

It almost made him feel like a Peeping Tom just looking at her. He was glad that Charlene hadn't been there to see his initial reaction to her, which was subsiding quickly. He started to place his hands together in front of his crotch, then realized the futility of it, and stopped.

It was obvious that she had seen him aroused.
She smiled a small *special* smile at him to let him know she had witnessed the subtly stopped gesture. It was a nice smile, free of malice. He smiled back. He instinctively liked her, but instinctively didn't trust her.

"Sorry!" she said apologetically, "I didn't know you were still married."

"Really?" Brandon asked seriously.

"No … not really." Cat shrugged eloquently, her large firm beautifully formed breasts rising slightly. Brandon had to force his eyes to stay on her face. "You *are* kind of cute, you know!" she smiled at him.

Brandon laughed and something inside him relaxed a little.

"*Kind* of cute? Nobody has ever called me that! Thanks for the compliment, Ms Nipp."

"You're welcome, handsome. And you can call me Cat." she purred back.

The bell tolled again.

"Mr. Garrett Hastings and Miss Natasha Gray!" Whitner announced to no one in particular from the doorway, then turned and discretely exited.

Hastings and Natasha entered the room hand in hand, Natasha beaming at Brandon and holding her doll, Dolly, in her other hand.

"Bye Whitner!" she yelled over her shoulder, just before he vanished from sight.

Damon touched a spot on his bare wrist, where a watch might rest, and three people suddenly appeared at the end of the table where there were no place settings.

One was Charlene Thomas, Brandon's ghost wife. The other two were, ghost husband and wife, Michael and Sylvia Brighton. They were holding hands.

Brandon was stunned, as was Hastings.

Hastings was the first to speak. "Commander, why is it that we can see them?" he went to touch Sylvia, but his hand passed right through her.

"I won't explain how; it is far too complicated. Michael and Charlene are wearing a special watch that I also wear. It only becomes visible in the *AfterLife Realms*. The watches are the reason you can see and hear them. Suffice it to say that you can see them and hear them only in this room and the library."

All present saw the Triangle Watches on Michael's and Charlene's wrist.

"I was able to set up some very sophisticated equipment to allow you all to see and hear them. Good morning, Michael, Sylvia and Charlene?"

"Good morning." They responded respectively.

"Wow!" Sylvia enthused, "It sure is great to be seen and heard by other living people. It's nice to know that I'm not just a figment of my own imagination!" Everybody laughed. "I'm holding my husband's hand so that you can see me also. I gave my watch to Charlene."

Brandon snapped out of his stupor. "Char, where have you been?" he asked automatically, his mind racing.

"Damon asked me not to appear until summoned, to allow you to rest and recuperate." She looked at her husband in concern. "Are you alright, dear?"

"I'm fine Char. Just shocked. I shouldn't have been. It appears that nothing is as is seems around here."

Everybody grinned in appreciation of that remark. And all for their own reasons.

"What shall we call ourselves?" piped up Natasha. "A team *needs* a name, doesn't it?" she asked seriously, then added, "We could call it the Commander's Seven Team, 'cause ... I mean '*because*' you're the Commander and there are seven of us." She paused in thought, "Maybe not ... sounds too much like seventeen, doesn't it? Maybe it could be ..."

"I'm not part of the group?" Damon interrupted, smiling at her word correction.

"Of course you are a part of the *group*," Natasha stated in exasperation, "you're just not part of the *team*. *We seven* are the *team* and all of you are the *Commander,* Commander!" as if it was perfectly clear. Damon just looked at her. "You are *our* team

Leader!" Natasha clarified, paused in thought; then added "and besides, you *are* your own team, Commander."

Brandon noticed that no one looked startled or took exception to that last statement. He kept his own counsel.

Damon looked around at everyone, smiled and said innocently, "I always did like the taste of Seven Up."

"I was thinking more like ... *the Magnificent Seven!*" Hastings announced theatrically with raised arm, "But that's been taken." His hand dropped in defeat, along with a dramatic pause.

"'*Seven Up*' it is then." Natasha piping voice announced seriously, then exclaimed excitedly, "And I'm part of it!" she unconsciously bent her head slightly in thought, then raised it and exclaimed, "I can be the *Cherry* Seven Up!"

"And for many, many more years!" Damon added fervently. Everybody laughed at that except Natasha. She bent and listened to Dolly, then sighed. "My Dolly said I will understand in time. In time for what?"

As the question was not directed at them, but rhetorical, no one answered, but all the adults smiled.

The '*Seven Up*' team was now assembled.

The bell tolled softly again.

"Breakfast is served!" Whitner stated from the doorway.

Suddenly his eyes widened as he saw Michael and Sylvia.

Just as quickly his eyes returned to normal.

Acknowledging Charlene, Lord and Lady Brighton with a smile and nod as if nothing was out of the ordinary, he turned to Damon and enquired politely,

"Shall I request the placing of three more settings, sir?"

Scene 38

They were all either seated or standing, depending on their preference, in the library of BlackStone, where they had retired to after breakfast to discuss the plans to rescue Angel Thomas. There had been a few pleasantries exchanged when Damon, who had been sitting, suddenly stood and took control of the situation.

"To business. As Brandon stated earlier, time is of the essence if Angelina Thomas is to be rescued ." Damon confirmed. "Time to *octo-team* them."

"And what exactly does that mean, octo-team?" Brandon asked.

"It means that we will have all eight tentacles or team members acting separately or as one, as circumstances dictate, in order to effect the safe retrieval of your daughter, Brandon. That means the Commander becomes a tentacle when circumstances dictate." Damon stated matter of factly, with no inflection in his voice. A Command voice.

"Commander! ...." Hastings started to interject.

"We would do no less if it was Natasha, would we not? This is no different, is it?" Damon asked his friend softly. Hastings paled again at the thought of Natasha in Angel's predicament and was silent in assent.

Damon smiled at his friend in appreciation. He knew that Hastings blamed himself for not being able to prevent the deaths of his parents or his grandparents, and was paranoid in his obsession to protect Damon from all harm. He understood what the cost was to Hastings for his silent acquiescence.

Damon continued. "We have received reliable information that the Dragon Lord, personal Champion of the Immortal Emperor of China, single handedly managed to abscond, undetected, with Angelina Thomas, under the very noses of Q's best agents.

Q has no idea where they are"

"How do you propose we find her, if her whereabouts are unknown, not only to Q, but to us as well, Commander?" interjected Hastings.

"I did not say her whereabouts were unknown to *us*, did I?" Damon chided his friend gently.

Hastings smiled back. "I'll shut my mouth, Commander. Speak on."

"Brandon, I have the items that you requested of me yesterday."

"You do? How can that be? You couldn't possibly have had the time!" Brandon blurted in total amazement, half *believing*, half *wanting to*.

"Oh ... don't get him started on *time*!" stated Natasha in a solemn voice. "He will talk your ears off and you won't understand *any* of it." She noticed Damon's amused look. "Hey! It's not just *me*, Commander!" she piped up in defense of her statement, "Even my Dolly doesn't understand most of it!" as if that proved it.

Damon nodded and turned to Brandon, "In a sense she is correct Brandon ... you probably wouldn't understand. Not that we even have the time to discuss it at present. You can believe the statement when we say that we have the items that you requested, plus a few that we feel might come in handy. I will show them to you after the War Counsel."

Turning to and addressing all of them, he began, "Cat, you work best alone, but this time there is to be an exception. I need you to cover someone's back. Here's what I want you to do ...."

**

"The plans are set. Everybody should know what they have to do. Any questions on what we have discussed?" Damon looked at each of the Seven Up team. None responded.

"Then this War Counsel is over. You all have your assignments. Go, succeed and return safely. If you need help, call. That is an order!" None smiled. They all knew that Damon was not jesting, he was deadly serious. He wanted them *all* back safe, even the dead ones.

"Brandon ... if you will stay behind, we have those items and others for you." Brandon nodded. The rest filed out or vanished.

**

Scene 39

I t was as black as fresh tar outside of the soft foggy glow of the *Fern Berry Truck Stop* lights. It was a moonless and starless night. The temperature was coolish, causing the heavy, low lying moisture-laden clouds to encase everything in a dense fog. The murky suffocating silence was deafening, as if all the animals and insects were waiting for something important to happen and they didn't want to miss it.

Semi tractor-trailers of every description were lined in rows with drivers sound asleep in the back, with their loads nestled behind. MotorHomes of every size and description were situated between them, depending on when they had arrived. With the exception of a one or two soft muted interior lights, the hundred plus vehicles were lightless.

All but invisible, a shadowy figure crouched down at the edge of the parking lot, completely encased in a dark dappled dusty grey non reflective bodysuit, with the exceptions of the matching grey camouflaged motocross style boots, gloves and silenced gun with gunbelt. There were no openings of any kind for eyes or mouth, nothing to give a clue as to the color of skin, eyes or teeth. It completely covered every inch of the body armor.

Even to an expert observer, the body armor under the bodysuit made the person appear male. Because of the broad shoulders, thick muscular waist and cod piece, all would agree it was a male figure.

Kameleon had designed it that way. The cod piece was a clever decoy. It had saved her life on more than one occasion when someone had kicked her in the groin thinking it would incapacitate her, only to find needles of steel porcupine like quills imbedded in their foot. Their screams of anguish were soon silenced.

She touched her crotch absentmindedly and smiled as she felt the needle tips. She then adjusted her muscular, *almost to the point of paunchy,* padded waist line, that further enhanced the male physique appearance, then made some subtle fluid movements and stretches to assure that it would not bind or restrict her movements in any way. She checked the buckles on her boots to make sure they were securely fastened and would make no noise when the special grip *silent step soles* propelled her soundlessly through her missions. Her aura was safely shielded. No one with *aura sight* would see her. She automatically continued through her final countdown checklist.

Finally satisfied, Kameleon started to rise and stretch, but paused and dropped down again as she saw a nondescript couple with a young girl who was carrying a doll *(much like one would do with a security blanket),* obviously the couple's daughter, suddenly materialize out of the fog and approach a gigantic featureless motor home.

She was surprised because she had not seen their aura's until she first saw them appear and even *then* their auras were very faint.

'*Strange.*' she thought as she went into defense mode, although the way they walked and acted made her sure that they seemed unaware of her at present.

Kameleon knew that they were *not* the owners of the Monolith. The present owner was in the Fern Berry Truck Stop doing a little grocery shopping and having a bite to eat. She eyed them curiously, relaxing slightly. From their aura's she read no hostile intent.

Kameleon focused in on the male.

The Eagle had followed her at one time, *undetected* so he thought. She had taken it for curiosity and allowed it. She had wanted to know him as well. They were the top and best of Q's Elite. She had reciprocated and followed him, undetected to the best of her knowledge, and confirmed that it *was* just curiosity. She knew his walk, stature and mannerisms in unguarded times, and all the little things that showed as much as a fingerprint to the right person.

Although his face was distorted by a strangely sculpted beard, her night vision glasses confirmed that the man walking with the two females was definitely *not* the Eagle. The two females, one adult and one child, were wearing matching eyeglasses also. It added to the *family image* that was created. They were wearing hooded dark gray jogging suits of a superior cut that effectively camouflaged their physiques, dark non-reflective silent footed jogging shoes and thin dark non reflective gloves.

In absolute silence they walked directly to the Monolithic MotorHome. The man, whose upper face was also slightly distorted by the thick black framed and thick curved lens spectacles, walked confidently up to the vehicle's door. Without looking around and without taking off his gloves, he punched in a series of keys on the blank keyboard embedded in the side of the passenger door. Silently the large door swung open.

It hit her suddenly that the man was not using any kind of flashlight! His thick feature hiding glasses were really NiteVision goggles also!

The man entered while the woman and child positioned themselves outside and stood in silence, backs to the Monolithic M Unit. Within seconds the man reappeared, with what looked like a large laundry bag or king sized pillow cradled lightly in his arms.

The door of the *'Munit'* closed as if on cue and the three exited the parking lot. Just as they were fading from sight, the little girl turned slightly as her small head swiveled around, her free hand pushing up her glasses that had started to slide down her tiny nose, revealing pure lavender colored eyes. Hand still raised, she smiled suddenly and waved a discrete goodbye in Kameleon's direction.

Kameleon sat there stunned for a split second, then laughed silently to herself in revelation.

Shela Pryce, *aka Kameleon,* knew that she had just been *privileged* to witness *the* slickest operation she had ever experienced. The trio, *whoever they were,* had just abducted Angelina Thomas from under the watchful eyes of the most feared Assassin in the world, Kai Akyi, China's dreaded Dragon Lord and the Emperors' personal Champion.

Kameleon pondered. Did the trio somehow know that she was there and proceeded with the operation anyway, as if they *knew* of her agenda?

Kameleon was not interested in burdening herself with the terminally ill girlchild. Kameleon had not been contracted to kill Angelina Thomas. The IceMan knew better. She also wasn't interested in being a babysitter. She was *only* interested in *shadowing* Angelina Thomas until her father, the *Eagle* came for her. Kameleon didn't care who had possession of her.

Kameleon, last of the Valkyr, had no desire to be there when Kai Akyi returned. She harbored absolutely no urge to pit herself against, from what she had garnered about him, quite possibly the most dangerous living person on the planet. With no time to erase her presence there, Kameleon quickly went into her *VState* (Valkyr State), arose and followed the abductors ... but with great care. The girlchild knew of her. Did the other two?

It didn't matter. It never did.

They had the girlchild and where they went, Kameleon went. To her it was the only sure path to Brandon Thomas, the infamous Eagle.

Kameleon's target.

Kameleon arose and followed.

***

Kai Akyi, China's dreaded Dragon Lord and Emperors' personal Champion, entered back into his body seated at a table in the Fern Berry Truck Stop, holding a newspaper, head bent slightly as if intently reading. Nobody in the restaurant seemed to notice him.

His eyes came back into focus in an instant and he sat in contemplation of what he had just observed at the Monolith. He had witnessed the liberation of the child. *'Impressive!'* was his thought. Who did the little girl seem to be waving to as they left? It looked like she was looking straight at him. Had she seen him?

Kai surveyed the room. None of the customers who were there had changed their position much or even seemed to notice him.

One fat bald sweaty trucker was trying to wedge himself out of his booth to leave and was having a hard time doing it. The Dragon Lord rose swiftly to beat the trucker to the cashier. From the lethargy of his actions, Kai knew that he would be taking awhile to pay. Kai didn't have the time to waste. He paid his bill, left an adequate tip and exited the building as the huge trucker came waddling and wheezing up to the counter to pay.

Kai smiled inwardly in victory. He had accomplished what he had set out to do. There was a homing device secreted on the unconscious child. No one would find it. He was assured that it was undetectable unless you knew exactly where to look. Kai knew and he still had a hard time finding it. It would take him to his quarry.

As he pulled out of the parking lot in the Monolithic MotorHome, Kai noted that the huge monster trucker was still at the counter, trying to hit on the waitress. *'The huge Trucker might get lucky, at that'*, was Kai's errant thought. *'The waitress is almost as big as the he is.'* Kai was happy that he left first. He would still be there, standing behind the bald trucker as he tried his moves on the waitress, if Kai hadn't moved as quickly as he had.

Scant seconds after Kai had paid his bill and left the truck stop restaurant parking lot, the huge bespectacled trucker, the very same one that Kai had just been thinking about, broke off his conversation with the waitress, paid for his fare, of which he had not partaken of, tipped his sweat stained, greasy baseball cap one last flamboyant time at the waitress and left the restaurant building at a slow lumbering knock kneed walk.

He laboriously climbed up and into the cab of a huge, brilliant red, eighteen wheeler hauling a long Box. It had been idling, waiting for him. He settled into the seat, took off his glasses, put the Kenworth HyBrid Semi-Tractor with trailer into gear and drove off smoothly.

The eyes of the monster trucker changed from liquid sliver to having one Golden eye and one swirling blood red eye. The oversized puffy face smiled.

Damon Gray was pleased with the way *things* were progressing.

***

Scene 40

"**M**r. President, the *Eagle* has landed!" spoke the scrambled mono-metallic voice.

"Great! Where has he landed? And turn off that blasted voice scrambler, IceMan. It grates on me greatly."

"As in cheese, Mr. President?" responded the IceMan's natural voice over the secure line. "He has landed in England. It has been reported that he is *just now* having a private audience with the Queen."

"Oh ... my ... god! How could that happen? I was lead to understand that we had the situation under control! What the hell is he telling her?" Wild Bill raged in a fury of fear.

"We don't know, Mr. President. It is in one of the Private Audience rooms, exactly which one we don't know. Not that it would matter. We have never been able to install any listening devices in any of them. And we have no idea how or why he asked for and received a private audience with the Queen. My apologies, Mr. President." finished the soft voice.

"Get some men over there and take him out when he leaves. I don't care how many have to die. Kill that sonofabitch *dead!*"

"Already structured and in place Mr. President. I knew that those would be your orders. The Eagles wings will be clipped when he is within range of any of Q's agents. He will never fly again. The Palace is surrounded with seven of Q's Elite and fourteen Agents." The IceMan paused.

"Out with it IceMan!" commanded the President in a voice that betrayed him and told Douglas of the sinking feeling in Williams stomach.

"He was wearing a Q disguise that we knew, Mr. President." IceMan stated quietly.

"Is that information *supposed* to make me quake in my boots, Douglas?" Bill responded with a relieved voice, followed by a soft chuckle, as if he hadn't been worried at all. "And if so, why should it, Douglas?"

"Because Brandon Thomas has never been seen *as a recognizable version of himself* in *any* his assignments. He purposely chose one of the disguises that we taught him in Q's Elite training. He *wants* us to see and recognize him. He *needs* us to know that it is Brandon Thomas, the *Eagle,* that is in the Royal Palace, in Private Audience with the Queen."

"Now why in the world would he do that?" Bill responded in kind. "Why would the infamous Eagle sign his own death warrant? I thought you told me that he would move heaven and earth to save his daughter's life?"

"I did. And I believe he will. What he is doing makes no sense, Mr. President. That is what worries me."

"Well ... what the hell!" Wild Bill Lantern suddenly laughed, "Don't let it bother you Chandler. We now *know* where he is and *if* you have *ordered done* what you say you *ordered done*, it won't be long before it is a moot point anyway! Just kill the cocky sonovabitch and call me when it's done, IceMan."

"Yes sir, Mr. Presid...." Wild Bill had already hung up the phone.

***

Douglas Chandler replaced the phone softly in the cradle and hit the *'Stop'* button on his recording device.

"*You* are the cocky sonofabitch, Mister President. *'If I have ordered done what I said I ordered done?'* I seldom *lie*, Mr. President. I did order it, but I am not convinced that the seven Q's Elite and fourteen Agents will be enough to bring the Eagle to roost." the IceMan spoke into the air, raising his right hand and pointing at the speaker mounted on the desk in front of him as if it was the President of the United States of America, William Lantern. He continued his tirade to empty air.

"This will no doubt come as a real shock to you *Mister* President, but ... just because you *are* the President of the most powerful nation on earth, doesn't mean that you are *Jean Luc Picard* and that your commanding words can *'Make It So'*."

Here the Iceman paused, took a deep breath and closed his eyes to calm and collect himself.

Then Douglas Chandler, Master Strategist, sat in intense silent contemplation for a long while. Suddenly his eyes flashed open and his fingers seemed to fly over some slightly recessed buttons on his desk, the nimble fingers tapping to an unconscious inner tempo. A large computer monitor angled up from his desk top to the perfect viewing angle for him. The screen was set up so that only someone sitting in his chair could view it. His fingers now flew over the touch screen keyboard on the monitor. He sat patiently as the computer processed his request. Finally the results appeared on screen. He nodded approval at the results on the computer monitor screen.

With a couple of key taps, he cleared the screen and sent it back into hibernation, sinking once again to be a part of his desk top.

He pushed another button.

"Pearl, please come in here."

***

Scene 41

"Enter!" Wild Bill commanded to the knock on the oval office door. The door opened silently.

An incredibly beautiful woman walked through. William Lantern marveled at how Karen's sparkling silver green eyes twinkled with humor long before the smile came. There was an innate calm happiness that emanated from her. The kind of calm of one very competent and secure with who they were.

Their eyes met and the full lipped smile appeared, matching the warmth and intelligence in her eyes. He never could fathom her age. Her thick shoulder length hair was of a pale, beautiful, unknown color. An errant beam of light from a window touched and highlighted it. It seemed to change the color even as she talked to him.

"Eye Em on Red One Mr. President." Karen Lynn stated, her soft southern Virginian accent barely noticeable.

"Thank you Karen." Turning to the three people seated in front of him, he smiled apologetically and rose. "I'm sorry Lady and Gentlemen, but I have a call that I must take. Ms Karen Lynn will show you the way out and reschedule." Karen turned and smiled at them. "This way please." issued the musical voice.
The three smiled and could not seem to take their eyes off Ms. Lynn. They arose as one and obediently followed her out.

Bill Lantern smiled. Karen could have sent them over a cliff and they would have smiled. She never would. It was not in her, and that was part of her magic. She was truly as nice as she seemed. He had flirted with her shamelessly when they first met. She had responded to it in such good humor, and in such a way that he was not offended when she turned him down, time and again, until at last, in embarrassment and acceptance, he finally gave it up.

He remained standing until they left, then sat and punched a button on his desk. A panel moved on his desk and a clear red phone arose with a flashing light.

He answered "… Hello Eye Em, this is William … Report!" There was a long listening silence and then the eruption. Wild Bill lived up to his name at that moment.

He surged to his feet and screamed into the phone, "May the Almighty God DAMN that cursed Brandon Thomas to the deepest and hottest Pits of Hell and Damnation, Fire and Brimstone for all eternity! What in Satan's name do you mean when you said … *'He just disappeared Mr. President'?*" his voice sarcastically mimicked the voice on the phone. "How can someone just *disappear* from under your best Agents very noses? Elite at that! Are your Agents really that incompetent, IceMan? Do they understand what this could mean? I …" he stopped cold.

If anyone had been watching at that exact moment, they would have seen William Lantern's face reflect his surprise at himself for his total loss of control, as he paused for breath. He paused and collected himself, before continuing in a calmer voice.

"I know … I know … I sounded more like a scared kid throwing a tantrum than the grownup President of the United

States, didn't I?" Not waiting for a response to his backhanded apology, he continued, "I also do recognize that you know the ramifications, Douglas. Please explain in detail how the Eagle escaped, or vanished into thin air."

He listened for a long while in silence until the voice on the other end of the phone stopped talking.

"Anything else that you can think of, Chandler? … Fine. Fine. I'll call you back shortly with instructions. Good day." With that he hung up the phone and punched a button on his desk.

"Karen, please contact Commandant JD Powder and have him come at once."

"Yes sir, right away Mr. President." The phone went dead. William Lantern lowered his head to his hands for a moment and then raised his head and eyes to the ceiling.

"Why won't *that* goddamned *Eagle* … that little cockroach sonovabitch … do me and my beloved Country just one *little* favor … *and just die!*" the President whispered in anguished prayer to the ceiling.

***

Scene 42

"**M**ister President," the IceMan stated, "the Eagle has been sighted going into conference with the Czar and *all* the top Russian leaders, at their ultra top security compound ... Yes sir, we do have KOLD Agents and Elite positioned strategically, and as you suggested, sir ... yes, Mister President ... I stand corrected sir ... as you *ordered* sir, we doubled the amount of Q Agents that we had before .... Fine, fine, absolutely, Mr. President, I will continue to keep you informed. Good day sir." Douglas Chandler hung up the phone.

The stress was showing on the IceMan. His lean face was inclining towards haggard and he had dropped in weight. His eyes were red rimmed from lack of sleep.

Douglas suddenly stood up, stretched and then started unconsciously pacing the floor in an erratic pace and random pattern.

Something was wrong ... terribly, dreadfully *wrong!* The Eagle had evaded Q's best Agents efforts to dispose of him, time after time, after time, after time, to the tune of *five times* since he had resurfaced, counting the time with the Queen of England. All in the space of less than two weeks!

Six times, if he counted the time at the hospital! The IceMan slammed one fist into the other palm in frustration.

'How in the Bloody Hell was he doing it?' the Head of KOLD pondered for the *nth* time. *'If I could just figure out that, we'd have him!'*

The question that the President had kept asking him popped into his mind again, "And what exactly *is*, or should I say *has*, the Eagle been informing or talking to them about, IceMan?"

He remembered his humiliating response, "We have absolutely no idea sir. No one is talking, and by that I mean exactly that. I repeat, sir ... NO ONE is talking! We have tried everything short of kidnap and torture. We would have tried that, except that immediately after the Eagle left, security increased ten to twenty fold on all the members and leaders involved in the meeting. They have *all* gone into seclusion. And that includes all the Leaders, in every country that met behind closed doors with the Eagle. No one is talking *and that*, in my opinion, is a very, *very* bad thing, Mister President."

Although it *was* extremely self-belittling and humiliating, it did accomplish one goal. It effectively shut the President up! No longer were there any tirades about consequences and threats. William Lantern was no longer acting the role of Wild Bill. He was *now* acting the very real role of the President of the United States of America. William Lantern knew that something *colossal* was in *global* progress and he was stepping up to the plate and taking Command.

It took a lot of the pressure off Douglas Chandler and allowed him to focus more on the accomplishment of their goals, which was the destruction of Brandon Thomas and his daughter Angelina.

The other goal being the obliteration, or at the very least, silencing or suppressing the information of the COW File.

'No,' the IceMan personalized, *'not the 'Destruction' of Brandon and Angelina Thomas.'*

'Cold Blooded Murder *was more the accurate or proper term.'* Douglas corrected himself.

He sat back down at his desk and looked at the yellow legal pad in front of him. It was filled with notes and questions. He flipped to the last page written on. On that page were all the unanswered questions that he had listed in random order. He looked at the first one.

Why was Brandon wearing the same disguise every time he was spotted? That told Douglas that he wanted to be seen by Q, but that wasn't the answer he was looking for. He scratched out that question and rewrote it to read, *why was that?* And by that he meant, what did the Eagle have to gain by risking positive recognition by Q? So many questions and so few meaningful answers.

He looked at the next question. Did Brandon Thomas suspect that Q was behind the garage bombing attempt on his life? The IceMan was fairly certain that Brandon had no knowledge of the identity of the bomber, as the bomber had been a freelance operator. The Bomber *had* never been an Agent of, or affiliated in any way with, Q. He had only been utilized personally by the IceMan for discreet missions that could not be traced back to Q. The *'had'* was used in the past tense, because *now* in the present tense, that Bomber was dead. Douglas unconsciously shook his head softly and smiled a small sad smile.

The Asian had been a great asset to him on many occasions. He had never failed to fulfill his contracts, no matter how tough they were. And he never complained, about anything. Douglas liked that about him.

That led to the next question. Did the Smoke Organization know of Q's involvement in the bombing? Douglas knew that Mr. Smoke had *'Smoked'* him by the traditional leaked photos to the News media. Did Mr. Smoke obtain any damaging information from the Asian Freelance Terrorist Bomber *before 'Smoking'* him? When asked at gunpoint or by torture, the IceMan knew from personal experience that many *will* tell *all, and more,* in an effort to avoid the pain and oblivion.

He wrote a tentative *'No'* beside that question. Recent information confirmed that there were no signs of torture or struggle concerning the Asian Bomber. Douglas knew, by gut feeling and supported by the man's profile, that the Bomber would not divulge *any* information when there was any chance of escape. To do so would be akin to signing his *own* death warrant by Q Assassins. The information received stated unequivocally that the Asian was caught unaware, and by surprise, and had no time to react. The blood work showed no elevated levels suggesting otherwise.

Douglas was satisfied. He stood and started pacing again, this time *not* in a random pattern.

'Could it be that the Eagle still thought that Red China was responsible for the bombing that killed his wife and was dressing in a recognizable disguise to let Q know that?' Douglas puzzled. It

would explain his behavior. The pacing stopped abruptly and Douglas straightened his head as realization suddenly dawned.

'Of course!' he silently enthused, *'When we put out that rumor that Brandon was a* mole, *he must have realized that it was because Q's top brass thought that there* was a mole inside Q, *and it was the Eagle's way of telling Q that he wasn't the mole and was trying to find out who it was for us, while protecting himself at the same time. It makes perfect sense!'*

The IceMan sat behind his desk and his hands flew over the keyboard. There was the only one thing bothering him. The fact that it *did* make *perfect sense* to him. *'Nothing is* perfect *in this world!'* he thought as he waded though the reports, double checking his information and instincts.

When he was finished, he sat back and softly sang, off key and with joy, "and that's close enough to perfect ... for ... me... !" Still smiling, he reached for the phone. He now had a plan.

'It was time for the Eagle to come home to roost.' He smiled again, this time in grim determination, then slightly altered and rephrased the last part of the thought to, *'come home to* roast!'

He touched a button on the desk.

"Pearly Anne ... Please get JD Powder on line one for me."

"Right away, sir!"

***

Scene 43

"**I** like your new lapel pins." Douglas stated casually. "They have the look of hand carved solid gold." His eyes focused on them closer as they shook hands. His eyes lit up. "A right Eagle wing on your right lapel and a left eagle wing on your left lapel. Incredible detail! A genuine handmade Johnny RainBolt *signature* set. You could retire in kingly style if you were ever to sell those." he enthused, noting the blended embedded Native Symbols signifying the name of the Legendary Native Medicine Man and Shaman, Johnny RainBolt.

Commandant General JD Powder nodded slightly in acquiescence although he knew that they were not questions, but statements.

"What do they signify, if you don't mind me asking?" Douglas finished with a question.

"These are but one of *seven* pair of individually hand crafted solid gold wing lapel pins that were just recently presented to me in a private ceremony by the President and Joint Chiefs of Staff, in recognition of and to signify my Commandant General Status. One pair for each day of the week. I was told that when I retire, my replacement will be presented with seven pairs of them, copied from the molds of these." JD rumbled softly as he touched them lightly, absently in memory.

"Right now, Douglas, these are one of the only seven pairs in existence. My initials are engraved on the back. My future

Replacements will be wearing exact copies of my wings right down to my initials on them." His erect, gigantic form seemed to swell and straighten slightly, an almost impossible feat.

"I feel honored to wear them, IceMan. And you were correct; they *are* Eagle wings ... the wings of the soaring majestic Eagle Symbol of the United States of America." He paused for a moment in memory. Douglas didn't interrupt. He knew *when* to be a good listener.

The Commandant continued, "They were presented to me behind closed doors, in a private ceremony, so as not to draw attention at this time. The President said that if I wanted to, they would conduct a more formal and public presentation in the near future." He chuckled. "I told him and the Joint Chiefs of Staff, that I would never let the public see the lump in my throat that I had then. They all laughed ... I'm not sure why. I told them I thought that it was best kept *low key*. They also agreed on my suggestion that only the ones that *needed to know* would know at present."

"Congratulations Commandant. May you live long enough to wear them out."

The Commandant smiled a smile ... a *hard* smile. "I am a survivor, as are you IceMan. I expect to go through *several* sets of these."

Now it was Douglas who smiled the *hard* smile, only his smile caused a small coldness to blossom within the stomach of the Commandant. It was a new sensation that he would study later.

"To business Douglas." JD Powder announced.

"To business, JD. I have the notion that we can send out a recall and bring the Eagle in. I think that he still thinks that Red China was behind the bombing. No one has come forward to dispute it. Mr. Smoke helped us on that when he killed that Asian Terrorist Bomber and publicized it around the world."

"I am not sure that I am following you, IceMan. What makes you think that he believes that the Red China was truly behind the bombing that killed his wife? Word has been put out, by us, that the Eagle was a mole in Q, which is why every Nation and Country is trying to kill him for us."

"Agreed Commandant, but that was all just surface ripples caused by us. We created the wind that caused the ripples that escalated to become waves. Everyone saw the waves, while deep beneath the surface where the *true* things happen, is the place where *we* do our *real* work, unaffected by the waves we created above." Douglas finished.

JD looked at him for a moment in amazement and then burst out laughing. Douglas frowned.

"Have I said something funny, JD?" he asked curiously.

Douglas stopped laughing, "No, IceMan, you didn't. It just suddenly struck me how palatable you can make things taste." and his eyes turned stone cold, "I felt like I was being served Caviar instead of that hand fed Horseshit! We are very different you and I Douglas. I don't understand what you are saying. Speak in terms that I can *comprehend*. See, I know a big word too!" his eyes went round with innocence.

Douglas laughed. He did not intimidate easily. "Well, you'll just have to learn to live with it Commandant. That is how I communicate. It has worked for me all my life." He slipped into a southern drawl "If'n it ain't broke, ah ain'ta gunna do nuthin' bout' fixin' it!" he grinned unabashedly.

Voice returning to normal, he continued, "I don't intend to converse any other way than the way I do. If you need clarification JD, ask for it. Please be specific. I find it draining to read minds."

JD sat completely still for a moment, torn by his silent inner struggle. He wasn't used to people disobeying him. He quickly quelled his instinctive mounting rage as he watched Douglas sitting in comfortable silence, watching him and giving him the time to think things over. *'No wonder he's called the IceMan. I'd wager he could freeze Hell itself.'*

JD Powder instinctively knew that Douglas Chandler was a man who would not respect or react well to someone who was ruled by emotions. And JD knew that the IceMan was someone who was on the same side as he was.

'Plus', JD opined, *'with his connections, he thinks could probably eat me for breakfast and still be hungry for lunch.'*

He stood, stretched greatly, sat back down and smiled an easy smile at Douglas. The smile never reached his eyes. In fact, they got harder and colder.

"Understood, IceMan. I wouldn't want you to expend any extra energy reading my mind." *'Can he?'* JD mused seriously, surprised that he *almost* believed Douglas. Without missing a beat his voice grated,

"Now, explain to me why the Eagle would trust us enough to come in."

Douglas knew when to back down. Now was that time. He was surprised and that was a very rare thing in recent years for Douglas. He had underestimated JD and found that the Commandant was not a man easily manipulated or intimidated.

His smile matched JD's.

"Well my friend, it's like this ..."

***

Scene 44

Brandon Thomas sat, lotus position, in contemplation. He had been seated thusly for some time.

Something appeared before him that brought his eyes back into focus. Seated opposite him, matching his lotus position, was Charlene Thomas.

"Why it's easy to do this when you're a Ghost!" she enthused in amazement. "When I used to try this when I was alive, it just about killed me." She saw the flicker in her husbands eyes. Instantly contrite she blurted "I'm sorry Brandon. I didn't mean to hurt you. I know it must be hard for you to adjust emotionally to my being a ghost."

Brandon smiled tenderly at his wife's concerned look. It turned to surprise when he responded, "It's not that, Char. I'm perfectly fine with you being a Ghost. When you said it, it made me realize that."

"*That* what?" she asked slightly confused.

"What *that*?" he asked innocently.

"The last *that*." she responded laughing.

"Which last *that*?" he asked looking confused.

"The *first* last *that*." By now Charlene was beside herself with laughter. Brandon joined, no longer trying to keep up the charade of innocence.

When they had laughed themselves out, Brandon continued.

"It made me realize that many things have changed in me since the explosion, Char ... or maybe I should say ... inside me."

He saw the concerned look cross her face again.

"No, no darling, it is nothing bad," He saw the relief spread instantly across her face. He continued, "just different. I'm still me, but with added parts. It is like the explosion triggered a metamorphosis in me. I am no longer the blending caterpillar. I am now the Dragonfly."

"You mean a beautiful Butterfly!" she corrected spritely.

He smiled back, "No, definitely *not* a beautiful Butterfly. More like the Griffin of mythology, made of many different parts." He saw her start to speak. He raised his hand slightly to ward off her question or statement. She recognized his struggle and acquiesced into silence, awaiting illumination.

After an intense few moments of reflection and contemplation, he continued.

"It was as if a mask had been lifted off my face revealing a completely different face underneath. It was the same face, yet completed. It was like I had been a jigsaw puzzle with pieces missing that I didn't know were missing. Pieces that had been growing subliminally over the years that I was unaware of. Pieces that may have been there all along, but just not clicked into place. Does that make any kind of sense?" Still looking inward, he did not respond to Charlene's slightly confused negative head shake.

"Although I speak as if it were my face, I am really talking about the total me. The *essence*, as it were, of who I was, or again more correctly, who I am *now*."

Charlene understood that analogy, nodded and sat in silence, trying not to break his train of thought, knowing instinctively that something as profound as this could be lost if interrupted.

Brandon's face suddenly lighted up in an epiphany.

"No, not a mask at all! I was right the first time. It was if the explosion had blown off a cocoon that had surrounded me. Only the cocoon had become more of a hardened shell instead of a pliable substance that I could emerge from."

"Close, but still not quite accurate." a cultured resonate voice responded from behind Brandon.

Brandon became instantly motionless, curbing his initial reaction, and sat in silence as Damon Gray passed by him and dropped in lotus position beside his Ghost wife.

Damon continued, "I sometimes think that there are no accidents. I came to discuss how to save your daughter when I heard you talking to your wife." He felt the question and answered it, "I have exceptional hearing."

"What did you mean when you said, 'not quite accurate'?" Brandon responded quietly.

"You are an *EH* Brandon. The day of the explosion was your thirty fifth birthday, give or take a day or two." Damon stated quietly.

"Close but no cigar!" stated Brandon.

Now it was Damon's turn to raise his hand for silence. Brandon nodded.

"I know what date they assigned you at the orphanage, but it was just a guess. They were out by sixteen days. You were a small baby. An easy mistake for anyone to make."

Brandon now sat speechless.

"What is an *EH*?" Charlene prompted.

"You are one too Charlene." Damon smiled at her. The smile transformed his face. It changed from statue cold to that of a vibrant and excited young man. If she could, it would have taken her breath away. As it was, she was rendered as speechless as her husband.

Appearing not to notice, Damon continued, "*EH* stands for *Enhanced Human*, which, as I said, both of you are. I won't go into the details now, I will at a later date if you wish, but I will give you an overview." Brandon and Charlene nodded in unison.

Damon's voice took on the style and intonation of a Master StoryTeller.

Brandon and Charlene Thomas sat in rapt attention as a child would, fearing to speak and break the spell.

"An Enhanced Human is born with extraordinary *Talents*, *Abilities* and *Gifts* that *Normals* don't process. I call them TAG's, for short. They varies with each *EH*. Some *TAG's* are great some are small. Remember the tissue samples I took from you Brandon, when I was doing some tests on the SIM Virus?" Brandon nodded.

"I used some of your samples for other tests as well. Although costly, I also procured a sample of Charlene's tissue." Damon saw their faces go into shock. "Initially it was in reference to defeating you daughter's SIM Virus." Their faces cleared.

Damon continued.

"My genetic research showed that both of you came from a long line of Planned *EH Joining's*, or Planned Parenthood. My research also suggests scores of generations. When two EH's breed, their offspring are usually stronger in *Talents, Abilities and Gifts* that their parents, usually a blend of both parents with a crossover effect which makes them stronger. A popular myth that has been widely propagated, that *Talents, Abilities* and *Gifts* cannot be passed down to the offspring, is just that. A myth. Now what *is* more accurate is that when a EH propagates with a Normal, all bets are off. If the child *has Talents, Abilities and Gifts*, they are usually lessened, or diminished. But such is not the case with either of you. My preliminary reports and the final ones, show *conclusively* that there is no sign of Normal cross breeding in your lineage. Are you with me so far?"

They both nodded, again in unconscious unison.

The Master StoryTeller continued, "Both male and female EH's go through a change or metamorphosis every seven years. Five for the male and four the female." He saw the questioning looks.

"Females mature quicker than men, as in Normals." He saw their understanding and continued.

"Their TAG's grow subliminally, working their way seamlessly into every fiber of the EH's being. When the EH's TAG's have completed matured, if all circumstances are right, they appear in full bloom and the EH knows instinctively how to use them. Much like the cocoon you spoke of Brandon."

Brandon smiled inwardly at the recognition.

Damon's expression then clouded. " There are not a lot of EH's left in this world. The ones that *are* left are extremely highly endowed with TAG's. We have to be to have survived." Charlene raised her hand in a question.

Damon smiled and continued. "EH's have been hunted and murdered for countless generations by an Organization known as the EHE, which stands for *Enhanced Human Exterminators*. An immensely powerful and wealthy global organization of fanatics who wished to purge, as in cold blooded murder, what they consider a plague on the purity of the human race." Charlene's hand went down.

"They are currently no longer a threat." Damon stated with a quiet certainty. As if he was a mind reader, he again answered their unspoken question.

"The EHE organization is in shambles," he shrugged slightly, more a bulging or swelling of his shoulder muscles, "but who knows what may transpire. Instilled bigotry and hatred are emotions almost impossible to eradicate. Time will tell, but for the moment the EHE are rendered powerless. They have disbanded."

"I take it when you say 'we' that you are an EH also?" Charlene smiled the question.

Damon paused for a fraction of an instant. Both listeners noted the small hesitation. Then Damon came to a decision and continued. "Yes, I *was* born an EH also."

"You say 'was' as if you are now *not* an Enhanced Human." The Eagle stated with a certainty of voice that brooked no argument.

Damon did not respond.

"How can he *not* now be an Enhanced Human, if he was born one?" his wife asked her husband, confusion and frustration showing in her voice.

"I don't know *how*, Charlene. I just *know*." her husband responded kindly. "As you are aware, *Knowing* is one of my Talents."

Her face cleared, then clouded. She turned to Damon. "Is my husband right Damon?" She already knew the answer before Damon spoke it.

"Yes," he acknowledged, paused, then continued, "and no." Both Brandon and Charlene were stunned. Brandon was the first to recover.

Damon raised a hand to stop the questions. "Let us proceed to more pressing issues, shall we? Like what do we do with your daughter, Angelina and how do we affect her cure?"

Charlene jumped right in. "I have been thinking about that!" she enthused, "Well, first of all we have to find out where...." Her eyes widened, "What did you mean when you said *'what do we do'*..." Her voice faded off in a soft whispered, wondering, wishing tone.

"We have secured her release from captivity." Damon stated quietly. He saw their disbelief turn to belief. And from belief to relief. And from relief to the beginnings of anger.

He raised his hand and sliced it through the air in a cutting motion that distracted them for a second.

"If I had waited to discuss it with you, the one chance we had to effect her rescue would have *evaporated*," his hands waved slightly in a fluttering motion, "like *steam* or *smoke* into the errant wind. Plus you both are far too emotionally involved to have been of any real rational help. You could have caused her death with your parental precautions."

He spoke in a firm friendly tone that brooked *no* argument. They felt the *truth* in his words and their anger vanished like the *smoke* he had just mentioned.

"Where is she and why can't I seem to feel her?" Charlene asked, concern in her voice.

"Miss Natasha Gray." stated Whitner from the doorway, then withdrew.

Natasha entered, wearing a pale green dress with lavender trim, looking every inch like a little princess.
All three arose to standing positions.

Carrying her matching attired Dolly, she walked quickly to the group. She looked up at Charlene Thomas.

"Angelina is still heavily *sedated*? That is why you can not *feel* her." She looked over at Damon. "Is that the correct word, Commander, *sedated*?"

Damon nodded and smiled a compliment at her grown up talk.

Natasha Gray returned his smile and turned back to Angelina's mother, still smiling.

"She is resting comfortably in a room. If you would like, I will take you to her now. Brandon will remain to discuss his plans with the Commander." The last was said with an air of authority that brought a smile to everyone's face.

"I would like that very much, Natasha." Charlene exclaimed.

Turning she smiled at Damon. "I don't know how you did it and I don't care how many nations you had to destroy to do it! Thank you." All laughed.

As they were leaving the room, the two men heard Natasha stage whisper, "The Commander said I could tell you that I helped in Angel's rescue." She put her hand slightly over her mouth and whispered lower, "He said I was a good *implement.*"

"*Instrument!*" Damon corrected automatically.

Natasha jumped slightly, half turned and craned her slender neck to look back at Damon with pink tinged cheeks.

"I keep forgetting how good your ears are Commander."

Turning back she skipped into a run to catch up with her ghostly companion.

She giggled infectiously as the two left the room.

"Isn't he wonderful?" they could hear the girl child enthuse,

"I'm going to marry .. him ... when .... I .... grow......." The voice faded into silence as they passed from Brandon's range.

Damon smiled softly as he heard the "...up" and the soft peal of Charlene's musical laughter.

***

Scene 45

"**W**hat in the world *is* that beautiful mechanized beast?" Brandon Thomas demanded of Damon in enthusiastic amazement as he paused halfway down the steps of the jet. Damon smiled at his new friends excitement.

They were in the process of exiting Damon's jet in a hangar in another part of the world when the machine in question cruised up and crouched on the tarmac. Moments earlier Hastings had exited the jets cockpit to bring Damon's vehicle around. Damon and Brandon had stayed on the plane for a final few minutes fine-tuning their next Plan of Action.

Damon smiled. He liked the vehicle also. He responded in kind.

"That '*mechanized beast*', my dear Brandon, is *my* highly modified version of this planets fastest Production Car. I modeled it after the Bugatti Veyron 16.4 Super Sport. That beautiful production model is nothing less than a twelve hundred-horsepower version of the one thousand horsepower Bugatti Veyron 16.4. Similar to its lesser sibling, the Super Sport is best explained through numbers: twelve hundred horses at sixty four hundred rpm; eleven hundred and six pound-foot of torque; zero to sixty two miles per hour in two point five seconds.

"Oh, I should mention that the production model has a two hundred and sixty eight mile per hour top speed, making it faster than any other production car on the planet. All for the low, low price of two point eight million US dollars. Worth every penny I hear. This beast is a step up from that with a lot more bells and whistles. I assisted in the design and implementation."

He saw the question in Brandon's eyes.

"Yes," he nodded in understanding, "and a lot more expensive. I won't go into the schematics; suffice to say it can go from zero to sixty five in well under two seconds. Special tires grip the pavement with superior traction. The top speed easily exceeds three hundred ten miles per hour, with computer assisted suspension, steering and breaking at those speeds. As I mentioned before of the other, well worth the investment."

"Wow!" Brandon blurted, stunned. Before he could say more, Hastings exited from the drivers door, showcasing the machines true proportions.

"Have we time to view it?" Brandon enthused excitedly.

"Of course we do. The Czar is not expecting us until tomorrow morning at eleven." Damon smiled one of his genuine smiles, an *almost bashful* smile of a proud creator caught by surprise by the Eagles genuine enthusiasm. He took Brandon through the vehicle and explained everything. When he was done, Damon asked of Brandon, "Would you like to drive it?"

"Is the Pope Cath .... I mean ... of course I would." Brandon saw the smile appear on Hastings face.

Damon had seemed oblivious to the word play, but Brandon had the feeling that he was not.

And away they went ......

Scene 46

Later that evening, seated at the table, in the dining room of the plane they had arrived in, Brandon looked up thoughtfully at Damon as he cleared the table from the dinner he had prepared. Hastings met Damon at the kitchen entrance and took the soiled dishes from him. It confirmed in the Eagle's mind the comfortable long association between the two of them.

"You are a strange creature, Doctor Gray. I would never have suspected that you were a world class gourmet chef." He saw the half smile questioning look from Damon. A smile that accepted the compliment, yet wondered why it was given.

Brandon elaborated. "I meant that I am surprised that someone with your schedule and obvious resources would ever take the time to learn to cook like this. It is unlike anything I have ever tasted, and believe me when I state that I have tasted some of the best culinary cuisine this world has to offer. Or at least I thought I did until now. The tastes were subtle but incredibly delicious. Thank you for wonderful dinner."

Damon surprised Brandon by laughing out loud. It was such an infectious laugh that it had all three laughing, two of the three without knowing why.

"Oh, I *do* manage to squeeze in the time for the occasional cooking lesson *whilst* jetting around the world, playing the piano and ravishing all the beautiful young groupies who throw themselves at me." He flipped his long hair back dramatically, placing the back of his right hand on his forehead and his left arm pointing at the ground behind his arched back. A truly tragic looking figure of a man.

"It *is* hard, sooo hard ... but I somehow manage."

Brandon laughed again. "I believe you *are* exactly who you are *pretending* to be Doctor Gray, a Master ShowMan ... hmmmm ... no, let me rephrase that. Not a *Master*, but a *GrandMaster*. My illusory hat is off to you, sir." He went through the taking off the hat motion, then added a quizzical *"Whilst?"*

"The women love that word!" Damon affirmed solemnly. All three broke into laughter again.

As Damon was speaking, a small, almost silent, oh so soft *'pop'* whispered across the room, like an imaginary breeze.

"Alright ... what did I miss?" asked a soft female voice behind them. Charlene had just then appeared.

Brandon spun in pleased surprise. The laughter had covered her entrance to all except Damon.

"Just the most wonderful meal, Char. You should have been here earlier to taste ..." the excitement in Brandon's voice died suddenly, as he realized what he had been about to say.

Charlene just laughed in genuine humor at the stricken look on his face.

"I wish my timing could be like this *all the time*. The look on your face is priceless darling .... ooooh, and look at you ... why, bless me if you're not *blushing*!"

That took away what *could* have been an awkward moment. All laughed in genuine humor at Brandon's slightly flushed face ... even Brandon.

A look of distaste crossed Charlene's face as a thought crossed her mind. "Besides, it's a good thing I can't eat. Imagine what it would do to my figure!" She posed primly and did a pirouette, showcasing her new dress. It was spectacular. A twinkle in her eyes replaced the distasteful look. "Besides, I wonder what the Ghost turds would smell like when I had to go potty? And besides that, *where* would I go pott ..."

"Charlene Thomas!" Brandon interrupted haughtily.

All laughed again at Brandon's pretended indignation. When the laughter had subsided, Charlene continued,

"Well, what *have* I missed since I was gone? Please bring me up to date."

Brandon went into his debriefing mode. Succinctly he brought his wife up to speed on the rescue of their daughter by Hastings, Natasha and Catherine.

"Do you know where the Emperors Assassin is now?" she asked.

"No." Damon answered for the group. "It bothers me to inform you that I have not been able to trace his movements after the abduction." He saw the question in her eyes. "I had Hastings leave devices on the Monolith that would have allowed me to get a reading on the Emperor's Personal Bodyguard and Champion of China and mark him in an undetectable way to enable us to track him. He foiled that by never returning to the vehicle after he parked it a few miles from the Truck Stop. He must have had another backup vehicle waiting, which leads me to surmise that he somehow *knew* what had transpired."

He paused a moment to let that information set in, then continued, "It was a setup to have us take the burden of Angelina off his hands and put her in ours. That is why Angelina is tucked away somewhere in the Rocky Mountains, still sedated for the time being. She needs to be brought out shortly or she will suffer damage. Knowing the new situation I did a physical on Angelina. As I suspected, and found, Angelina has some almost undetectable *organic* tracking devices that were implanted in her. They were brilliant. I would like to meet the person who created them."

He saw the look on their faces and went back on track, assuring them, "I completely disabled them and will remove them at a later date. They pose no health problem. Catherine and Natasha are now with her."

"A little girl and a fitness instructor slash swimsuit model?" Charlene asked anxiety showing in her voice and posture. "Dr. Gray, do you really think that they will prove to be enough to protect her?"

Damon smiled at the *'fitness instructor/swimsuit model'* label that Charlene Thomas attached to Catherine Nipp.

He replied gently, "Your daughter has two of the most qualified and dangerous beings on this planet guarding her." The way he said it harbored no uncertainty.

Both Charlene and Brandon froze in stunned disbelief for a moment, then Charlene blurted, "That's impossible! ... I mean ...." She paused at a loss for words.

Brandon picked up where she left off, "Damon, I think what my wife is trying to say is that she has a hard time believing that a seven year old girlchild and twenty year old woman are two of the most *'dangerous beings on this planet'.*" He nodded slightly to cement his next statement. "With all due respect Damon, I have to agree with her."

He paused for additional effect, then continued, "I should know. As you already aware Damon, I am the infamous *'Eagle'.* I *know* who the most dangerous people are on this planet. Now the woman, Catherine may be highly qualified at what she does, but I seriously doubt she is a match for China's Champion. I am not sure anyone, including myself, is capable of stopping him."

"I finished Cat's combat education myself." Damon stated quietly. "I was about to go to the gym for a workout. Would you care to put my skills to the test?"

Brandon smiled at the prospect. "I would love to see what a concert pianist can do against me." He paused in thought, then added, "What are the rules?"

"That is the most difficult part, for you. It is to total defeat, not death. To assure that there is no question of luck or cheating involved we will go through a series of competitions, the first being armed, then unarmed. We will wear specially designed combat suits. Both of us with use the same specially designed weapons that will incapacitate the area where we are hit. Then we will proceed to the full contact unarmed combat part. We will be using special tear away clothing that will not restrict us in any way. Do I need to clarify further?' Damon asked with a small grin.

Brandon Thomas looked at the concert pianist opposite him, trying to evaluate what he had just heard. Dr. Gray was far more than he seemed to be at first glance, but to find out how much more, Brandon had to rise to the test.

"I am ready whenever you are." He stated quietly. He was not afraid of being beaten. He had never been beaten, even throughout Q's training. He knew Damon thought that he was superior. Was that the confidence of a good warrior or that of a talented untried student? Only the test would tell.

"Don't hurt him Brandon!" Charlene burst out in fear. "Damon has done so much for us!"

Brandon smiled at his wife's concern and responded gently. "Don't worry Char, it is not to the death."

Damon looked at Brandon with puzzlement, then nodded slightly and smiled in understanding. "No, but you will wish for it by the time we are through. I do not take this lightly, Brandon. Do not be so confident as to put yourself at a disadvantage. I do not."

Damon paused in thought and continued, "It is possible that you could best me. Anything is possible, given the right set of circumstances. A wise man once said that if he had to choose an ally with skill or luck, he would choose luck every time. No matter what, you and I will both learn from each other." Damon smiled again. It was a different smile this time.

This time the hair stood up on Brandon's arms, as though an electrical jolt went through him. Something, an *almost knowing*, told him that there was no way he could beat Damon. He had never felt that way before. He filed the thought away for future reference.

Smiling back at Damon, he nodded slightly, an almost bow of acknowledgement, letting the Master Pianist know that his warning had been noted and would be acted on accordingly. There would be no quarter given. It would be to *total defeat*.

***

Scene 47

"**B**randon? .... Brandon? How are you feeling Brandon?" Charlene Thomas was hovering over her husband, her face clouded with high concern.

Brandon slowly opened his eyes and looked up at his Ghost wife. He started to give her a flippant answer but stopped abruptly when he moved. He sat up slowly and looked down at his body in wonder. He looked back up at his wife.

"What the hell happened Char?" he demanded suddenly. "Why am I sitting in BlackStone, in perfect health, when I should be in a hospital in the IC Unit?"

"What do you remember, dear?" Charlene asked her husband solicitously.

Brandon stared at her, not really seeing her face, as he brought forth the memories.

"I remember it all except the last, Char. Being easily bested by Damon on all fronts, the weapons range and then being just as easily beaten to a pulp in Close Combat. I remember the bones being broken in both my arms and legs!" he looked in amazement at his unmarred legs and arms. There was no sign of discoloration or swelling. In point of fact, he admitted to himself, he had never felt better.

"How long have I been unconscious to heal this quick?" he asked in consternation, a new fear pulling at him.

"About an hour." Charlene announced in a matter of fact voice.

"That is imposs …." His voice faded off. He sat in silence for a few moments striving to recall. His replay abilities had shut down on the last part of the battle, the pain had been so great. He shook his head in amazement and sighed.

"Okay darling, tell me what you saw. My mind's memories are a little fuzzy at the end."

"He kicked your ass!" Charlene exclaimed, "I didn't think anybody could do that! And you are right, he made it look simple. Whatever he is Brandon, he is definitely *not* human! No one can move like he did … and no one's body can do what his did!"

"Damon is a *human* Char, he just isn't a *normal* human. Remember he talked about EH's? And that we were EH?"

"Why, yes, now that you mention it, I do! I do believe you are right Brandon, Damon Gray is an EH. Why didn't I tweak on that?"

"Because my dear, I see, now that I look back on it, that Damon was, and is, a consummate actor. Flawless in fact. He skirted the issue. Now back to what happened. What happened to me after I lost consciousness?"

Charlene's eyes went big. "It was the darnedest thing I ever saw. He picked you up like a rag doll, as if you weighed nothing and brought you to this room. You started to moan and he touched a nerve and you stopped moaning." Charlene's eye's closed as she remembered, and her hands started circular waving motions. "He started touching you. No, not touching, more like laying of the hands, if that makes any sense, like he was a diviner looking for water. Only he was looking for pain and disruption in your body. When he found it …. he … oh, I don't know how to explain it," she muttered to herself, eyes still closed, hands paused as if over a body.

She continued pantomiming Damon's movements as she continued, "My EH Ghost vision covers more of the spectrum. I could actually see Ghost tendrils of energy extend from his fingertips and into your body, reversing the damage he had committed."

Charlene's lips curled in a softened smile. "I even saw him fix *things* in you that *needed* fixing. *Things* you didn't know you had. *Things* that I could only see *needed* fixing *after* he had *altered*, or *fixed* them. Some of the *things* were physical and some were, aah … other *things*. Oh, Brandon, I don't even have any meaningful words to explain or describe it. He sort of made you complete, if that makes any sense."

Now she seemed to be talking to herself as she half whispered, "I don't care what logic dictates, Damon Gray is definitely *not* human."

She opened her eyes and looked into her husband's eyes. "He also took some *thing* or *things* out of you Brandon."

Brandon did a quick mental, psychic and physical check on himself. "Nothing seemed to be missing, Char, yet I feel that something, an essential part of me has been *taken*, then altered … or added to, if that makes sense, and then had been returned."

"No, not *taken Charlene. Copy Pasted* is a more correct or accurate term."

Both spun to find Damon standing in the doorway. Once they made eye contact, Damon proceeded into the room.

"May I sit?" Brandon nodded assent. Damon sat. He turned his head to Charlene.

"Did you tell him what I asked you to?" he asked quietly.

Charlene looked aghast, "I'm sorry, Damon! I forgot in my concern." She turned to her husband, "He asked me to tell you he was brutal with you to prove a point. He says Catherine is almost his equal in fighting skills. He wanted both of us to rest assured that our Angelina was in good hands," and then she finished primly, "and I for one *now believe him!*" Brandon could not help it and laughed in spite of himself and the situation. He regained his composure quickly.

Turning to Damon he spoke, "I believe you as well, Doctor Gray. Now what do you mean when you said *'Copy Paste' is a more correct or accurate term?*"

"We *'Copied'* all of your *Talents, Abilities* and *Gifts*, or *TAG's* as we like to call them, and *'Pasted'* them into us. As a way of recompense, we brought out and matured *all* of your TAG's, some hidden, damaged and buried TAG's that you were unaware of. You will also know how to use them completely. We blended that knowledge into your being as well. Think of it as payment for what we had gained from you. We also heightened and strengthened all your TAG's, your bones, and also enhanced your Healing Ability. You lost nothing. You are as you were and more. We have never had the opportunity to gain TAG's from a male before today. Thank you."

"You have done this before with females?" Charlene asked in surprised curiosity.

Damon did not answer.

"Well?" she insisted.

"Well, what?" Damon answered in a neutral voice.

"Aren't you going to answer me?" she demanded.

"Why?" asked Damon, again quietly.

"Because I *asked!*" she stated emphatically.

"Oh ... because you *asked!*" Damon emphasized the word 'asked' as she had.

"Yes!" Charlene announced in exasperation, as if it was obvious.

"And *why* is that?" Damon continued.

"Why is what?" Charlene asked in momentary confusion.

"Why do you ask?" Damon elaborated.

"To get an answer! What part of the question don't you understand?" Charlene asked in frustration.

"The *why*." Damon stated flatly, and before Charlene could respond, he added "as in *'WHY'* is it important for you to know that information?"

"Oh, I understand now! ... I was ... um ... just curious, that's all."

"Oh." Damon responded noncommittally.

"Well?" demanded Char.

"Well what?" answered Damon quietly.

"Are you going to give me an answer?" she was starting to sputter.

"No." Damon stated flatly.

"Why not?" she asked in furious exasperation.

"How many times have you had sex with a man in one day?" Damon asked suddenly, leaning eagerly forward for her answer.

Charlene's face darkened in anger. "That, sir, is none of you busine ....." Astonishment replaced anger as the answer hit home.

"Exactly!" Damon stated succinctly.

Hiding a grin at the look on his wife's face, Brandon spoke to Damon.

"What did you mean when you said *'We' Copy Pasted* ... Who are the *'WE'*?" He asked quietly.

Damon looked at him and said nothing.

Brandon grinned and looked at his wife and finished with, "Eleven times in one day and it was with my wife, Charlene!"

All laughed.

When the laughter died, Damon answered. Both were not sure which one he was speaking to when Damon answered, "Perhaps ... when we know you better ... perhaps."

At that moment Hastings entered the room.

No more was said of the matter as the POA came under discussion.

***

Scene 48

Damon was seated at his desk working on his computer when Charlene Thomas appeared behind him. Her entrance was silent. She had learned not to announce her presence to people who had Ghost Sight, (people and animals that could see and sense Ghosts) someone like Damon. She smiled to herself as she watched his seemingly slender fingers fly over the keyboard. He had taught her the trick.

"Hello Charlene." Damon stated casually, fingers still flying, not taking his eyes from the screen. "What brings you by?"

"You said no one would feel me blip into the room!" she responded indignantly, startled.

"I didn't hear you 'blip' into the room. I felt your *presence* appear." Damon turned his leonine head and smiled at her in amusement. "You do have a distinct *presence,* Charlene ... Unnaturally, yet delightfully, pure." he added as an afterthought.

"How *dare* you!" she sputtered, "How could you even think that?"

Damon started to speak, but Charlene interrupted quickly, "Never mind. Don't you *dare* tell anybody that, Damon!" She glared at him. "I have an image to uphold. I am definitely *not* an *'innocent',* that I can assure you!" she stated vehemently, stamping her tiny foot in agitation. "And I have been known to be *'not good'* a time or two!" She smiled and awaited his shocked response.

"I didn't say you were an *'innocent'*, or even *'good'*, for that matter." He stated mildly. "I said *'pure'*."

Charlene was, and looked, confused.

"We find that almost all humans are riddled with contradictions." Damon clarified simply. "You are not. It was not meant as an insult or slight ... or even a compliment, for that matter. It was just a statement of fact." He still observed her confused look. "An observation of ours."

Her face cleared. "I think I understand. You mean that I am pure like Yellow Gold and not like Silver Gold or Red Gold. I am still metal but of a different color, or mixture."

Damon nodded slightly. "Not even close!" he stated softly, negating the nod, but then confirmed it with a small chuckle, "but close enough in a very broad sense ... and in re-evaluation, it could be interpreted as a compliment, if you so desire."

Charlene laughed and added, "I think I will. Thank you, each."

Damon's face froze for a flicker of an instant, then smiled back. His fingers had stopped typing, paused over the key board. She *felt* the presence of *three* looking at her intently, curious and *almost alarmed*, but without any trace of malice.

"When did you find out," three *almost* identical voices issued forth quietly, "and more importantly, how did you find out and have you told anyone else?"

"That is what I came to talk to you about, Damon ... or should I say, *Mister Smoke?*"

His hands moved away from the keyboard and settled lightly on the desktop.

He looked keenly at Charlene Thomas for a few moments in silence, this time his face betrayed no emotion.

Finally he broke silence.

"Damon will be just fine Charlene." the three voices answered neutrally.

***

Scene 49

"**W**hoa ... slow down ... no ... hold it! Stop for a second, Commander." Hastings stated in confusion, holding his right hand up. "Can you please explain or restate that again? This time in a way that I can fully understand?"

"I'm not understanding ... what part don't you understand Hastings?"

"Wait ... let me tell you what I *think* I understand and then you can continue from there? Maybe my telling of it will help clarify it to me." Damon nodded and remained silent.

"Charlene came to you and informed you that she had just experienced a sort of *'Celestial Visitation'* and was told that, now that her daughter was out of enemy hands, so to speak, that it was time for her to move on. The *'Celestial Visitation'* informed her that you, *and only you*, could somehow take Brandon and her to ElseWare to be together one last time. And that certain circumstances dictated that it had to be at once or be lost forever. You explained that in ElseWare, with a lot of technical and paranormal mumbo jumbo gobbledygook, about how a spirit or ghost could, for a short time, become flesh under certain circumstances. And that this was one of those times. Charlene's ghost could become flesh one last time to be with her husband before she moved on. You mentioned that she actually gave you the *Celestial Visitation's* explicit instructions on how exactly to perform the task." Hastings paused and shook his head in confusion.

"Correct. Continue." Damon prompted quietly.

Hastings sighed, and continued "That is where you lost me, Commander. I would like you to start *from* there and speak in words that I can understand. Forget the process of the *Celestial Visitation's*. Carry on with the story, but please, mostly do Headlines. "

Damon laughed, "We do tend to get technical sometimes, don't we? Or should I say '*I*' instead of '*we*'? Golden and Garnet are not detail oriented." He saw the look and small smile from Hastings and laughed again. "I'm doing it again aren't I? Alright, let's start from there, shall we ..."

***

Scene 50

"**N**ow let me get this straight, Commander ... are you telling me that you had *sex* with Charlene Thomas in *ElseWare*? And that her husband, Brandon Thomas, agreed? That just doesn't seem to make sense!" Hasting expostulated in amazement. "Okay, now is the time to drop the Headlines and go to the Fine Print."

Damon looked at his friend in amusement. Hastings was one of the deadliest humans on the planet and yet was an innocent in so many other ways. He understood the consternation, though. It was *not* something Damon would have normally done. He went into the Fine Print.

"As I told you, Hastings, when I took Brandon and Charlene Thomas to *ElseWare*, it was for the purpose of leaving them for awhile to be together, in the flesh, before they said their goodbyes. We left them in ElseWare and returned to earth. Charlene contacted us when to return. Only *we* could have taken them to ElseWare and only we could bring them out. As you know, in *ElseWare* time travels *differently* than on earth."

He saw the look on Hastings face. "Rest assured, I won't go into that, my friend." He saw the relief on his friends face. "Let me start in when I went back to get them ...."

***

When Damon arrived in *ElseWare*, Brandon was dressed to return, but Charlene wasn't.

Except for her high-heeled shoes and makeup, Charlene Thomas was utterly and completely nude.

The high heels made her legs and butt muscles stand out spectacularly. The high-heels caused her back to arch, which she accentuated dramatically by sucking in her stomach and thrusting out her large breasts with engorged and aroused and protruding bright pink thickened nipples.

It was obvious to Damon that Charlene's body was still stimulated from their lovemaking. All in all, one of the most exquisitely *almost* overpowering and provocative pictures of *pure sexuality* that Damon had ever experienced. He looked at her posed body for a moment, and then his eyes rose to meet Charlene's.

When he had first brought Brandon and Charlene to ElseWare, Charlene had been attired in the outfit that she was wearing as a Ghost. Those clothes were now folded neatly on the floor. Charlene's thick red mane glowed with a light catching, unearthly sheen. Her pale translucent skin was flawless, void of freckles, moles or any of the normal earthly imperfections. Charlene Thomas seemed to have left them behind when she had passed on. Her *ElseWare* flesh and blood body was that of a woman in her peak, or prime, physical condition. It was the body of a woman in her late teens or early twenties with a figure that defied gravity.

"You rang, madam?" Damon stated in a butler's voice, as if nothing was out of place.

Brandon laughed and looked at his wife. "I told you that he wouldn't show surprise." Looking back to Damon, he finished with, "Well done, Damon!"

Damon smiled in response. "Alright, what is going on?"

Charlene relaxed her pose and smiled sheepishly, almost bashfully.

Brandon filled the silence. "Damon, Charlene shared some secrets with me. Some I knew, some I guessed, and ... some I did not know. Secrets I swore to her that I would keep, except to only those involved, unto Death and beyond ..." the Eagle reached out, put his hand over Damon's, and continued, "and I have *never* broken a promise in my life ... Mr. Smoke. Your secrets are safe with me."

Damon looked from Brandon to Charlene. "And what secrets might those be?" he asked softly.

Brandon looked to Charlene. She took over, "Damon," she answered with no trace of humor; yet with a kindness and caring in her voice that was clearly evident, "before we answer you, please answer a question from me. You never once demanded, suggested or even asked for a *Vow of Silence* of any kind from me, yet you must have known, or guessed by things I said, that I must have harbored information that could seriously compromise and jeopardize you and your friends. *Knowing,* which is one of my *TAG's*," she smiled a wonderful smile at him, "of your extreme protective nature towards you friends, my question to you is, why did you not, at the very least, ask for a *Vow of Silence?*"

"I had *not* that *Right.*" Damon responded quietly, yet with absolute authority. "The information you have, whatever it might be, is yours. I did not share any information with you that I did not want you to have ..." he paused for fraction of a second.

Both Thomas's felt Damon's struggle. Nothing showed that he made a choice, but they felt it just as Damon seemed to look at them both at the same time and continued.

"As you are both aware, I have *Talents, Abilities* and *Gifts* also. I trust them as you trust yours; absolutely and implicitly. That is as it should be. To doubt one's own TAG's is suicidal, an open invitation to disaster."

Damon's eyes lost focus in memory. "I had to learn that the hard way." His eyes refocused on Charlene. "A long explanation to a simple answer. The simple answer is that I trust you ... and as you probably know, I trust only a very few people in this world."

"Do you trust me also?" Brandon asked in the same tone.

"I trust your *word*. So does Natasha. That is more than enough for me ... Brandon Thomas ... aka the infamous *'Eagle'*. Although you have not asked for it, as I have not asked you for yours, you have my *Vow of Silence* that your *'Eagle'* identity will remain among Hastings, Natasha and Catherine."

He saw them look at each other and then back at him.

"How can you speak for them, Commander?" Brandon asked the question he and his wife were thinking.

"I asked each of them for a *Vow of Silence* on the subject and received it personally *from* each of them with no hesitation."

Husband and wife both nodded in acceptance and relief.

Damon looked at Brandon's wife and asked again, softly, "And so I ask again; what secrets would those be, Charlene?"

Charlene Thomas turned to face Damon squarely, thrust out her impressive chest and spread her incredible legs in an extremely provocative pose.

***

Scene 51

Hastings looked at his Boss in disbelief. "I don't understand some of this, Commander. Let me again tell you what I think I understand, and then you can fill it in from there, alright?' Damon nodded slightly once.

They were seated on a bench in the gymnasium where Damon and Hastings had just finished an intense workout. Hastings needed the workout to help let his subconscious mind assimilate the information overload that Damon had provided. It was a technique that he used successfully many times.

Hastings Held up one sweaty finger and began. "First you tell me that Charlene Thomas was *buck-naked* when you appeared in *ElseWare*. Your description brought visions, that's for real and for sure, as the young kids say today." He added another sweaty finger and smiled with and *at* Damon's smile.

"Then you said that she *Knew* of your *Ability* to absorb," he saw Damon start to speak, and corrected himself hastily, "I mean '*Copy/Paste*' a woman's *Talents, Abilities and Gifts* into yourself by bringing them to the Ultimate Orgasm, when all their defenses were down for that flicker of an instant. Correct?" ... "Correct." Hastings finished for his boss, then adding another finger, he continued,

"Then you said that she and Brandon had talked it over, and that Charlene had convinced Brandon that Angelina's best hope for survival was for her to '*have sex*' with you, as you so bluntly put it, so that you could Copy/Paste all her *Talents, Abilities and Gifts* into yourself, on the promise from you to do your best to help her daughter and her husband stay alive and healthy."

Hastings sighed and shook his head, "I understand *what* you said, but it just doesn't make *sense* to me. I mean, how could she possibly *know* that? I mean there is no way .... unless ...."

He saw Damon's slight nod. Hastings eyes widened, "Are you implying that she *witnessed* you making love with a woman and saw the Copy/Pasting process?" he demanded incredulously.

"She has *never* witnessed us making love to *any* other woman." Damon stated emphatically. He saw confusion on his friends flushed, perspiring face and continued "but she did witness *us* having sex with a few. And she witnessed the Copy/Paste *TAG* transfer from Brandon. And that was a strange experience!"

"*And that was a strange experience*?" Hastings mimicked in almost humor. "Really? Copy/Pasting a male EH's *Talents, Abilities* and *Gifts without* having sex with him? Go figure." The look on Hastings face was too much for Damon.

Damon laughed with his friend and replied, "Okay, okay, I know that '*we*' are different Hastings. By '*we*', you know I mean Golden, Garnet and I. We are who we are. Three beings who are *almost* one. I admit that we have enjoyed having sex with the EH females, but we had, or have, *no* urges or feelings for them ... well ... except for the *almost* overpowering craving desire to gain their *Talents, Abilities and Gifts*." He paused in thought. Hastings sat patiently.

After a moment of contemplation, Damon continued, "And that *craving desire* is becoming a monstrously *great* one, my friend. Approximating Vampirism, as you so succinctly stated before." Hastings nodded, understanding and believed him. "I now seem *almost insanely* attracted to EH females, since I obtained this EH *Copy/Paste Ability*. There are *not* a lot of EH left in the world, but they ones that are, are very strong in TAG's ... And I have this *FEELING* Hastings ... the *FEELING* that I *need* to acquire all the *TAG's I can*, as well as all the *tools*, *skills* and *knowledge* that I can acquire, to survive what I must ..."

He looked at Hastings and shook his head slightly, "I don't really have the words to describe it, my friend. If I could, I would ..." He smiled at his friends sweating, after-workout face. "Well, for now, let us move on to something else. Something was *different* when I *gained* Charlene's *Talents, Abilities and Gifts*."

"Different?" Hastings grinned, "I'm all ears, boss. In what way was it different? And don't leave out *any* of the details."

Damon grinned back. "I am not going to go into *all* the details, my lecherous friend. Let your imagination fill in the blanks." He went serious again.

"Maybe it was *because* Charlene Thomas was a Ghost," he stated softly, almost as if to himself, then continued in his normal voice, "but her *TAG's* were *unbelievably* strong, Hastings. And some are very different from *anything* that we have ever heard of, *or* experienced. Almost Alien in nature." Damon shook his head.

"No, I correct *us*, not '*almost*', they *are* Alien in nature. Their assimilation into my system was unbelievably difficult, and different, to say the least. It was the first time that I was so injured by them, that Golden and Garnet almost *didn't* hold us together. But they did and it did make us stronger, although the recovery time was the longest it has ever been." Ignoring Hastings intense disapproving look, he persisted.

"I am convinced that Charlene did *not* have those Alien TAG's when she was alive, Hastings. I have the strong *sense,* one of *our* newer *TAG's,* is that Charlene acquired some of her TAG's *after* she died. Charlene Thomas also has some TAG's that *she* was totally unaware of. I brought these to fruition."

"Are you sure, Commander? I mean, how could Charlene acquire TAG's *after* she died?" Hastings asked, lecherous thoughts gone the instant that he heard Damon express almost dying, in his calm way. "Is it even possible for a Ghost to do that?" Hastings paused as he realized what he had said. "I'm sorry Commander, I don't expect you to have the answers. The questions were rhetorical. Please continue."

"I think someone or some*thing used* Charlene Thomas, as a sexual vehicle, to pass those Alien TAG's into me on purpose. I also think that the idea to Copy/Paste her TAG's to me was *not* hers. I think it was subliminally implanted into her."

"Why did you do it, then?" Hastings asked curiously. He knew Damon was not the type of person to take undo advantage of anybody.

"Because I didn't know it at the time." Damon answered simply. He explained further, "As I explained, after I had Copy/Pasted, I was totally incapacitated for a short time, as was Charlene. That, in itself, was a shock to me. I recovered first and laid my hands on Charlene to make sure that she was alright. She was, but I immediately noted that the *Alien TAG's* were *gone* from her. That is why I am convinced of third party action. She awoke shortly, and as with the other EH females, with no memory of the Copy/Paste experience. She asked if it had been accomplished. I affirmed that it had. She was relieved."

Damon paused as a new thought came to him, then continued, "As I just mentioned, I think the idea was somehow implanted in her subconscious, but I am now also firmly convinced, by her actions *afterward,* that she was completely in agreement with that suggestion."

"*How* did her actions show?" Hastings asked.

"By the *kiss* she gave me before we walked back through the portal. It was unlike the other *EH's* that I have had sex with in the past. It was the most loving and passionate kiss I have ever experienced, Hastings. The other EH women wanted *nothing* to do with me afterwards. Charlene was exactly the opposite. She was warm and loving and compassionate and thankful that I would protect her family. Most definitely a strange experience for me."

Damon's face took on a thoughtful expression. Subtle though it was, Hasting noticed.

"You are leaving something out, Damon. Out with it!" Hastings demanded.

Damon nodded. "Something happened while were having sex during the Copy/Paste experience, Hastings. To *us* and to Charlene Thomas. We somehow *bonded,* in a sense. It went from having sex to *almost* making love. It was a true first for me Hastings."

"Are you inferring that this is the *first* time in your life that you actually made *love* to a woman?" Hastings asked incredulously. He corrected himself quickly when he saw Damon's look. "I meant, you *almost* made love to a woman?"

"I am not *inferring* anything, Hastings," Hastings looked relieved. "I am stating it emphatically." Damon finished. Both laughed.

"Probably a good thing that you had returned Brandon back to the Triangle Cave *before* Charlene and you performed the Copy/Paste." Hastings added dryly.

"Agreed." Damon acknowledged quietly, "Brandon might not have understood."

"Oh, I think he would have. He agreed, also." Hastings chided his friend gently.

Damon took it literally and sighed slightly, "No, if *you* don't understand, my friend, I doubt that Brandon would."

"Explain." Hastings stated softly.

Unconsciously mirroring his friend Damon responded just as softly, "Charlene Thomas could *never* love *us* the way that she loves her husband and daughter. Hastings, the love and lust that Charlene has for *us* is *different*. Our love for her is ... *different*, as are our sexual feelings for her."

"What do you mean when you say, different?" Hastings asked, genuinely interested and confused.

"Do you love Natasha?"

"Of course, who wouldn't?"

"Many, but that is not the issue. Did you love my parents?"

"Yes."

"My Grandparents?"

"Of course."

"Did you love them equally?"

"Of course I did!" Hastings exclaimed indignantly.

"How can that be? How is it possible that can you possibly love five completely different people equally?"

"That's easy. Because they are not the same, they are each different and individual. The love I have for each of them is diff ...." Hastings eyes went from confused to understanding. "Because it is a *non* possessive love, far different from mate love."

"You are a wise man Hastings. Yes, *now* you understand ... but would you understand if it was *your* wife?"

Hastings thought for a moment, then, in agreement, shook his head. "No ... probably not. Thanks for clarifying, Boss. By the way, did Charlene come back to earth with you when you returned?"

"No, she didn't." Damon said, a little sadly it seemed to Hastings. "She slowly started to fade as we approached the portal. She was dressed in the dress that you saw on her the last time you saw her, the iridescent one that was cut to the waist at the front and back?" Hastings smiled acknowledgement. He remembered it well.

"Even though she and Brandon had taken leave of each other earlier, Charlene stopped suddenly, turned and looked up at us with the most imploring look. She asked that we say goodbye to Brandon for her, and to tell him of her great love for him and their daughter Angelina."

Damon looked at Hastings strangely. "Charlene then said something that we shall only share with you, my friend, and only this once. This, we feel, needs to be spoken of, because we feel it is important ... It needs to be repeated ..."

Hastings spoke not a word. Although his face did not change expression, tears appeared in Damon's eyes and roll down his face, unfelt and unheeded.

Whatever it was, Hastings wanted to hear it.

"The last thing Charlene Thomas said to us was *'I am so glad that a part of me lives on in you, Damon.'* Hastings, it touched me in a place I have never been touched before. I did not know what to say, so I said nothing. She seemed to understand and smiled that angelic smile. We are telling you because that statement of caring needer to be shared with another, if only once. We *mattered* to her Hastings. And it felt *good* knowing it."

Damon paused a moment to collect himself, then continued. "She then turned away and ran for the portal but vanished before she made it half way there. It was strange Hastings, but I could have sworn that I saw something start to protrude from her upper back at the last moment."

"What did you see?" Hastings queried.

"I'm really not sure. Charlene had become so faint that it was almost impossible to tell ... for certain." Damon stated.

Hastings noted the slight hesitation and inspiration hit him. "What did you *feel* you *almost* saw?" he probed gently.

"You won't believe it." Damon stated gently.

"Yes I will." Hastings stated emphatically. He knew from experience that his friend and employer was seldom wrong.

Damon shrugged slightly, his massive shoulder and neck muscles writhing and leaping to life.

"We felt that they were the beginnings of wings." came the low response.

"I don't believe it!"

"Neither do *we*," Damon agreed, picking up a towel and handing it to Hastings to wipe his sweating body, "but it is what *we* felt *we* saw. Life, and even Death, can be confusing, can't it?"

"You said a mouthful!" Hastings heartily agreed as he wiped his face and body quickly. They both arose at the same time to go about their different missions.

As they were leaving the room, Hastings asked casually, "Boss, if Charlene came back, would you make love with her again?"

Damon turned his head towards his friend and both of his eyes started to separately kaleidoscope from Liquid Silver to Blood Red and then to Golden Cat Eye in a random, mesmerizing fashion.

"What a *strange* question." three distinct voices issued from one throat.

***

Scene 52

Brandon Thomas was definitely *not* having a good day. He had just survived being killed by agents of Q as he was leaving the Kremlin building. How in the world Q knew he was there, he could only begin to hazard a guess.

If it hadn't have been for Damon and Hastings, he would not have survived the assassination attempt. How they knew of it, he did not know or care. They did and he was alive. It was enough for him.

He was seated on the floor, lotus position, in his bedroom at BlackStone. He had asked to be alone for awhile. While nothing was mentioned, both Damon and Hastings understood his frustration at being caught unawares and had acquiesced.

Brandon was highly concerned. As the Eagle, he should *not* have been caught unawares, but the fact was, he was. The Eagle was no longer on top of his game. That concerned him greatly. It was absolutely unacceptable to him. He could be of no use to Angelina if he was dead. He *could* have put the culpability on his going through his last *EH* metamorphic Cocoon like *Change*, as Damon put it, with the addition of his new *TAG's*. But instinctively he knew that was not the case. He reveled and gloried in the changes it had made, both *to* and *in* him. The Eagle was no longer a *blender*. Oh, he could still be an invisible *blender* if he so chose, he had not lost that *TAG*, but his last *change* and new *TAG's* were so dramatic that he could hardly fathom them.

Damon had explained them to him. Brandon knew, on an *instinctive* level, what they were, but not on the *intellectual* level that Damon did.

At that time Damon had informed him that he had *Copy/Pasted* Brandon's *TAG's* while he was repairing the Eagles unconscious body after their personal battle. Damon informed him that it had been an instinctual action, that what had happened or was triggered *instantaneously*. He apologized and assured the Eagle that he had *no* conscious control over it. Brandon smiled at the memory of their conversation.

"You mean to say you would *not* have done the instinctive *Copy/Paste TAG* thing, if you had the choice?" he chided Damon slightly. Truth be known, he didn't care that Damon had done the *Copy/Paste*. He would have done it in a heartbeat if he had been in Damon's place.

Damon's answer had surprised him.

"*No*, we *wouldn't*, Brandon. If it had been anybody else, the answer would have been a resounding *yes*." He smiled at Brandon's surprised look. "We consider you our *friend*, Brandon. When we took on the task of helping you, your wife and daughter, we brought you into our circle of friends. You may or may not consider us *your* friend, we know and understand that, but we consider you *our* friend." Here Damon paused for effect. "And we would never take anything from a friend without asking first." It worked. The Eagle was impressed.

"And would you have asked?" Brandon asked curiously.

"Absolutely." Damon answered.

"And if I'd have said ... *no*?" Brandon *had* to know.

"I would have apologized and *then* Copy/Pasted." Damon stated quietly, as if it was just a matter of fact.

Brandon was amazed. "*No* doesn't mean *No* to you, even if it is a *friend*?"

"Not if it doesn't *hurt* our friend in any lasting way and can benefit us greatly. I *thank you* by the by. You have great TAG's. We appreciate them greatly. Would you like us to explain them to you?" Damon asked excitedly, leaning forward.

Brandon remembered laughing at the simple logic that Damon Gray had. The Eagle could find no flaw in it. Any anger that might have been generated by the act was dispelled as if by *Magik*. The true *Magik* of honesty between friends. It was because of that very *Magik*, at that vary *instant*, that Brandon Thomas, the infamous *Eagle* of Q, included Damon Gray into *his* circle of friends.

He reached out and touched Damon lightly. "I agree. Please *do* explain to me about *our TAG's* ... friend. Both new and old."

At that exact moment, the instant of touching, of contact, time seemed to stand still for Brandon. He thought he *saw* an innocent, almost childlike, look of *welcome* flicker across Damon's face; then it was gone. Maybe it was more a *'feeling'* than a *'saw'*, Brandon rethought later, in retrospect, but whatever it was, *it was real*.

Damon went on to explain Brandon's, and now also Damon's, *TAG's* in great detail. Brandon was mesmerized.
Brandon snapped back from the memory. No, it wasn't his new *TAG's* that were hindering him; it was something far greater.

He cleared his mind and looked deep within himself and still could not see it, yet he felt *so* close to seeing it. What was he missing?

Frustration was starting to set in. The Eagle recognized it immediately and calmed himself down. *'Maybe I am* too *close to the problem.'* was the errant thought that passed through his mind.

Like an epiphany, the light switch of understanding clicked on.

Brandon Thomas stepped back from himself and looked again. Still nothing. He stepped back farther. Nothing ... a little further. Suddenly he saw it.

The illumination of understanding dawned like a cloudless morning after a black and starless night.

Delayed reaction set in and his whole body started to shake uncontrollably. He had witnessed it in others but this was a first for him.

The loss of his Ghost wife was devastating him. It was affecting his judgment in all things, the most important to him being his daughter's safety and health, and that was unequivocally *unacceptable* to him on every level and fiber of his being. He sat in silent battle, striving mightily with all his TAGs, intelligence and tools, to understand, and with that understanding, the ability and capability to master and overcome. Now was not the time to fall apart!

Time seemed to stand still. Finally, after what seemed like an eternity to the Eagle, he started to come to grips with it. Slowly the shaking subsided. He now had a handle on it. It was under ntrol. A small handle to be sure, but a handle, none the less. He felt he could now function.

"Can I be of assistance?" a sultry voice asked softly from behind him. The soft caring voice of one he knew well.

He turned slowly, unbelieving, and looked up squarely at the smiling person behind him.

Into the smiling face of his Ghostly wife, Charlene Thomas.

Gone was his small handle on it.

***

Scene 53

"**A**re you are alright, Brandon?" Charlene Thomas asked her husband in high concern.

"Of ... of course I'm sure." Brandon stated, somewhat shakily. He had been stunned, almost speechless for an instant, then his legendary iron control was exercised. He arose smoothly and walked to a chair. He repositioned it, sat and stared at his wife closely.

"Should I go get Damon?" she asked in high concern.

"I said I was fine." he stated softly, not taking his eyes from her.

Charlene looked uncomfortable under that scrutiny.

"You haven't taken your eyes off of me. What is the matter?" she asked in trepidation.

"'*What is the matter!?*'" he repeated.

"Yes." she answered, confused.

Brandon shook his head, as if to clear it.

"Am I dreaming, Char? Is it really you?"

"Yes, it's really me. Aren't you glad to see me?"

"Of course I'm glad to see you ... but ..."

"But what? Is there a problem that I don't know about?" she demanded.

"Problem?" Brandon repeated her again, stalling, struggling, trying to get a *new* grip on things.

"Yes, *problem*. Is there a problem that I am unaware of? What part of that question are you unsure of darling?"

Brandon looked at his wife closely. She seemed subtly different somehow.

"The last time we were together, you said you had to *move on*, correct?"

"I know what I said!" Charlene stated in growing agitation.

"You said that you would *not* be coming back, *correct?*"

"I said '*I know what I said*'." came the same agitated response.

"But now you are back." The statement was spoken flat voiced, with no emotion. It was not a question.

"Finally!" Charlene stated, almost with a sigh of relief.

"*Finally?*" Brandon exclaimed, in confusion. "Finally what?"

"Finally you've moved on. Yes, Brandon, I'm back. I must say, darling, that you don't seem overjoyed to see me." Again the irritation showed in her voice.

Brandon unconsciously shook his head in frustration.

"This feels like an Abbot and Costello skit." he muttered, almost to himself. He looked closely at his wife and said very slowly, "Let's start again shall we?"

"Oh, alright, *if we must*." Charlene muttered, as if to *herself*.

Brandon couldn't help it; he smiled.

"Bear with me Char. I'm struggling here. Let me work this out in my way, so that I can understand, alright?' Charlene nodded silently.

"You said that you were *somehow* told, or *knew*, or *something*, that you had to *move on*, and that you felt the *pull*. We made love one last time and then I left while you passed your *TAG's* on to Damon." She nodded again.

"Damon told me what you said. Thank you for that." The last was said softly. Charlene smiled a *'You are welcome'*.

"And that you then *vanished* before his eyes and moved on." She smiled and nodded her head again.

Brandon did *not* return the smile. "What am I missing here, Char?" he asked in frustration.

"Nothing so far. Everything you said is as it happened."

"But ... you ... are ... back!" he stated slowly, emphatically.

"I ... know ... I'm ... back!" she responded in like. "And it doesn't seem like you are all that *pleased*!" she added irascibly.

"Char," he stated forcefully, "of course I'm happy you are back ... I'm ecstatic! I'm wondering, and therefore *asking* you, *why* you are back? You said you had to go ..."

"I know what I said!" She stamped her little foot in exasperation. "I know I told you I had to go, but as it turns out, *I can't.*"

"When will you be going?"

"I don't know." she answered in a despairing voice.

Brandon paused, shook his head and took a deep breath. "I'm asking the wrong questions aren't I?"

"Yes you are. Why not try a question that I *can* answer?" her voice rose slightly in pitch and volume.

Brandon knew she was upset, but could not figure out why.

He paused again in thought. Then, something clicked inside. Inwardly he smiled. The Eagle was back in control!

"Alright," he stated quietly, "Let's approach this another way, shall we? You don't know *when* you are going, but do you know *why* you couldn't go ... on?"

"The answer to *that* question, I *know*." she said, miserably. She paused and her head dropped slightly.

"Well?" Brandon prodded gently. He was not sure he wanted to know the answer, if his wife didn't want to tell him. He could feel and see her tension.

She looked at him with beseeching eyes.

"Because ... because I'm *pregnant!*" she whispered.

"PREGNANT!" the word exploded out of his mouth. "How in the seven hells can you be pregnant, Charlene?"

He took a deep calming breath, and then stated very, *very* slowly.

"Darling ... you ... are ... a ... Ghost!"

Her face darkened like a thundercloud. Her soft voice went as hard as tempered steel. "I *know* that I am a *Ghost, husband,* you do *not* need to remind me of *that.*"

She placed her hands on her hips and glared at her husband. "And just because I'm a *Ghost* doesn't mean that I am ... well, that I'm *omnipotent or something!*"

Here she paused again, as if trying to think of something else to say, then finally finished with, "and believe it or not, *husband,* I am most definitely *not* having a *good* day!!!"

***

Scene 54

"Wings?" Hastings asked again as they were heading for one of the small dining rooms for dinner.

"That is the feeling we got." Damon acknowledged quietly as they entered the dining room. "And we feel that we are correct in that sense."

"Doctor Gray and Mister Hastings." Whitner announced from the doorway, then turned and exited discreetly.

"Why does he *always* do that?" Hastings whispered to his boss.

Damon smiled and whispered back, "Because Natasha told Whitner that is what a butler *should* do in a Castle."

"But BlackStone is not technically a ....." Hastings paused, then continued, "but to Natasha it is, isn't it."

The question was rhetorical, but Damon surprised him when he whispered back "Yes ... and is, in the same way, to us."

Already seated at the round table and talking, was Catherine Nipp, resplendent in one of her gravity defying, breathtakingly seductive dresses, Natasha dressed in silver and Lavender, replete with her Dolly, and Brandon Thomas.

At first glance Hastings could see that *something* was vastly different about the Eagle. The last time Hastings had seen him, Brandon had seemed unusually solemn. Hastings figured it was his near death experience on his last mission.

The Legendary Eagle *now* seated at the table looked like a different man entirely. There was about him an undeniable inner glow of confidence and strength that hadn't been there earlier.

No, Hastings corrected on second glance; not an inner glow of *confidence,* more like light reflecting off a brilliantly polished and honed, razor sharp, deadly sword. There was no sign of the weakness or despondency that he had sensed in the man earlier.

Damon and Hastings sat down.

Dinner was served immediately. And what a meal it was!

***

Scene 55

Later they all adjourned to the Library at the request of Brandon Thomas.

Once seated in their respective chairs, Whitner provided beverages for all and discreetly departed.

All present waited for Brandon to speak.

Brandon arose and walked to a position where he could view all of them at the same time.

"If you would Damon, would you please call Michael and Sylvia to join us?"

Damon nodded slightly and touched his left wrist lightly with his right hand middle finger and made a quick design on it. Instantly Michael and Sylvia Brighton appeared, both dressed to the nines, as if interrupted in the middle of attending a Royal Concert or Play.

"Hello everyone!" Sylvia stated brightly. "You caught us at precisely the perfect time. The last curtain call had finished and people were pushing through us, like stampeding cattle, to exit the building." She held herself and shivered at the memory, then smiled.

"Their emotions and memory glimpses, as they passed through me, always makes me shudder slightly." Here she paused in reflection, then continued, "Although sometimes those memories have helped us in gaining vital information." She smiled again.

It was like sunshine permeating the Library.

All returned her smile. She turned to Brandon. "What's up Brandon?"

"I need to ask a favor of you Sylvia."

"Absolutely. What is it?"

"Can I have your Triangle Watch back for a little while?"

Sylvia looked shocked. "My Triangle Watch won't work for you Brandon. We tried it, remember? Just after Charlene took it off and returned it to me?"

Brandon smiled slightly at the memory. "I do, Sylvia. I remember it well. It is not for me, that I am asking."

"Well then, who are you doing the asking for?" Sylvia asked for everyone present (with the possible exception of Damon Gray).

"It is for me." Charlene's velvet voice responded from behind them.

She advanced into the room. Shocked, and happy faces greeted her. Sylvia rushed over and hugged her. So did her husband Michael.

Natasha impulsively jumped from her chair, and clutching her Dolly, rushed into the hugging melee. Everyone (with the possible exception of Damon) looked shocked, even the Ghosts.

Michael was the first to respond in word.

"I didn't know you could do that, Natasha." he stated in a surprised voice.

Natasha smiled and shook her head depreciatingly, "Aw, it's nothing, really! I can do *lots* of things. It's a small TAG, but it *is* a *fun* one." she finished excitedly.

She turned to Charlene and continued enthusiastically, "When are you going to have the baby, Charlene? It's a boy, by the way. His name is *Karman*! At first I thought he said *Karma* and repeated it, but he said *'No, Karma is a Bitch and I am Male'*. So that's how I know he is a Boy! How big are your wings going to grow?"

Natasha saw everyone looking at her in shocked amazement, with the possible exception of Damon.

The Eagle noted later, in memory replay, that Doctor Gray seemed to *almost* have a small smile playing at the corner of his lips.

"I'm sorry!" Natasha blurted in abject apology. "I should have said *'Welcome Back'* first, shouldn't I?"

***

Scene 56

"**T**hat *sonovabitch* has visited, and talked to, all the leaders and top officials of *every* major power in the world, even China! Why, just today he has been sighted in *China. Leaving* the *Royal Palace of the Emperor!*" Lantern screamed in rage. "Nobody even saw him *enter!* We don't even know how long he was there. Nobody is talking. *Why* in bloody blue blazes is nobody talking? What the *hell* is going on?"

Wild Bill Lantern was almost frothing at the mouth. He was pacing back and forth in the Oval Office.

JD Powder sat in silence. He was upset also, but knew enough to keep his mouth shut. Not that he could have said anything anyway. His best Agents were but rank amateurs compared to the wiles of the Eagle.

He knew, in retrospect, that trying to kill a man of the Eagles caliber was exceedingly foolhardy, to say the least. *'More like it was downright FUBAR stupid.'* was the ex sergeant's random military thought. He was always a little surprised when he slipped back into those old military thought patterns in times of extreme stress. JD remembered a psychiatrist stating that excessive stress has a way of making you revert to early life Primal Survival Patterns, when threatened.

Mentally he shrugged. *'What the Hell, they always worked for me before'* was always the response to that surprise.

The Commandant had never understood, or agreed with, the Eagle's Extermination Order from the very beginning, and he still didn't. Brandon Thomas had never given *any* indication that he would ever use *any* information to harm the United States, *even* with the mythical COW file.

But JD Powder did not argue with the Presidential decision. He never argued with his superior. JD *always* followed Bill Lantern's orders, as the President knew he would. He looked down at the hand carved golden wings on his lapels, and brushed them absently. Made expressly for him by Johnny RainBolt, legendary Native American Shaman, they glowed with an unearthly beauty. Looking at them, JD could almost believe the Magical Myths and Legends attributed to the man. He wondered idly how much longer he was to wear them. Would they be given to his replacement, placed on display or buried with him?

"Well?" was the angry question.

JD snapped back to the present.

"Well, Mister President ...." the Red Phone rang.

Gone was the blustering and posturing of the President. Both looked at each other in amazement. *No one* was supposed to be calling on that line. No one had called it in over sixty years. Presidents had used it to call out occasionally, but no one living remembered a call *coming in*. It was a secure line that only a select few had the number to. The Red Phone was a line that was to be used only under Catastrophic Circumstances.

The phone continued to ring. It had a strange ring, JD thought to himself

Finally the President shook himself and pressed the speakerphone button.

"This is the President. Salamander One Delta Two." He waited for the response code.

"Seminole Alpha Four Four Three Two." Came the calm response.

The President blanched. The response meant "Cataclysmic Situation."

"Continue." the Presidents voice remained firm.

"Mister President, this is the Eagle. I am calli ..."

"The Eagle? Is this some kind of joke? How did you get this number?" the President demanded, all pretense at composure gone.

"That is *unimportant* Mister President, and please do not interrupt again. I don't have much time." The voice spoke commandingly.

"Continue." Wild Bill acquiesced.

"Mister President, I know that Red China was behind the bombing that killed my wife, injured my daughter and tried to kill me because of the information that I gained on my last mission. As you may or may not be aware, the Emperor's Champion, Kai Akyi, kidnapped my daughter and has her in his possession, to force me to try to rescue her so that he can eliminate both of us.

"As long as I am alive she is safe. She is the bait." The voice paused for a moment, then continued, less confident this time.

"It is a point of Honor with the Emperor. And it is a bait that I have to rise to, Mr. President. I have no choice, if I am to save my daughter's life." His voice changed slightly, and the power came back into it. "But before I move against them, I have information that I need to pass on to you in person, Mr. President. That is the reason for this phone call."

The Commandant started to object, but a quick gesture from the President silenced him.

"You can tell me now, over the phone. It is perfectly secure. In fact, it is the most secure line in the world." The President announced with surety.

"Really?" came the humorous response. "Then how is it that I am on it, if it is so secure?"

The President was silent.

"Are you *absolutely sure* that you want me to tell you this information over this phone, Mister President? I happen to know with *absolute certainty* that it is *definitely* NOT a secure line. Note that I did not mention my real name when I called. Please do not speak it either. Note that I knew what passphrase to use to capture your attention. Therefore, know that *everything that* is being said on this phone and line is being heard by others *even as we speak,* Mister President. They don't call me the *Eagle* for nothing. I am the best at what I do. You, of all people, Mister President, *should know that.* I *will* tell you the information over this phone line, if you insist, Mister President, but once I do, it will be known by many, if not *all* of our countries enemies."

"What do you suggest ... Eagle?" Bill responded quietly, struggling to maintain composure.

"I suggest that we meet at Langley, your secret, secure Air Force Base, sir, at a time of your choosing. I do have certain requirements, though. I want the Head of the US Military there, the Head of the CIA, FBI, Q as well as the Head of the entire United States Health Care System."

"The last is a strange request." The President interrupted. "Why the ..."

The Eagle interrupted him, "Mister President! I am not sure if you are aware of it, but I have just finished visiting *all* the Major Powers in the world. Political and Financial. The information that I have discovered, sir, is of *global* importance!" his voice dropped in volume.

"GLOBAL, with potentially *catastrophic* consequences to our country, if we don't act *immediately!*" The Eagle paused dramatically after the last statement.

Silence reigned supreme.

The President and the Commandant looked at each other. Both recognized the conviction in the Eagles voice. No one spoke. The silence became deafening. After what seemed like an eternity, the President spoke one commanding word.

"Continue."

"I have certain demands that need to be met, to protect my safety, when we meet, sir."

Bill Lantern looked over meaningfully at US Commandant General JD Powder.

"Continue." repeated the President, this time with a smile.

***

Scene 57

"**G**OTCHA! You *sonovabitch!*" Wild Bill exclaimed as soon as he hung up the Red Phone. He looked over to JD. "That god damned *sonovabitch* is walking right into our hands!" he slammed his hands down on his desk to release more of his pent up energy.

He looked up at the Commandant and laughed, "He still thinks that Red China was behind his assassination attempt! That and the fact that the Emperors Champion now has his daughter confirmed what we told him. How perfect!"

Suddenly his face went dark. Very dark. JD marveled at the transformation. It never ceased to send a small thrill of fear tingling down his spine.

"I want that man *dead*, JD. He is *not* to leave Langley Air Force Base alive." He looked at his friend meaningfully. "But *not* until he has given us *all* the information he has. I, and ONLY I, will give the signal as to when I feel he has given all and to be exterminated. *Nothing* is to be done, under ANY circumstances, until *after* I give that signal, is that clearly understood, Commandant?"

"Understood completely, Mister President." JD Powder nodded affirmation and smiled softly in admiration of what he said next. "The Eagle's requests were simple. Brilliant, but simple. He even provided for *your* safety as well, sir."

Bill's face cleared up and he laughed again. "Yes, he did, didn't he? It's almost a shame that we have to eliminate him." He saw the surprised look in JD's eyes, and laughed again in high good humor.

"Just kidding, my friend, just kidding." He waved his hand in a dismissing way. "Go do what you have to do, Commandant General. You don't have much time to set things in place."

"Yes, Mr. President."

JD Powder turned and left the oval office.

As JD Powder exited the building, he paused for a moment and looked out over the grounds. He was now a man on a Presidential Mission. A Mission to murder a *MAN*. And to JD, a *MAN* in today's world was a *rare thing*. He felt that there weren't enough of them. He subconsciously shrugged his massive shoulders.

'But then again' he concluded, *'there never was and never will be. So be it.'*

Suddenly JD ducked, and dropped to the ground and rolled as a large caliber automatic hand gun suddenly appeared in his hand, as if by magic.

What made him do it, he did not know. He just *felt* that someone had just taken a shot at him with a silenced weapon.

He looked around *quickly*, then again *very carefully*.

Nothing.

Slowly the Commandant rose and proceeded to the waiting limo, his gun leading the way, only to disappear upon entering.

***

Scene 58

"**I**mpressive!" Damon stated softly. "It appears that Commandant General JD Powder is an *EH!*"

"How could you possibly know that?" the Eagle demanded. "Is it a calculated guess," then smiled at Damon's enigmatic smile. "or is it one of your TAG's?"

"A little of both. We are sure to within ninety nine point nine six percent." Damon *felt* the next question and answered, "The way the Commandant General ducked, dropped and rolled, when I used the *burst* to gather their conversation into the ring, should not have happened. That burst should not have been felt by anybody, the power is so minute."

Brandon Thomas looked at the ring Damon was talking about. It looked like a simple star sapphire ring, set in what appeared to be muted titanium; a tasteful ring that you could pick up in any expensive jewelry store. Its subtle simplicity made it remarkably *unremarkable.* Only extremely close examination would show that it was beautifully and exquisitely made.

It was unbelievable to him that the ring, just minutes before, had been attached, through almost invisible wires, to the integral part of a unique, collapsible and telescopic tripod flexible tubular device, with a circular dish mesh antenna mounted at the end.

The device that Damon had used to retrieve certain specific *information* stored in Johnny RainBolt's *golden wings* attached to the Commandants uniform.

Once Damon's hand had started to close around the handle, Brandon witnessed two monofilament wires sprout from the ring and enter into matching pin-sized openings in the handle. To Brandon, the wires had seemed alive.

That information in question being the conversation in the Oval Office that JD had just had with the President.

The Eagle looked at Damon Gray with new eyes. Ruefully, it seemed to the Brandon, he was doing a *lot* of that recently, with his new friend. Not that it was an unpleasant feeling; it was just that it was very unusual for him.

The Eagle had always functioned best alone. In this case, he knew he needed help, and was grateful to get it. He knew his limitations in this instance. It was personal ... he was too close to it. But he did not feel that it lessened him. It, in fact, empowered him. He looked again at his newfound ally.

The Eagle had *always* been able to figure people out. It had been his job and Brandon felt he was the best in the world at it. Damon Gray, he had already decided, was nothing like the image he portrayed to the public. Doctor Gray continued to surprise him on an ongoing basis.

Brandon Thomas mentally noted that Damon Gray always wore monochromatic clothing, usually in soft smoke gray, that made him almost invisible in a crowd. The Eagle noticed this because it was also how *he* dressed when he was on a Q Assignment.

'Interesting ... and delightful!' was Brandon's thought to that observation.

This and many other thoughts flashed and passed through his mind as the two of them left the high rise building, half a mile from the White House; where the two of them had just completed the *information retrieval* and takedown process from an apartment located on the buildings top floor. An apartment that, Damon readily admitted, was owned by one his many companies, along with the building.

Brandon found it more than just a *little peculiar* that Damon should have an apartment that had a clear view of the entire front of the Presidential Whitehouse.

What was even *more* peculiar was the way the flexible, telescoping, tripod mounted, broadcasting and receiving antenna was somehow connected to and with, an overhead orbiting space satellite that was somehow *invisible* to the US Government ... correction ... all global Governments, Brandon mentally amended.

There was a small LCD screen mounted on the tripod device that showed JD leave the building and proceed to the car.

Damon split and zoomed two boxes on the screen to the two Eagle Wings attached to JD's uniform lapels. The images were frighteningly clear. The boxes on the screen remained locked on the wings as JD Powder moved.

When Damon caressed the *send* button, the Commandant *instantly* dropped to the ground, gun *magically* materializing in his hand.

Hastings held the car door open as they entered one of Damon's oversized nondescript limos.

Later at BlackStone, in the Library, the three of them gathered and listened to the entire conversation between the President, JD and the Eagle.

***

Scene 59

"**G**OTCHA! *You sonovabitch!?*" Hastings exploded. "The President of the United States of America actually said 'GOTCHA! *You sonovabitch!?*' That does it! I will *never* vote for that creep again! *Ever!*"

Brandon smiled at Hastings fervent reaction. A warm feeling permeated his body. He had never had many friends, so it was a new experience to have someone, other than his wife, step up to the plate for him. His unique job with Q had precluded that.

Damon laughed, "What ... you didn't think the President was human, Hastings? That being the President automatically excludes all prejudices, like narrow-mindedness, bigotry, shortsightedness, blind anger and stupidity, to mention just a few?"

Brandon and Hastings both joined in his laugh.

"I guess you are right Commander, Wild Bill Lantern *is* just human after all. I guess I was but one of the many that bought into his media *'Legend'* hype." He mimicked the Presidential Campaign Slogan, "Wild Bill Lantern. *At Last! An Honest Man!*" Hastings paused as another thought struck him. "Will this change our POA?"

Damon shook his head, "Not in the least. This *could* prove advantageous in the planning and effecting of our strategies." he paused in thought.

Abruptly Damon stood and stated, "I am going for a workout. It helps clear the mind. Shall we meet back here in ... say ... one hour?"

"Mind if I join you?" both Hastings and Brandon asked in unison. The shocked look on their faces as they looked at each other, caused Damon to smile inwardly.

"Welcome. Both of you." With that, they headed for the Gym.

***

Scene 60

"**Y**ou'll need *more* of *my* help on *this* one, Commander." Natasha stated in her high crystal clear voice.

"And why do you assume that, my Natasha?" Damon asked her quietly. There was no disrespect or parental humor in his voice. He asked the question as an adult to an adult. An adult whose opinions and thoughts he respected and valued.

They were in a park and Natasha had been playing with some of her friends, when suddenly she nodded to her Dolly and made a bee line straight to Damon.

Damon had not missed the exchange between Dolly and Natasha. He did not have to question it. He never had. If he had, he would *never* have let her go on the Retrieval Mission, as Natasha called it, on the rescue of Angelina Thomas from China's Champion.

Natasha looked up at Damon with her pure lavender eyes that seemed to glow with an unearthly light. That she loved the Commander, there was no doubt. What Damon *did* doubt, was that it was a child's love for a parent. He *had* heard her say to her Dolly that she was going to marry him when she grew up.

That definitely did not sound like the love of a seven year old for a parent.

Not that he *was* her biological parent. She was the highly Gifted EH offspring of an EH female Assassin (named ShabNab at the time), and another EH male Assassin. ShabNab had killed the biological father immediately after she found out that she had accomplished her mission in getting pregnant by him.

Damon mentally smiled at the memory of how they first met; then returned his attention back to the conversation.

"I liked it when you said *'my Natasha'*, Commander." she piped, "No ... not so much what you said but the way that you said it." She tried to deepen her voice, "my Natasha." She failed miserably and giggled infectiously. Then she returned Damon's smile with *her* special smile. He smiled back.

Then Natasha got down to business. Her little face got serious.

"I don't *assume* it, whatever that means." Her pretty face frowned at the word, then it cleared, like the sun suddenly appearing after a spring shower, shining through the moisture-laden air, making everything glow.

"I *know* it!" she finished triumphantly, smiling up at him.

"What do you know?" he prodded gently.

"I know *how* to cure Angel!" she enthused.

Damon was shocked! And he was not one to be easily shocked anymore.

"You know how to *cure* Angelina Thomas?" he restated to clarify.

Natasha shook her head. "No, I didn't say I know how to *cure* Angel ..."

She looked at Damon expectantly, as if he understood. Damon said nothing, waiting for her to continue.

When she saw he truly did not understand, she spoke slowly, as if speaking slowly would help in his understanding.

"I didn't say I know how to *cure* Angel."

"Then what *did* you say?" Damon asked softly.

"I said I know *how* to cure Angel." she ended triumphantly.

Damon's face cleared. "Ah ... I am beginning to see. You are saying that you know *how* you can cure Angelina. Please explain."

Now it was her turn to pause. Then she continued, "Yes, I don't know how anybody *else* can cure what Angel was ... *infected? (Damon nodded)* with, I only know of a way that *I* can cure Angel."

"And how is that?" Damon again prodded, quietly.

Natasha smiled at him, *knowing him.*

"Oh, you don't have to worry, Commander. *I* won't be in any danger. But when I do it, I have to do it alone with Angel. Others would be hurt by what I will be doing. Dolly said I may *only* be able to do it once." She giggled.

"That's funny. Dolly sometimes says the *funniest* things. Why would I want to do it *twice* when one time will do it?"

Something happened inside Damon that only Natasha could see. He relaxed, his concern for her welfare vanished as if it never was. He matched her smile.

"Can you explain it?" he asked excitedly, leaning forward.

She straightened to her full height, leaned forward ever so slightly, placing one foot slightly forward, put her hands on her hips and glared up at him.

"*I'm only seven years old*, Commander! Give me a break!" Damon heard Hastings in that last statement, and broke into laughter.

"I will record it." he stated to her.

"Okay, but the sound won't register." Natasha stated matter of factly.

"It has to do with sound?" he persisted.

"Only part of it Commander," she responded spritely and with a big smile, "but I think it is a *big* part. And some of the sound is not *really* sound. That's what my Dolly said. She will be guiding me through it."

Damon nodded. "When would you like to do it? Now?"

"Oh, no!" Natasha stated in a decisive voice, "Dolly says to tell you that she will tell me when the timing is right ..." here she paused and looked at her Dolly intently for a moment as if listening, then continued in a voice of one repeating something she had been told to, "and then, only *after* your POA has been completed with Brandon. Dolly says that what *you all* are trying to accomplish ... is *very important*."

Natasha Gray giggled, "She sounded *very funny* when she said that, Commander. *'you all' (she repeated in a soft southern drawl).*" Then her face clouded again in concentration.

"Dolly *also* said some things about my TAG's, magnetic lines of force and cos-cosmological placement." she stumbled on the word.

Then her face cleared, "Anyway ... I'm going to play now! Bye ..." She waved as she ran back to play with the other children.

Damon noticed that the other children didn't seem to miss her and continued playing as if she hadn't left.

He looked down at his wristwatch and then back at Natasha.

'Hmmmmmm, Interesting'...

***

Scene 61

Langley Air force base: Tuesday, 12 o'clock high noon.

The thermostat registered one hundred eleven degrees in the shade. The sky was cloudless. There was no breeze. Plethora were the military and electronic eyes that watched as, what appeared to be, an expensive, softly muted, dark metallic smoke gray Land Rover silently pull up to and stop at the front gate.

Brandon Thomas, the infamous *'Eagle'* exited the vehicle from the rear passengers side, closed the door silently and the vehicle soundlessly glided away. None tried to stop it.

It was part of the agreement.

Brandon was not wearing a disguise of any kind. He was wearing a muted non reflective grey body suit that clearly disclosed that he was unarmed, sporting only his usual color coordinated gray titanium wristwatch on his left wrist and wearing his plain, ruby embedded, titanium wedding ring, now on his right hand in memory of his wife's passing. Nothing flashed on him. He was like a shadow, hard to focus on. Brandon looked down.

Handcuffed to his right wrist, and connected by a short thick flexible woven metal cord, was a small, thin, dull gray briefcase. He looked back up.

The Eagle approached the monstrous front gate. Silently, it opened for him. *'Impressive,'* he thought, *'a gate that size that was silent!'* As he walked through he heard nothing, but he knew that he was being scanned by every known device that the United States Military had access to. They were taking no chances on the Presidents life, or the welfare of the powerful people with him.

Just inside the gate was a table fitted with security scanning devices. He placed the brief Case in the slot provided. It started glowing, scanning the brief case with a superfluity of exotic equipment. The table was encased in a clear Plexiglas type substance, so that he could view the briefcase through the entire procedure. This was also one of his demands. There was a click and a green light flashed on the table, which meant he was allowed to remove it.

Brandon turned away from the table and commenced walking. All around were military snipers, assassins, and soldiers, just out of clear visual range. Most had telescopic rifles of all descriptions at their side, in the *'at ease'* position, ready to be whipped up and fired in a fraction of a second. The balance had sniper rifles resting on tripods, with the snipers leading the Eagle's progress across the tarmac through eye pieces of their telescopes.

Although the Eagle had been in some extremely dangerous positions in his career, this felt like this was the longest walk of his life. Everything seemed to go into slow motion. A spot between his shoulder blades itched intensely, like multiple lighted red *sniper* dots were resting there, tracking his progress. He resisted the impulse to reach back and scratch it.

No one approached him. None were supposed to. The Eagle knew *exactly* where to go. He approached a small, compared to the rest, thick, rounded, squat building, in the middle of a square. The automatic sliding door opened, as silently as the other, as he approached.

Brandon Thomas paused for a moment at the entrance and looked in. Then he slowly entered. He knew he was being scanned again.

Inside, the room was sparsely decorated, as per his order, with only one round table off to one side.

In the middle of the room stood the President of the United States and surrounding him in a half circle were the people that the Eagle had demanded be present.

There was JD Powder, Commandant General and Head of all the United States Military Armed Forces, second only to the President. There was Alex Wainscot , Head of the CIA; Roger Moline, Head of the FBI; Lawrence Quantrell, Head of Q; and last but not least: Stephanie Guilderas, Head of the entire United States Health Care System

Brandon had told Wild Bill that, if attacked or detained, he would immediately activate the instantly acting poison capsule that Q had implanted, so may years ago, *(to be activated in the event of capture and/or torture)*, and that the information he now had, would die with him.

What was in the brief case would be useless without Brandon alive and well to code in the passwords. The Eagle had told the President that he felt it was his *only* Asylum at this time.

The Eagle's flawless reputation preceded him. The President believed him and took no chances.

The President left the group and approached the Eagle with a smile of genuine warmth. Wild Bill Lantern grabbed Brandon's hand, politician style and wrung it warmly with both of his.

"Welcome home son!" he boomed in his Presidential voice. He placed his arm around the Eagle *in a protective way,* and walked him back and formally introduced him to the others as the 'Eagle', not once mentioning his real name.

After all the introductions and hand shaking, the President got down to immediate business.

"Alright son, as you can clearly see, I have everybody here that you asked for. Now *what* is this *vital* information that you have for us?"

***

Scene 62

Brandon did not answer immediately. He walked to the small round table and placed the briefcase on it.

"Mister President, if you would do the honors?" The Eagle, Brandon Thomas, looked to William Lantern.

The President walked over and placed his thumbprint on the fingerprint reader on the briefcase; the very briefcase that the President had provided for the Eagle with the Presidents fingerprint transferred to the reader. There was a confirming click from inside the briefcase, and both handcuff and case opened as one. That had also been the Eagle's stipulation. None present were to be able to open the case except the President of the United States. That was for the William Lantern's protection as well.

Brandon opened the case wider. Inside were eight Android PDA cell phone's, identical except for color. Brandon handed them out, seemingly at random, to each of them. When he was done he faced them all, holding the eighth one in his left hand. His was a gray color, matching his outfit.

"Well gentlemen, and lady, it proceeds like this. First you need to fire up your phones. Hit and hold this button ... Good! Now you need to hit the Red Skull Icon to access the Internet. Now click on the site that has been saved." Brandon checked all their phones to make sure they had all done it correctly. "Good. Now turn on the devices camera like this ... Yes ... good ...and now take a picture of your left thumb. Great! Now you wait a moment while your individual files load."

The smiles on their faces faded as soon as the files loaded and opened. The ashen look on their faces told it all. To a person, they pulled their cell phone close so that no one else could see what was on theirs.

The President was the first to recover. "What is the meaning of this..." he started to bluster.

"Can it Bill!" came the sharp retort from the Eagle. He seemed to be looking at all of them individually at the same time.

"In case you haven't figured it out yet ... I *did not* and *could not* have created those files. Yes they are part of the mythical COW file ... therefore ... I am *not* the only one who has access to the COW File."

"So ..." JD stated in surprise. "You *did* find the Mythical Cow File! I didn't think it existed. And even if it did, I didn't think you would have kept quiet about it. Your record shows your *loyalty* and *commitment* to the United States of America."

"You are right and wrong JD. Can I call you JD?" JD smiled and nodded, though sweat was pouring off his face. All the others were sweating, though the temperature was cool.

The Eagle was in full Control. "Let me clear the air. And I don't want any of you to speak or interrupt in ANY WAY until after I have finished. I will tell you when I have finished. Nod if that is that understood." To a person, they nodded.

"Good. Now where shall I begin? Oh ... yes." He turned to the President. "first and foremost, Mr. President ... I AM NOT

YOUR SON! ... Well, not that I am aware of anyway. Do *not* call me that again ...

"Next ... I do know that it was Q who killed my wife and injured my daughter in the home bombing, and that it was set it up to look like a Red China assassination attempt." He *felt* the surprise in the appropriate people. "This was done because Q had received information that I had been privy to the COW File. A mythical file that was rumored to contain *all* the dirt on *all* the important people in the world today."

The Eagle looked directly at the President and growled softly, in the deadliest voice any of them had ever heard, "You fool! Contrary to the propaganda propagated by Red China and now popular belief ... I *didn't* have access to the COW file *at that time!*"

He almost whispered the next. *"All you had to do was ask."* Again he felt the surprise in the appropriate persons.

The President paled a little, as the realization set in that he had tried to kill one of the most dangerous men on the face of the earth, for no good reason, and had failed. Not only failed, but that man was now standing just in front of him. His hand twitched for the gun on his belt. The eyes of the Eagle stopped him.

"As you can see, gentlemen, that is no longer the case. I found the Mythical COW File." He could see some of them starting to shake.

With no remorse the Eagle continued. "If even a *particle* of the information that you are looking at, was to reach the outside world, *all of you* and *all of your entire families,* would be annihilated. And I am sure you will all agree that I am stating it mildly." The shaking increased.

He held up his right hand. "Lady, " he nodded at the shaking Stephanie Guilderas, "and gentlemen, this Watch is also a Health Monitor. If I die, those files will automatically be posted all over the World Wide Internet. You and all of your entire families would follow me within the week."

"Now see here so ..." the President stumbled as the word 'son' almost crossed his lips, "I mean Eagle. I don't know what you are talking about. What do you mean Q tried to kill you? Why ... I'll have a Presidential Investigation into this! No stone will be left unturned until I get ..."

"Stop it!" came the soft reply from the Eagle. Bill Lantern was effectively silenced.

"Don't play those games with me Bill, or I won't tell you the *really bad* news."

The still shaking Stephanie Guilderas looked around wildly at everyone and whispered in a hoarse voice, "What does he mean by that?"

Clutching her iPhone to her breast, so no one else could see it, she turned from the Eagle to look at the rest of the men.

Stephanie Guilderas voice rose in volume.

"What does he mean by that? What the hell could be *worse* than this?" she quickly waved her phone and then quickly clutched it to her breast again.

"Calm down, Stephanie." The outburst had given the President enough time to regain some of his composure. He turned back to the Eagle.

"Alright Eagle. This information will keep you safe from us, but the rest of the world powers are still hunting you. Even if we tried, and used the best of the United States elite, they could never protect you from China's Defender." He saw and felt no reaction in the Eagles eyes. Fear tingled down his spine. "And I don't believe anything you say you can say could be worse than this. This *(he motioned his iPhone like Stephanie did)* could topple the Government and destroy the US in the eyes of the world. I think all of us here would agree to that." Bill looked around.

Every head nodded, except JD Powder's. Huge body tensed like a crouching panther, sweat continuing to pour down his face, his cold slate eyes never once left the Eagle. The IPhone in his hand was crushed beyond recognition, looking like a piece of scrunched tissue paper in a child's hand.

"Oh ye of little faith." murmured the Eagle. He held up his right hand, spread his fingers, and turned the outside of his hand to face them, showcasing the titanium wedding band surrounding the glittering eye clear oval diamond encased within it, on his ring finger.

"I am sorry about your wife and child." the President stated quickly. "We can help you get your daughter back!" he looked around quickly.

Everybody nodded eagerly, again with the exception of the Commandant General, who maintained his statue like pose, stone cold eyes glittering dangerously, waiting patiently.

The President continued, "Now tell us about this other informatio ...." he paused in shock as, realization set in. "The stone in *that* ring used to be a dark, blood red ruby!" he exclaimed to no one in particular. The President looked around frantically as if to find reassurance that he was right. They all looked at him blankly, again with the exception of JD Powder ,who stood statue still, awaiting his *kill order*.

"You are absolutely right Mr. President!" Brandon stated quietly. All eyes focused on the Eagle. "It *was* red when I arrived." He smiled a friendly smile at everyone. The smile, though warm and friendly, chilled each and every one of them to their core. Even JD was affected, although he did not outwardly show it. All present felt it. Brandon felt it in all of them.

None spoke, awaiting illumination. The tension became unbearable. It was the President who finally broke under the strain and whispered the question.

Sometimes a whisper is louder than a scream.
"What in Gods Name have you done, ... Eagle?" came the anguished question.

"This ring is special." Brandon stated, as if he hadn't heard the question.

"This special ring was specifically made, just for me." He turned his hand in a way that seemed to mesmerize everybody. Their eyes were glued to the ring.

"It is an almost exact copy of my wedding ring. When I shook hands with all of you, this *special* ring secreted an instantaneous numbing solution. A solution that masked the needle that punctured your skin and deposited a small amount of the red solution into you bodies." They stood spellbound, all leaning slightly forward, as if they were hearing the best story ever told and did not want to speak so that they would miss nothing.

Brandon Thomas paused again. The infamous Eagle was still in perfect control, surpassing his legend.

"The red liquid that all of you now have in your system is nothing more than a small amount of blood." He felt the disbelief and confusion mixing in their nervous systems.

"That blood is the last of a vial of blood that I took from my daughters arm when I last saw her in the hospital." He saw the look of dawning comprehension on some of their faces. He clarified for the rest.

"That was just after I had been informed that my seven year old daughter had *accidently* been infected with a bag of blood containing the SIM virus. The deadly toxic SIMIAN virus that kills *all* within six weeks to a few months of infection."

The look of total disbelief that was on all their faces changed to belief.

All started speaking at once.

The Eagle raised his hand and made a sharp cutting gesture and silence reigned supreme again.

Wild Bill didn't look so wild now.

JD Powder looked slowly down at his hand and felt a new sensation. Fighting a man did not faze him. JD Powder was afraid of no man, but this was not a man. What JD Powder felt was terror. It immobilized him for a moment.

He looked up at the Eagle with pleading eyes, as if to say, *"This is a joke, right?"* They all had that look.

The look in Powders eyes changed as realization set in. Gone were the cold stone soulless eyes. Insanity now flared in them. He unconsciously set himself to attack Brandon.

Brandon recognized it before it happened. He had been waiting for it. He turned and looked fully into JD's eyes and whispered, "Go for it, JD! Do it now! *Please!*"

The insanity in JD Powder vanished as if it never existed. As was his intent to attack and kill the Eagle.

The look that the Commandant General saw in the Eagles eyes was *not* the *threat* of death. Threats meant less than nothing to him. To JD, death threats were meaningless, laughable. That would *never* have stopped him. Nor was it the look of insanity. He had faced both many times without flinching. He had even laughed at some. JD knew without doubt that the Eagle's look was not one of insanity.

No ... this look was different than anything that he had ever experienced. In fact, it was not a *look* at all. It was the entity DEATH staring back at him. CERTAIN DEATH. JD Powder's death.

It was DEATH itself looking the Commandant back in the face that took away his insanity as if it never was.

Until that very moment he had never considered *death* as the entity DEATH. All his formidable strength and speed and quickness of mind were as *nothing* before that FORCE of nature.

Something inside him told Powder he would never be the same again. JD Powder now felt lessened ... *mortal.*

With one exception, none present noted the mask he erected to hide his feeling of vulnerability. They were all dealing with their own Issues. It was doubtful that they even noticed the exchange.

The lone exception was the Eagle.

Dismissing JD, the Eagle turned his head, eyes and attention back to Wild Bill.

"Mister President," he continued as if nothing had occurred, nodding to the rest, as if to include them, "you are *not* the *only ones* infected with the SIM virus. *Without exception*, every major Power Figure in the world is now infected."

He saw the looks of disbelief. "You have received messages from your Agents in the last few days that the Eagle was seen *leaving every major government building in the world* and had been in contact with all heads of Power, is that not so?"

William Lantern nodded absently, his mind still in shock.

"You are the last. I have infected the heads and leaders of every major country in the world. When I infected the first, they were more than happy to set up meetings with other countries leaders for me to infect, in hopes of finding a cure. They kept the knowledge of their own infection secret. Their very lives depended on it. You will each be getting a call from your counterparts from the other countries shortly to bring you up to date on their progress."

He looked hard at the President. "You, Mister President, will be receiving a call within moments, from the Czar, to confirm my statements."

Suddenly, the Eagle seemed to vanish from his face and Brandon Thomas surfaced and smiled. "Lady and gentlemen, find a cure for my daughter. You will all be heroes if you do. I have faith in you." He looked at his watch. "I must depart now or what you have in your hands will be broadcast world wide."

He looked directly at JD Powder and added, "Please do not try to stop or detain me. I am on a time schedule. I need to report in within a certain time to deactivate the COW File release."

He turned to leave and then paused and turned again to speak directly to the President enunciating each word and sounding exactly *like* the President,

"GOTCHA ... *you sonovabitch!*"

William Lantern's face went grey with shock. His nature was such that, being untrustworthy himself, he never fully trusted anyone. He felt everyone was like him, always after the BBD *(Bigger Better Deal)*.He instinctively turned, looked over and glared at JD Powder.

Powder was the only one in the Oval office with him at the time he said those words. It could *only* have come from JD Powder, the United States Military Commandant General.

Gone in an instant were the years of trust. The seed that had just been sown in the Presidents fertile and always distrusting mind, by the Eagle, had grown to full bloom in that flicker of an instant. Rage and Vengeance took its place. It showed on Lantern's face in that flicker of an instant and then was gone.

The Commandant General just returned his stare. JD saw the flicker in the Presidents eyes and recognized it for what it was. Powder knew that he was now in the Eagle's shoes, but without any COW file to protect him.

JD Powder knew his life was over, that it was just a matter of time. He knew he could never convince the President that he had not repeated that conversation in the Oval Office.

'*Hell,*' he thought realistically and fatalistically, '*I wouldn't even be able to convince* myself!"

With that fatalism came a small, hard, inward smile. *"It ain't over 'til the fat lady sings. I guess it is about time to make a few plans of my own.'*

As the Eagle turned to leave the building, the i Phone in the Presidents hand rang. The stunned and angry President answered automatically.

Pre-programmed, it automatically came on speakerphone, so all present heard.

"Mister President," the Czars distinct voice boomed, "vee need to talk ....."

The voice faded as the Eagle exited building, and the compound, with no interference.

***

Scene 63

Brandon Thomas looked hard at his new friend. He didn't have many friends. In point of fact, before now, his wife, Charlene Thomas had been his only *real* friend, Brandon realized suddenly, in shock! He had never really thought of it before. His particular line of work precluded any and all real friends. He admitted to himself that he did have business associates, but that was all they were to him.

His new friend looked back at him without expression.

"'*Thank you*' seems like such small recompense for all that you and your friends and associates have done Damon. I won't ask you how you acquired access to the mythical COW File." He saw the suggestion of a small *almost smile* that seemed to *almost* tug at the corners of Damon's full lips. Brandon could not be sure. "But as sure as your shooting, it saved my bacon. I would have been fried. Without it, I would never have left that facility alive."

That brought a real smile to Damon's face. "As sure as your shooting? Bacon? Fried?"

"Well, I've never seen you miss. And the rest ... well they are each ... just an expression." Brandon supplied.

"I know, I have just *never* heard them actually used." responded Damon with a smile.

"What can I say, I love old movies and I love to read. And Readers are Leaders, they say."

"I talked to *They* and *They* claimed he never said that at all! *They* said it was *Them* that just made it up one day, and then pinned it on *They*! *They* said he was getting tired of *Them* abusing him all the time." Damon responded seriously and then paused as if in thought. "*They* did say that he wished he *did* say that one though. *They* said it had the *Ring of Truth* to it. And you know how *They* love rings!"

Brandon couldn't stop himself, he started to laugh.

"What are you laughing about, Daddy?" came a small musical childish voice behind him.

Brandon spun as if attacked. Coming through the doorway was none other than Angelina Thomas, looking as pretty as a picture. She was wearing one of Natasha's plum colored dresses and it fit her beautifully.

Beside her walked Natasha Gray in a Coordinating lavender outfit, replete with a matching Dolly under one of her arms. They were almost identical in height and size. Both were wearing feathery hats and looking very sophisticated.

Brandon looked back at Damon. Damon's face gave away nothing.

"Is she alright? Is Angelina cured?" the words poured out of his mouth without Brandon even being aware of it.

"You are asking the wrong person, friend. You will have to ask Natasha." Damon responded with a smile in his voice.

Brandon turned back to the two girls as they approached. From the look on Natasha's face he didn't need to ask. She was beaming a beautiful smile at him.

"Thank you, Natasha." Brandon said helplessly.

"You are very welcome, Mister Thomas!" came a soft high woman's voice out of Natasha. "I am not supposed to talk much until my vocal cords heal. The Commander said he wouldn't have to heal them, that they would heal all on their ..." she looked up at Damon looking at her and then finished very softly, "own." She gave Brandon a big smile and primly curtsied her *final* acceptance of his *thank you.*

She leaned down and seemed to listen to her Dolly. She smiled at her Dolly, and then raised her hand to her neck and felt it. She nodded again to her Dolly and spoke.

"My Dolly says my voice is fine now!" said the voice that was that of Natasha, but with more resonance in it than before. "Better, in fact!" she said excitedly.

"Now I can tell you how I fixed Angel. She told me to call her Angel. She said that only *you* call her Angelina."

She looked sternly at Brandon. "You've got to get with it!" She piped. "She's only a kid!" she giggled. "You can call her *Angelina* when she grows up!"

Brandon smiled and shook his head slightly, "I'm afraid not Natasha," he said kindly. "As her father, I have an obligation to call her Angelina so that she won't forget who she is." he finished solemnly.

Natasha bent and listened to her Dolly and nodded.

She then straightened up and looked up at Brandon and stated clearly.

"Dolly says you are joking, but that what you say is true. She says for you to remember what you told me. And that you are a wise man and don't know it!" she finished proudly, as if it was a rehearsed speech that went off as planned.

Then Angelina Thomas ran into her father's gathering arms. No more words were said for awhile.

None present *could* speak.

***

Scene 64

Later that night, as Brandon was tucking her in, Angel looked at her father and said, "I had a dream when I was asleep for so long. Can you explain dreams, daddy?" she asked in a curious voice.

"Well ...." stumbled her father.

"If he can't, maybe I can!" came a voice behind Angelina.

"Mommy!" shouted Angelina, spinning around and jumping out of bed and throwing herself at her mother.

"I was afraid to ask about you! You are ali ..... you're pregnant and have wings!" Angelina went sailing through her mother. She staggered to a stop.

"You are a Ghost also? How long was I asleep?" she asked in concern. "I feel like Sleeping Beauty." Fear started to cross her young features.

Charlene read the look and responded.

"I am all those things, and I am still your mother, young lady. Back to bed!" Charlene finished in mock anger.

Angelina lost her fear and giggled. That was *definitely* her MOTHER speaking. She ran and hopped back into bed.

"Okay, what is this dream you had?" Charlene asked her daughter.

Angelina fluffed the pillows and settled herself comfortably under the covers. She looked at her parents, took a deep breath and began.

"Well, I dreamed I was watching a young man walking down the middle of a Golden road."

"Well ..." began her father.

"No ... not yet Daddy! It is a long dream. I will tell you when it is over."

"Oh ... okay. Continue." he said in a mock abashed voice. Then his face went serious.

"I remember it very clearly ... well, mostly. Here goes:

***

Scene 65

young man was walking down the middle of a Golden Road. He came to a set of golden stairs that spiraled up the side of a mountain. At the top of the mountain was the most beautiful golden palace that you can *ever* imagine.

It was so high up it looked like it was in Heaven.

The young man ... I didn't know what his real name was at that time so I will call him Boy ... you will see why later.

Anyway ... Boy started to climb the stairs. After awhile he came around a large boulder and approaches a huge golden gate set into, and between, a large natural cleft in the mountain.

There were two big muscular men there with thick, black, bushy beards that were well trimmed. They looked like identical twins. They were dressed in golden armor and had golden swords. That is how I knew that Boy was young. He had no hair on his face.

Boy looked through the gates and saw more twins lining the golden steps, one on each side of the steps, going up the mountain until lost in the distance.

One of the Guards stepped forward with his hand on his sword to the young man, "Why are you here?" came a voice like thunder out of the Golden Soldiers mouth.

"To go up to the Golden Palace, of course."

"Are you a Righteous Man? You don't look like a Righteous Man. In fact, you look hardly more than a Boy."

"A Righteous Man?" Boy repeated. "What is a Righteous Man?" Boy asked.

"Do you *not* know what a Righteous Man is?" demanded the guard.

"I am not sure I do." responded Boy politely. "What is a Righteous Man, kind sir? Can you explain it to me?"

The golden guard looked down at Boy. *(Angel smiled at her parents smugly.)*

That was because the golden guard was standing on the step above Boy. They were actually about the same height. The guards were just more muscle-ee.

(Brandon and Charlene smiled but did not interrupt.)

"A Righteous Man, or Righteous Woman are the only ones who can enter the Golden Gate to have an audience with the Emperor. Boy," he growled in a dangerous voice, "no one goes up the Golden Stairs without being a Righteous Man or Woman."

The guard looked at Boy with distain. Boy was clean and passably dressed in old faded clothes and boots. He wore a sword at his hip, encased in a battered sheath. The plain handle on the sword showed much use, as if passed down from generation to generation. It looked very, very old but clean and well cared for, just like Boy's clothes. The clothes looked slightly big on him as did the sword belt, but Boy wore them well, as if long accustomed to them. The leather food pouch that hung from his shoulder looked depleted, but the water skin was full. A guitar like stringed instrument hung from his other shoulder by a leather strap. They too were very old, yet beautifully cared for.

"How do you know who are Righteous People?" Boy asked in amazement.

The guard laughed in genuine good humor.

"Righteous People have a letter from the Righteous Center in the heart of the city behind you. Every Righteous Person knows that!"

"If that is the case, then no, I am definitely *not* a Righteous Man. How do I become one, so that I can pass through the Golden Gates?"

"There are only two ways Boy. One is to spend years in meditation and study. The second is the way we did. And that is through Mortal Combat at the Testing Games, the ones that are to start tomorrow. In those two weeks, the Testing Games choose the Righteous one, and that, of course, is the Victor. Thirty one Golden Guards are added to our ranks each year.

"When you advance up the stairs you must present your Righteous Man Diploma to each Guard. At the end of the Golden Guards, there are twelve steps that lead to the Golden Palace Gates. One large, the Main Gate, and one small, the Golden Guard Gate.

"Each of the twelve steps to the Main Golden Gate has two Golden Warrior Priests. One on each side. Each priest will ask only one question. The questions vary. No two are the same. There is no set pattern to them, so there can be no cheating your way in. To enter the Main Gate, you must correctly answer each one of their questions. We, the Golden Guards, never go through the Main Gate. We cannot answer the twenty four questions. We are billeted in a Soldiers building through the smaller Golden Gate. There we live and practice our Warrior Arts."

Then he patted his shiny Golden Sword.

Boy nodded his head in understanding, thanked the golden guard and turned away.

The golden guard smiled and watched him go.

(Angel smiled at her parents. "I could tell the golden guard liked the Guitar like instrument. No one behind him could see, but I saw his face as he looked wistfully at it swing as Boy walked away".)

Blam!

(It was that quick!)

Suddenly it was two weeks later and Boy had returned. He looked the same as he did previously, except that his food bag looked fuller.

One of the golden guards started to step forward.

"It is my turn." He grunted to the other golden guard.

"'s okay Bro. I know this one. I'll handle it." grunted the other Golden Guard. He stepped forward.

It was the very same Golden Guard who had stepped out to meet Boy the first time.

"What are you doing back here Boy! Leave. Now. We are expecting someone." thundered the golden guard. "Someone important!"

"I am here to pass through the gates, kind sir, but I will wait until after the Important person has come and gone if you prefer." Boy answered respectfully.

"Are you a simpleton, Boy? Did you not hear and understand what I told you the last time you were here?" stormed the golden guard furiously. "I do not and *will not* suffer *fools!* Begone from here, Boy."

"To answer your question sir, I *did* hear all the words you spoke last time I was here. I pondered them greatly. As to whether I understood them as you do, is ... uncertain at this time." Boy answered calmly.

"What in Harrods Hades is that supposed to mean, Boy?" roared the golden guard in vexation.

Boy reached into his food bag and produced a golden tubular device and handed it to the Golden Guard. The Golden Guard accepted it automatically.

The Golden Guard was struck dumb. He could not seem to find his voice for a few moments. He just stood there looking at the Golden tube in his hand.

Boy removed it from his hand and pulled a pale golden paper like substance out of it that had markings on it that I did not recognize. Apparently the golden guard did.

"How did you get this, Boy? Did you discover a way to steal it?" he demanded.

"You know it can't be stolen, sir. Only one who has been treated can hold it. As you are treated for it every day. You can feel the deadly tingle but it won't kill you until your treatment has worn off tonight when your shift ends. I won it in the Arena at the Testing Games." Boy paused here and frowned. He didn't look happy at that moment. "I was unaware that the Testing Games were a death sport until I enrolled. If I had known, I might not have entered. I had no wish to kill anyone."

"You are him!" the golden guard gasped. "You didn't kill any of your opponents, just rendered them temporarily incapacitated. They all had to be carried out and they all completely recovered. It has *never* been done in the history of the Testing Games before. Nobody even knew there was an Incapacitation Rule in the Testing Games Rules. It has *always* been assumed to be a Death Sport event." He shook his head in wonder.

"There is talk of taking out that Incapacitation Rule in future Testing Games. Why it was ever put in there, I'll never know. It's a disgrace. That's what it is, a disgrace to the Testing Games."

He glared at Boy.

"Be that as it may, I passed." Boy replied quietly.

"You, Boy, are a disgrace to the Testing Games!" the Golden Guard insulted.

Boy looked back at him calmly, not responding.

That irritated the Golden Guard. "You *do* know that a Golden Guard at the main gate can challenge anyone that he feels is a threat to the empire or to the Emperor, don't you?" He said it viciously, not like a question at all.

Boy treated it as one though and thought about it for a moment, then replied hesitantly, "Well …. No, sir, I'm afraid I don't think I do." Boy answered quietly.

(Boy, it sure did look to me like he was unsure at that moment.)

"Is there a threat to the Emperor, or the Empire, that I should be made aware of?" Boy asked in an anxious voice.

The Golden Guard smiled. *(It was not a* nice *smile. Not* nice *at all. It was sort of creepy scary.)*

"Well, we have been told to always be on the lookout for enemies against the Emperor or Empire. And I think your cheating at the Testing Games qualifies. What do you say to that?"

"I'm not sure how to react to that." Boy said softly. Then his face cleared.

"Ahhh ... yes! I do believe I know of that Rule. Any man guarding the Golden Gate has the right to challenge the Games Champion to a Duel to Death if he believes there is a chance that the Games Champion is a threat to the Emperor. Believe me sir, I am no threat to the Emperors life. I want him to come to no harm. May I now pass?"

"It looks to me like a real man would scare you to death. *Would* a real man scare you to death, *Boy*?"

Boy looked at the Golden Guard and said very seriously.

"I'm not sure sir."

(At that exact instant, Boy's face went really funny, and I mean not in a nice way. He turned slowly and looked all around and his eyes got really big and round looking, as if in fear, but not really.)

"If you would be so kind as to point one out to me, I might be able to answer you."

(He was now looking at the golden guard with that round eyed innocent face with that funny, not funny, look on it. I thought the golden guard was going to faint, he went so white with fear. The

front of his uniform pants got wet looking. Boy even scared me real bad at that moment and I wasn't even there!)

The Golden Guard with the wet pants turned his head so the other Golden Guard would not see his wet pants and said:

"Let him Pass."

***

Scene 66

Damon and Natasha entered the room at that moment, with Damon carrying some refreshments and snacks. "Is anybody up for some chocolate chip cookies and warm unicorn milk?" Natasha piped.

She was carrying her Dolly with her. Both were adorable in Royal Purple pajamas with lavender trim. Damon was dressed in a flattering dark grey hooded sweat suit, as if he had just come or was just on his way to the Blackstone Gymnasium.

"I hope we are not intruding?" Damon stated softly. "We heard voices as we were about to put Natasha to bed and Natasha thought we should be 'neighborly' and bring by some bedtime snacks for everyone."

"No, you are just in time to hear the end of my dream!" Angelina announced excitedly.

"You are too late for that, Angel. I already told him *all* about it." Natasha stated matter of factly, "but I know he will want to hear it from you also. It is a strange habit of his, liking to hear it First Hand, that is." She sensed the effect it had on Brandon and Charlene. Tasha smiled at them.

"It's okay. Angel said I could tell him."

Angel nodded enthusiastically. "I thought that everyone here should know of it, because I *need* it explained to *me*. I really, really need to understand it. Soon! I have a feeling it is important."

Brandon smiled and patted his daughter's hand.

"Let's have some warm milk and cookies first though ... shall we?" he smiled at her.

"Absomundo!" Angel saw Natasha's puzzled look.

"It's daddy's Fonzie impression, whatever that means. It means *yes*."

Natasha smiled in complete understanding. Both girls knew grownups did and said some weird things.

When they had finished the snack, Angel spoke.

"I know that Natasha told you the dream earlier and you asked me to tell it again tonight, that I might have missed something the first time I told Natasha. Shall I retell the first part again, Commander?" Damon smiled at the *Commander* title. "Or is the recording good enough?"

"The recording will do fine. How did you know about that?"

"Natasha told me. She said you monitored *everything* in BlackStone to keep me safe. I knew my room would be the *most* protected. I feel very safe in BlackStone, and even more so in this room." She clapped her hands together in glee as a thought struck her. "I was right about the recording! I like it when I'm right." She said to no one in particular. None responded, though all smiled at her enthusiasm, especially her father.

To Brandon Thomas, at that very instant it seemed like forever, but it was just the day before that his daughter was one step through DEATH'S doorway. Now she was whole again and injury free, and happy with her new friends. Natasha had cured his Angelina of the SIM virus in the place called *"ElseWare"*. Brandon had not been allowed to be there. None were *except*

Damon, and Brandon was thankful for that. Although Natasha told Damon that he shouldn't go, that it was dangerous, he went anyway, although he told Brandon that he had taken appropriate precautions.

Damon later confirmed that he *had* been *slightly* injured but was able to heal and restore himself to full health. Brandon had doubted the validity of the word *'slight'*. It was confirmed when Natasha told him that without Damon, she could not have healed Angelina completely. Natasha stated that the Commander was deeply injured at one point, protecting both her and Angel, but Natasha said, about Damon, that *they* did not give in, and that *they* won the day, whatever that meant. Brandon did not ask who *they* were. It didn't matter.

When Brandon Thomas tried to express his appreciation to Damon, the Commander did not seem to understand.

Damon's statement was, "I would expect no less from you if the situation was reversed."

That simple logic and faith that Damon had in Brandon, humbled him. The Eagle gained much more than knowledge about Damon Gray from that statement. It cemented their friendship in a way that went beyond mere words. Brandon *understood*. He was not sure that Damon *understood*. Damon Gray just *was Damon Gray*, and whoever or whatever that Damon Gray was, it was perfectly fine with the Eagle.

He came back to the present and watched as his daughter milked her captive audience. In the back of his mind, he questioned some of the adult language and phrasing mixed in the story telling. He would address that later.

He looked lovingly at his daughter as she worked her audience. Angelina was an instinctive entertainer.

"Well, what are you waiting for?" Brandon prodded his daughter. "You have us all hooked. Enough with the theatrics! On with the dream!" Everybody laughed.

Angel continued:

***

Scene 67

Boy passed through the gate and presented the Golden Scroll to each of the Guards. All felt the buzz, authenticating it. All Golden Guards read it. All Golden Guards passed Boy on, until at last Boy reached the Golden Palace.

When Boy finished showing his Golden Scroll to the last Golden Guard, he stepped back and looked at the Palace.

Up close, it looked more like a Great Golden Castle than a Palace, although I am not sure of the difference. It was Magnificent! Boy took a long time looking closely at all of it.

The last Golden Guard finally spoke.

"Move on Boy. We have better things to do than watch you ogle the Golden Palace walls."

"As you wish, sir." responded Boy in a respectful voice. He abruptly turned and walked towards the Twelve Steps; to where the twenty four Warrior Priests guarded the Main entrance.

"Boy!" roared the last Golden Guard he had showed the Scroll to, "Yours is the Smaller Door. That Entrance is for an Audience with the Emperor."

Boy stopped and turned to the soldier. "Thank you for that information sir, but I have already been told about the doors from the first Golden Guard."

"Boy, beware!" shouted the last Golden Guard as Boy turned away and proceeded toward the Priests. "The Warrior

Priests guarding the main entrance were trained in a special way. Their skills in Battle are to ours as ours are to a peasant with no training. If you fail to answer correctly the minimum amount of questions, they will kill you or turn you away without hesitation, never to be allowed back."

That stopped Boy. He turned and looked at the last Golden Guard. He then turned to the Warrior Priests and called out. "Is what he says true?"

"Yes Boy," said one of the Warrior Priests. I could not tell which of the twenty four Warrior Priests had spoken. None of them seemed to move.

Boy turned and walked back to the golden guard who had warned him.

"I know that none of you liked what I did in the arena. Why then did you warn me sir?" he asked this question quietly, politely yet with deep interest.

The last Golden Guard looked a little uncomfortable. He didn't speak for a few moments. I think it was because he was hoping Boy would go away. Boy continued to wait for the answer. The last Golden Guard started looking more and more uncomfortable.

Finally he mumbled something.

"Pardon me, sir?" responded Boy, not understanding. I heard him because I went up close.

"Because you are one of us, dammit!" he roared. "No matter how you won, you won. And now you are one of the Golden Guards. We are family. We don't always like what our family does, Boy, but we *always* stand by them." He said the last part fiercely and with great pride. For some reason, I was proud of all the Golden Guards.

Boy turned towards the Warrior Priests and called out to them, "Do you feel the same way about each other?"

No voice answered Boy.

He turned back to the Golden Guard and said very quietly, so quietly that only the Golden Guard could hear, "I will heed your warning. Thank you, sir."

Boy then turned away again and approached the first step of the main entrance. The first Warrior Priest stepped down from his step and waited.

Boy approached him and handed him the scroll. The Warrior Priest took it, read it, but did not return it. He held it loosely in his left hand. His right hand had dropped down to rest lightly on his sword handle.

"We have heard of you also, Boy. You are a warrior, not a scholar. Why do you seek audience with the Emperor?"

"Is that the First Question?" Boy asked quietly.

The Warrior Priest was startled. He was not used to being questioned. His face darkened, then cleared. His face went calm again.

"Good for you, Boy! No, that was *not* the first question. Forgive my tongue slip."

Boy did not respond. He just stood there calmly. Waiting for the first question.

After a few moments, the Warrior Priest spoke. "Are you not going to respond to my apology, Boy?"

"I didn't realize it was a question. It sounded like a statement. Of course I forgive you."

Boy then put forth his left hand. The Warrior Priest's face darkened again and his Hand tightened around the handle of his sword.

His grip was so hard that his knuckles went white. Boy had not moved his right hand at all. It hung limp at his side.

Slowly the blood faded from the Warrior Priests face and his grip lessened on his sword. He put the Golden Scroll in Boy's hand and announced.

"Pass."

Boy then turned and went to the second Warrior Priest who had stepped down to meet him.

Boy approached him and handed him the scroll. The Warrior Priest took it, read it, but did not return it. As with the first Warrior Priest, he held it loosely in his left hand. As with the first Warrior Priest, his right hand dropped down to rest lightly on his sword handle.

"Question two, Boy: What are Dreams?"

Boy thought for a moment, then responded:

"Dreams are exactly that; Dreams."

The Warrior Priest pondered his answer. He could find no flaw in it. Finally he spoke.

"There was no flaw in the answer, only in the phrasing of the question. Pass."

He handed Boy back the Golden scroll. I won't go into the ritual for the next questions. It was the same; the holding of the

Golden Scroll in the left hand and the gripping of the sword with the other.

The third Warrior priest was ready. Sound traveled well here. All present heard all the answers.

"Question three: What *one* thing do you feel one should know about *true* Personal Dreams?"

Boy thought about that for awhile before answering.

This was his answer:

"To me; One should know that:

True Personal Dreams are: *Goals.*

"Pass."

The next eight Warrior Priests asked him the same question, but asked for a different answer..

These are his answers:

Personal Dreams are: *Hopes.*

"Pass."

Personal Dreams are: *to be strived for.*

"Pass."

Personal Dreams are: *to be cherished.*

"Pass"

Personal Dreams are: *to be loved.*

"Pass"

Personal Dreams are: *to be guarded.*

"Pass"

Personal Dreams are: *to be followed.*

"Pass"

Personal Dreams are: *to be believed in.*

"Pass"

Personal Dreams are: *to be lived.*

This Warrior Priest actually frowned.

"You know the Nine!" he spoke almost incredulously.

He handed Boy the Golden Scroll.

"Pass."

The next twelve questions were different.

Question thirteen took him the shortest time to answer. The question was:

"What is Love in all its forms?"

"The answer can only be:

Love is Love and nothing else."

That really ticked off the Warrior Priest. I could tell that he expected a long meditation on that question.

"Pass." He said grudgingly.

Question fourteen was:

"What is Death?" The Warrior Priest who said it said it smugly, as if he had been waiting to use it for an occasion like this. He said it like it was a trick question.

Boy seemed to recognize this, because on this one Boy took some time. When he answered, he did not repeat the question as he had for some of the previous ones. He just said two words:

"The Beginning."

The Warrior Priest actually took a step backward in shock. He tried to find a flaw in those two words. He tried for ten minutes. He even looked at the other Priests for help. None came to his aid.

"Pass."

Question Fifteen: What is Friendship?

Answer: "A Choice"

"Pass."

Question Sixteen: What should one do if they see a poison snake in a crowded room of important decision makers.

Answer: "Kill it immediately, before any conversation starts."

"Pass."

Question Seventeen: What is more important than the *'Will to Succeed?'"*

Answer: *"The Will to Prepare."*

"Pass."

Question Eighteen: "What is considered the One *Just* Use of Power?"

Answer: "To Serve People."

"Pass."

Question Nineteen: "What is Religion?"

Answer: "A Man Made Institution."

(Boy sure caused a commotion with that one! But none could find a flaw with it.)

"Pass"

Question Twenty: "What are the Best Three Ways to avoid Criticism?"

Answer: "Say Nothing. Do Nothing. Be Nothing."

"Pass."

Question Twenty-One: What is Failure?

Answer: "Failure is the Opportunity to Start Over Differently."

"Pass."

Question Twenty-Two: "What is a True Test of a Persons Character?"

Answer: "Give Them Power".

"Pass."

Question Twenty-Three: "What makes Greatness in a Strong Person?"

Answer: "Greatness Lies Not in Being Strong, But in the Right Use of That Strength."

"Pass."

The Warrior Priests were beside themselves. Many were the numbers they had turned away because they had failed to answer correctly the minimum amount of questions. That minimum number was twenty-one. If twenty-one questions were answered correctly, they would allow that person an Audience with the Emperor in the Audience Chamber.

Boy approached the last Warrior Priest. No one had ever had a perfect score. Boy was going to get an Audience, but they had to beat him at their Game.

They would be ridiculed if a mere Boy could answer all the Questions that had baffled some of the Greatest of Minds of the times.

The top seven Warrior Priests got together for a consultation. They knew Boy had won and they all agreed they wanted to pose the *one* question that had never been answered to anyone's satisfaction.

After they dispersed, Boy was allowed to approach the Last Warrior Priest.

The Last Warrior Priest looked at Boy with New Eyes. He asked the last question:

Question Twenty Four: "Why?"

This one question took Boy the longest to answer.

Finally he shrugged his broad shoulders slightly, as if in defeat and answered, very, very softly, so that only the Last Warrior Priest would hear his words.

The Last Warrior Priest's eyes got very round and he stepped back also.

"Pass."

The Warrior Priest then gave the special knock and the Monstrous Double Golden Doors were opened.

Boy was facing the door when it opened. I went around him to see his face when he looked in the Castle for the first time. Then the strangest thing happened. Boy turned slightly so the Warrior Priests couldn't see and then straightened up to his full height, he was taller than the Warrior Priests, and then he looked right at *me* with his *real* eyes and said,

"Tell my Father that I will be waiting for you, my Guardian Angel. Tell him that I have walked the walk, have seen a need and I will come. In the beginning, I will need your help, girl-child. Please bring unto me that which shall be the heart of me, the NullStone, my soul vestal."

The Warrior Priests looked around but none saw me, because I wasn't there.

"Heed my words well. Only you will be able to handle it. Let none other touch it. It will devour their very Soul." That sure scared me! Then Boy smiled a beautiful smile at me to take away my fear. And it did, it really did! And then Boy turned and walked through me and into the Golden Castle.

Just as the doors were closing, the Warrior Priests Heard loud voices Proclaiming;

"The Emperor has returned through the front Gates! The Emperor has just returned through the *front Gates!* Praise the heavens, *they* are back."

Then I went back to sleep.

***

Scene 68

"Well .... What did you think of my dream?" asked Angelina excitedly. "Who can explain it to me?" she asked eagerly. No one spoke for a moment. Then Natasha bent and listened to her Dolly. She looked back at Angel.

"Dolly wants to know if you heard the Answer to the Last Question. Did you?"

"Yes I did. I didn't mention it because it didn't seem important ... well, all *that* important. Boy only said two confusing words. I even understood the words. I just didn't understand their meaning. And the way he said it sounded almost like a question - a question! How do you answer a question with a question?" Angelina shook her small head in frustration, black curls flying everywhere.

"That is why I told all of you the dream, so that one or all of you could please explain it to me."

Angelina seemed to be looking at all of them at once.

"Why did Boy say what he did? How could he see me? How long did he know I was watching? What is a Null Stone? Why was I scared and then not? What does it all mean? It wasn't like a dream at all. In fact I *know* it wasn't a dream. It was *real*, only I *wasn't. I was the Dream.* Oh, somebody tell me so that I can understand! I feel the answer is just out of reach, but so close. I feel will *know* it when I hear it."

All present were pondering the Dream.

Charlene was the first to speak. "What were Boy's words?"

"What? ... oh yes, Boy's words." She smiled and stated it in a whisper, like Boy did; "Why Not!?"

"That's it? *'Why Not?'* What kind of answer is that? It says absolutely nothing!" Charlene exclaimed in irritation. "The rest of the answers made at least some kind of sense!" holding her swollen belly she stated "It was just a dream, Angel. Just a dream."

"I am not so sure." Damon stated softly. "Angelina?"

"Yes, Commander?"

"Tell me about Boy's eyes."

"His real eyes?"

"Yes. His real eyes." Damon said gently, hypnotically. He ran his long fingers through her thick dark curly hair.

Angelina Thomas seemed to suddenly get very sleepy. Her agitation suddenly seemed to disappear.

"He had the most beautiful eyes I have ever seen." She yawned a big yawn.

"Before they changed they were cold looking, a swirly kinda shiny silvery. Like yours Commander. When they changed to his *real* eyes, one was the most beautiful Golden Cat's eye I have ever seen and the other one was like a beautiful red sun burning and swirling and spinning in Boy's eye socket .... the most beautiful eyes......" Angelina was asleep.

Damon put a finger on the middle of her forehead, leaned over and whispered in her ear.

"Sleep a calm, peaceful and restful sleep, Angelina Thomas, and awaken feeling fully rested, happy and alert."

Angelina smiled and nodded her head ever so slightly. "As you wish, Commander." she mumbled, then rolled over. Quietly, they all left the room.

***

Scene 69

B lackStone Library.

One hour after Angelina had fallen asleep.

Physically present were Damon, Hastings, Catherine, Natasha and Brandon. Spiritually present were Michael, Sylvia and a very pregnant Charlene Thomas.

They had all just arrived. After they had left Angelina's bedroom, Damon had invited all of them to repair themselves and meet in the Library in one hour, with the exception of Brandon. Brandon had accompanied Damon.

In the Library, all present were in various positions of standing or sitting, whatever suited their temperament at the moment.

"Thank you all for being so punctual." Damon started with no preamble. "What I am about to tell you will stretch your belief system to the breaking point. I was unsure whether to tell Brandon earlier or to wait until all were present. I asked him and he assured me that he could wait."

Damon looked around the room at all his friends. "Let me first say that what I am about to tell you stretches my belief system also, but I see no other explanation." He paused again.

"For some reason, this is hard for me to tell you. Yet I know that I must. It is vital that I do. Lack of anything less than complete disclosure with all of you could prove *Catastrophic* to all concerned." He paused again.

Brandon could not help himself. He put his hand on Damon's shoulder and said quietly. "I think I know, friend. It is alright!"

All felt Damon relax, though to the eye, nothing changed about him.

"Let me bring you all up to date first." Damon now looked directly at Brandon. "First of all Brandon, you should know that I am Mr. Smoke."

There was a moment of stunned silence from the Eagle. Nothing had prepared him for that bit of information. Finally realization set in.

"You are Mr. Smoke, the terrorist bomber assassin?" Brandon almost shouted in disbelief. Damon nodded slightly. "You *are the* Mr. Smoke." The Eagle actually shook his head slightly in wonder and awe and finally in belief. Then he recovered, and smiled at his friend in genuine happiness.

"Wow! That is Great, Damon!" He paused again as something else came into his mind and clicked into place. "You created the COW file, didn't you?"

Damon didn't answer immediately.

"What is the COW file?" asked Natasha innocently.

Brandon answered, "It is a file that contains a lot of important and damaging information about the bad things that very Important and Powerful People in the world do. Information that could destroy each and every one of those Important and Powerful People, Natasha. All of those Important and Powerful People want to have it found and destroyed. The COW File was rumored to be Myth. I learned firsthand that the COW File is, in fact, not Myth. It was the Cow File that saved my life and the lives of my family."

"What does a cow have to do with it? How can a cow be that dangerous to anyone?" asked Natasha, again with the innocent curiosity of a child.

Damon now answered, "COW stands for *'Can of Worms'*."

"That's a strange Name for a File, Commander!" piped Natasha. "That's a funny name! *'Can of Worms'*!" She burst out giggling. "Why is it called that?"

The giggling was contagious. All laughed.

"You will find out when you get older, Tasha." Damon stated when things quieted down. "I thought it was fun too, when I named it and put it out there that it existed." Damon turned to the Eagle, "Yes Brandon, I guess that answers your question. That I have it, we all now know. How I acquired and acquire the information stays forever with me."

Damon walked to one of the Book Cases and removed a nine by twelve inch slender, nondescript, leather bound volume. At first glance, it looked disappointingly ordinary, like an accounts ledger. The only unsettling thing about it was its lack of writing anywhere on the cover. The edges of the pages were blackened to match the color of the leather.

"I recognize that!" Michael Brighton announced. "Been in the family forever. Nobody could ever decipher the bloody thing. It was only kept because of the leather binding and pages. No one could ever figure out what kind of leather it was. It never got stiff with age or collected dust like the rest. The same is also assumed with the pages. Nobody liked the feel of it. All who felt or held it said it made them nauseous. I felt the same way, when I viewed it. Repulsive feeling thing." Michael shuddered at the memory. "The pages felt like a fine leather also, but smooth on both sides. A kind of a novelty piece, you might say. The very repugnance of it saved it from being destroyed or discarded."

He looked at Damon curiously. "I assume that you have deciphered it?"

"You assume correctly, Lord Brighton, although I never experienced that feeling you mentioned. It felt ... natural to me."

Opening the book, Damon thumbed through it until he found the page he was looking for.

"This is the NullStone." He announced quietly, turning the book so that all could see the pictures. The pictures were on both sides of the snow-white pages and showed a compilation of, what appeared to be, an artists renderings of a round shaped black flecked, black rock. A rock perfect for skipping across a pond, so slender was it, the tapered edges rounded.

"It looks like a telescope lens!" stated the surprised voice of Charlene Thomas. "I feel that I have seen that stone before!"

"I'm afraid not, Charlene." stated Michael. "That book has never been photographed or copied. Ever. We have never allowed that with any of our Library. Family tradition and all that rubbish."

"I know that I have never *seen* it on earth." agreed Charlene. "I said I feel that I have seen it before, as in a dream that I can't remember."

"Those pictures are three dimensional." stated Cat, with childlike wonder in her voice. "Although they *must* be hand drawn, if the book is that old, the pictures in it look so real! Like I could just reach out and pick any one of them right out of the page. It looks more like a bunch of black flecks stuck together, rather than a rock that was worn down by the elements and time."

Damon nodded. "I hadn't thought of it quite like that Cat. Brilliant observation. A true stroke of genius insight. Thank you for that Catherine." Cat looked puzzled but pleased at the compliment.

Damon immediately walked over to a large desk, opened a drawer and took out an incredibly large magnifying glass out of it and took a closer look at the pictures.

"It does look like a black jigsaw puzzle skipping rock, with all of the black interlocking jigsaw flecks composing and completing the forming of the NullStone. There looks to be no spaces between any of the jigsaw pieces. They fit together flawlessly. Unbreakable, and indestructible if I am right."

His head dropped slightly and only Natasha was short enough to see Damon's liquid silver eyes change. One changed into a large golden cats eye and the other into a shining, blood red swirling star.

Damon ran his hands over the pages and illustrations lightly. His eyes returned to liquid silver and his head rose. "And you are also right in assuming that these images are not hand drawn. Somehow they were carved onto or into the pages. In every angle of the NullStone images, the jigsaw pattern is perfectly the same in the dimensions and shape ... interesting."

Natasha's head dipped, as if listening to Dolly. "What else is *interesting*, Commander?" asked Natasha curiously.

Damon glanced at her and smiled. "I don't think they are ready for that yet, Tasha." he said softly.

"Dolly says *I* am though. I'm seven, you know!" she stated with imperious meaning.

Damon nodded his understanding, turned away, walked over and put the Magnifying glass back in the desk drawer.

All present knew it was to take time to make a decision. Damon walked back to where he had been, to where he could look at all of them at once.

"I feel Natasha is right. If Dolly feels Natasha has the right to know, I feel I must share it with all of you. Whether or not you believe me doesn't matter. At least you will have the knowledge if the time comes that you need it."

Hastings chuckled, "It's gotta be a real doozy if you think we might not believe! Go ahead Commander. This I gotta hear."

Damon laughed with him. The mood lightened.

Without any further preamble, Damon looked at Michael and stated bluntly, "The reason you felt repulsed, was that the book cover and pages are made out of leather. But it is a very special kind of leather. I didn't even know one existed until now."

Like a teacher Damon looked at Hastings, "What is leather made from?"

"Depends." Hastings answered carefully, "Usually tanned animal hide."

What is animal hide?" Damon prompted.

"The skin of the animal?" Hastings answered hesitantly, not understanding where this line of questioning was going.

"Correct!" stated Damon. Holding up the Book, he continued, "The reason this Book has no writing on it is because none will stick to it."

Pulling a needle pointed, razor sharp knife out of the air Damon put the book on a nearby coffee table and slammed the knife into it. The blade crumpled like wax. The table shuddered terribly and almost collapsed. Damon held up the book. No indent of any kind could be seen. "This book is made from the heart pouch skin of a full grown Male Dragon Lizard, taken while he was still living, a supposedly impossible thing to do. The heart of a Male Dragon Lizard is encased in an almost indestructible protective heart pouch. Makes them almost impossible to kill, unless their head is totally separated from their body. They regenerate quickly because the heart keeps pumping their highly regenerative blood. They seldom die of old age.

"The snow-white pages of the book are made from the unblemished skins of unborn Female Dragon Lizards, *before* they develop shells within the mother. They are not near as durable as the males heart pouch cover, thus were able to be engraved."

"Who cares about a bunch of lizard skins." announced Cat without emotion. "What has that to do with us, Commander?"

Damon smiled and shook his head slightly in amusement. Catherine Nipp was not affected with things that would make everyone else shudder and scream uncontrollably.

Cat was a pure soul, but pure in a way that humanity had no label for. A highly Enhanced Human, born without morals or conscience and trained by circumstances from birth, ShabNab *(her real name)* was the Perfect Assassin.

"This Book is not of this world, Catherine. Therefore logic dictates, with a great deal of certainty, that the NullStone is not *on* this world."

***

Scene 70

"How do you know that for sure, Damon?" Lady Sylvia Thomas asked for everyone present.

"I can state for certainty because I was there, on the world where this came from, for awhile." Damon answered matter of factly. "It is a very dangerous and hostile place. Even for me. I had, and have, no urge to return."

Hastings face went dark. Damon noticed. "That was *before* you accompanied me, Hastings." Hastings nodded understanding and his face returned to normal.

"I was on that world with the Commander." stated Catherine. "I would not care to return there either." She looked at her Commander keenly, "We're not are we, Commander? Going back there, I mean ...."

Damon held up his hand and continued, "Please, hold all further questions until I have finished. It gets a little complicated. If at that time any one of you has any questions, I will try to answer them." All nodded. Damon continued.

"You all should know that I am an EH, which stands for Enhanced Human as were both my parents and their parents, and so on, for uncounted generations. EH's had been mercilessly hunted for almost as long as they first evolved. Because of this, while in my mother's womb, my father made some changes, enhancements, additions and adjustments to my basic DNA structure. I am not as you are. As you may or may not know, EH's mature differently than normal humans, or *Normals*, as I call them. EH's have Talents, Abilities and Gifts as well as different strengths in each of them. Many EH's have TAG's that are similar to others." Damon sensed a question.

"As I have no doubt told you all before, I refer to an EH's *Talents, Abilities and Gifts as TAG's* to keep it simple. Also to protect those same EH's. Some TAG's are physical in nature and some are *not*. There are countless TAG's out there, ranging from small to *huge*. EH TAG's usually mature every seven years. After each cycle, their new TAG's grow subliminally for seven years, working their way slowly throughout the EH's nervous system, then spring full bloom on or about the EH's seventh year birthday, with the EH having full knowledge and control of them, much like a butterfly coming out of its cocoon." Damon grinned at Natasha's smile at the butterfly analogy, and continued,

"Upon exit of the cocoon, the butterfly *instinctively* and *immediately* knows how to fly. With EH's, sometimes their TAG's get stunted because of circumstance, accident, injury and mixed breeding, among a multitude of other things. The EH female TAG's mature faster than EH males. The EH females have *four* Cocoons for their TAG's to reach full maturity. Their TAG's mature at age twenty-eight. To my knowledge, with one exception, all male EH's have five Cocoons and their TAG's mature at age thirty five. For many reasons, some due to the genetic manipulation and additions made in the womb, I am that one exception. To date, I have experienced seven ... but then, I never was normal."

He saw Hastings amused look at the understatement. Damon smiled back in acknowledgement as he continued, "Some of the worlds we have visited have different time lines. I am older than this worlds time says I am by some fifteen years."

He saw all their looks. According to this worlds time Damon Gray, Concert Pianist, was thirty-five years old. He knew he still looked to be in his early to mid twenties. He was over fifty years old in real life time and experience, according to his calculations. And Damon Gray's calculations were extremely accurate.

"The reason we tell you all this, is because of *our* latest TAG cocoon maturity. One of the recent TAG's we acquired, was the Ability to assimilate *ALL* of a Female EH's TAG's by ..." he suddenly became aware of the children in the room. " ahhh ... coupling with them and at a particular point in the coupling, Copy Pasting all of their TAG's in us. After the Copy Paste, they lose interest in us."

"The *lose interest* thing doesn't work with *all* EH women who *coupled* with the Commander. I know of one EH who *coupled* (*Catherine smiled and enunciated the new word with relish*) with the Commander prior to and after all the Commanders latest Cocoon maturities and didn't lose interest." Cat corrected, "I didn't, and the Commander gained *all* of my TAG's. It didn't bother me at all. Not one whit! In fact it was kind of stimul...."

"Yes, Cat. You are one of the exceptions ... so far. I stand corrected." Damon hastily interrupted.

"*One* of the exceptions?" asked Cat with eager interest. "Ooops, I know, no questions until the end. Sorry Commander."

Damon looked discomfited.

Hastings couldn't help it. He started laughing. It had been a long time since he had seen Damon get even slightly embarrassed or off balance. The rest joined in, even Natasha.

Last but not least, so did Damon. He immediately saw the humor. All trace of embarrassment disappeared.

"Let's move on, shall we?" he stated. All became silent.

"Thank you Catherine for understanding. The reason I tell you these very personal things is for a reason. You will all understand shortly. The reason I asked for no questions was for this exact scenario. If I was to answer that question without first explaining, your minds could jump to erroneous conclusions. Snap decisions can be very limiting, especially if they are wrong. It takes the brain awhile to discard emotional responses to statements." He saw the look on their faces. "Okay, okay! Enough with the Lecture Tour. On with the show!" they all grinned. Damon continued.

"As an experiment, I took Brandon and Charlene Thomas to *ElseWare* to be together one last time before she was to move on. I was correct in thinking that ElseWare was a place where spirit became flesh. Brandon and Charlene made love one last time. Before Charlene was to go beyond she told me that she and her husband had talked it over and that Charlene should *couple* with me so that I could gain her TAG's to help in the rescue and cure of their daughter. I agreed. We coupled." Damon paused and looked at the group.

Each one felt that Damon was looking just at them.

"We find that we do not make love as normal people do. By we, I mean I." Damon stated emphatically. "Charlene and Brandon did that. They made love. We coupled. I gained her TAG's. I thanked her and she left."

His face relaxed slightly when he saw they all understood.

"We are always amazed that humans confuse coupling with making love." He stated absentmindedly, his eyes losing focus and slipping back into the 'we', as he gathered his thoughts to continue. After a moment, he continued.

"I *was* going to go into the whole process that brings me to what I am about to tell you, but I have changed my mind. It would serve no purpose except to muddy the waters. You will just have to take my word on what I am about to tell you. I am asking you to trust me in this and believe what I say. Are you all willing to do that?" the look on their faces answered his question.

Damon smiled his *'Thank You'* at them and continued.

"In a delayed answer to your question Cat, yes, you *will* have to go back to the Dragon Lizard world. Natasha and Angelina will go with you, to bring back the NullStone." His face took on a look of anguish for the first time. It was gone almost before it started, but all saw it.

"I will not be able to make this journey with you. There are vital and critical things that we must do right here and right now. As with most important things, timing is critical. I wish it was otherwise."

Natasha bent her head slightly and listened to her Dolly and nodded but said nothing.

"Wait a minute!" exclaimed Brandon. "If this world is so dangerous, why would you want to send my daughter there?"

"I didn't say I wanted to. I don't want to, my friend. I have gone over it many times in my mind and it is the *only* way that we have a chance to retrieve the NullStone and bring it to earth."

"But ..."Brandon started to say.

"What are we missing in this equation, Damon?" Charlene interrupted her husband quietly. "Please finish," She looked at her husband with great meaning. "*we* will not interrupt again." Brandon kept his mouth closed and his thoughts to himself.

With a smile of gratitude at Charlene, Damon took a great breath and continued. "Thank you Charlene. I will only tell you highlights. You can all question me later. One of the reasons the NullStone needs to be brought to earth is that if it isn't, your baby will die, and quite possibly *you* as well. If you die as a Ghost or Spirit, you will die the *final death*."

Everyone gasped slightly at that bald statement.

"Another reason is that your unborn son, Karman, can not exist for long once or if he is born. Karman shouldn't even be able to exist at all! But he does. The only thing that can possibly keep him alive is the NullStone. The knowledge of this comes from the writings in this DragonHeart Book."

Damon held up the Black Dragon Skin bound Book.

"This DragonHeart Book foretells of a time when a *Child of the Universe* could be born. It doesn't say '*will*' be born, it says '*could*'. It also says without the NullStone the child will perish within a few hours of the birth. Even when he has fully matured, Karman *may* never be able to live without the NullStone for any more than a few days at a time. According to the Book, the NullStone was constructed and created, in a place before time began, to *be* Karman's Heart, should he be born. The NullStone is a construct of unfathomable power that many have tried to possess. If a male touches it and tries to possess its power, they are consumed instantly by the NullStone. Only a pure of heart female can hold it for a short period but must relinquish it within a short time or be consumed also. The Book says the reason for that is that the NullStone *must* be carried *by* a PureHeart *to* a PureHeart without a heart."

Damon shook his head, "At first, it didn't make sense to me. Then I realized that it *could* have been designed to *be* the Heart of Karman."

Damon looked at Charlene and stated softly, "Your child has no heart, Charlene. Karman could *never* have been conceived on this earth in an earthly body. That is why he was conceived in ElseWare."

Charlene just gaped at him. "What are you talking about? Of course Karman has a heart!" She looked down at her stomach.

Something happened at that moment. A strange look came over her face. Charlene Thomas looked at Damon.

"Karman, just now communicated with me. It was not a baby's voice. It was young but ageless, actually more like a series of thoughts than a voice. He imparted that his sister remembered the dream with great accuracy and told it well, with only a little of his help. Is he talking about the dream Angelina just told us about?"

"Yes, I believe so." Damon answered.

Brandon smiled and now knew from what source the adult language and phrasing originated from that had issued forth from Angelina during the DreamTale. The language and phrasing that he had mentally questioned earlier. His instincts had been right on the money.

Charlene continued, "I *somehow know* that to live he would have to have the NullStone brought to him. Karman is being nurtured by my essence right now, but that will cease at birth. I believe that you are right Damon. Karman has no heart."

She turned to her husband, "What am I to do, Brandon?"

"I don't know Char." Brandon turned to Damon. "Can you stop or abort the pregnancy without hurting Charlene?"

"That is a moot question, my friend. Even if we could, we wouldn't. We will do everything we can to aid and bring the birth of Karman to fruition."

"I will not lose my wife!" stated Brandon emphatically. "I am not in favor of aborting, but if my wife's life is in danger, I will sacrifice my unborn son's life rather than my wife's life!"

"It is not your choice to make, Brandon. You are in no position to affect anything at present. And although we might be able to, we won't." Damon stated quietly. "And it is *not* your unborn son."

"I know." Brandon stated just as quietly. "I knew it the moment the words came out of my mouth. Karman is as much Charlene's as mine, if not more. I'm sorry Char."

"I understand, Brandon." Charlene acknowledged kindly. "I would have said the same if our positions were reversed."

"Then you would both be wrong!" Damon stated sharply. All present looked confused. Damon was not one to speak sharply to friends.

"I do apologize." Damon stated quickly. "But I had to get your attention. The child you carry Charlene is not Brandon's. It is mine! And I will not let my child be killed if I can prevent it. I would do the same for all of you. I can do no less for my son."

"What in the world are you talking about Damon." Sylvia now spoke up. "Did you couple with Charlene using the 'Family Jewels'?"

"Yes, I did." stated Damon.

"Then she couldn't be carrying your Child!" stated Sylvia. "They are artificial ..." she saw the look in Damon's eyes, "aren't they?"

"They were." stated Damon. "A lot has happened in the last fifteen years. Although they are still removable, the *Family Jewels,* or *Jewels* as I now think of them, are as much a part of me as the rest of the enhancements I have added over the years."

Sylvia was speechless. Michael took over, "Damon? Do you mean to tell us that you are no longer sterile?"

"Great question, Michael. The truth of the matter is, I don't know. I can only assume that I am sterile for humans and EH's, but apparently not for Alternate Entities. And the *Jewels* are an Alternate Entity."

"How do you know you are the father?" Brandon asked in a slightly demanding voice.

"Boy's eyes in Angelina's dream." Damon stated simply.

All but Brandon and Charlene understood. They looked at Damon uncomprehendingly. As they looked at him, Damon looked back at them. They saw one of his eyes change to a beautiful Golden Cats eye and the other change to a Burning Swirling Red Sun.

Brandon and Charlene were both struck speechless.

"Say hello to Golden and Garnet. They are entities that are now an integral part of us." The eyes switched back and forth between eye sockets.

"Hello." said three distinct voices out of Damon's throat. Two voices said, "Pleased to finally meet you both."

Brandon and Charlene were still speechless. Charlene's wings, now fully grown, instinctively spread wide, as if to take flight. The Golden eye and the Red eye went crossed as if to look at each other and then vanished, leaving only Damon's liquid silver eyes looking at them.

"You can now understand why we feel ... no, wrong word ... not *feel'* ... why we KNOW that Karman is our son." Damon stated quietly; then added, almost as an afterthought, "And *why* I have a propensity to say '*we*' a lot."

No one seemed to know what to say. Silence permeated every part of the room. Every nook and cranny and every crack. No hearts seemed to beat. No breaths seemed to be taken. It was so quiet that their ears started to ring softly to create sound.

Brandon came out of it first. "Wow!" was all he could say for a few moments.

Charlene's wings had unconsciously wrapped around the front of her, covering her stomach as if protecting her full term child.

Brandon took a deep breath. Then he smiled. Then he laughed. All except Damon, thought he had lost it. Then Brandon spoke.

"We sure do know how to pick our friends, don't we sweetheart?" he said looking at his wife.

Charlene's eyes, eyes that *had* been affixed to Damon's face, turned to look at her husband with a look of incredulity. The look faded and both started laughing hysterically.

No one moved. Damon had motioned them to stillness.

Finally the hysteria turned to genuine laughter. Then it too faded into silence.

Brandon suddenly smiled at everyone and broke the silence.

"Does this type of thing happen every day around here?" All started laughing again at that statement.

When it calmed down Brandon continued in a serious voice, "I mean, isn't anybody except Charlene and myself, just a little blown away by what is happening here?"

That started a whole new laughing session.

When things had calmed down again, Brandon once more started the conversation.

"Yes Damon. I now believe that Charlene is carrying your child, not mine. It is a relief in a way. Heaven knows, I would never want to kill a child. Even as I said it, I was not sure that I could live with it. Knowing what I know now makes me understand that the decision is Charlene's and yours to make, not mine. I am very thankful for that. Whatever you two decide is fine with me."

Charlene and Damon looked at each other. Unspoken words passed between them.

Charlene spoke, "Karman will live!"

***

Scene 71

He was situated in his royal exercise dojo. Just finished a strenuous workout, he was seated lotus position. He took another slow calming breath and then pulled a cord hanging from the ceiling. A servant glided in on silent feet and presented him with the device on a golden platter. Not looking at him, the Emperor of China removed it from the plate and the servant retreated just as silently as he had arrived. It was doubtful if the Emperor even remembered that the servant had come in. Or left. He had other things on his mind.

Quan Chi Hanoi, the Immortal Imperial Emperor of China looked down at the PDA in his slender hand. A PDA that had been personally delivered to an Imperial Palace Guard by none other than Brandon Thomas, the infamous Eagle! Dangling from the bottom of the PDA on five slender silken threads, were five engraved, ancient looking, ivory colored human hand bones. The Emperor recognized them immediately as Oracle Bones.

These Oracle Bones were actually a note written in the Emperor's Script. A secret script that only China's Imperial Emperor could write or understand. An ancient and secret script that Imperial Emperors used to pass secret information and wisdom down to the Royal descendants, the future Reigning Imperial Emperors.

The Emperor sat stunned. He looked again, not quite believing his eyes.

Yes, it *was* written in the Secret Royal Variation of the Royal Chinese *Jiaguwen* (甲骨文), or Oracle Bone Script!

This was the earliest form of Chinese writing, used from the Middle to Late Shang Dynasty approximately fifteen hundred BCE to one thousand BCE. This script was usually hand etched into Turtle Shells or Special Animals Bones, which were then used for Divination in the Royal Shang Court, hence the name *'Oracle Bones'*.

Scholars have been using Oracle Bones as historical documents to investigate the reigns of later Shang monarchs, and surprisingly, confirmed the veracity of the traditional list of Chinese emperors that was deemed, by many, as mythological rather than historical.

The shapes of these were often described as *'pictographic'* characters, in that they resemble stylized drawings of the objects they represented.

The script on the PDA bones was one that was written and understood *only* by Chinese Emperor's. The Oracle Bones said that only the Emperor's fingerprint would open the PDA. And that *only* the Emperor should view the information that was in the PDA and that he, Quan Chi Hanoi, should be alone when he viewed it.

When he had been informed of it, the Bones intrigued him.

At the Emperors command, the PDA had been put through a series of inspections to identify if there were any dangers to the Emperor, but all were under orders that none were to attempt to open it. None of those tests had proved fruitful. There were no explosives in it, or poisons. It was as it appeared to be, a sophisticated, state of the art, PDA. *'Made in China'* as well. Much as he disliked it, the Emperor was forced to smile at the brazenness.

Quan Chi had read the instructions on the Oracle Bones. The Bones stated that only his left index fingerprint would open the PDA. That statement alone intrigued him. It was a little known fact that Ancient Emperor's had used their fingerprints to sign messages.

Quan Chi Hanoi activated the PDA and put his right index fingerprint in the blank square.

Nothing happened except an X appeared in the box indicating an incorrect print. He continued with all his fingerprints except the left index finger. None opened it. On the ninth one, a warning came up. In Royal Script, it said:

They are all your fingerprints, but not the correct one.

The choice is yours. China's fate is yours.

'We fear what we do not know'.

Right now you are in fear.

You will have to open it.

You have to know.

That also made the Emperor smile. He was *not* afraid! He knew it was a psychological ploy to get him to open it. He also knew that the Eagle *knew* he had no choice. He had to open it. That part made him angry, and the Emperor was not used to getting angry. Quan Chi Hanoi was not used to being forced into playing the pawn in any game!

The Emperor calmed himself. He reminded himself that Kai Akyi, son of Zuki Akyi, would take care of the Eagle for China. The Emperor's Champion had never failed him.

At last he placed his left index fingerprint in the box. The PDA opened. The Emperor went pale at what he saw. He read until it was finished. He sat there shaking. He sat in real fear. It had been a long time since he had felt that emotion.

The Emperor caught the flicker of a movement in the corner if his eye. He flowed to his feet in an electric movement and turned to face his visitor.

Mister Smoke stood in a corner of the room that *no one* could *possibly* have gotten to unobserved!

***

Scene 72

The Emperor blinked his eyes, slowly and on purpose. Mister Smoke did *not* vanish. Quan Chi had recognized him immediately.

In the ancient language of the Emperors, Mister Smoke spoke fluently to the Emperor of China. His accent and speech patterns were flawless.

"Greetings, Imperial Emperor. I come bearing a choice of two wonderful gifts."

"And what gifts might they be?" the Emperor asked quietly, but his mind was in a turmoil. *'Mister Smoke was Chinese! And of Royal Blood at that! Which of his offspring could he be? There were so many.'*

"The Gift of Life or the Gift of Death." answered Mr. Smoke. *"Shall we sit? You look troubled. You should be."*

The Emperor started to move sideways. The arms that were crossed on Mr. Smoke's chest blossomed with two automatic handguns that pointed unerringly at the Emperor. The Emperor hadn't even seen the man's arms move.

"You know some Martial Magik." It was not a question.

"I know that you know some Martial Magik. And you think I that also know some Martial Magik, but in this you are in error. I not only know all Martial Magik, I am Martial Magik. Could I have appeared here if I didn't? Please have a seat." came

the slightly mechanical voice response through the mask, altering the voice.

The calm face of the Emperor looked at Mr. Smoke thoughtfully. The size of the silenced guns staring at him told him they were not toys. Each gun was a simplistic work of genius, a professional workman's tool. They could even conceivably penetrate *his* defenses and that was unacceptable. He sat quietly.

Mr. Smoke did likewise.

"I see you have read my PDA." Mr. Smoke started the conversation.

The Emperor blinked in surprise. *"This is your work?"*

"I did not say that. I take no credit for that. I said that it was my PDA. The information on it came from ElseWare."

Quan Chi broke with his usual formal patter and spoke plainly.

"My life is obviously not what you came here for Assassin. Otherwise I would not still be alive. So ... what is it that you want Ninjitsan?" (Ninjitsan translating to mean 'MasterKiller'.)"

Quan Chi held up the PDA with a slightly shaking hand. He was humbled to see his hand shake thusly.

In a voice trembling with emotion barely held in check, he spoke.

"Mister Smoke, this information must never get out! The Chinese Dynasty would be destroyed! All our secrets revealed. Billions would suffer and die. China itself could well be destroyed!"

"You still haven't chosen. What wonderful gift shall it be? The gift of Life, or the gift of Death?"

Mr. Smoke spoke not another word. The Emperor started to sweat with real fear. He could smell himself. Fear sweat has a distinctive odor. He had smelled it many times on others, but *never* on himself. He knew that Mr. Smoke smelled it, as Quan Chi had on others.

It had been long since China's Emperor had felt shamed and lessened. He felt that way now. Quan Chi immediately calmed his emotions and looked within himself and saw the truth.

He had been isolated from the real world for too long. He had isolated himself. He seemed to shrink in stature. He seemed to age suddenly. Ignoring Mr. Smoke, China's Imperial Emperor bowed his head in thought.

The words *"You still haven't chosen. What wonderful gift shall it be? The gift of Life, or the gift of Death?"* kept ringing in his ears.

A broken man slowly looked up at Mister Smoke. Quan Chi Hanoi understood. China's Emperor *no longer* was the man he once was. *'That must be the first change!'*

Quan Chi spoke. *"I have lived too long in the past. It is not the past that I should have been looking at. I now realize that. It is now a different world. I need to learn her new ways."* He smiled a small, pain filled smile at Mister Smoke.

"In a way, I thank you for that, Mister Smoke. It has been a long time since I have been broken. And though I am broken, as always, I will heal. Remember this well, Assassin. I always heal, no matter what the pain or cost." He bowed his head in ritual capitulation.

"I surrender Mr. Smoke." He looked closely at Mr. Smoke with ageless eyes.

"I choose the Wonderful Gift of Life. Life for us and life for China, for we are China. And as such, China will survive.

"Name your terms Defeater."

***

Scene 73

"**G**ood evening everyone. I am Fred Connelly. We are interrupting the regular programming to announce that the Queen Mother has announced that there has been a *cure* discovered for the SIM virus!" Fred announced in an excited voice.

"As you all probably know, we have all been told that there *was* no cure for the deadly SIM virus. While only a few thousand people globally had the SIM virus, it was suddenly important enough to someone to find the cure." Fred looked right into the camera knowingly. "Makes you wonder a little, doesn't it!" Fred winked, "and now, back to your regular programming ..."

***

"A cure for the deadliest disease known to man has been found! Stand by for an important announcement from the Czar ......"

***

"Extry! Extry! Read all about it!

"President Lantern declared a Hero!

"The world rejoices! President Lantern has announced that at his instigation, US doctors have discovered the cure for the SIM Virus, deadliest disease know to humanity.

"Extry! Extry! Read all ....."

***

Scene 74

"What do you mean, the Emperor of China has called off the hunt for the Eagle? He has never done that. He would rather commit ritual suicide than do that!" the Eagle exclaimed in awe.

Brandon Thomas saw the noncommittal blank look in Damon's eyes. He was not fooled. "Does it have anything to do with that PDA with the dangling bones? The one that you dropped off at the Royal Palace, when you were dressed in one of my recognizable disguises, so that Q would think I was there and forward that Intel to the President?"

Damon nodded slowly in agreement.

"A true stroke of Genius, by the way. Thank you for that, Damon." he added as an afterthought. He knew that once Damon had removed his disguise and discarded it, the Chinese would never guess that it wasn't Brandon. If questioned, Damon Gray could truthfully answer that he, Damon Gray was there to negotiate a new China Tour with his Chinese Agent.

Brandon later found out that Damon had instead changed into another disguise to escape. He was actually one of guards sent out to find himself, that is to say, the Eagle in disguise. Damon fit in perfectly. Most of the Chinese Imperial Royal Guards were his size or bigger.

Damon nodded again, as if reading Brandon's mind. Brandon looked around the room trying to gather his thoughts and put them in coherent order.

They were seated in the BlackStone Library. Each had a cup of coffee.

Damon loved the BlackStone Library. He had once told Brandon that he had read every book in there and some twice, just for fun. Looking around at the thousands and thousands of volumes, Brandon found it *hard* to believe, but he *did* believe. He focused back on Damon's face.

Finally, he just blurted. "Okay ... Out with it Damon. I need to know. All the pertinent highlights would be fine. For my protection, I need to know."

Damon paused in thought and then nodded at the wisdom in that statement and spoke.

After he was done, Brandon questioned him.

"How did you get in?"

"I dressed and acted and looked like one and passed myself as of the existing Palace Servants. I knew his pass codes and I had a copy of his fingerprints copied onto my fingers." Damon replied. He held up one hand and peeled off a thin layer of skin on one finger to show him. "I kept this one on so I could show you. Fingerprints are easy to get. They have a record of all their employees on their computers. I can be any of them who come close to me in height." Brandon nodded understanding. He had done it many times himself. He knew that people never really looked at anyone closely after knowing them for awhile.

"I can understand the Servants Pass Codes, but how did you know the *Emperor's* pass codes? The ones that he changes daily."

"I have access to his home computer. In fact, I have access to *all* of their computers." He saw Brandon's incredulous look. "We supply them to all the Palace servants and staff. The Emperor likes to shop outside China for his computers and software. He doesn't trust some of his underlings. And some of those underlings run, or own, the computer factories."

Brandon nodded. "How did you escape?"

"I wasn't in there." Damon answered.

Brandon was rocked by that answer. "What in blazes do you mean, you weren't in there? That doesn't make any sense."

"I went in earlier, as that servant, and set up the equipment in a number of rooms so that, if he was in one of those rooms when he opened the PDA, I would be able to appear to him. The digitally altered voice made it easy for him to be fooled. If I tried to use a regular speaking voice, he would have heard the mechanical part of it in the speakers and realized it was a holographic image he was talking to. This way he would think it was a Chinese person trying to disguise their voice to avoid recognition."

"Okay ... I won't ask any more questions about how you did things, although I'm itching to know. But we don't have time. What did you talk to him about?" Brandon finished.

"I got him to agree to help in the SIM Virus cure. I also *persuaded* him to call off the contract on you and your family. He is now convinced that if you are killed, the information in the PDA will become common knowledge. He will move heaven and earth to stop that. You are safe ... well, almost."

"What do you mean by '*well ... almost.*'?" Brandon asked.

"Quan Chi Hanoi told me that he had no way of contacting the Dragon Lord, China's Champion, his Personal Bodyguard and assassin, Kai Akyi, to take him off your trail. He volunteered that he had indeed sent his Personal Champion after you, but I am sure that *he* knew, of that that *we* knew. Quan Chi has put out the word, but I don't hold out much hope that he will succeed. He informed me that the Dragon Lord never returns or contacts the Emperor until after he has successfully completed his mission. It is a point of Honor with the Dragon Lords. As it has been for many thousands of years." Damon looked keenly at his new friend and continued.

"Next to myself and Catherine, Kai Akyi is the most dangerous and cunning Assassin in the world." Damon saw the blatant disbelief in Brandon eyes. Damon elaborated. "We have fought, friend, so I know your skill level, as you know of some of mine. In my opinion, Brandon, your combat skills rivals or surpasses the best of the best. No offense intended my friend, but I am not convinced that even your vaunted skills and improved body and new TAG's are adequate enough to stop Kai or even slow him down." He looked at Brandon. The Eagle was listening with an open mind. "You need to understand this. Kai Akyi is EH as are his children. That is one of the reasons they are almost unstoppable. Although I knew it, the Emperor confirmed it to me at our meeting. Whereas you have trained and honed your skills for many years to become the Eagle, you were not *trained* in them from birth on, and had to increase, add to, refine and hone those skills every waking minute of every day of your life, like China's Dragon Lord has had to. He only mates with Chinese female EH Assassin's to have successors. And those fully trained Dragon Lord Successors are waiting in the wings even now."

The Eagle's mind took an epiphany shift. The information Damon just provided changed his whole attitude. It was a hard pill to swallow, but the Eagle was used to swallowing hard pills. Brandon did not get to be the Best of the Best by thinking inside the box. Brandon Thomas knew that he was fallible. That was one of his greatest strengths. He now believed Damon. He nodded understanding and agreement that his skills might not be enough. That knowledge made him stronger. That was why he was the Eagle.

Damon nodded back and continued. "Kai Akyi will not be dissuaded. His combat skills may rival mine. That is one of the reasons why he was chosen by the Emperor as his Champion, as was his father before him. If I had a really bad day and he had a really good day, Kai Akyi could possibly defeat me." He saw Brandon's skeptical humorous look and smile, and Damon smiled back in a serious way. "I never take someone that good lightly, my friend. Don't you."

All kidding aside, Brandon nodded in serious agreement.

"We can only hope that the Emperor can contact him." Damon finished. "Until we know for sure that he is off the trail, we will have to prepare for him." Damon gave a little sigh. "I would dearly hate to have to kill a warrior of his criterions and caliber."

"Me too." Brandon mumbled jokingly, sarcastically, under his breath.

Then he smiled at Damon. He knew Damon heard. Damon smiled back.

"Let us prepare for both!" Damon stated seriously.

Brandon nodded. "For both!" he repeated.

'Who the hell is "Both"?' was the Eagle's thought as they exited the library.

***

A lright driver, you may proceed now."

"Yes madam!" the driver replied respectfully, in a tone that reflected that he thought she was royalty, or at the very least, an American media star of some kind.

Ms. Shela Pryce had been sitting in the unmarked taxi-limousine a block away and around a corner, hidden from view and the front gates of BlackStone. They had been parked there for some time.

The black limo pulled up smoothly and paused at the front gate and the driver pushed the intercom button. "Ms. Glistin to see Doctor Gray." the driver announced in response to the mechanical voice.

The massive gates opened, quickly and soundlessly, Shela noted. That impressed her, and Shela was not one to impress easily. Most would not even have noticed. Most didn't.

The Kameleon did not need to glance at the time on the taxi's dashboard as she exited the vehicle at the front door. She knew she was precisely on time. The Kameleon always knew exactly what time it was. It was one of her TAG's.

Shela mentally shook her head. Kameleon was *off duty* tonight. Tonight was a date!

Ms. Pryce had done due diligence on researching her first date with Damon. She learned that Damon Gray was extremely punctual.

As she raised her hand to knock, the door opened. An elderly man in a three piece formal black suit smiled.

"Welcome to BlackStone Ms. Glistin. You are precisely on time. My name is Whitner. Please come in."

She almost gaped in childlike wonder as they entered a breathtaking foyer. Whitner closed the door behind her, accepted her Glittering midnight black evening coat and then led her to a sitting room off to one side. It was as beautiful as the foyer.

Shela had been around the world and had seen many beautiful buildings and many beautifully *decorated* buildings. None had come close to the combination she had witnessed upon entering. She estimated the cost of the two rooms she had seen would beggar most small countries treasuries.

The exterior of Blackstone was largely hidden by the weather and the hour she had arrived. The night was dark and the sky was overcast, as London was wont to be, on many an occasion.

Bereft of her bottled golden tan, Shela's pale flawless skin glowed in the soft lighting. As she walked her leg muscles rippled beneath her satin white skin. She was dressed in a simple, low cut sleeveless and seamless black evening mini-dress. It was made of the same material and liquid black color as the ankle length evening coat that she had given Whitner. Like the coat had, it hugged her body as if designed for her. Both had been.

Wearing black, stiletto style, high-heeled shoes, she walked to the sitting room as though they were flat sandals, so perfect was her balance. That was the extent of her clothing.

She carried a small black clutch purse that she wore at he hip, suspended there by a thin black cord draped over one bare muscular shoulder.

Shela was wearing a single, huge amber and diamond, spider shaped pendant necklace. With slender diamond encrusted legs, the huge amber spider pendant was suspended on an intricately handcrafted, double chain. The top chain was chocker tight. Suspended on the lower chain, the large amber spider nestled just above, thus showcasing, her ample cleavage.

The huge spider sparkled brilliantly as the lights hit and rebounded off its many jeweled facets; drawing the eye to it, making it perfectly obvious to Whitner that Shela Pryce's incredible physique was not hindered by undergarments of any kind. His face did not change in the least. ShabNab had cured him of that.

Whitner held a chair for her and she lowered herself to perch on it, arching her back slightly and sucking in her stomach.

"Thank you, Mr. Whitner." she smiled at him. He smiled back, nodding ever so slightly, as befitted his status and station.

"You are welcome." He responded in like, then added. "It is just Whitner, Ms. Glistin. Doctor Gray asked me to tell you that he was delayed and would be here in," Whitner glanced down at the pocket watch that he had just taken out of his vest pocket as he had started his speech, "six minutes and thirty four seconds."

Whitner noted Shela's amused look. "Aaah, I see you know something of Doctor Gray's ... peculiarities. Good!" He pocketed the watch, bowed slightly, turned and left the room.

Shela rose quickly and took inventory of herself in the wall mirror that she had noticed as she walked through the sitting room door. She posed and straightened herself, fiddled with her thick, natural platinum blond hair slightly, and then repositioned herself on the edge of the chair. Why had Whitner not reacted? She stood again and reviewed herself in the mirror. She shrugged and sat.

'He must be Gay,' was her only conclusion, *'or a Eunuch!'*

As she awaited Damon, Shela revisited their first meeting.

***

Scene 76

I t had started as a hunch actually, and Shela Pryce *always* followed her hunches. It was a part of her Valkyr makeup. Fresh off a flight, Shela was checking into at an expensive London Hotel, under an assumed name, when the young hotel Night Manager asked her if she was staying in the room alone. It was a strange question. She looked at him strangely and asked why he asked. The young man grinned.

"It is not a pick up line Ms. Glisten." He grinned and held up a wedding ring. "A family checked in awhile ago and the gentleman said that his pregnant wife had taken sick, *morning sickness* he called it, and she wasn't able to make it to a concert that he had tickets to. Tickets to the Sold Out 'Damon Gray' Concert that is going on tonight. His wife insisted they go without her, so only he and his daughter went. On his way out he called me aside and gave me this ticket and asked me to give it to someone who *I* thought might appreciate it."

He laughed softly, nicely and held up the ticket. "I would have used it myself but I couldn't find anybody to take my shift."

He sighed unconsciously, "If I was still single, I think it would be worth the chance of getting fired as Night Manager to see it. I hear the Gray Ghost's concerts are unbelievable."

Shela felt a red flag go up. This was too coincidental. "I have heard that also." She answered brightly, smiling a dazzling smile at him. "It is strange you would ask that. I was about to enquire at the front desk as to how to get a ticket for it. How much for the ticket?" Shela asked softly almost breathlessly.

She saw the look cross his face. The flag went down. Shela relaxed. It was the look of greed. An honest look and reaction, slight as it was. Then he looked slightly crestfallen. He smiled at her and said cheerfully.

"I'd love to charge you but I told the man and his daughter that I would give it to someone who I thought would appreciate it." He held out the ticket to her. "You can thank *them* when you get there. Please don't offer to pay.'"

He paused, and added somewhat regretfully, "Well, you can try if you want, but I wouldn't be able to accept. They did make it perfectly clear that it was a *free* ticket. I just can't seem to help it, I am a man of my word, Ms. Glisten." He smiled boyishly at her. "Not that I would have it any other way. I wouldn't think of charging you for it." he held out the ticket.

Shela laughed and accepted the ticket gracefully, without paying. She went up to her room and repaired herself; then changed to eveningwear and left. On the way out, she dropped an envelope off with one of the bellmen to give to the night manager. In the envelope were two one hundred Euro Dollar bills with a note that said, 'Samuel, here is a small tip for you for you kind and expert advice on an evenings entertainment.' She did not sign it. Shela Pryce liked to pay her own way.

She did not have a chance to talk to the man and daughter who had given her the ticket through the Night Manager. She was seated when they arrived at the last second and took their seats in the dark.

Shela did meet them briefly at intermission and she did thank them for the FREE ticket. The man just brushed it off pleasantly and nicely, as nothing, stating that he was just glad that someone with a taste for the Arts had gotten it instead of a Scalper who sold it at the door. He mentioned that he had been given Back Stage Passes upon entering and presented her with the extra one, and introduced his daughter, as "my Daughter". His daughter put forth her little hand. Shaking Shela's hand formally, his bonneted daughter said nothing. She just held onto her matching attired doll, replete with bonnet also, and continued to look up at Shela with big eyes behind her slightly tinted thick-rimmed glasses. The tinted glasses made her eye color unrecognizable. Her doll was wearing matching tinted glasses also.

Doctor Gray had met her at the reception after his concert and had gone out of his way to speak with her for a long time; much longer than he had with any of the others that Shela had seen him chat with, prior to their first meeting.

Ms. Pryce remembered that she almost *hadn't* accepted the proffered backstage pass, until the young child with the doll had piped up from beside her. "Wow! Are we ever lucky!" The excitement in her voice was contagious. Shela accepted the Pass.

Shela smiled at the memory.

In retrospect, Shela knew she would *never* have given Damon Gray her cell phone number if it had been based on her first impression of him. A world renowned Concert Pianist and Mystery Man, Doctor Gray seemed like such an airhead when she had first seen him chatting up the other guests.

'A prime entertainer, all surface glitz and fluff with nothing of substance beneath.' was her first thought and impression.

She also assumed the *no photo's allowed* of Damon Gray was a publicity stunt. Many were the rumors that it was.

She had just been preparing to leave the reception when she saw out of the corner of her eye that Damon seemed to recognize someone that he wanted to see in the distance.

He broke off the conversation he was having, abruptly and in mid sentence; excused himself and immediately turned away from the person he was talking to and walked away, in her direction. Damon passed by so close to Shela that she caught a slight whiff of his cologne. It immediately somehow excited and intrigued her. She had never smelled anything like it.

"Nice cologne." Shela casually mentioned, without thinking, as he was passing and asked him what it was called.

Damon immediately stopped where he was going and turned to face her. Up close and personal, Damon Gray was much larger than he appeared at a distance. It startled her, because she was a great judge of sizing up people. She mentally complimented Damon's tailor. She also mentally complimented his plastic surgeon. No scars showed. She couldn't tell their color exactly, because of the slightly tinted glasses, but she *could* clearly see his large slightly sunken eyes. The glasses seemed to enhance them. A more physically beautiful man she had *never* met.

He smiled, his full lips revealing what had to be show business white perfectly capped teeth.

"Thank you Ms. Glistin. It is a custom made blend." His voice startled her and brought her back to reality. She realized that he was talking about his cologne. The resonance and tones in his voice were that of a professional speaker and singer. Shela could actually hear the music in his voice.

Unaware of it, she smiled back.

That started the conversation.

Damon had mentioned at the end of their discussion that he would like to see her again. Surprising herself, she had agreed. Nothing firm had been set up, but she had given Doctor Gray her cell phone number.

He was the first one, in recent memory, that could actually hold her attention in a conversation, and make her genuinely respond, and more importantly to Shela, the first one *ever* that she had given her private cell phone number to.

What had started as an incredible performance in the theater; to the initially boring reception afterward, had turned into a wonderfully surprising and totally refreshing evening's experience.

It was such a wonderfully delightful experience that it had escalated into the setting up an actual date. She shook her head at the wonder of it.

This was a first for her.

Shela Price's first date that wasn't job assignment related.

***

Scene 77

D amon Gray entered the sitting room exactly on time. Shela rose to meet him. Damon was not wearing his glasses. His large liquid silver eyes took her in at a glance. She smelled his cologne as he came near. His smile told her that *he* was not a eunuch or gay. She relaxed a little.

"Shall I have the temperature raised a little?" he asked her.

Shela caught a glimpse of herself in the mirror. Her nipples were standing erect and sticking out a full inch. What could she do? She just smiled.

"The temperature is fine. I am not cold." Damon looked pointedly at her nipples. No one had ever done that before. At least no one she liked. She couldn't stop them, they stuck out another half inch and thickened tremendously. Her voice got husky.

"If you keep looking at them they will swell until I topple over!"

Damon looked up and into her radiantly glowing amber eyes that locked onto and into his. "Well my dear, we can't have that now, can we?" he responded with a picture perfect upper crust British accent and look, and then he laughed.

Shela laughed also and that broke the painful sexual tension she was feeling and softened it down to a fun thing that she could handle. She looked away.

Damon put on his tinted glasses and held forth his arm, "Shall we set off for dinner, Ms. Glistin?"

"I think so Doctor Gray. I'm feeling very horn ... hungry!" she hastily corrected, her whole body blushing furiously.

"The pink is a great look against the black dress." Damon teased. "It becomes you."

Shela kept her mouth closed and took his arm and they exited the sitting room together. Damon retrieved her coat from Whitner, who was waiting for them and handed it to Damon. Damon held it as she slipped into it.

"The car is parked out front waiting, sir." Whitner announced.

"Thank you Whitner. Don't wait up."

"It's nice to know you still believe in fairytales, sir." Whitner held the door as they exited and closed it after they left.

Damon opened her door and settled her in her seat and then went around and entered the driver's side.

"What did he mean by that remark?" Shela asked curiously.

"It means he will wait up all night, or until we come back." He smiled at her. She smiled back. A genuine smile.

"I think I like Whitner. Where are we going?" Shela asked her *date*.

"To Conflamation." Damon stated quietly, eyes on the road.

"Don't you need reservations to the most exclusive club in London?" Shela asked in surprise. She had tried to get in various times and had not succeeded. The waiting list was too long. She was never able or willing to commit to a two week to a month waiting list.

"We need reservations?" Damon asked in a shocked voice?

"Of course we do. Didn't you know?" she asked surprised.

"I don't get out as much as I should it seems. May I borrow your cell phone for a moment? I seem to have forgotten mine. Something or *some things* must have distracted us." Shela smiled at the reference to her nipples. She reached into her purse and produced her cell phone and handed it to him.

"Would you mind steering?" he asked as he took her phone and dialed it.

Shela held the wheel with her right hand. It felt strange to the American girl to be steering a car down the wrong side of the road from the wrong side of the car with someone else controlling the gas and breaks.

Damon punched in some numbers and waited. "Whitner? Please make a call to Conflamation and see if you can get us an immediate reservation. I will text you the phone number and my credit card information should they require it. Call me back at this number. Thank you."

He hung up and his hands flew over the small keyboard as he sent the text message. As he started texting, he said, "Look at that! I keep hitting the wrong keys. Your phone sure has small letters. I'm glad piano's don't have keys as small. I would be a terrible pianist. I'd have to have chop sticks tied to my fingers to play. It is a good thing you are driving. They say that it is against the law to text and drive at the same time. They say it can be dangerous. Ah, but what do they know?"

He handed Shela her cell phone when he finished his call. She laughed at his frustration and his humor. "I have felt it myself many times. As you can see I don't have small hands either." she held up her shapely muscular hands.

"Strong hands. Beautifully formed." Damon agreed inferring that her fitness helped to make them more attractive than they naturally were. She looked down at her hands in a whole new light.

A few minutes of silence went by and her phone rang.

"This is Ms. Glistin ... One moment please." She handed the phone to Damon and again took the wheel.

"Hello? Thank you Whitner ... Yes ... Yes ... Yes, I will ask her and call you back within two minutes if the answer is *no*. Goodnight Whitner." He hung up, handed the phone back and took over steering.

"Is it alright if Whitner uses your number for tonight to contact me if something comes up that he needs to talk to me about?"

"Of course it is alright. Do you need to call him ... no you don't, do you? Only if the answer is no."

"Correct. And thank you." Damon responded sincerely.

"For what?" Shela asked confused for a second. "Oh, you are welcome, Doctor Gray." She said in a teasing way to cover her confusion.

"Please call me Damon."

"Of course ... Damon." Shela paused for a moment and came to a decision. "And please call me ... Shela."

"Thank you for that, Shela."

"What fo ... never mind ... you're welcome. You are a strange one Damon Gray ... in a nice old fashioned way. It's kind of refreshing." She shook her head slightly. "Well Damon, where are we going for dinner?"

"To Conflamation." Damon stated quietly, eyes on the road.

"You got reservations that quick?"

"I know the owner." He replied, again quietly.

"Oh, I should have guessed. You are a famous person and meet a lot of people." She racked her brain for a minute. "For the life of me, I can't remember who the owner of Conflamation is. Who is it?"

"It's a corporation actually."

"Really? And who owns the corporation, or is at a board of directors?"

"Both really. I have the board run it mostly. They are very competent."

It took a moment for the message to sink in. "You own Conflamation?" she asked, just to clarify.

"In a round about way, yes." Damon answered simply. "It was a beautiful old building that was going to be torn down and a Projects was going to be put in. I bought it, restored it and rented most of it out to the Project people that were already living there. They do very well. At first we had to have experts come in and train them. Most took to it like a duck to water. The ones that *didn't* had the ones that *did,* help them. It has worked very well. The empty space I turned into Conflamation. Who would have guessed that it would turn out to be London's hot spot?"

Shela laughed. "You continue to amaze me Docto ... Damon. I am looking forward to our evening. Maybe later you can work on my nipples until they go down."

Damon adjusted his custom made bolo tie. In doing so, he depressed a small button in the back of it. They had just finished an incredible meal at Conflamation and Damon had ordered a specialty coffee for them while they both leisurely perused the desert menu.

Shela's cell phone rang. She answered.

"Yes he is. One moment, please." She handed her cell phone to Damon. "It is Whitner." Damon nodded and took the call.

"Hello? ... Who just arrived? Mr. Thomas and his ... why that's great! Tell them ..." She could hear Whitner's voice interrupt although the room noise made most of his words indistinct. She saw Damon's face alter subtly at the news, whatever it was.

Damon's voice changed, raising slightly, as if in agitation.

"Really ... and he wants to see me now? Did you tell him I was on a date? ... That important? What can I do, I'm just a concert Pianist?" Shela heard the placating tone of Whitner, but again could not hear the words. "I don't care! I ... I ... Tell him I don't want to get involved! ... You did? ... When did they arrive in the country? ... Does anyone else know?"

He listened for a moment, worry starting to show on his face. His eyes looked off into the distance.

"Okay, please take Brandon and Angelina to the Guest House and tell them I will arrive shortly. Oh, and give him my condolences on the tragic death of Charlene. Tell him I was going to send a card. Yes ... yes, I shall return at once. Thank you." He ended the call and returned the phone to Shela and signaled the waiter. His hand was shaking slightly.

"Bad news, I assume?" his date asked in a concerned voice. A slightly *different* voice. A controlled voice.

"What?" his eyes refocused on Shela and he tried to smile valiantly. "Dessert will have to wait for another time, Shela. It seems that I have just had a couple of unexpected guests arrive, very, *very* unexpectedly, and they are *demanding* to see me. I *must* attend to this matter immediately! If you like I can take you back to BlackStone and can have someone drive you home, or I can pay for a cab from here if you prefer."

She smiled a warm radiant smile that lit up her face. "I thank you for that, Damon. I would feel a lot more comfortable if you took me to Blackstone with you and had one of your staff drive me to my Hotel. It *is* on the way and I would feel much more secure. Besides, you might be able to fix things so that we may be able to continue our evening. As you can see, my nipples are still rock hard and growing." She arched her back slightly, accentuating them.

"Every male in here has been looking at them since I took my coat off." And then finished in a voice that only he could hear. "Not that I mind."

Damon's face brightened visibly. "Well, maybe ..." then his face fell again. "We'll see. I sure hope so ..." the waiter brought their coats. When Damon went to put Shela's coat on she could see the tremors in his hands. She took the coat and draped it over her arm. Something in the phone conversation seemed to be terrifying him.

When they approached the car, the doorman opened the drivers door and handed the keys to Damon.

"Would you like me to drive?" she asked in the same soft, concerned, controlled voice.

"Do you mind, terribly? My mind and hands aren't all that steady right now." Damon smiled gratefully.

"Not at all." She smiled in return.

She turned and sat on the driver's seat. She looked straight at Damon and lifted her left leg slowly and swung it gracefully in first, showing Damon that she was truly wearing no undergarments. Slowly the second leg started to follow. Damon stepped in close and blocked the leg from closing.

"Thank you for offering to drive." He stated softly. He looked down intently for a few moments and then back up and into her eyes. She knew where he was looking. She made no move to cover up. When he went to step back she spread her leg wider to accommodate him. He took another look.

"And for the incredibly beautiful view." he added as an afterthought. She smiled a *'You're Welcome'*, waited an extra moment and then swung her leg in slowly. As Damon walked around the vehicle, she looked over at the Conflamation Doorman and smiled candidly at his open mouth and bulging crotch.

Shela Pryce had entered Conflamation with Damon Gray.

It was *Kameleon* who exited the building with him.

***

Scene 79

At Blackstone, Whitner met them at the front door. "I will have the vehicle put away, sir." he stated formally, accepting the vehicle key from Kameleon and putting it in his jacket pocket.

"Very well, Whitner. Thank you. Please show Ms. Glistin to the sitting room and I will attend to her shortly." Turning to Shela, he continued, "Is that alright with you?"

At that moment her phone buzzed. She reached in her purse and looked at it. She looked back up at him and smiled. "Of course it is, Damon. I just received a text. Is there a computer handy that I can check my messages on? I don't have internet on my phone."

"I don't blame you. The international rates are really quite high." Damon still looked a little distracted, as he had been for the entire trip back. He seemed to rally and smiled back at her.

"And in answer to your question; yes, there is a computer in the sitting room that you can use. It is on the desk facing the door, for complete privacy. Whitner will fire it up for you. He has the security code. Anything else?"

She shook her head slightly.

"Until later then?" Shela nodded.

"Take your time. I will be waiting." Kameleon smiled.

Damon Gray's eyes brightened for a moment and then seemed to glaze slightly as he turned and left. He kept shaking his head slightly and muttering "unconscionable" under his breath as he hurried away, walking a little stiffly, unconsciously, as one would in great distress.

"This way Ms. Glistin." Whitner announced. "Shall I carry your coat?"

"No thank you, Whitner. I will carry it."

"As you wish, Ms. Glistin." Whitner bowed slightly, turned and preceded Kameleon to a different room than she had been to before. It was sumptuously decorated in a mixture of old and new.

As with the rest of BlackStone that she had seen, it had a timeless feel to it. This sitting room also took her breath away. Whoever decorated BlackStone was a genius, or geniuses, of design and color. As if admiring the Sitting Room, she scanned it quickly yet closely for hidden cameras or viewing devices. She saw none.

"Who did the decorating?" she asked impulsively.

Whitner smiled a sad smile. "Ah ... yes, that is the question, isn't it? Folklore has it that Blackstone was old when time first began. I am not sure I could give your question justice. Please forgive me."

"You are forgiven!" Kameleon smiled at him. "I'll ask Damon."

Whitner brightened, "By Jove, that is *exactly* the right person you should ask!" he smiled back at her and continued to the desk.

"The computer is right here. Let me *'Fire It Up'* for you as the Master would say." He suddenly smiled and his face changed immediately to that of a friendly older man.

"Actually, the Master *did* say those exact words!"

"Master?" Kameleon queried.

Whitner's face regained his composure. "As in *Master of BlackStone*, Ms. Glistin. Doctor Gray. Anyone who rents or stays at Blackstone, I usually refer to as Master or Madam. "

"Ah, yes. Formal speech is strange to my ears after living so long in America." She conceded.

"Not to worry, Ms. Glistin. I have heard that Doctor Gray is a Colonial, as well. Although, I must say, he seems to have taken to it rather quickly. Must have been his English parent's upbringing."

"So, Doctor Gray doesn't own BlackStone?" she asked curiously.

Whitner shook his head slightly. "A Corporation owns it."

That confirmed her knowledge of BlackStone.

He went around the desk, leaned over and turned on the computer; put in the Password and then stood back.

"There are writing instruments and paper in the desk, should you need them. Is there anything else you need, Ms. Glistin?"

"No thank you, Whitner. And please call me Shela."

He nodded in acknowledgement to the '*thank you*' and bowed slightly.

"I must leave you now. Duty calls. If Madam needs anything, please push the red button on the desk and either I or one of the staff will respond immediately."

"Thank you, Whitner, but I will be just fine." She smiled inwardly at the *'Madam'*. It seemed that Whitner had taken a liking to her.

Kameleon sat down at the computer screen as Whitner left the room. She waited until he was beyond sight before she rose up and circled the room again looking for any *hidden* or *camouflaged* viewing or listening devices.

Again she found none.

She again seated herself in front of the computer screen; activated *'Private Browsing'* and went to her email. Her phone had a cryptic message on it that concerned her greatly. Only Q knew her cell phone number and the code to send her that message. Shela had told them, at the beginning of their relationship, her third assignment to be precise, *never* to attempt contact with her while Kameleon was on assignment.

Q had on her second assignment and it had almost caused her death. She would contact Q *only* if she needed more information or help. She was adamant on it. Although it went against protocol, they agreed and never had. Until now, it seemed.

In code, it fundamentally said, *'Kameleon. Check your private email account for vital updates on current assignment'.*

After a lengthy and complicated process, Kameleon logged onto her account. On it was a link to another ultra secure site.

She triple clicked it. Double clicking would have erased the site. Plethora were the safeguards that Q put into their sites.

The site came up. What came up, she was not expecting.

Shela Pryce sat stunned for a moment, and then settled downed and started reading.

Scene 80

Kameleon sat in deep contemplation. When she had first seen the site, she knew it was not from Q. In fact, it stated immediately, *'This information is not from Q'*. The site showed all the information she had been given on Brandon Thomas, only *this site* had all the *missing* information that had been intentionally omitted by Q. Information clearing Brandon of all the false allegations and charges that the IceMan had used to convince Shela to go forth as Kameleon to kill Brandon Thomas.

After absorbing the information, Shela used other methods to verify the additional data, now that she had it. It was accurate. She relaxed a little. Kameleon faded and Shela re-emerged. Q's assignment was now null and void in her mind. Douglas may or may not have known. She would deal with the IceMan later.

Shela's head snapped up. She heard someone coming. She had already exited the computer and made sure that all her information was not in the computer. She knew who it was by the footsteps and the scent.

Damon Gray walked through the door. He smiled at her, but he still looked a little nervous. He had changed into a soft looking, muted dark grey hooded body conscious lounging suit, replete with
matching rubber soled footwear. The hood was lying flat over his shoulders, cape like, with his long hair flowing over it.

Shela smiled inwardly at the, over the top, custom made designer combat, workout outfit. Damon did not suit it. She knew he was wearing it to impress her.

"I'm back!" he said, trying to impersonate a famous actor. Shela smiled. He came close to her. His scent made her loins ache for him. Her nipples engorged and extended more, almost painfully arousing. It shocked her. She had never felt like this in her life. It confused her. She shook her head slightly, as if to clear it. Damon noticed immediately.

"Excuse me. I must use the facilities for a moment." he said softly and walked around her to a rest room situated off to one side. As he receded, so her desire did also. She heard the water running. This gave her the time she needed to exert an iron control on her desires and suppress them. *Now was not the time!*

When Damon returned, he smiled again. As he came close, Shela could smell his cologne, but now just faintly. It had worn off with time and dissipation, she surmised, yet it was still refreshingly tantalizing.

Shela again smiled back. Her desire was still there but was now under her complete control. She studied Damon closely. He still looked a little nervous.

"How are your guests?" she asked bluntly.

Damon looked at her, startled for a second. "Pardon?" he asked, as if postponing while searching for an answer.

"Brandon and Angelina Thomas ... they *are* your new guests aren't they?"

"How in the world did you know that?" Damon asked in an incredulous voice.

Kameleon laughed a little at his expression, "You told me." she stated quietly.

Damon looked startled, "I did? ... I don't remember..." Damon shook his head slightly in puzzlement, trying to remember.

"No ... I'm sure I didn't." He looked her in the eyes. "When did I tell you?"

"You didn't tell me *personally*, Damon. It was in your conversation with Whitner. First you repeated their last name, trying to remember. Then you mentioned both their first names in your conversation."

Damon smiled in obvious relief. "Ah ... yes. Really quite simple actually." Then his face took on an anxious look. "You won't tell anybody will you? They just informed me that their very lives are in mortal danger. That they are being hunted, even as we speak," Damon sighed. "and I can't even help them." The last was said in a helpless and hopeless tone.

"Maybe I can." Shela stated, again quietly.

Damon's eyes got wider. "How can *you* help? ... Who *are* you?" he whispered.

"I am someone who *may* be able to help." Shela stated opening her purse. She reached in and withdrew a photo ID that stated that Shela Glistin was a Top Ranking United States of America, Consulate of Diplomatic Foreign Relations (CDFR) Agent. She presented her credentials to Damon.

Damon went to the computer and researched her credentials. It appeared that she was exactly who she said she was. He seemed to relax.

"Did you know that they are being hunted?" Damon asked.

"I was not aware of it." Shela stated with authority. "But I can find out for you."

"Could you? ... That would be great!"

At that moment, her cell phone buzzed again. "Would you excuse me for a moment? Thank you." She announced as she walked to the other end of the room and took the call. Her face took on a relaxed look as if she was talking to an old friend.

"This call had better warrant the breach. Hmmm .... alright ... yes ... I understand. Apology accepted. The total balance of payment will be deposited tomorrow, as agreed? ... With the bonus ... excuse me, you are not listening, I said *with* the bonus. It was your choice to discontinue, not mine. Full payment only ... uh huh ... yes ... good ... fine ... then I will contact you tomorrow upon confirmation. Goodbye, and give my love to all your family. Don't work too hard." Kameleon finished sweetly and hung up.

Shela walked back over to the computer that Damon had just vacated and sat down. Her hands flew over the keys. A few minutes later Shela shut the computer off and turned to Damon.

"Brandon and Angelina Thomas are not in any danger from the United States. There was an S and D, which stands for Seek and Detain, Warrant out on them, but it has since been withdrawn. However, it does seem that the two of them *are* in mortal danger from *other* countries." She looked at Damon meaningfully.

"How long have you known these people, Damon?" she asked bluntly.

"Ju ... just a short time. I met them at a concert a few years ago in the US." Damon stuttered.

"A few years ago is *not a short time* to me. How well do you know this Thomas family, Damon?" she asked, her voice a little warmer and softer.

Damon seemed to relax at her softer voice.

"Not all that well actually, Shela." he announced quickly, too quickly, as if to distance himself from the situation. "I have only seen them a few times in those years and it was when they were over here on vacation or holiday."

He was reacting as she thought he would, given the circumstances. She had heard of his unreasonable fear of public exposure and used that knowledge to unsettle him slightly.

"This is way above your head, Damon. I had better talk to them personally and explain. The less you know, right now, the better it is for you. Please take me to them now. I need to talk to both of them immediately."

Damon looked uncomfortable. "Brandon and his daughter are not together right now. Angelina is currently ... ElseWare."

"Elsewhere?" Shela asked.

"Close, but no." Damon answered somewhat absently, eyes roaming all over her face in distraction.

"Pardon?" Shela asked in pique.

Damon's eyes came back into focus. "Angelina is currently at an unknown location for medical and security reasons ... reasons I am sure you are far more aware of than me. She left just after they arrived here. I only found out Angelina was gone when I just now went to see them."

"I understand completely. Take me to him now. Is he in BlackStone? Or has he left?"

"Brandon is on the property but not *in* Blackstone proper ... allow me to go ask him first. Please wait here." Without a backward glance, Damon left the room in a hurry, again stiffly, as if his emotions were stretched to the breaking point and ready to snap at any time.

When Damon disappeared from view, Kameleon took over full control and went into 'VAS' and followed him.

***

Scene 81

Damon Gray approached Brandon Thomas. "Kameleon is on her way. She followed me when I left her. She is better than excellent. I was unable to spot her." Damon smiled in appreciation. "She will be here shortly. Do you want to meet with her?"

They were in an enclosed courtyard within Blackstone. The night was black, showing no stars. A dank heavy mist was in the air, giving the garden an unearthly aspect. The fog eddied and swirled slowly, making everything seem distorted. They were standing amidst a group of bushes that shielded them from view.

Damon used the courtyard for some of his many training exercises. Devices were perfectly secreted around the courtyard to camouflage, therefore negate, auras. EH's with aura sight would have no advantage here. He had designed it for that as well as the esthetics. In daylight it was breathtakingly beautiful, with plants, trees, shrubs and flowers of every description and color imaginable.

The Eagle was dressed in one of Damon's grey combat outfits. Hastings was there also dressed identically. Damon had pulled up his hood also, shadowing his features into facelessness. Brandon smiled to himself in appreciation at their outfits. If one was to view the three of them in the open, the three of them would look like identical triplets. Anyone trying to discern Brandon, or any of them for that matter, would have a hard time doing it.

"Did she get the message you sent?" Brandon asked Damon.

"Yes she did. It remains to be seen if she will still pursue her Assignment, but I doubt it. She received a call when I was there and it appeared that it was a family matter."

"Shela has no family." Hastings noted.

"Correct." Brandon confirmed.

"Exactly." Damon agreed, "I took the liberty of tapping into her phone conversation. Q cancelled the Assignment and agreed to pay the full balance of the Contract plus a bonus that was offered for quick execution. Whoever she was talking to wasn't happy. I think the only reason he paid her was to keep her happy. She is Q's top independent Assassin. Perfect score so far. I think she had mentally cancelled the assignment before the call. The information I supplied her, also gave her the links and the access to verify the supplied information. From what I've garnered about her, Kameleon will not be happy at being manipulated."

Damon smiled slightly. "I am curious as to what her actions will be towards Q, or more importantly, to her Handler, the IceMan? Kameleon has been known to exact deadly payment for being deceived. At this point, Q doesn't know that Kameleon knows the full state of affairs." He saw Brandon's look. "I know it is supposed to be impossible to tap into Q's phone calls and have this information. When one supplies Q with all the hardware and all the software, from different companies of course, one can circumvent ... certain things."

Damon smiled again in genuine good humor, and continued, "Well, actually, everything they have access to, I do also. Even though the voice was electronically modified, I knew it was a he by the phrasing of his sentences. That is how I knew it was the Iceman who called the Kameleon." He smiled slightly at the Eagles reaction.

"You are a strange, strange man, Doctor Gray!" the Eagle stated with genuine admiration. Used to acting alone, the Eagle felt a little out his element and wasn't used to feeling like this. Not that this friendship thing was a bad thing. It just took a little getting used to. This friend, this Doctor Damon Gray, if he still was a man, continued to amaze him.

"As do both of you, we live in a strange world, Eagle."

"Both of us?" Eagle questioned.

"Are you not Brandon Thomas when at home, and the Eagle when on Assignment for Q? Two distinct and separate entities?"

"I hadn't really thought of it that way before, but yes ... I believe you are right, Damon!" the Eagle acknowledged. "If, as you say, Kameleon has had the Assignment terminated by Q, why then do you think she still wants to see me?"

"What would your surmise be?" Damon countered. He did so to get the Eagle back on track quickly.
Damon knew that too many things may be happening at one time for even the Eagles brilliant mind to assimilate all at once.

The fact that Angelina, Brandon's seven year old daughter, along with Catherine Nipp as bodyguard and Natasha as guide, had departed this world to a dangerous one, to find a mythical heart for Damon and Charlene's unborn ghost-child, Karman.

An unborn man-child who was almost full term inside Brandon's very pregnant ghost wife. Brandon Thomas had a lot on his plate.

Damon was impressed that the Eagle was functioning as well as he was. Most professionals in the Eagle's circumstances would be totally incapacitated. Brandon was functioning close to his full capacity.

"Because she's pissed." the Eagle surmised, cutting into Damon's thoughts. "And maybe she wants to kill me because she may feel that I may really be worthy of killing, because of the fact that Q pulled her off assignment. She may feel that they fed her they information to back up their story, so that she would agree to cancel."

"Or?" Damon prompted.

"Or the Kameleon believed the information that she received and has additional information that could benefit me, possibly information that she has not shared with Q!"

"My feelings exactly." Damon agreed. "Q's phone call came at an extremely inopportune time, for us. It could be construed the way you explained." He looked hard at the Eagle. "What is your decision?"

"I will see her." Eagle announced. He stepped out of the bush and headed for the entrance to the building. In the middle of a small clearing a figure flew out of the bushes and slammed into him, knocking him to his knees. He rolled to his feet, gun in hand and spun to face his assailant.

Shela Price, aka the Kameleon, lay dead at his feet a small neat bullet hole in her chest, a smoking silenced gun still clutched in her right hand. Another sound spun Brandon and he dropped to a crouch, looking around.

Damon exited the bushes, also with a smoking silenced gun. Hasting was right behind, his weapon at the ready. The Eagle realized that the impact of him being hit and knocked down had muted the bullet sounds. The sound he had heard that spun him around was the impact of a body hitting the ground. Brandon walked over to it. Hastings followed.

A dead body it turned out to be, with two bullet holes in the head. One bullet hole was situated in the exact center of the forehead and one exactly between the eyes. The dead eyes of Kai Akyi, China's Emperors Champion, looked up at the Eagle as if he was still alive. Hastings walked up and calmly pumped six more silent shots into Kai's chest, three on each side, just for extra measure.

While they were doing that, Damon bounded to Kameleon's limp form in one long leap, knelt and scooped up her body as if it weighed nothing and raced into BlackStone proper.

Entering one of the sitting rooms, the nearest, Damon quickly cleared a large coffee table with one arm, and laid Shela down gently and straightened and adjusted her body.

Damon then dropped immediately to lotus position and placed both his hands over the bullet hole and closed his eyes. A slight pulsing of air seemed to emanate from beneath and around his hands, making them blur slightly.

If anyone had been watching Damon at that exact moment, they would have seen Damon's whole body start to blur slightly also. Suddenly Damon's eyes flew open and his whole blurred body started to shake. His eyes changed from red to gold and back again as Golden and Garnet strove to keep their body together.

Damon had to fight with all his might to remain sitting erect and keep his hands over the wound. Sweat beaded on his brow and his face seemed to shrink ever so slightly, as if he had just instantly lost some weight and his body seemed to alter beneath the combat outfit. A few moments went by. The shaking subsided. Slowly his body came back into focus and firmed up.

During that time Hastings and the Eagle had been busy. Guns at the ready, they searched the parameter of the courtyard and found no one else there.

They entered the sitting room just as Damon was removing his hands from Kameleon.

Hastings cried out in fear and started to rush to his friend. He had never seen his friend look so changed. Damon's whole body seemed to have changed. To Hastings, Damon looked like an exotic animal. Like a cat man. Damon looked at his friend, shook his head slightly and raised his hand. Hastings stopped immediately. Damon's face suddenly filled out slightly and his body seemed to change and swell subtly under his clothes. He now looked like Damon Gray again.

Damon continued his hand movement and touched where his triangle watch would be on his wrist and looked up at a point in space and said. "You can come back to your body now Shela Pryce. I have repaired the damage to your body."

Both men looked at where Damon was looking and saw nothing. Damon flowed to his feet in that impossible movement and reached over and placed his hands on each of their shoulders.

Kameleon's ghost was standing there looking at all of them. Still sported the bullet hole in her chest, Shela Pryce looked slightly stunned.

Charlene Thomas suddenly appeared beside Shela and immediately put her hand over the bullet hole for a few moments. When she removed her hand the hole was gone.

'Thank you for calling me, Damon." She smiled at Damon and raised her arm slightly, the one sporting the Triangle watch.

Charlene turned to Kameleon. "Damon healed your earth body. He called me. I came and healed your Spirit or Ghost body. You can now return to your earthly body. In fact, you must. You are no longer linked to it. It will not last long without your Spirit Soul inside or at least linked to it. No body can."

Shela Pryce looked down and touched her healed chest. Suddenly Kameleon hands flashed out and grabbed both of Charlene's arms and she looked directly into Char's eyes with a strange intensity, as if judging her. Something passed between the two women.

Seemingly satisfied, Shela let go of Charlene and turned to face Damon, her crystalline amber eyes glowing dangerously. Gone was the stunned look.

"I felt you healing my body as I was leaving it. You took something from me, didn't you, Damon?"

"No, I took nothing away from you, Kameleon. Our body automatically Copy/Pasted all your Talents, Abilities and Gifts into us before you had completely left your body. We had no choice. It happened automatically. You lost absolutely nothing. Although it almost killed us this time because you were in VState when you died, the Copy Paste actually helped me in repairing your body so quickly."

Damon shook his head slightly at the memory, as if in revelation. "Instinctively turning Primal was the only thing that saved our life and allowed us to make the repairs to your body, before any major damage was done by the chain reaction that should have been caused by the impact of this bullet."

Damon opened one hand, exposing a distorted, blood-smudged slug residing on his palm.

Shela's eyes lost their dangerous look. She turned back to Charlene. "What did you just do to me?" she demanded.
Charlene Thomas smiled a gentle smile and placed her hand on Shela's.

"You knew you were dead, Shela. The bullet hole in your ghost body confirmed that to me. It gets a little complicated. Because your ghost bullet hole originated in your earthly form, you could not return to your healed body that way. So I did to your Ghost body what Damon did to your physical body. I healed you."

Charlene lifted one of her hands and patted Shela's.

"Here, take this." Char's other hand placed the ghost bullet, matching the one in Damon's hand, in Shela's other hand. Shela instinctively took it and tucked it under one of her shoulder straps.

"Now you must return to your body quickly. It must be your choice Shela. When you died and left your body, you severed your connection with it. It will not draw you back as it normally would. The connection is gone. Do you understand me Shela?"

Charlene asked, concern in her voice, taking both of Shela's hands in hers.

Shela did not respond immediately. She just stared intently at Charlene Thomas. When Charlene went to remove her hands, she could not. Shela was gripping them so strongly that she couldn't. Charlene relaxed her hands and let Shela sort things out.

Suddenly, Shela smiled, released her hands and leaned forward and kissed Charlene's cheek.

"Thank you for caring Charlene. It has been a long time since someone has cared about me." Her smile turned humorous. "And I had to die for it to happen."

Then her face went serious. "No, Charlene Thomas, I will not return to that body. It is a beautiful body and has served well its function for me. It no longer holds any appeal to me. It is time for me to move on to ... other things. Thanks for healing me Charlene. I feel strong again, stronger than I have ever been and I can tell that I still have my Talent's, Abilities and Gifts, as Damon called them." Shela turned her head and smiled at Damon. "Thank you for maturing all of them to full strength and making them stronger, Damon."

Damon smiled a return *you are welcome* back at her, but did not speak.

Shela turned back to Charlene. "I have a feeling that I will need them where ever I am going, and I am usually right. I have used some of them to discern your predicament."

Shela looked deep into Charlene's eyes and spoke with great care. "Take my body and have your child Charlene Thomas. Live the rest of your life with your husband and take care of each other in the future as you have in the past. Believe me when I tell you it is a good body."

Shela put her hands on Charlene's cheeks and put her forehead to Charlene forehead. Charlene's head snapped back as if she had been physically struck by a baseball bat. Almost as if something had passed between them again.

Something far stronger this time.

Shela turned back to Damon.

"You called me by my real name, Damon. Do you know my information and where I live?"

"I do, Kameleon." Damon replied softly.

Shela smiled at that. "It seems you do, Damon. Remember that to Q, she will still be Kameleon, freelance Contractor."

Damon nodded understanding.

She turned back to Charlene who stood stunned in shock.

"Take the body." With that said, Shela Pryce, aka Kameleon, turned and started to fade as she walked away.

"Wait!" Damon commanded. Shela stopped fading.

"I can't hold this form for long, Damon. What is it you want? Speak quickly." The strain showed in her voice.

"Charlene, quick, give Shela your Triangle watch!" Damon commanded.

As one in a trance, Charlene quickly made the transfer.

Shela looked at the watch on her wrist and smiled.

"Thank you, Damon. It is beautiful. As are you ..." she turned and started walking. As she walked, she faded.

She looked back over her shoulder one last time and smiled at Damon. "I do regret not knowing you inside me, Damon. It would have been ...." Shela Pryce was no more.

***

Scene 82

Charlene? ... Charlene? ... How long do you have?" Damon asked sharply.

Charlene snapped out of her daze. "Pardon me?"

"How long do you have to enter your new body?" Damon repeated. It had been a few minutes since Shela had faded and Charlene had been frozen as still as a statue. Damon had summoned Michael and Sylvia, but they had not appeared as yet.

"How long was I gone?" Charlene asked.

"Three minutes fifty six seconds." Damon informed her.

"It has to be shortly then." She shuddered a little. "It seemed like I was gone forever." She stepped over to Shela's body and touched her forehead to Shela's forehead, as Shela had done to her. Upon contact she vanished!

"Charlene!" screamed her husband in anguish. He went to grab the body but Damon seized him.

"Give her time, my friend." he whispered in Brandon's ear. The whisper penetrated where a scream wouldn't. Brandon froze, then relaxed.

Damon continued, "Look, my friend. She is now breathing softly. Look closely at her chest." Brandon looked could see small movements in the chest area. Otherwise, nothing.

Damon and Hastings brought some chairs over and they all sat vigil.

Hours passed, when suddenly Damon spoke. "It is happening."

"I don't see anything." muttered Hastings.

"Look at her stomach." Even as Damon finished speaking all present could see the swelling of the stomach. It gathered momentum until it was the same size as when Charlene was a Ghost. The black shimmering dress stretched to accommodate.

Crystal Amber eyes flew open and her chest took a slow, deep, long great breath. The sparkling eyes focused on the three of them and the lips smiled.

"Hello boys. Nice to see you." It was Charlene's voice that spoke, but it was in a slightly different timbre. She tried to sit up. She couldn't. She looked to find the reason and saw her stomach.

"Oh ... my ... god! It feels so different in the flesh. I'd forgotten how clumsy one gets at the end." She looked at her husband and smiled.

"Well, don't just sit there like a lump on a log, husband. Help me to my feet!"

Brandon smiled and jumped to help his wife.

***

"Hello everybody! We're back!" piped a small clear voice from the doorway.

Damon spun with a choked cry of joy. Walking into the room was Natasha, Angelina and Catherine. He ran to them and grabbed Catherine and threw her in the air and caught her as she came down, spun her around and gave her a hug.

"Cat, thank you for bringing them back safely." he said softly to her.

Catherine Nipp laughed delightfully at the rush it gave her, then sobered.

"I would never allow anyone to hurt Natasha. She is your daughter, Commander, and has TAG's. Not like mine, but hers. I would not let anything happen to either of them. You told me to protect them. I protected them as you commanded." she stated simply, then looked over and nodded toward Charlene.

"Who's the pregnant bimbo?" she asked curiously.

***

Scene 83

"Mommy!" screamed Angelina rushing to her mother and throwing herself into her mother's arms. Charlene caught her daughter and staggered, still not used to her earthly weight. Coming to the rescue, her husband grabbed and supported her before she fell.

After a few moments, Angelina stepped back, looked at her mother and announced. "I love your new body. Where did you get it?"

"From a friend." Charlene answered softly.

"I knew it," Angelina replied, "I was just checking." She touched her mother's swollen stomach with one hand and turned to Damon holding out her other hand. It contained a small dark red leather bag that she had just removed from one of her pockets.

"We brought the Null Stone back for my brother." Angel stated quietly.

Damon nodded. "Thank you, but you had better keep it for now, Angelina. You are the only one who can handle it." Angelina nodded in understanding. Anybody could handle the bag, but only Angelina could handle the bag's content.

"That is Charlene Thomas?" Catherine's voice tone demanded explanation.

"It is a long story, but ... yes it is." stated Charlene before anyone could rally. "Nice to meet you in the flesh, Catherine." She waddled over to Cat and put forth her hand.

"Nice to meet you too … Charlene." Cat met and held her hand for a moment. Then she let go of Char's hand; turned and nodded at Damon.

"I'm going to have a shower. Call me later if you would like Primeval or I to come to you, Commander. You have our number." With that Cat smiled and nodded to everyone as she left the room.

After she had left, Charlene announced in awe, "I have never seen any woman walk like her … Wow!" everybody laughed and the tension was broken.

Angelina had walked around her mother and announced. "You are taller, mommy. Will your wings still be able to lift you?"

Everybody looked at Charlene in surprise, with the exception of Damon Gray. No one else there could see any wings.

Charlene's face was as surprised as the rest at first and then went still. "I'm not sure, Angel. Let's find out shall we?" she answered with curiosity.

Suddenly there was an almost flickering or fluttering of invisible wings silently beating the air. Everyone present could almost feel a breeze in the air.

Charlene Thomas feet slowly lifted off the ground and she rose to a height of two feet above the floor before she slowly settled back down softly.

"I guess my wings can lift my new body." She said jokingly. Suddenly she grabbed her stomach and bent over in pain. "Oh my god. It's happening!"

"What is?" her husband demanded with genuine fear in his voice. Fear that he was going to lose his wife again.

Charlene managed to smile at him as she held her stomach.

"I am not going anywhere Brandon. I am giving birth. Is there a Doctor in the house?" she asked in mock humor.

"Ohhhh!" she moaned and stumbled back to the coffee table. "This is different. I can't hold him in. Karman is coming!"

Damon quickly laid her on the table and had everyone stand

back. He rolled up his sleeves.

"Hastings. Please get my bag and have Whitner bring some blankets and a pillow."

"At once Commander." Hastings fled the room.

"Lay there and try to relax. Breathe." he spoke soothingly to Charlene Thomas.

"I am breathing, dammit. Oh God, the pain. I have never experienced anything like it. I need a doctor, for real!" Charlene grated in agitation and pain.

"I am a doctor Charlene." Damon responded, again quietly.

"Not a Doctor of Music or Philosophy, but a medical doctor, Damon."

"I am a certified medical doctor and surgeon, Charlene."

"You are? Oh thank heaven. And thank you Damon."

Charlene seemed to relax slightly and her eyes looked into Damon's with complete trust.

"You just put yourself in my hands and everything will be just fine." Damon did not break eye contact. His placed his hands on her stomach and she relaxed a little more.

Whitner came hurrying into the room with the requested supplies. His eyes popped at Shela Pryce's body at nine months pregnant. His face suddenly went blank and he left the room immediately.

Damon lifted Charlene as if she was a child and had Brandon set up a delivery bed for her. Almost as soon as he laid her back down, Charlene went into her final contractions. Damon went down to the birth canal to assist. Something in his face changed slightly. Nothing altered but all present felt the change in him.

"What's wrong?" Brandon cried out, stepping forward impulsively.

"Nothing that will affect Karman or your wife, Brandon. Please stay back and give me some room." Damon's voice was commanding as he looked at Brandon. Brandon Thomas stopped moving. Why he didn't know. He stood helpless and watched.

Forty two minutes later, Karman came into the world.

***

Scene 84

Charlene Thomas held the small child in her arms. She looked down at Karman and smiled.

Looking up at her, he smiled back. Then after looking at everyone else in the room, Karman closed his liquid silver eyes.

"Is it the right Time, now?" Angel asked Damon.

"Yes it is, Angelina." Damon responded

Angelina opened the drawstring, reached into the pouch and withdrew the NullStone from within. She held it aloft, showing it to everyone present, turning it over and over in her small hands.

Made of a black unknown substance, the NullStone looked exactly like the illustrations of it, a Puzzle Rock. No light reflected off it. No one would touch it. Damon said that there was something different about the NullStone's dimensions. The rest all agreed that it was hard to focus on.

"Strange" was their feeling of it.

"Different" was Damon's feeling of it. They all agreed both words described it.

It was suspended by a dark red leather unbroken cord running through a small round hole in the very center of it, filling and fitting the hole perfectly. The perfectly round cord was made of the same Dragon Heart protective sheath leather as the red carrying case, Damon had informed them.

With the exception of Damon, no one present could hazard a guess as to how the unbroken Dragon Cord had been strung through the hole. There was no bonding line.

Damon's only explanation, and a strange one to all who heard it, was that the heart cord might have somehow been actually grown through it.

Angelina had placed the cord over Karman's head and around his neck. Karman's eyes flew open at the touch. One changed to that of a swirling solid blood red miniature sun and one changed to that of an incredibly beautiful golden cat's eye.

The cord had immediately shrunk so that the NullStone was positioned directly above the baby's breastbone, in the hollow of the neck. It then melted or was absorbed into his tiny body. No sign of it, or the cord, showed. Karman's eyes changed back to silver and looked fleetingly again at each person. Karman smiled at each of them in recognition and closed his eyes again.

Later, after everyone had left except Damon and Brandon, Charlene turned to Damon.

"Damon, why does Karman not have a belly button?"

"I would hazard a guess that it is because Karman was born of Magik and Magik sustained him throughout your pregnancy Char."

"Magic?" Charlene asked incredulously. "Please Damon! Do you really expect me to believe in magic?" She looked at her husband. Brandon remained mute. This was not his discussion.

"Magik with a K." Damon corrected.

"What difference does a letter make?" Charlene demanded in confusion.

"Magic with a C is all illusion." Damon explained patiently, gently. "Magik with a K is real." The last was said with absolute authority.

Charlene paused in contemplation. "I think I see the difference. I believe you, Damon. How simple. True Magik is all around us isn't it?"

Damon smiled back, "I see you see, Grasshopper!" he said gently putting his palms together, prayer style.

"Grasshopper?" then she giggled infectiously, "Damon Gray, are you actually referring to that old Kung Fu TV show?"

She saw Damon's response look.

"You are!" All three of them burst out laughing at the same time.

"Thank you Damon." Charlene spoke softly after the laughter.

"For what?" Damon asked back.

"For making me laugh. For making us laugh." She looked at her husband. He nodded in agreement. "And for helping me give birth. For ... for ... oh, hell... for everything that you have done for me and us."

Brandon again nodded to that. He still maintained his silence. The Eagle felt something was coming and did not want to mess with the chain of events. The Eagle watched and listened.

Damon answered, "I understand. You are welcome. And thank you, Charlene."

"What for?" Charlene asked genuinely surprised.

"For carrying and giving birth to our *Child of the Universe*, Karman." Damon Gray stated simply.

Charlene was speechless for a moment. Then understanding dawned.

"*Child of the Universe*. That's right! I had forgotten about that. You are welcome" She smiled back at him. "Will I be able to breast feed Karman?"

"I'm afraid not. But Natasha should be able to get some unicorn milk that should suffice. From what I've read, human milk will not nourish Karman. Besides, your new body has no milk to give. It was only Karman's temporary Birth Vessel. Your new body has not been harmed in any way, Charlene. Karman made sure of that on the way out.

"I see." Charlene remained silent as she struggled to digest what he had just told her.

"Karman won't be staying with me, will he?" she said, smiling a little sadly.

"Why do you say that?" Damon exclaimed.

Charlene looked at him uncertainly. "He is your child Damon. He belongs with you. I wouldn't even know how to raise him." Her voice took on a despairing undertone. "I now understand that." her eyes showed her anguish. "It hurts ... oh god, how it hurts," her eyes cleared, " but I do understand and accept it Damon. I really do. I know that I belong with Brandon and Angelina. As you said, I was just the birth vessel for you child; your son ... Karman, Child of the Universe." Charlene stated, still a little sadly.

"You were, and are, far more than that Charlene Thomas. Yes , you new body was the birth vessel, but you carried Karman to full term. You, Charlene, not your new body. You are far more than you can even imagine right now. And Much, much more important than just a simple birth vessel. I now know and understand what Shela's lasts words were going to be."

"Aha!" stated Brandon. "I knew there was more to this than meets the eye."

"What do you mean? What are you talking about, Brandon?" Charlene demanded, the grief in her voice turning into exasperation.

"I don't know," Brandon stated. Before his wife could speak, he continued. "but Damon does, don't you Damon?"

Damon nodded. "I think it will take all of us together to raise Karman ... all of us together meaning both of you as well, if you so choose." he stated with conviction. "Karman will need all our wisdom, patience, raising, help and love."

Charlene's face lit up like a Christmas tree.

Brandon was not to be deterred.

"You are good, my friend, and you said all the right things, but on this I will not be deterred, Damon. I noticed your almost reaction when the birthing of Karman started. Something you kept quiet about at that time. When I questioned you, you stated 'Nothing that will affect Karman or your wife, Brandon' and you continued as if nothing happened. Is that why you sent the rest away for dinner and asked me to stay behind?"

Damon answer was his smile.

Brandon smiled at Damon's smile. "Out with it my friend. What did you see that was so unusual that it could shock someone like you?"

Charlene burst out, "Is it because this has never happened before?" she queried in high concern.

"No, as far as I know, this type of birth has happened before although not quite under these circumstances. That is what concerns, yet excites me."

"Please Damon!" begged Charlene. "It can't be that bad, can it? Don't analyze this. Please, Please ... just tell us."

Damon paused. He had his speech all planned out. He threw it away.

"Kameleon's last words were going to be: *'my first time'*. You were a virgin when you gave birth, Charlene. The body of Shela Pryce was, and still is ... a virgin."

The End ... for now.

Robert Preston Walker

JIGSAW

PM

3rd in the 'Smoke' series

A new novel Novel by
Robert Preston Walker

SCENE 1

Tanner Wild reached down absently and scratched Shadow behind his ears. Shadow wagged his lion's tail and looked up at his master, his lime green eyes glowing in contentment. His master did not look down. Wild's mind and black eyes were focused on the exterior of the building in front of him.

It was night. The sky was overcast. Heavy fog tendrils wafted through the chill, calm night air. No light exited from the huge building. It stood dark and foreboding, parts of it seeming to blend and vanish into the black night sky.

"Something definitely doesn't seem right, Shadow! I feel like I should know this building! But I don't. We've never been here before, have we? " Tanner whispered softly to Shadow, finally looking down at him and meeting his gaze. Shadow seemed to shake his head softly.

Tanner's lips curled up slightly and he crouched down beside the smoky canine and whispered even softer.

"Let's check it out, shall we?"

Tanner now finished the smile at Shadow. "This is what we get paid the big bucks for, partner. You take the main floor and basement. I'll take the third and second floors." Shadow looked over at the building Tanner was talking about, looked back at Tanner, shook his large head slightly and padded off towards the building. He started to fade as soon as Tanners hand lost contact with him. Before Shadow had gone ten paces he had faded into thin air.

Tanner chuckled. He knew Shadow wanted to check all the floors, with or without him, and shook his head and vanished *just* to show his irritation. He knew Shadow could hold his form for up to forty five minutes after contact with his master. Tanner was the battery that charged Shadows physical body.

He cupped both his hands around his mouth.

"Okay, grumpy!" he called out softly, "You can do them all! Just make sure you don't get sidetracked. I'll give you ten minutes. After that I'll meet you back at the hotel."

Tanner stood and watched as Shadow turned visible for a moment as a confirmation response, then he disappeared again. Tanner switched to his GhostSight and followed Shadow's progress to the building. Slightly larger and much more muscular than a full grown Poodle, Tanner lost sight of his large GhostDog when Shadow passed through the outer wall of the boarded up, supposedly empty old boardinghouse.

Tanner stood for a moment as a thought struck him.

'Am I getting soft and lazy in my old age? Or both? Should I be in there with him?' he laughed softly at himself and flexed unconsciously. Turning forty two in a couple of days, he knew he still had the body and face of a twenty five year old body builder or gymnast. He should, he was both.

Wild knew he wasn't soft *or* lazy. He was just indulging Shadow. A gift. A Birthday Gift.

'And Shadow would be turning thirty five on our birthday.' he justified to himself. *'What better gift can you give a dog! It's what he wanted. And besides, Shadow loves this kind of thing!'* Tanner now felt at peace with himself.

Shadow had been born on Tanner's fifth birthday.'

And if there *were* any *ghosts* in there, well then, Brandon's Shadow: part Wolf/ part African Lion/Part Fox/ part Full Grown Poodle mix, who just happened to be a thirty five year old Ghost, would sniff them out.

'What evil lurks in the hearts of men? Only the Shadow knows!' the memory of his dad's voice wafted spookily through his mind. He chuckled to himself, remembering that it was his dad's favorite radio show and Tanner's favorite movie.

He turned, walked slowly back and entered his Silver Grey Honda Element. He looked at his watch and then sat there staring at the black building.

Tanner suddenly realized why the old boardinghouse had looked so familiar. It vaguely reminded him of his childhood home.

Tanner Wild continued to stare at the building. He wasn't *really* staring at the building. He was staring *through* the building and into the distant past. To the time when his father had first brought Shadow home to him.

It had been years since he had revisited those memories. The years had not dulled them. In fact, it seemed that the years had done exactly the *opposite*. Father Time seemed to have honed them to razor sharpness.

***

"Daddy, you really got me a puppy for my fifth birthday?"

Tanner saw his Daddy's smile. "You did, you really did! You got me a puppy for my fifth birthday!"

"I sure did son. I didn't have a choice. He was born this very morning, just a few hours ago. On your birthday JigSaw. His mother died during the birth. As he was one of our lab experiments, there were no female dogs there that could suckle him. I knew you had been pestering me for a dog for the last year and I did say I would think about it." his father smiled and looked down at his son.

"The other scientists wanted to put him down. The pup could never reproduce because it was a Hybrid so they had no use for him. Son, dogonit, it really bothered me, the way they played God with the animals lives so callously. I believe all life is special. Even a HyBrid LionDog. Well Jig, I thought about it and thought about it and it just seemed plum wrong to me and strange also, maybe because he *was* born on your birthday, to let the lab technicians put him down on his birthday."

He looked lovingly at his wife. "I phoned your mom and asked if she would be in agreement. And I have to tell you JigSaw, I thought I was in for a long one," *(meaning discussion)*

He paused and looked down at his small son, put up his hand to hide his lips and said in a loud stage whisper, "She didn't argue at all! She said that she *knew* it would happen. Can you believe that? I was almost tempted to buy some of that Microsoft Stock she's always talking about." He winked at his son. Tanner winked back, not having a clue as to what was going on. He was just happy to have his very own dog. His dad continued.

"So I brought him home. He is your fifth birthday present from you mom and I. You should name him, son. And a name is important, Tanner. It should only be *his* name you choose, not another. Think hard and long before you name him. Take your time. There is no rush."

"Boy, I'm sure glad you're the janitor there Daddy."

"What makes you think you dad is a janitor?" his father asked humorously.

"Cuz yor always sayin' you have to clean up all the messes that those meerons, that's whut you called them, get into. Meerons and idjits.!'" He smiled at his father with great pride.

"I'm shur proud of you daddy. You always bring home all kinds of great stuff, but this is the *best one yet*. My very own dog!" He paused, then said graciously, "I mean the frogs and mice and rabbits are great, but *nuthin'* beats this ... this ... " he looked in the big cardboard at the shapeless sleeping bundle of grey fur. "Whut kinda dog is he Daddy?"

"Well Jig, my boy, this here experiment is a mixture of four animals. He is one quarter Fox, one quarter full grown Poodle, one quarter Wolf and one quarter African Lion.

As Tanner looked again into the cardboard box at the large newborn, his shadow fell across the puppy. The pup opened his brilliant lime green cats eyes and looked at Tanner. Something happened inside of Tanner Wild. The pup closed its eyes yet the feeling stayed within Tanner. He didn't understand it but he liked it. He looked in again and again his shadow fell across the pup. This time the pup ignored it. That is when Tanner noticed.

"Why," Tanner exclaimed, "he is 'zackly the same color as my shadow. Wudja lookit that! Come see!" They both did.

His father said, "He sure does, boy. He sure does look like your Shadow. That is a good name for a pet, Jigs. What do you think, dear?" he asked his wife.

"Why, I think it's a beautiful name!" she enthused. "Is that what you are going to name him, Tanner?"

Tanner put his hands on his hips and frowned at the sleeping newborn pup. "Can a special animal, like him, have *two* names like a person?"

He looked up at his parents.

"Well ... " said his mommy slowly. "I guess so. Why would you want to give him two names, Tanner?"

"I got two main reasons." Tanner said seriously, looking down at the sleeping shapeless lump of fur. "One is that I don't want him to be a pet, like a rabbit or a frog. I want him to be my friend, cause I don't have any, "he saw their concerned look, "Sept for you, and yore just my parents ... which I *guess* is okay .. but it ain't like a real live friend! And friends have two names. A first and a last, like me,"

He saw them both smile. His father picked up the ball next. "Well then, Jigsaw, I think your friend should have two names. What are his names going to be?"

He looked up at his father with wide happy eyes, and stated with great pride, "Shadow Dollar."

He caught his mother's questioning look.

He looked at his father and mother seriously and clarified, "Shadow is his First Name and Dollar is his Last Name."

"We had that figured out son," stated his father, "and we understand the first name, but why Dollar for the Last Name."

Tanner smiled in pride, "Aw, I'da thought at least *you* could figure it out Daddy. You are the one who really came up with his last name."

"Really? I did? And how do you figure that, Jigsaw." His daddy chided him.

Tanner just smiled, his large black eyes shining. "See, you did it with me and helped me with Shadows last name!" he waited.

Finally he spoke, as if to a child. "Daddy, mommy said you nicknamed me 'JigSaw, cause I just love puzzles mor'n anything, right?" His daddy smiled, nodded and waited. This was just too good to pass up. He wanted to remember this memory.

Encouraged, Tanner continued. All was not lost. They were with him so far. *'Parants!'* he thought to himself, 'can be *frustrating! Sometimes they just didn't get it!'* he continued.

"Daddy, 'member that time when I needed a Dollar to get that Puzzle at the Dollar Stop'nShop?" his father nodded. He really didn't remember which particular time Tanner was talking about, there were so many.

"Well you didn't have a dollar, so you gave me four quarters. I got mad, remember, and I said that I needed a whole Dollar not four quarters. You said that four quarters made a Dollar."

Tanner saw his dads smile of understanding, but let him finish what he had started.

"And shadow is one quarter Wolf, one quarter Full grown Poodle, one quarter Fox and one quarter African Lion. You told me four quarters makes a Dollar! So you helped me choose his name Daddy."

"Will you take good care of him, Tanner?" his mother asked. "An animal is an awful lot of work, you know."

"Aw, mom, you don't gotta worry none. It'll be a snap!" he snapped his little fingers to show just how just how easy it would be. "Shadow ain't no *animal*! NoSirReeBob, 'cause Shadow Dollar is family. He's my friend. I named him. I guess that's like I *dopted* him, right Daddy? Right, mommy?"

What choice did they have?

"..... Right!" they answered in unison.

"Happy Birthday Tanner!" both parents said together.

Suddenly Tanner's face looked stricken! Backing up, he held up his little hands as if to ward off bad news.

"Hey! He's not *all* I'm getting for my birthday ..... is he?"

***

READER REVIEWS

Robert Preston Walker has created a book that you're compelled to finish quickly. The scene layout, the structure, and one of the most potentially iconic characters in recent memory draw you in, and before you know it, you find your left hand holding more pages than your right. It is complex, but not difficult to follow, and crosses typical genres smoothly. Mr. Smoke is quite simply, a wonderfully distracting and thoroughly enjoyable read.

Rev. Rob Warren - Louisville Kentucky

***

When I read Mr. Smoke, after a few Scenes I was addicted and I wanted to figure out what happened in the end. Damon Gray in the end was not only a hero to the world but to himself, Natasha, and Cat without ever knowing it. He saved himself by crawling his way out of the black hole that had become his life and he saved Natasha and Cat from the darkness that they had lived in for so long.

Gabby Templeton, New Albany, Indiana

***

Mr. Walker,

I wanted to tell you how much I enjoyed your book, Mr. Smoke! I used to read books to my children so they now enjoy reading, but I have let that part of me be distracted by other "stresses." This book was so interesting and took me away from this life to Damon Gray's world.

The language, while being a little raw, was just what you would expect from the assassin world. I found myself cheering for the murdering of assassins. Of course, with all of the bombing around the world and 9/11, my feelings have changed somewhat. The terrorists in the world NEED to be stopped, and I truly want to believe that there may be a "Mr. Smoke" organization somewhere that could assist the world governments. As a Christian, I know God can do anything to help us as long as we do what we should.

In anticipation of the new book, I am ready for you to finish it. I am glad that you enjoy writing because I will enjoy reading your next book. The brief snapshot of "Gotcha" in the back of the book just "wet my whistle" for more reading. Meeting you was a joy for me and I thank you for autographing my copy of the book.

Ready for the next *Mr. Smoke* adventure,

Peggy Harper

***

Sir Robert Preston Walker...

Your book, Mr. Smoke, was fabulous! So fabulous in fact.. I have yet to come up with words worthy of describing it.

I am sending this so you will have my email address AND to let you know I have not forgotten about the review I promised.

Fan & Friend, Natalie Beumer

***

Robert,

You signed a copy of Mr. Smoke for me in Louisville Kentucky Thanks for a very entertaining story.

I truly enjoyed the characters in Mr. Smoke.

This was a truly different story line, and I have read many hundreds of books. I just wanted to let you know that your MR Smoke was a great book.

I so hope you will write a sequel....I just have to wonder about what is on the other side for Mr. Smoke and Misty.....

I am also looking forward to your next book "GOTCHA".

Lynn Lee

***

My name is Iola Belt. My girlfriend and I met you and your wife at the Louisville Street and Rod show. We both purchased your book, 'Mr.Smoke'. It was great; can't wait to read your next book 'Gotcha!' If it is anything like 'Mr. Smoke' I know I won't be able to put it down. Keep writing the great books.

Iola Belt

***

I just finished reading your book "Mr. Smoke". I bought a copy at one of your Book Signings. (Thank you for so graciously signing my copy!) I enjoyed it very much and look forward to your next book! I finished reading the book over Christmas vacation. When I got to work today, I couldn't wait to tell my friends how much I enjoyed reading it. While this isn't typical of the type of book I enjoy reading, this captured my attention immediately and kept me engrossed to the very end! If you ever visit Indiana University Southeast, I hope you will let me know so that I can look for you. I would like to buy a copy of your next book and would love to have you sign it as well. Could you please tell me when I could expect the next book and where I might find a copy?

Alice K. Watson

Office Services Assistant

Indiana University Southeast

***

Bonjour Robert!

FYI I did read and finish the book, Mr. Smoke... Waou!

You have quite an impressive imagination!!!

It is crazy but with a great profound meaning and I enjoyed reading it very much.

Cheers,

Estelle Arnaud-Battandier

Consular Affairs Officer | Agent consulaire

***

I will put a "Rave Review" out on Amazon.com as I think the book, Mr. Smoke, is well worth reading.

Had I known you would put a review in your next book, I would have written a bit more about some of the exciting and strange things I like about the characters.

Let's just say I really love this character and I do hope for a sequel down the road. I can't stop thinking about Mr. Smoke.

Also, as far as "Gotcha!" is concerned, I hope you will be in Louisville when it is published so I can have you sign this one too! If there is any way that you can keep me on a list, so that when Gotcha! Is released, you will let me know where you might be. I would love to get my copy of 'Gotcha' signed by you.

Lynn O. Lee

***

I have read many books and I can say that by far Mr. Smoke is one of the best books I have ever read. This book has an amazing plot line with lots of twists and turns. Robert Preston Walker has created many interesting characters. I congratulate Robert on this fantastic piece or work. Robert Preston Walker is an amazing author and I look forward to his next books in the Mr. Smoke series. I had the privilege of meeting Robert and I can say that he is one of the nicest people I have met and I thank him for signing my book. I had fun reading Mr. Smoke and I look forward to reading Robert's other Books.

Alexis Eicher,   Louisville, Kentucky

***

I just finished Mr. Smoke today. I will have to say it was hard to put down. It only took me so long to finish it because I was only reading it during my breaks and lunch hours at work. I have had several people already intrigued and interested in the novel. I made a promise to provide you with a brief review for your book:

"An astonishing masterpiece!"

I think those three words pretty much sum it up. I was engrossed in what Mr. Smoke/Damon Gray would do next. Just when you think you have him figured out, he evolves. He is truly the most interesting and complex character I have ever read about. I am looking forward to seeing what adventures you might write up for him next. I am very glad to have met you and to have a signed copy of Mr. Smoke. It was definitely a pleasure to read!

Megan L. Foye

***

To all who sent Rave Reviews:

Thank you, all of you, for your kind words.

I wrote a sixteen word song (or poem) that says it all:

That thoughtless Act of Kindness

that meant so little to you;

Meant so much to me.

Robert Preston Walker

10369276R10321

Made in the USA
Charleston, SC
30 November 2011